THE
HIDDEN
VALLEY

*Other Five Star Titles
by Jeanne Williams:*

The Underground River

Beneath the Burning Ground

Book II

THE HIDDEN VALLEY

A Frontier Story

Jeanne Williams

Five Star • Waterville, Maine

First Edition
First Printing: December 2004

Published in 2004 in conjunction with
Golden West Literary Agency.

Set in 11 pt. Plantin by Elena Picard.

Printed in the United States on permanent paper.

Library of Congress Cataloging-in-Publication Data

Williams, Jeanne, 1930–
     The hidden valley : a frontier story / Jeanne Williams.—1st ed.
     p. cm.—(Beneath the burning ground ; bk. 2)
     ISBN 1-59414-016-2 (hc : alk. paper)
     1. Kansas—History—Civil War, 1861–1865—Fiction.
I. Title.
PS3573.I44933H53 2004
813′.54—dc22   2004057980

For my cousins, Francis and Albert Billings

Chapter One

A dry winter and bone-dry spring. Swift rain in April roused grateful pungency from plowed fields, encouraged people, fingerling corn, and greened the grass, but the moisture vanished at once in the thirsting earth.

The hungry grass, Dan O'Brien thought. That's what they called grass in Ireland where some poor soul had died, mouth stained from trying to feed on it. If you stepped on such sod, unknowing, weakness melted your knees, and, if someone didn't quick pop a bite of food in your mouth so you could break free to untainted ground, you'd perish like one famished.

Dan still cringed to remember his baby sister on her knees, trying to eat grass at the door of the schoolmaster's hovel the day that kind man found them, took them in, and shared the little he had.

A swell of longing made Dan's throat ache till he thought he would strangle. Bridgie, little Bridget, who couldn't grow up like Beth Ware and Letty Parks! Any wee bone left of her rested lonely beneath the sod an ocean away, not even near their parents who'd been tumbled into a ditch with dozens of others who lacked kin able to see their burial.

Homesick? No. Dan never yearned for Ireland even when the sun beat down day after glaring day. Heartsick was what he was when he thought of Bridgie. He doubted anything could ease the pain he felt when he had to face the fact that no matter how fine the crop, she could not eat of it, that all she had known in this world was hunger.

No one was that hungry yet in Kansas this droughty summer of 1860, but, as corn and wheat shriveled and potato vines and gardens burned, wagons began to roll along the Military Road, mostly folks who'd come in the last few years, heading back to Ohio, Iowa, Illinois, or even farther East.

"There won't be much grain to grind this year," Simeon Parks said, looking around the supper table. Instead of succulent new potatoes with peas, Lydia had concocted a stew of shriveled turnips and the tender inner part of cat-tail stalks and root shoots.

Still, the fare was sumptuous compared to that of many households. There was cheese, milk, butter, and eggs, although cornbread, hominy, or mush was only served once a day. The family had agreed to cut back on this main staple in order to give cornmeal to near-starving folk. The Parkses also probably gave away more dairy products than they used.

"I've been studying and praying on it." Simeon's voice was weary but determined. "Seems our best chance is to turn the cows in on all but three acres of corn . . . let them get some good of it rather than just have it burn up."

Cows grazing over seventeen acres that had been so laboriously cleared? Seven years after the first sod-corn crop, men and oxen and horses had wrestled out the last stumps just that February, then plowed, harrowed, planted, and ceaselessly cultivated in that yearly race with weeds.

"We'll starve!" Mildred Morrison cried, clutching at her full bosom. "I knew we should never have come to this awful place! My poor daughter. . . ."

That daughter said roundly: "You could have stayed in Ohio, Mother. Uncle Bart would be glad to have you go back and keep house for him."

"And leave you expecting after two miscarriages?" Mildred gasped. "What kind of mother could do that?"

"Lydia's right here, and Catriona's a fine midwife. Don't stay on my account."

In spite of Simeon's polite indifference, Mildred had still not given up hope of him. She cast him an appealing look. He paid close attention to spooning up the last of his stew. Lips thinning, the widow turned to her daughter.

"I know my duty. You need a mother's support and comfort."

"I do," retorted Harriet. "So if you're going to stay, please don't gloom and doom."

"Pa," Owen argued, "it could rain! And there'd be all that corn wasted!"

"Not as wasted as it'll be if it doesn't rain and the cows have no use of it, either." Simeon let that penetrate. "We'll have to let the acre of sorghum cane go, but we'll try to save our acre of potatoes, haul water from the river and run it along furrows to reach the roots, mulch with dry leaves and grass to keep the ground cooler around the plants and hold the moisture. If it rains, we'll give thanks. If it doesn't, we'll have a decent chance of lasting till next summer."

"What if it doesn't rain before then?" Owen demanded. He put his hand protectively over Harriet's. After the miscarriages since almost-five-year-old Letty's birth, they were happy that Harriet was expecting a baby that fall, about the time Susie and Andy McHugh would have their first child.

Letty scrambled onto Owen's lap. She was a leggy child with Harriet's yellow-brown hair and blue eyes. She gripped her father's shoulders, and peered at him. "Daddy, we won't dry up and blow away like Gran says, will we?"

He smoothed her hair and laughed, although he shot his

mother-in-law a stern glance. "No, honey, we surely won't!" He caught and held his father's gaze. "All right, Pa. We'll do what you say. But if we don't get enough rain to make a crop next summer, I'm taking Harriet back to where it rains enough to make a living."

"You're a man grown," allowed Simeon. "You have to do what you judge best for your family." He leaned over to smooth his granddaughter's hair. "Don't worry, Letty girl. We won't go hungry while our good cows give us milk. Tomorrow you can help bring them to the corn. They'll be happy, if we aren't."

The cows, Jerseys traded for with the Wares, indeed thought the foot-high corn and sorghum cane was paradise. Joanna was dry but Honey, Lucinda, and Bridie had calved in March. After suckling their big-eared, knobby-kneed young, they still gave plenty of rich milk for the household.

The corn in the lower field promised best. Simeon plowed a furrow along each row as close to the stalks as he could get without hurting the roots. Sweating and swatting at pesky insects, Dan, Owen, and David hoed up wells around the potato vines. Small Letty, sunbonneted like her mother and Aunt Lydia, helped them fill the wheelbarrow and baskets with dried leaves and grass and spread them around the vines.

"Always the 'taties!" Dan said, resting on his hoe a moment, flexing his cramped shoulders. "In Ireland, there was water aplenty but they rotted in the ground, a stench like the dead, and thousands died for lack of 'taties whilst the landlords shipped off grain and swine and sheep to England." He swung the hoe deep. "It was the same in the Highlands and Western Isles, Andy and Catriona say, but most lived near enough the sea to live by gathering seaweed and shellfish."

"Those who hardened their heart against the poor will answer at the Judgment," Simeon returned.

"I'd liefer they answered for it now," Dan growled. "Uncle Simeon, it must be as desperate at the Wares' as it is with us. I want to let Mister Ware know what we're doing to try to grow at least some food. Being more of a teacher and preacher than farmer before they came here, he may not have thought of it."

"He only has Thos to help, and of course the womenfolk," Simeon pondered. "We'll start hauling water this afternoon. Owen and I can keep on with it tomorrow, but you'd best head on over to the Wares, Dan. Stay and help them get set to irrigate if they decide to try. Davie, you'll go help Andy if he wants to water some of their crop. Generally he gets paid for his blacksmithing in grain or such, but it looks like he'll have to wait till next year for that and had best grow what he can himself."

Zephyr and Breeze were needed to haul water, so Dan struck out on foot, fiddle in its homemade case under his arm. The trees any distance from the river were sparse-leaved. Some were yellowing as if it were autumn. The river ran, sparkling and cool, but was down at least eight feet from the usual level marked on the limestone through which it had worn its way. A doe and fawn raced away from drinking and a belted kingfisher dived, showing the rusty breast band of the male.

Whether humans came or went, so long as there was some water, wild creatures would live here. Birds would sing. And what had people brought here anyway, but fighting and trouble? We cleared the trees for fields, crowded the Indians out, tried to make the country fit the way we live, instead of fitting ourselves to it. Maybe white folks were never meant to spread away out here. If you're merciless in what you want from the land, won't it be merciless in turn, like the wearied soil of Ireland, like a bitch suckled too hard, too long?

11

Plaguey, uncomfortable notions. Dan felt almost a traitor for having them, but hadn't God told Cain: "Now thou art cursed from the earth, which hath opened her mouth to receive thy brother's blood from thy hand. When thou tillest the ground, it shall not henceforth yield unto thee her strength." Brother's blood. Osawatomie. Marais des Cygnes. Scores of other killings, and what was yet to come? It seemed to Dan the outraged earth cried out: "You have given me blood, not water. Now see if you can eat the harvest!"

The heavy sense of doom mingled with his bittersweet belief that whatever became of people, fawns and bear cubs, wolf pups and panther kits would be born in season. Parakeets would flock, chattering, and passenger pigeons would darken the skies in autumn and feast upon the acorns.

He wished he could tell these thoughts to Christy, but, during the two days he stayed to help, they never were alone. He found Jonathan Ware plowing a deep furrow along the corn rows while Christy hoed wells around the most promising potato vines. Thos had left a few weeks ago to sign on with the Pony Express, the exciting mail service from St. Joseph to Sacramento that the freighting kings, Alexander Majors and William R. Russell, had started in April.

"Thos is skinny," Jonathan laughed, "not quite eighteen, and, though he's not an orphan, the kind of rider the company prefers, they hired him when they saw how well he rides. Can you believe the pony boys cover two thousand miles in as little as eleven days, the route that takes mail wagons eight weeks?"

Dan shook his head. "Sounds like greased lightning!"

It was 13,000 miles, a four-month steamship journey, from New York around the Horn to San Francisco, and three to six weeks to cover the well over 5,000 miles if you took the jungle railroad across the Isthmus of Panama. The overland telegraph was being laid from both directions, racing to meet and span the nation, but it would be at least a year before that happened. There was river travel up the Missouri after it thawed in spring till it froze, but from where the railroad had reached St. Joseph last year on Missouri's western border, mail, goods, and people had to reach the West Coast by wagon, stage, horseback, or on foot.

There was the joke of the five-mile railroad from Elwood to Wathena, the first in Kansas, that opened in April with great fanfare after the locomotive was ferried across the river. Railroad financiers planned great things, but the bill to admit Kansas to the Union had not carried and Lincoln's May nomination as the Republican candidate fanned the embers of Secession talk into open flame. If war came, railroads would be blown up instead of built.

"When the drought made it look like fool's work to fight weeds, Thos reckoned he'd better earn some cash money to help out," explained Jonathan. "We're trying to rescue enough to get by."

"That's what we're doing." Dan nodded. "Uncle Simeon can spare me a couple of days. Shall I plow or start hauling water?"

"I'd sure appreciate your hitching up one of the oxen and getting water to the potatoes," Jonathan said.

"Danny!" Beth Ware came out, hurrying as fast as she could without spilling the contents of a crockery mug. "Mama says you have to drink this buttermilk!"

"It'll be my pleasure, sweetheart." Dan grinned into the long-lashed hazel eyes. "Thank you kindly and thank your mama, too."

"Can you stay to supper? If you can, Mama says she'll make Indian pudding!"

"Well, I'd have to stay for that, wouldn't I? You tell your

13

mama I'll be around a few days if she doesn't run me off."

"She won't!" Beth rejoiced. "She likes you, Danny! All of us do, especially when Thos and Charlie are both gone and we don't have any great big boys." She regarded him with a furrowed brow. "Are you a big boy, Danny, or are you a man yet? Charlie says he'll be a grown-up man when he turns twenty-one 'cause he can vote then. He says he'll never vote for that black Republican, Abe Lincoln. He says. . . ."

"Beth," said her father, "we don't call Mister Lincoln a black Republican."

"Charlie does."

"I've asked him not to at his mother's table." Jonathan Ware, who must be in his early forties, had very little gray in his thick red-brown hair, and was as handsome as his wife was pretty. To Dan, they had always seemed the way he'd have dreamed his parents to be, just as he thought of the cabin he'd helped to raise as the happy house. Jonathan waggled a finger at his youngest daughter. "Anyway, Elizabeth Ellen Ware, you aren't almost twenty-one, so for a few more years I trust you will graciously follow the customs of your ancient fuddy-duddy parents."

She laughed so hard she hiccoughed. "Papa! You aren't an-shunt!"

"Fuddy-duddy?"

She gazed at him thoughtfully. "Luke Hayes says that's 'cause you're a parson, and a Uni-univers-a-list at that."

"*Mmm.*" Jonathan quirked a wry grin over her head to Dan. "Always refreshing to know what your neighbors think. Go help your mother, Beth. You can pester Dan tonight. Take his fiddle to the house, please."

She took the mug, gave Dan's knees an ecstatic hug, and gripped the fiddle carefully, moving to the cabin with Robbie at her bare heels. Dan's eyes met Christy's. In the sunlight, the deep gray looked brighter. The sunbonnet hid her hair except for a few vagrant ringlets. She smiled, like sun edging out from under a cloud. His heart stopped, lurched, and began to pound till it hammered in his ears. Dirt smudged her face and rolled-up sleeves. The skirt of her gray homespun was stained from hoeing and the sweaty bodice clung to her, but he'd never seen her so real and — and beautiful. Not even in the blue silk dress.

Jerking his head toward Beth, he teased to cover his feelings and give him an excuse to speak to her. "Were you like that when you were little?"

"Thos and Charlie say I was worse." Her laugh was a silver rippling like small bells. "I don't believe it! She's had all of us to spoil her." Sobering, she went back to work. "It's good of you to come. Good of the Parkses to spare you when they have twice as many to feed."

Maybe it was best for her brothers to be off earning wages, but Dan couldn't keep from feeling one of them should have been home so Christy wouldn't be doing men's heavy work. He said gruffly: "If it gets to be more than you and your dad can manage, promise you'll let me know. Uncle Simeon's got Owen and Davie besides me."

She paused and looked at him. Again his heart stopped, caught, and began to thump. What would it be like, to take her in his arms, feel the promise of her wind-molded body against him? Would the beaded moisture on her upper lips taste of some private essence as well as salt? She was at once the girl-child he'd refuged with in the cavern and the sweetest mystery in all the world, in some ways known like the beat of his pulse, in others secret as the underground river.

"Thank you, Dan. I'll remember. I'm glad you brought your fiddle."

Full of pride and delight, he laughed as he started for the

pasture where Noah and Pharaoh grazed with sun dazzling off the knobs on their horns. "Sure, and we'll have earned some music by nightfall, Christy."

He loved saying her name. He loved her. Suddenly he could admit that. It wouldn't change however far he ranged, however many women he came to know. It wouldn't change, no matter if they both lay under the hungry grass of this starving earth so far away from Ireland.

They had Indian pudding that night, sweet with Sarah Morrow's honey, pungent with cinnamon, one of Charlie's gifts. Ellen Ware knew how to make the best of plain fare — sweet potatoes were whipped with butter and cream, cottage cheese sprinkled with finely-chopped green onions, and the turnips Dan was sick of tasted different with cream and watercress. Maybe, too, because Christy was across the table.

When those rain-cloud eyes touched him, he couldn't have said what he was tasting, except the closeness of her, sweeter than Sarah's honey, headier than a nip of hard cider. After supper, he offered to dry dishes while she washed them, but Beth got the dish towel and hopped on a stool.

"I'll dry, Danny! You play 'Froggie Went A-Courting'." That was her favorite.

Christy groaned. "Go ahead and get it over with," she urged.

Beth made a face at her sister, but her lip quivered. Jonathan scooped her into his lap, chuckled, and sang lustily while Dan bowed his liveliest. Ellen lent her crystalline soprano. Well before the last verse, Christy shrugged, grinned at her sister, and joined in.

They finished, laughing, and it was one tune after another, with Ellen playing the piano, and Christy, Jonathan, and Beth singing. "Oh, Susanna!", "Sweet Betsey from Pike", "Comin' Through the Rye", "The Lowlands Low", "Gypsy

cks, I would go between you and the wind, I would go between
u and death.

He finished, drained, as if he had wept again all the tears of
s life, as if he had played his dreams and offered them to
ιristy. Had she understood? Almost in dread, he looked at
r.

Tears sparkled on the homespun patchwork in her lap.
e had stopped sewing to listen. "Dan." With only the light
the fire and the candle on the piano, her eyes were dark as
ght. "Oh, Dan! That was the loveliest song I've ever heard."

Ellen watched him as if he had sprouted horns or wings.
Vhy, Dan, you're a composer!"

He raised a hand in denial. "A little scrap of this, a little bit
that. Nothing grand."

She laughed. "What do you think composers do? Franz
szt is creating his wonderful rhapsodies out of Hungarian
k music. Where do you think Chopin got his mazurkas and
lonaises? Schubert drew from folk music." She smiled on
n with such kind encouragement that he wished she was
mother, and immediately felt shame for disloyalty to that
ιdowy sweet-voiced woman of the lullabies.

No. He wanted no other mother. But his heart swelled
en Ellen said: "It's wondrous, your weaving a pattern from
ιr memories. Don't apologize, my dear. You're in exalted
npany."

Beth was almost asleep, hugging Lambie. Jonathan rose
h her in his arms. "That music will be a heritage for your
ldren, Dan, a song out of Ireland. We thank you for it." He
nced toward the loft. "It's probably hot up there for
ping. Maybe. . . ."

"I already made his pallet on the dogtrot." Christy put
le her work. "Good night, Dan. Thank you."

She had understood. Somehow that was more important

Davy", "Sourwood Mountain", and more.

"Here's one you'll like," Dan said, after a res
gers. "For all that an Irishman wrote it last year
York minstrel show, it's a mighty good tune. Folk
from the East say you hear it all over the count
what words I remember, but I'll have to hum a lo

> In Dixie land where I was born
> Early on a frosty morning. . . .

On the second chorus, the Wares joined in,
end, Beth cried: "Again, Danny! Play it again!"

He did, wishing he knew the words better. The
laughing and clapping. "I never heard the South
before," said Jonathan. "But with a song like that,

"Do you know some Irish tunes?" Christy ask

"Not real ones," Dan regretted. He decided
private song with her, although he'd never pl
anyone; it came from so deep within. "I've mad
thing, though, from what I remember." Christy
quilt pieces together. He pointed his bow at he
smiled. "Sort of like that."

His mother's faintly remembered Gælic lullab
sense chants, snatches of a haunting lament for a
away by fairies, airs gay or lonely Da played on hi
— these Dan had put together in what he thoug
Song". It changed every time he played it, but alw
soft like his mother's voice, jigged and flourish
mourned them, but lullabied small Bridgie, m
too, and shrieked of loss and anger. But these a
solved into hope, the hope of America, and this ti
his feeling for Christy, the sad-sweet promise he
mind from Gælic to English: *I would go between*

17

Davy", "Sourwood Mountain", and more.

"Here's one you'll like," Dan said, after a rest of his fingers. "For all that an Irishman wrote it last year for a New York minstrel show, it's a mighty good tune. Folks coming in from the East say you hear it all over the country. I'll sing what words I remember, but I'll have to hum a lot."

> In Dixie land where I was born
> Early on a frosty morning. . . .

On the second chorus, the Wares joined in, and, at the end, Beth cried: "Again, Danny! Play it again!"

He did, wishing he knew the words better. They wound up laughing and clapping. "I never heard the South called Dixie before," said Jonathan. "But with a song like that, it will be."

"Do you know some Irish tunes?" Christy asked.

"Not real ones," Dan regretted. He decided to share his private song with her, although he'd never played it for anyone; it came from so deep within. "I've made up something, though, from what I remember." Christy was sewing quilt pieces together. He pointed his bow at her work, and smiled. "Sort of like that."

His mother's faintly remembered Gælic lullabies and nonsense chants, snatches of a haunting lament for a baby stolen away by fairies, airs gay or lonely Da played on his tin whistle — these Dan had put together in what he thought of as "My Song". It changed every time he played it, but always it began soft like his mother's voice, jigged and flourished with Da, mourned them, but lullabied small Bridgie, mourned her, too, and shrieked of loss and anger. But these at the end resolved into hope, the hope of America, and this time he added his feeling for Christy, the sad-sweet promise he turned in his mind from Gælic to English: *I would go between you and the rocks, I would go between you and the wind, I would go between you and death.*

He finished, drained, as if he had wept again all the tears of his life, as if he had played his dreams and offered them to Christy. Had she understood? Almost in dread, he looked at her.

Tears sparkled on the homespun patchwork in her lap. She had stopped sewing to listen. "Dan." With only the light of the fire and the candle on the piano, her eyes were dark as night. "Oh, Dan! That was the loveliest song I've ever heard."

Ellen watched him as if he had sprouted horns or wings. "Why, Dan, you're a composer!"

He raised a hand in denial. "A little scrap of this, a little bit of that. Nothing grand."

She laughed. "What do you think composers do? Franz Liszt is creating his wonderful rhapsodies out of Hungarian folk music. Where do you think Chopin got his mazurkas and polonaises? Schubert drew from folk music." She smiled on Dan with such kind encouragement that he wished she was his mother, and immediately felt shame for disloyalty to that shadowy sweet-voiced woman of the lullabies.

No. He wanted no other mother. But his heart swelled when Ellen said: "It's wondrous, your weaving a pattern from your memories. Don't apologize, my dear. You're in exalted company."

Beth was almost asleep, hugging Lambie. Jonathan rose with her in his arms. "That music will be a heritage for your children, Dan, a song out of Ireland. We thank you for it." He glanced toward the loft. "It's probably hot up there for sleeping. Maybe. . . ."

"I already made his pallet on the dogtrot." Christy put aside her work. "Good night, Dan. Thank you."

She had understood. Somehow that was more important

18

than whether she'd someday let him kiss her.

There was music again the next night, although Dan was sure Jonathan and Christy must ache from their labors as much he did. Christy, of course, couldn't heft barrels of water, but she had carried buckets of it to fill the potato wells.

By noon of the third day, the remnant crops were watered. After dinner, Jonathan shook Dan's hand. "Much obliged, son. We'd have gotten it done in time, but that time could have cost us corn and spuds that will make it now, by the grace of God." He chuckled. "Tell Simeon we hope to have some corn for him to grind, but he won't get fat off his share!"

"He won't keep a share if you need it," Dan said. "You can make it up next year."

Their eyes met in the knowledge that another year like this would drive them out. Ellen Ware caressed the crude fiddle case. "Thank you for the music, Dan. Thanks for your song."

Beth hugged him and gave him a moist smacking kiss. "Come back, Danny! Soon as you can!"

Christy gave him a wax-sealed crock. "Take care with it, Dan. It's honeycomb. Sarah says her bees won't make much over what they need themselves this year because flowers are scarce."

Their fingers brushed as he took the jar. A warmth golden as honey, slow-moving and sweet, glowed deeply inside him. He wished he could tell her the Parkses could have the honeycomb. He only needed her smile.

"Thanks," he mumbled. "Thank you kindly."

"We're the ones to thank you." Her gray eyes borrowed the blue of the sky. "Thank you, Dan. For everything."

He went off, floating on air, heedless of blisters on his heels, the ache of his shoulders. He whistled his song, his own song. For the first time, in spite of the drought, there was more joy in the song than sorrow.

Chapter Two

Her mother smiled thanks as Christy drew water from John Brown's well to pour around the rose bushes Charlie had brought two years ago, a gift from Lavinia Jardine. "I hate for you to work so hard, dear. We can do without roses."

"No, we can't!" said Christy.

As if she hadn't seen how her mother loved the velvety crimson flowers, the pink-tipped ivory ones. It wasn't fair that Lavinia Jardine had so many roses, a hundred different kinds, when her mother might lose these cherished two. As long as she could crawl, Christy intended to keep them alive. They'd stopped blooming in this dry heat, but the leaves stayed green. They'd bloom again when it cooled off. The roses usually got the water from the wash basin and dish rinsing, but that now went to the onions and carrots.

Rinse water from laundry went to the maiden blush apple trees and grape vines, but, when the leaves began to curl, Christy drew extra water for them, too, even when she was so tired she could barely make her feet move or her arms pull the rope.

The cows, oxen, and horses feasted on abandoned corn and sorghum cane. "Bless them," her father said as he and Christy paused from filling buckets from the barrels and watched the animals feeding blissfully. "They deserve a treat, but I wish it didn't cost so much in work and hope." His ruefulness deepened. "Are you through pulling up the beans and peas for the sheep and pigs?"

"Not quite." Christy wanted to roll her shoulders, loosen the knotted muscles, but that would make her father feel badly. He hated for her to do heavy outside work. "And there's still the potatoes we can't water."

"Why don't you pull them up while there's good nourishment in them?" Jonathan asked. "I can finish here."

It was his way of sparing her part of their arduous daily chore, but it was also true that each unrelenting hour baked moisture from the dying plants, so she nodded and walked up the slope to the garden where three hunger-emboldened deer had jumped the fence and were enjoying the fare. They sailed over the fence at Robbie's barking. Christy was dismayed at the vines they'd ravaged, but she couldn't grudge the food.

The pods that should have been plump with juicy peas encased tiny nubs, and the green beans were scrawny and tough. Christy winced as she pulled up a vine, shook earth — dry earth — from the roots, and tossed it in the wheelbarrow. If it rained tomorrow, how they'd regret this, the waste of all their labor! But they'd hoped and waited, waited and hoped.

Mildred, Cleo, and Nosey snuffled greedily as Christy scattered the vines from the wheelbarrow so all the sheep would get a mouthful. She had to smile at the lambs playing king of the hill, butting their little heads, although this was one year it would have been better not to have them. Apart from their appetites, if the natural prey of panthers, wolves, and bobcats dwindled enough, the hunters wouldn't all be kept off by Robbie's brave efforts.

Patches' and Evalina's family had increased again, too. Jonathan had traded off all the pigs he could, but more than one would have to be slaughtered that fall. As the black and white animals grunted their pleasure at this surprise, Christy hoped this wouldn't be the year her father decided that Patches' and Evalina's ages doomed them. The Wares had a special affection for the creatures that had traveled the long road with them to this new home.

When I grow up, Christy thought as she trundled the wheelbarrow back to the garden, *I'll try to live from the garden and fields, orchard, vineyard, and dairy. There could be eggs, too. I wouldn't kill the hens when they got past laying age. Even when they didn't calve any more, the cows could go on grazing.*

What if there's a year like this when grazing's pitiful and the chickens can't scratch up enough to live? Would you scant your producing animals to save the worn-out ones? The voice of what-everybody-else-thinks grew jeering. *Even if you're such a fool, what man would put up with that? Your father's so kind he can't believe anyone will go to hell, but even he has to give in to the plain hard facts of living.*

Dan's thin face, nose ridged to one side by old brutality, rose before her. Out of all the people at the cabin-raising, he'd been the other one who couldn't endure that the bear and her cub should be torn apart by hounds — and the bear hadn't even hung around his home, listening to music, as she had at the Wares'. He, unlike most folks, didn't joke about the Wattleses' vegetarian ways, although he'd looked dazed when the women wore bloomers to Andy's and Susie's wedding.

Christy giggled. Probably she'd looked a little dazed herself. Then she sobered as she pulled up vines. Strange how they came up in seconds when each one represented hours of labor. It wasn't only sweat that stung her eyes. To console herself and fret less over this task, she relived every moment of Dan's visit, imagined that he smiled at her, that those eyes the color of autumn haze on the hills had rested on her.

22

Humming, she tried to remember the melody of his song. She'd capture some of it before what followed eluded her. Her mother had been right. Dan had made something beautiful out of his pain and loss. That set him a world apart from her brothers, not to mention snooty, spoiled Travis Jardine or cruel-smiling Lafe Ballard.

She hadn't thought of Lafe in weeks and shivered now as she did so. Lafe would make pain out of beauty just as he'd scarred her flesh. Always, like an obscene brand, she'd carry his livid white mark above the pulse of her wrist. To banish that ugliness, she fixed her mind on Dan's song and tried to call it back.

As if drought wasn't enough, bugs erupted overnight on the potato vines. Her mother had hit on the notion of turning the chickens into the patch. It was Beth's chore to shoo Cavalier and his wives along if they started pecking leaves instead of bugs, but there were enough of the pests to keep the chickens occupied till the bugs were vanquished.

There was never much visiting among neighbors during summer. This year, there was even less, although the Hayeses, Barclays, Hester Ballard, and Emil and Lottie Franz usually came to Sunday services and stayed to share a meal with whatever they had brought. Being together raised spirits and hopes.

Dan O'Brien came when he wasn't too tired to walk. "The horses need their day of rest," he said. "If I took it, I'd be a hypocrite to sing hymns."

Ethan, Mark, and Luke Hayes were so busy with the tannery that Ethan had to let the crops go. "So many animals are dying or being slaughtered and divvied up fast before the meat spoils that we can't keep up," he said with a shrug. "Allie and Mary tote water to some spuds and garden. Other than that. . . . I'll swap tanned hides for food in Osceola. As long as the Osage River doesn't get too low, steamboats bring supplies that far."

Other neighbors watered some crops from the creek except for the Madduxes and Watt Caxton. The Madduxes expected their congregation to feed them, and borrowed from family back East to eke out the contributions. Caxton let his few acres wither. He'd made his usual rounds that spring to buy up mules and slaves and sell them at a profit. After that, rather than battle the drought, he organized cockfights for a share of the winnings and located runaway slaves and brought them back for the reward.

It was the longest summer Christy could remember. When she and her father weren't watering, they walked the creekbanks, cutting young willow and cottonwood limbs for the sheep and cows. The oxen and horses ranged outside the fences, feeding on grass that had already cured like hay.

The potatoes yielded well, but the family ate sparingly of them, carrots, sweet potatoes, and turnips. Most would be stored in the root cellar for winter. They did feast for days on roasting ears. The buttered tender corn tasted more delicious to Christy than anything she'd ever tasted. She and her father stripped the blades from the ears, let them dry, bound the sweet-smelling fodder, and hauled it to the barn. Only a fraction of what had been stored in previous years, it would be doled out to the milk cows and animals that needed it most.

Christy and her father were cutting willow limbs one searing late August afternoon when she heard Beth give a whoop. Glancing up, she saw her little sister run to hurl herself at Dan who picked her up and whirled her around before he set her down and started for the creek, Beth on his heels.

He stepped into the shade as Ellen Ware came out with a jug and cups. He took the sassafras tea with thanks as Ellen poured more for her husband and older daughter.

"Churches and folks from the East are fixing to send food and other supplies to Kansas," Dan said, beaming around at the Wares. "Each township is forming a committee to be in charge of what comes in and split it up as fair as they can."

"Well, that's a mercy," Ellen said. "Without help, it'll be a cruel winter for some poor souls."

"You folks around here are hit as bad as those in Kansas." Dan hesitated. "Uncle Simeon's on the committee for our township. He's got the others, Sam Nickel and Andy McHugh, to agree to share with people across the border."

Jonathan Ware straightened. It was only then Christy noticed he was bending so much with the watering that his shoulders were getting a forward slant. "We thank Simeon . . . and you . . . for thinking of us, Dan, but we'll manage."

"Well, if it gets bad later on, let Simeon know. I guess wagons will be hauling grain and such in till summer, but it won't be regular." He handed his cup back to Ellen. "I'm supposed to leave word at the tannery so Mister Hayes can spread the news. The committee needs to know as soon as possible how many families will need help."

"Stop for supper on your way home," Ellen invited.

Beth seized his hands. "Yes, Danny! Stop! If you do, we'll have potatoes! Won't we, Mama?"

"Indeed, we will." Ellen laughed. "And you, Elizabeth, may peel them."

Looking forward to Dan's company seemed to make the work go faster and easier for Christy. "Why don't you have a swim and freshen up?" Jonathan asked as he started to haul a last load of browse to the sheep. He added with a chuckle: "It might startle Dan speechless to see you in a clean dress, but why not try it?"

The beloved blue foulard had grown too tight for any artifice so it had yielded a shirtwaist for Christy and best dress for Beth, with material left over to make the dress "grow" with Beth till it was worn into quilt scraps. Christy's Sunday dress was now a green-gray plaid Charlie had brought last winter. To wash her hair later, she drew water from the well and left it in a tub and bucket to grow warm while she took her dress, clean underwear, and a towel to the swimming hole.

She couldn't swim more than a few strokes in any direction without hitting the limestone bottom, but even that was refreshing. Rubbing with the towel till her skin tingled, she tried not to think of what would happen if the creek ran dry. They'd have to haul water for themselves and for all the livestock from the Marais des Cygnes a mile away, or take the animals to the river morning and evening.

Would it never rain? The last blazing of the sun gave a pitiless answer, darkening Christy's pleasure at Dan's visit. She hurried to wash her hair and towel it as dry as she could before gathering eggs, feeding the chickens and pigs, and fetching in water and wood. Only then did she change from homemade work shoes into slippers, another of Charlie's gifts.

She sighed as she did so. It was sweet of him to bring the family presents when he finished long distance freighting in late autumn, but Christy would give all the luxuries for him still to belong to them, not the Jardines. She combed the tangles out of her hair and hurried to help with supper that would be special because of Dan.

Robbie escorted him in with joyful barks. He'd splashed water over his face at the creek, and his damp, unruly hair showed the efforts of a comb. He must be tired from working all morning and walking seven miles that afternoon, but his eyes lit at the sight of Christy like deep water struck by sun.

They sat down to potatoes whipped fluffy with butter and

cream, crisp carrot sticks, and a dish Ellen had devised — tiny dumplings of cottage cheese, eggs, and a sprinkling of corn-meal boiled first in water, then scrambled with eggs and watercress.

As soon as Jonathan said grace, Dan said appreciatively: "This sure smells and looks good, Missus Ware. We're still getting milk, but the hens have about quit laying."

"We'll send some eggs home with you," Ellen promised, although some of her hens weren't laying and those that were didn't produce as regularly in the hot weather. "How are the Hayeses getting along?"

"Hanging on. Lige Morrow and Watt Caxton brought in some hides while I was there. Lige says he took some fish to the Barclays and found them packing up."

"To go East?"

Dan nodded. "Lige tried to encourage them, but Mister Barclay said what settled his mind was when he went to dig up some potatoes. Instead of potatoes in the hill, there was a great big rattler."

"Good heavens!" Ellen gasped.

"He tried three more hills. Each one had a snake. He told Lige that, even if it wasn't a sign his land was cursed, he sure wasn't trying to farm where you raised rattlers instead of spuds."

Christy would miss her quiet brown-eyed schoolmates but she hoped they'd find a better place. "The Barclays asked Lige to tell their neighbors . . . especially all of you . . . good bye for them," Dan explained. "The snakes were the last straw. They just wanted to be on their way as soon as they could. Lige went home and brought them some jerked venison and smoked turkey for their trip."

"Lige is a good man," Jonathan said.

"Caxton isn't. He was hanging around Westport with Lafe

Ballard . . . yes, that's where he is now. They caught a couple of runaways and turned them in for the rewards. Then they happened onto a Negro whose master had freed him and given him a new coat and a hundred dollars. They beat him up, stole his coat and money, and burned his free papers. Then they sold him to a planter."

"That awful, awful man!" Christy choked. "Oh, I hope there's some way the first owner finds out and gets his man free."

"Ethan picked up Caxton's hides and slung them at him. Knocked him down in some fresh cow pies." Dan grinned at the memory. "Ethan told Caxton never to set foot on his land again. Lige said that went for him, too. He helped Caxton fly up in his wagon by shooting around his feet."

"Hester thinks Lafe's mining in the Rockies," Ellen said. "It would grieve her to know her son had a hand in such evil."

Christy's scar throbbed. "I hope he never comes back!"

Jonathan shook his head. "It's a hard thing to say, but the kindest thing for Hester may be if she never sees or hears tell of Lafe again."

"But it's terrible not to know," Ellen sighed. "I worry about Charlie and Thos all the time they're out on those dangerous trails." Meeting her husband's concerned eyes, she added with a little smile: "I start to worry, dear. Then I pray for them, instead."

Beth jumped up to help Christy clear the table. "We've got de-sert! I picked wild plums, didn't I, Mama? A whole pan full! And there's cream to pour on them." Since the ripening of dewberries and golden currants in mid-June, followed into July by raspberries and blackberries, Beth, guarded by Robbie, brought home sweet wild fruit whenever she could find it.

"These are a de-licious de-sert," Dan complimented Beth

28

as he raised a spoonful of the reddish-orange fruit to his lips. "I'll tell Letty she needs to find a good thicket and bring some home."

He didn't have his fiddle, but he stayed to sing along with the piano after dishes were done. How Christy wished she could see him every day, that he could sing with them every night.

When he left in the shallow light of a crescent moon, Jonathan cautioned: "Watch out for wolves. Ordinarily they're shy of humans, but, with prey scarce, they're getting bold. Two came up and watched us cutting willow limbs today."

A chill crawled down Christy's spine. "I didn't know that."

"They were on that bluff across the creek, still as could be. Didn't see any use spooking you, honey. I don't intend for you to be by yourself very far from the house. There's panthers out there, too."

"I've got my Sharps," said Dan. "But I'll find me a club, too, a good shillelagh."

He went off whistling that sad happy song of his own. Christy watched him fade into the trees. Then she did what her mother said. Instead of worrying, she prayed that he would get home safe this night, and all the nights of his life.

Now it was time to plow under the roots of the sacrificed wheat and oats. There wasn't any stubble. The animals had eaten the stalks into the ground. "I hate to put seed into such dry earth," Jonathan regretted, "but, if we don't get rain and make a crop next summer, I'll have to go freighting to get us through."

Ellen smiled at him across the supper table. "We'll do what we have to, Jon."

"Ethan traded some of his hides for seed in Osceola," Jonathan went on. "He'll swap us some for what corn and potatoes we can spare, and for teaching Luke and Mary. The boys'll come over soon with their corn knives and a wagon. I thought we could let them have the stalks they cut for fodder."

"Sharing's the only way any of us will get by," Ellen said.

To be freed of watering crops was like a holiday, although Christy put on one of her father's old shirts, and gloves Charlie had left behind before she used a sharp, murderous-looking corn knife for the first time. She cut the stalks close to the ground, broke off the stripped ears, and tossed them in the wheelbarrow. The family was almost out of cornmeal. As soon as the kernels were hard enough to grind, they'd have to shell a bushel to get to the mill.

A chance to see Dan. Christy hoped her father would let her take the corn. Apart from seeing Dan, it would be fun to visit with Lydia and Harriet. Wiping away sweat and itching chaff, Christy hummed as much of Dan's song as she could remember. In spite of dreaming of him, though, she was so hot and weary when she went to the house for dinner that her parents looked at her in concern. Even before grace, Ellen got a jar of Hester's ointment and smoothed it on Christy's blistering hands.

"I hate for you to do such work." Jonathan scowled. "But I have to finish plowing so the roots will pretty well decay before I plant wheat in a month or so. . . ."

"There's too much for you to do alone, Father," Christy argued.

"There is, but we don't want you worn to a nub, either." Her mother brightened. "Listen, dear. This afternoon, you can take Beth and gather wild fruit."

Now that would be a holiday. Then Christy sighed. "There won't be a lot this year."

lucky to have corn at all."

There wasn't much luck to losing most of the growing crops and hauling water for the rest, but Christy refrained from saying so. Her cheeks grew warm as she summoned up courage to make her request.

"When . . . when we have enough corn shelled, may I take it to the mill?"

Her parents exchanged startled glances. "I'd like to see Lydia and Harriet," she said truthfully enough, but blushed even before her father grinned.

"And Dan O'Brien, perhaps?"

"We . . . e . . . ell . . . yes!"

"I was wondering if you'd mind going," her father said. "Some shingles blew off the barn and smokehouse in that last high wind. I'd like to repair the roofs before I plant wheat."

"I saved some of Beth's baby things," Ellen said. "I'll send them for Harriet and Susie to share. That'll be nice to have cousins the same age."

"I wish I did," Beth said.

"You do, on your father's side, but they're in Ohio," explained Ellen. "I was born late to my parents, an only child. They were carried off with scarlet fever the year Charlie was born. I cried for weeks because they never got to see him." She sighed. "Unless families move together as the Wattleses did, once some move West it's likely they'll never see each other again."

Jonathan took her hand and pressed it to his cheek. "Yes, Ellen, but, when our children marry and have little ones, we'll be a big family again." He gave one of Beth's curls a playful tug. "You can be an aunt. That might be more fun than being a cousin."

The child bounced with excitement. "Who do you think'll get married first? Charlie or Thos or Christy?"

Ellen smiled at Christy with tenderness and a hint of sadness. "We'll just have to wait and see, won't we?"

"I won't move away!" Sudden moisture blurred Christy's eyes. "Not so far that we can't visit often and be together for holidays." She laughed to clear the lump in her throat. "Maybe I'll be an old maid."

"No," said Beth. "You've got to marry Danny."

Chapter Three

To Christy's disappointment, Dan had taken a plowshare to
Andy McHugh's forge for sharpening, but she did enjoy
hearing about the doings of the Moneka Women's Rights Society as she sipped sassafras tea and worked on the socks she
was knitting for her father. Harriet was so unwieldy that she
moved with effort, but she glowed with happiness. She, her
mother, Mildred Morrison, and Lydia were all sewing or
knitting baby things.

"I think I'm going to be able to carry this baby." Harriet's
blue eyes shone. "If it's a boy, we'll call him Owen Daniel
David Simeon."

"A lot of names for a tyke!" Mrs. Morrison snorted.

"There are four men we want to name a son after, Mama.
As hard as it is for me to have a baby, we'd better give this one
all the names."

Tossing a head that was still as much yellow as gray, Harriet's mother gave her daughter a reproachful look. "It hurts
me that you'd pass over your own two dear brothers to name
your child for an Irish orphan."

"Mama, how long is it since you've heard from either of
my own dear brothers?"

Mrs. Morrison reddened. "Young men who're freighting
don't write letters."

"Maybe not, but they can visit their families like Christy's brother does. Dan's a brother to Owen and he's been like one to me." Harriet smiled at Christy. "It was sweet of your mother to send those nice baby things. Between Susie and me, we'll need them all."

"I suppose," said Mrs. Morrison, tight-lipped, "that you have a name ready for a girl, too."

"Lydia Susan."

"Well! What's wrong with *my* name?"

"Mama! We gave Letty your middle name, Leticia, and used Owen's mother's name, Mary, for the middle one."

"No one calls me Letty. To outsiders, it looks like a slight."

"Outsiders can mind their own business!"

Lydia stepped between two pairs of angry blue eyes. "Would anyone like more tea?" Pouring from a treasured china pot, she said to Christy: "You may not have heard, but Eli Bradley and a friend have opened a saloon over at Trading Post. It's a hang-out for riff-raff from both sides of the border, and the Women's Rights Society is upset about it."

"You mean those bloomer-wearing Wattles girls are sticking in their noses where they don't belong," sneered Mildred.

"I mean I went with them to reason with Mister Bradley and his partner."

"I'd have gone, too," Harriet assured her mother, "except I was afraid of losing the baby."

"Praise be you have a pinch of sense!" Mildred Morrison frowned. "If women don't keep their place, they can't expect to be treated like ladies."

Lydia grinned. Her thin, high-browed face grew almost pretty. "That's more or less what Mister Bradley told us in a nicer way. He and his customers said that's why they'd never vote for giving the women the ballot. 'The minute you could vote, you'd outlaw whiskey, wouldn't you?' he asked." Lydia chuckled.

"Emma Wattles said . . . 'That's exactly what we'll do, sir, and then there won't be so many beaten, abused, hungry, and neglected wives and children!' "

"What did he say to that?" asked Christy. Her mother would relish hearing of the women's courage. It was a shame the Wares lived too far from Moneka to attend the society's meetings.

"Mister Bradley vowed that, if he heard of a customer beating his wife, he'd personally horsewhip the man." Lydia really was quite attractive when she laughed. "Then, most politely, Mister Bradley bowed us out the door."

"Which you should never have darkened!" scolded Mildred.

"Even without rain, our sorghum cane made a fair crop." Lydia was obviously experienced in evading Mrs. Morrison's onslaughts. "I'll send a jug home with you, Christy."

"You may need it." Not guessing that the cane would make a crop, the Wares had turned their livestock in on the field.

"We have enough to last till spring when we can get sap from the maples. Besides, you brought that good butter and cheese. What do you hear from Thos?"

"Just one letter with a few lines." Christy pulled a face. "He says he's too busy carrying mail to write, but he'll try to come home at Christmas."

Everyone laughed except Mildred whose sons neither wrote nor visited. At dinner, conversation centered on whether Congress would ever admit Kansas to the Union. "If it does," mused Simeon bleakly, "I fear it will herald the exodus of Southern states. They won't tolerate being outvoted in the Senate."

"Let 'em go and good riddance," growled Owen.

Simeon shook his white head. "With the Democratic party split, Lincoln's almost sure to win. He won't let Secession wreck this country."

"A war won't wreck it?" Owen asked.

"It could heal back together."

"In a hundred years?"

"That's as God wills."

David's green eyes caught fire. "If there's war, I'm going!"

"David, we're Quakers," chided Lydia. "Besides, you're barely sixteen."

David didn't answer, but the mutinous set of his smooth young jaw spoke louder than words. Simeon studied him in troubled silence before he turned to Christy. "I have to finish grinding for Hughie Huston and Sam Nickel, but I'll have yours ready well before dark. Or, if you'd rather get on home, I can give you meal that's already ground and keep yours."

"Oh, do stay if you can," urged Harriet. "It's lovely to have company! Mostly men bring the grain, so Papa and the boys get to visit, but we don't."

Christy's parents didn't expect her back till dusk. She was enjoying the little holiday, and, besides, Dan might return before she left.

"I'll wait," she told the miller.

The afternoon passed pleasantly. When David came to say the meal was ready and that he'd caught and saddled Lass and fastened the meal sack behind the cantle, the women said their good byes and Lydia tied a jug of molasses into a bag.

"You can fasten this to the saddle horn," she suggested. "Thank your mother for the butter and cheese, and do come any time you can."

"Thank her for the baby clothes and blankets!" Harriet called.

"I will." Christy nodded. "We'll be waiting to hear you have your new baby, and we'll pray that all goes well."

"Your little mare ran into something sharp and cut her shoulder while she was frolicking with Zephyr and Breeze," David told Christy. "Didn't much more than pierce the hide, but it bled some. I washed it with soft soap. You might want to do that again after you're home."

"Oh, poor Lass!" Christy stroked the chestnut's soft nose and moved around to the shoulder. A seep of blood marked a long scratch.

"She probably ran against a snag sticking out from one of those dead trees we haven't cleared off yet," David said. "I'm sorry."

"It wasn't your fault." Christy rubbed her cheek against the mare's as David secured the jug to the saddle horn. "We'll put some of Hester's coneflower salve on it and it'll heal with just a thin line. Thanks, Davie." She hesitated. "Tell Dan hello for me."

David grinned and looked with understanding. "Dan'll be sorry he missed you."

At sixteen, David was losing the angelic look of his boyhood, changing along with his voice into a strikingly handsome young man with dark-lashed green eyes and a mass of curly black hair.

Let there not be war, God. Don't let Davie go to fight, or Dan, or Charlie or Thos . . . or Owen or Andy or . . . or anybody.

She led Lass to a stump and mounted astride, pulling down her skirts as much as possible. The Wares had no sidesaddle, and Christy didn't want one. They looked dangerously uncomfortable and off-balance to her, but she did wish for the Wattles girls' ugly but practical bloomers.

Would her mother let her make a pair for excursions like this? She was going to have to dismount to pick some of those ripe red haws yonder, and then climb again into the saddle. Oh, for free-swinging, unencumbered legs!

She popped a few of the small tartly sweet scarlet fruits in her mouth and savored them while she filled part of one deep pocket of her knitted cape. A little farther along, she was tempted off Lass again by a nice clump of elderberries. As she struggled back into the saddle, her delight at having filled both pockets was chilled when she noticed that twilight was hazing the timber.

"We won't stop again for the best fruit in Missouri," she promised Lass. "Let's move along, girl."

Her parents would be worried. That was a poor way to make them think she could be trusted with errands. Something moved at the edge of her vision. When she turned, it wasn't there, but, in a moment, a shadow took form on the other side.

This one didn't vanish. She saw the glow of eyes. Lass snorted and broke into a gallop. Christy hung on to the jug to keep it from banging against the mare. The color of dusk, four wolves broke from the woods and raced after them. Two were bigger than the others. The biggest one of all hurled itself at Lass' throat as a scream ripped from Christy.

Lass rose up in the air, squealing, and struck at the wolf with her front hoofs. It was all Christy could do to cling to the saddle horn. Lass missed, but the big wolf fell back. The mare galloped on. Wolves weren't supposed to attack people! But maybe they were drawn by the smell of Lass' blood. They'd have less prey because of the drought. That could make them desperate. Or — perhaps the big wolf had hydrophobia. Any creature with that dread, foam-mouthed plague, even a normally timid squirrel, would attack anything or anyone.

The big wolf leaped again at Lass' neck. If he brought her down, the other wolves would finish her. Lass reared again and struck down as her wild ancestors must have done. The wolf fell. Lass whirled to kick him with both hind hoofs before she lowered her head and plunged on.

She'd gotten rid of the biggest wolf. There was no more jumping at her throat, but the other wolves pursued. Christy didn't use the reins. Lass knew better than she did what to do. Gripping the saddle horn, hugging the molasses, Christy prayed more fervently than she ever had in her life.

There was the crash of a shot. One wolf yelped, faded into the brush. Another shot. Christy ventured to glance around. All the wolves were gone.

"Christy!"

Dan! His shout sent such a flood of relief through her that her bones went weak and wavery. "Christy!" he called. "Are you all right?"

"Yes! We're fine." Christy leaned over, caressing Lass' neck, drawing gently on the reins. "They're gone, sweetheart. You can slow down now. What a brave girl!"

Dan rode out of the gloaming. Christy didn't know how she got down, but in a moment they were in each other's arms, holding tightly, tightly, as if the other might disappear.

"Oh, Dan! How come you to follow?"

He ran his fingers along her face. "I was so disappointed when I heard I'd missed you that I told Uncle Simeon I was going to catch up and see you safely home."

"Thank goodness you did!"

He reached out to pat Lass' sweaty neck. "Oh, I think Lass would've gotten you away. She brained that big wolf . . . just as well for him, because she broke most of his bones." He took his hand away from the mare and stared at it. Even in the heavy dusk, the stain showed on his fingers. "Did the wolf do that?"

She explained.

"Good!" He released Christy to examine the cut. "Even a scratch like this could be the end of her if that critter had hydrophobia. Christy, when Zephyr shied at that dead wolf, I was so scared. . . ." He took her in his arms again, finding her eager lips with his hard, tender ones. This time her bones melted from sweetness, not terror.

"If anything happened to you . . . ," he muttered at last. "I love you, Christy, sweetheart, darling. I guess I've loved you since the night we let those bears go and walked that underground river."

She laughed tremulously. "I guess I've loved you ever since then, too, Dan, in spite of getting mad at you when you scolded me for not changing Beth fast enough."

"Did I do that?"

"You certainly did!"

He cradled her against him. So wonderful to be like that, to hear his heart pound beneath her cheek, feel the muscle and bone and flesh of him, and all that still just the clothing for his soul, his spirit that made songs.

"I'll change the babes myself when we have some," he teased.

"Danny!"

At her happy cry, he shook his head, burying his face in her hair. "Christy, Christy, I pray above all things that you'll marry me, but it can't be till we can see straight ahead for a time."

"We're old enough! I turn seventeen in a few weeks. You're close to twenty!"

"Neither any great age, love." He laughed huskily. "But for sure, were it not for the great troubles roiling up, I'd ask your parents if they were willing."

"War?" He nodded. She held him closer, although in some way, in his being, he moved away from her. What she held

44

was not what she wanted. "Dan, there's been war on the border for years."

"Yes, and men have died on both sides and left widows and orphans." He put her away from him. "I'll not do that to you."

"But Dan, no one can be sure of living."

"Some can be surer than others."

"You weren't born here, Dan." It was an ignoble argument, but she couldn't keep from making it. "No one could blame you if you didn't fight."

Her shame filled the silence before he spoke. "I'll fight, Christy. Isn't it here I have a way to live free of landlords and have a chance to amount to something? How can I take those gifts and not try to deserve them?"

"We can still be married . . . have whatever time we can together."

"And you have a baby while I'm off, God knows where, not able to take care of you?"

"But. . . ."

He gripped her by her upper arms till it pained. "Christy, if I can help it, no child of mine will starve as I and my sister did."

She swallowed and blinked. "So because of a war that may not happen and a baby we might not have, we won't love each other while we can?"

He kissed her quickly and helped her mount. "We'll love each other. At least I'll sure love you. I ache to show you every way there is. I dream. . . ." He broke off, turning away. "Your folks'll be worried. Let's get you home."

What? What do you dream? I dream, too. Only her dreams stopped with embracing, mouths on each other's, breaths mingled, bodies close as they could be with garments in between. Beyond that, she dare not venture.

45

Lass still snorted now and then, flinging her head up, as if remembering the attack. Christy stroked her sweat-soaked neck. "You're a brave beauty, Lass. A brave, brave girl. You get some corn tonight."

"She's earned it," Dan said. His voice twisted. "If she hadn't fought off that big wolf. . . ."

Christy began to shiver, cold to the bone, although the night was warm. *If Lass had run on till the wolf pulled her down. . . . If the other wolves had grown bolder before Dan's shots scared them off. . . .* She held to the saddle horn as she had during the onslaught when her only hope was Lass.

Dan's voice roused her. "Look, Christy. Yonder shines a lamp in the window. Your mother's put it there to help you home."

Christy had only been gone since morning, but she felt changed entirely. Swift death had run beside her. Then Dan had come — and he'd declared his love in the same breath that he said they must wait to marry. Christy sighed. It was hard to believe life would ever run smoothly on this border.

The light shining from the cabin was like her parents' love, and love and gratitude for them warmed Christy, melting the chill of shock. "Dan?"

"Yes, sweetheart."

It seemed, at least, he'd allow endearments. "If . . . if we were married, and, if . . . something happened, my parents would help me."

"To be sure."

"Then. . . ."

"They'd help if they could." He added slowly: "Just as my parents would have helped Bridgie and me."

"Oh!" She recoiled. Her mother and father had always been in her life. She couldn't imagine otherwise. Wouldn't.

"But Dan, they're young, almost. Father's . . . *mmm* . . . forty-three. Mother's forty."

"Christy, I'd rather be whipped than say this, but my poor young parents weren't all that much older than I am now. Da, I recall, was twenty-five."

She winced but persisted. "That was Ireland. In the starving years!"

"If this drought lasts, folks will starve or leave. And what will a real war bring when, even without one, we've burnings and murders?" His voice turned grim. "Don't try to wear me down on this, girl."

"What if I'm not available when and if you finally come around to thinking we might run the terrible, unheard-of risk of getting married?"

Even in the dark, she could almost see his angry look. Her heart faltered and her mouth dried in the moment before he answered. "If you would marry someone else . . . maybe that rich puffed-up Travis Jardine? . . . then you weren't, in truth, for me. I'd wish you happy from the roots of my heart. I'll always wish you that, God knows. But don't you expect me to dance at your wedding."

"I'll never have one," she retorted. "Not if you must wait till all the woes of the world are over!"

"Not quite that long." He chuckled and his hand came out to brush her cheek. "How's this? If Lincoln's elected and the Southern states don't secede, and if things calm along this border, then we'll marry as soon as your folks agree and I can claim some land and get a cabin up."

Christy thrilled, remembering the raising of her family's home, such a happy, friendly, neighborly day. Except for Lafe's burning her. Except for Watt Caxton's planned bear-baiting. Well, maybe in life things were never altogether one way or the other, a little bad streaking the good, a flash of good lighting the murk of evil.

"So?" prompted Dan.

"I'm sure Father would like to have you farm with him. It looks like Thos and Charlie won't. There's too much for him to do even with what help I can give him."

Dan considered. "You have to know it's a long dream of mine, Christy, to own a bit of land. But it would be grand to buy land joining or close to your parents', and there's no man living I'd sooner work with than your father."

Robbie dashed to greet them. Jonathan and Ellen appeared in the cabin door, Beth rushing past them.

"Christy! Christy! Daddy was about to go looking for you!"

"I'm fine!" Christy called. Beneath Robbie's joyful clamor, she asked: "Shall we tell my parents, Dan?"

"Whatever you want."

"Let's keep it a secret for a while." She couldn't explain the way she wanted to hug it to her, let their understanding grow almost like a baby, warmed by her heart, hidden from the world. "Our secret, Danny."

"No harm in that, I reckon." He greeted her family, swung down, looped Zephyr's reins to the post, and helped Christy dismount. "I'll unsaddle Lass and rub her down," he said. "Mister Ware, when you hear what this little mare did, I think you'll say she can have some corn."

"I'll say so now if you think it, Dan." Jonathan untied the cornmeal and hefted it over his shoulder while Christy loosened the molasses jug. "When you finish with Lass, come in and have supper. We've kept soup warm for Christy."

Ellen held out her arms and Christy ran into them. "What happened, child?" her mother smoothed her hair. "What did Lass do?"

They went inside and Christy told them. "If I hadn't

picked the haws and elderberries. . . . Gracious!" She reached inside her pockets and brought out handfuls of berries pulped over the firmer red haws. "The haws are all right," she said, crestfallen, and tried to laugh. "Patches and Evalina ought to love the berries."

"Beth," said Ellen, "dip a pone in molasses and give it to Lass." She rummaged on a shelf. "Take Hester's coneflower ointment and rub it on that scratch . . . or have Dan do it." Her face crumpled. "Oh, Christy, if. . . ."

Jonathan put his arms around them both. "Our girl's safe, Ellen, thanks to Lass, Dan, and the grace of God. That wolf had hydrophobia or went crazy at the scent of Lass' blood. We'd all better be careful till the drought breaks."

Drought. It seemed to Christy that's what the threat of war was — a harsh blast shriveling what would otherwise thrive — but she knew her love for Dan would grow even without more nourishment than what she had already in her heart.

She hoped it would be the same for him as he came in, holding Beth's hand, light setting his hair aflame, making his eyes glow as they fell on Christy.

"Sit down, you two," Ellen said. "It's more than time you ate."

Jonathan cleared his throat. "We've always thought a lot of you, Dan, but, after this, you're . . . well, you're dear to us as a son."

Christy almost blurted: *He's going to be.* But then she met Dan's eyes, smiled, and hugged their secret.

Chapter Four

Outside was winter, but Lavinia Jardine's rose room was warm and bright, sun shining through the glass to caress every bloom from buds to full blown and woo from them the sweet odors that permeated the conservatory and wafted into the house.

Emmie napped on the wicker bench, nose tucked into her fluffy tail, but, when Charlie came in with Melissa, the gray cat dropped to the floor and came to rub against his legs. He bent to scratch behind her ears with fingers that would always bear the scars of her frantic clawing when he'd saved her from the hounds. Hither and Yon raised red-cheeked yellow heads from the apples they were devouring and grouched in parakeet.

Charlie's heart thrilled when Melissa took off her shawl and sun lit the amber around her throat, the necklace he'd given her four years ago. Four years? That made her twenty.

How long could it be till she married some gentleman farmer or one of the Bentons' St. Louis friends that Melissa's sister kept parading past her? Charlie saved all he could. At Jardine's invitation, he'd invested in the freighting company and that should bring returns in time, but here was Melissa past the age when most girls married.

He hadn't been able to save money that year at all. He and

Thos met in Independence as they'd earlier agreed and loaded a wagon borrowed from Seth Cooley with expensive wheat and corn, coffee, dried fruit, and other supplies. Thos volunteered to drive the mule-drawn wagon home while Charlie made his usual visit at the Jardines' before joining the family. After Christmas, the brothers had to get back to their work.

"Father'll have saved what he could of the crops," Thos had panted as he wedged in a barrel of molasses. "But since neither of us was there to help, I'm glad we can do this."

"Sure." Charlie had nodded, heaving on a sack of oats. He was glad, but losing a year's savings put him that much further away from the time he'd dare ask the bishop if. . . .

The soft tap of Lavinia Jardine's cane sounded on the polished floor. Charlie hastened to give her his arm. He thought her limp was worse this year, but didn't say so. Her hair was spun silver now, no hint of auburn left. She smiled up at him with soft blue eyes.

"It's dear of you to come see us, Charles. We're so far from Oregon and California that we can't expect Miles and Sherrod to visit, but that rascal, Travis! We're lucky to get a few scrawled words once or twice a year."

Charlie blushed. "I'm not much of a hand for writing home myself," he admitted, although if it had been acceptable to correspond with Melissa, he reckoned he would have. "Where is Travis, ma'am?"

"Who knows? If young men could just understand how mothers worry! The last we heard, he was at the Comstock in Nevada."

"When he strikes it rich, he'll come prancing up on a fancy horse flashing silver from its saddle and bridle, all loaded down with presents!"

"Seeing him would be better than any present." Lavinia

Jardine leaned on Charlie as he helped her into her wheeled chair by a trellis of ivory roses. She smiled over a twist of pain. "I suppose I should be grateful that Yvonne and Henry visit, but I must admit that the four children, dear though they are, are rather like an invading troop."

"They're brats, pure and simple," declared their aunt. "James and Tod can go to a military academy and learn some manners but Becky and Annette! I can't imagine men brave and foolish enough to hazard marriage with either."

"Melissa!"

"They're little beasts, Mama! Becky slapped Lilah last time they were here because Lilah pulled a tangle while brushing Becky's hair. Let me tell you, I grabbed Becky and shook her till her teeth rattled."

"Is that why Yvonne wouldn't speak to you the last day they were here?"

Melissa shrugged. "Don't fret about it, Mama. She gave me a scold for shaking Becky, and I gave her one back for raising such little monsters. Of course, with Henry for a father. . . ."

Lavinia touched her finger to her lips although her smile was sympathetic. "*Shh,* darling. Henry may be a trifle. . . ."

"Dull!"

"Unimaginative, perhaps, but he's good-natured."

"Lazy!"

Lavinia's smile faded. She straightened and gazed at her younger daughter in a way that made Melissa drop her head and mutter: "I'm sorry, Mama. But he is such a. . . ."

"Husband for your sister," Lavinia finished. She softened the rebuke with a pat of Melissa's hand. "Will you take Aunt Zillah her beef tea? Phronie says she spits it out at her and Lilah." Wheeling toward a bush of deep crimson, Lavinia selected the most beautiful flowers and snipped half a dozen.

"These are her favorites. I think she still sees a bit of the color, and she loves their smell."

Charlie started to excuse himself and follow Melissa, but Lavinia gestured at the wicker bench. "Won't you keep me company a while, Charles? I know you have to be off soon to your family. Thank goodness, the terrible drought finally broke. We had nothing to sell this year, but at least none of our folk went hungry."

Much as he liked and admired Lavinia Jardine, Charlie couldn't help thinking that, through the drought, black hands fetched water for the roses while his father and sister battled to save a little corn.

Charlie sat down and stroked Emmie who jumped into his lap. "It's a long while yet till harvest, ma'am, even if spring crops are good."

"At least the drought ran a lot of Abolitionist rabble out of Kansas," Bishop Jardine said as he strode in and stood beside his wife, arms behind his back, cider-colored eyes fixed on Charlie as if trying to read his mind and heart.

Charlie groaned inwardly. This was no accident, the bishop happening by when Melissa was sent on an errand. The Jardines were going to tell him their daughter wasn't for him. Kindly, of course, so long as he didn't get obstinate. He'd rather have been whipped than hear such words from Lavinia.

But the bishop didn't get to that message right away. "Glad as I am that plenty of thieving Free State rogues starved out of Kansas, it's sure to be admitted as a free state since that lanky ape, Lincoln, won the election last month. And that mealy-mouthed State of the Union swan song Buchanan made! States have no right to secede, he says! But the government has no legal right to stop them. What kind of wishy-washy drivel is that?"

"The kind he's used his whole term," shrugged Charlie, who had brought the news and suppressed one bit that he knew would enflame the bishop. The same day Buchanan addressed Congress, December 3rd, the bold former slave, Frederick Douglas, organized a rally honoring John Brown that was broken up by a mob. "Buchanan said one good thing, though . . . that the Union cannot be cemented by the blood of its citizens."

Jardine made a throwing-away motion. "Mark my word, Charles. By the time that black Republican takes office, states will be seceding right, left, and center."

"Do you think Missouri will, sir?"

"Who knows? To balance the big plantations along the Missouri and Mississippi, Saint Louis's thick with Germans. The lop-eared Dutch are against slavery almost to a man. Missouri was settled from both the North and South. Rests on a hair, I'd guess, how it swings."

"Mordecai," intervened his wife. "Could politics wait till we've discussed other matters?"

Charlie's guts tightened. Braced for rejection, he wished the bishop would get it over with.

Hands still behind him, Jardine puffed out fleshy red cheeks. "With everything so unstable, Charles, I feel it wise to take all possible measures to assure the future of this plantation and my womenfolk."

So he'd picked a suitable son-in-law, probably a neighbor. The words husked in Charlie's dry mouth. "I understand that, sir."

"Could you run this plantation?"

Charlie gaped. Had he heard aright? "Why," he floundered. "I . . . I never thought about such a thing."

Jardine's lips puckered up a bit at the edges. "Well, think, my boy! You've farmed. You know livestock and crops."

"Not cotton or hemp or tobacco."

"You'd learn."

"Travis. . . ."

"Travis is the main reason I'm asking, Charles. My other sons are doing well out West. They and Yvonne will inherit my shares in the freighting company. Travis and Melissa get this place. But Travis is too flighty to manage it. He's never taken the slightest interest in farming. The only livestock that brightens his eye are fast, mettlesome horses."

"You'll run the place for a long time, sir. Travis is bound to steady a lot in a few years."

"He takes after my younger brother," Jardine gloomed. "Knifed in a card game when he was twenty-two." He regarded Charlie as if planning to buy a horse or ox, weighing good points against bad. "Travis won't resent your being put in charge the way he would anyone else. You're a good influence on him. In time, he might even decide to help you."

"You have an overseer."

"Blake's all right, but he must have direction." The bishop spread his hands. "What I need, lad, is a young man to help me, one who can take over when I'm feeble."

"I . . . I'm honored, Bishop. And flabbergasted!"

Jardine smiled. "Think it over, Charles. If you accept, we'll let Seth Cooley know you won't be back."

Charlie swallowed, head awhirl. Live at Rose Haven? See Melissa every day? But there were the slaves. Jardine treated them well, but it didn't seem right to Charlie to own people the way you did livestock. It wouldn't be right to take the position without telling Melissa's folks how he felt about her.

"There are two things, sir, that won't be changed by any amount of thinking."

The bishop lifted his scraggy eyebrows. "What things, lad?"

55

Heart tripping, throat tight, Charlie blurted: "I love your daughter."

Both Jardines laughed. Lavinia squeezed his hand. "Lord love, you, dear! Don't you think we've seen that?"

"What's more to the purpose," grunted Jardine, "is that she's set her heart on you."

"Oh. . . ." Charlie felt as if his heart were bursting right out of his chest.

"You might as well know we tried to budge her . . . or at least I did." The bishop's voice held an edge of disgust. "The way you've been raised . . . from Illinois, Universalist minister for your father and all . . . is bound to have rubbed off some."

"Mordecai!"

"Yes, yes, Vinnie, but it's best to be honest."

"While we're being honest, sir, I should tell you my parents won't favor my marrying into a slave-holding family . . . but they won't try to talk me out of it. I know they'll welcome Melissa with all the loving kindness in the world."

Jardine turned a deeper crimson. "Then I wasn't as generous as your people, Charles. I tried, I surely did, to match our daughter with young men of the same background and views, but she turned up her nose at them." The bishop smiled at his wife and placed a hand on her shoulder. "Lavinia was the same. Insisted on me, Lord knows why, till her parents finally agreed."

Charlie's feet scarcely seemed to rest on the floor. It was as if he could float right up to the ceiling. But he had to state his other difficulty, the one that might ruin this dream.

"So, Charles?" Jardine crossed his arms again, standing behind his wife. "What's the other thing that can't be changed?"

"I don't . . . I can't . . . believe in slavery."

The bishop swung away. Lavinia looked distressed. Into

the silence, the bishop spoke at last. "Well, that does leave us with a problem. I tell you right now that I won't be coaxed or connived into freeing my colored folks. How would the work get done?"

"Free people can work."

"Not freed slaves. They have to leave the state." Jardine swung around. His eyes bored into Charlie's. "Would it be kind, even decent, of me to free Aunt Zillah who has no place to go, no one to take care of her?"

"Not if she can't stay here," Charlie had to admit.

"I have up to a thousand dollars a head invested in my prime hands. They're worth more than all the rest of my property. I can't just turn them lose."

According to the bishop's lights, he couldn't. There was no way of giving him any other lights. Charlie knew he should be high-minded and refuse to live where slaves were worked, but Melissa. . . . And the slaves would be there whether he was or not. He applied salve to his conscience, something to mitigate his parents' horror.

"You have the legal right to own slaves, Bishop, but you should know that . . . well, if I ever have the say around here, the slaves go free."

Jardine smiled. "By the time I'm dead, you may view things differently, Charles, but that'll be up to you, Melissa, and Travis." His tone hardened. "You do understand that I'll tolerate no encouraging or aiding my people to run off?"

"Of course." Charlie took a deep breath. "But, sir, if someone runs off, I can't let them be hunted down with dogs."

Veins corded and pulsed in Jardine's temples. "You'd interfere?"

"I'd have to."

"Then. . . ."

Lavinia caught her husband's arm. "Dearest!" So softly Charlie barely heard. "You know I've always begged you. . . . Please."

After a long moment, Jardine pondered: "Only one slave's run away . . . that proud-necked Justus. I'll always think he was hid by someone."

Charlie didn't want to encourage that line of thought. "The hounds didn't catch him, sir."

"No, but I think knowing I can get Caxton and his hounds after them keeps some of the restless ones from straying."

"I suppose," ventured Lavinia, "that they could go on thinking that even when we knew hounds wouldn't be used."

Jardine stroked his chin, gave Charlie a side glance. "Can you live with that?"

It was a compromise, but Jardine had already conceded more than Charlie could have imagined — in fact, this whole conversation was past belief. It would never have taken place, Charlie knew, except for Lavinia, and Melissa's defiant love.

She loved him. That was the lucky, unbelievable, amazing thing that made him feel at once humble and unworthy, yet exalted above all men. He couldn't wait to see her.

"Can you live with that?" Jardine repeated.

"Yes," said Charlie. "I can live with that."

He found Melissa wiping Aunt Zillah's mouth as Phronie held a cup with only a scum of pungent beef tea in the bottom. His face must have told her everything. Melissa gave a squeak and turned red.

"Charlie! Did Papa . . . ?"

He nodded. She dropped the washcloth. "Did you . . . ?"

Aunt Zillah raised on an arm like a brown-barked twig. "Who be it, missy? Who make you sound so glad?"

He went down on one knee by the bed and gently cradled

in his own hands the pair that were gnarled and dark as ancient roots. "I'm Charlie Ware, Aunt Zillah."

"Who?"

"Charlie Ware," he said as loudly and distinctly as he could.

She freed a hand and traced his features with spidery lightness. "Don' matter your name, child. My fingers see your face. You the boy my missy love."

"I sure do hope so."

Whether she heard or not, the old, old woman smiled. "You'll be a good man to her, honey. Your face tell me. Run along and let me smell the roses Miz Vinnie sent."

"You put on this shawl, Miss M'liss." Phronie took one from a peg and draped it around the girl's shoulders. Green eyes glinted at Charlie from the withered yellow face. "Won't hurt you to chill a speck, Master Charlie. That way you won't wander off and worry Miz Vinnie."

"Aunt Phronie!" Melissa sputtered. "We're going to be married!"

"All the same, no use stirrin' up them devils stoked away in any man who can totter."

Phronie might have been remembering her own daughter, born of a drunken guest of the Jardines', so beautiful that to avoid "problems" for himself or his sons, Jardine had sold her to a neighbor. She died birthing Lilah, her master's child. Phronie couldn't be blamed for her low opinion of white men. Charlie gave her what he hoped was an honest look.

"I'll never harm Melissa, Aunt Phronie. I'll do my best, always, to take care of her."

Her face softened. "I knows that, honey boy. Don't you still have the scars from savin' her foolish cat?" She patted his cheek. "You'd be out of the wind . . . and away from windows . . . on the back side of this cabin."

So that was where they walked, and where the clasp of hands turned to an embrace, holding each other as closely as they could, so closely they could scarcely breathe. Her lips and breath were sweet as warm honey, headier than the whiskey that had got him so drunk-miserable once that he'd kept away from it ever since.

He'd been with painted women some, mostly during winters in Independence, and he'd been grateful to them for relieving his throbbing hardness. That was there with Melissa, so insistently that he ached, but with it was such adoration and tenderness that he ached with that, too. He'd be careful with her, oh, so careful. He went dizzy at the thought of lying with her in bed, freed of all restraints but those of loving. He had never dared dream of that, never dared hope beyond a kiss.

He was the one who drew back at last with a soft groan that came from the roots of his manhood. "Oh, Melissa!"

She recovered faster than he, smiling up at him. "I hope Papa didn't have to propose for me."

"No, once I figured he wouldn't run me off, we sort of talked it out."

"You haven't asked *me* yet!"

He blinked. "By grannies, I haven't! If you won't, sweetheart, you'll sure make monkeys of me and your pa."

"I couldn't do that, now could I?" she teased. She offered her lips again. After what was both a long time and a short one, they walked toward the big white house.

Next day, he rode home, nerving himself to break the news. Just think . . . the wedding was set for New Year's Day, January 1st of 1861. Yvonne's family was coming for the holidays, so no special message need be sent to the Bentons. There was no way of reaching Travis, and his brothers were too far away to come. Thos probably wouldn't be fired from the Pony Express for turning up a few days late, and, if he were, they'd likely take him on again at the first chance. There was a lot of coming and going in that breakneck occupation.

After the way Charlie had insisted that his father take part with the bishop in performing the ceremony, he certainly hoped his father would consent. Charlie could live with the compromises he'd made, but he wasn't sure his parents could. One thing comforted him. They might not attend his wedding, but they wouldn't cast him off. He'd always be their son.

He had purposely delayed at the Jardines' till he figured Thos would be home with the mules and wagon, and, sure enough, the borrowed mules grazed in the pasture and the wagon was near the barn. Thank God, the horses, oxen, cows, and sheep feeding on the drought-cured grass seemed in fair shape.

Robbie's ecstatic barking brought the family out, Beth streaking ahead of the others.

"Why don't you ever come see us first?" she demanded as he swung down and scooped her up.

"Because you ask so many questions." He knuckled her hair and laughed. "Hey, I won't be able to do this much longer! You're big as a yearling calf."

"*Mooo-oo-oo.*" She giggled.

"Go on and eat before the corn pone gets cold," said Thos, taking the reins. "I'll see to your horse."

"Thanks, kid." Charlie shook hands with his father and kissed his mother, startled to notice gray in their hair. Even a brother had to notice how Christy had bloomed although she was thin.

They swept him inside, praising the supplies and presents

he and Thos had got, telling him how they'd managed through the drought. It shamed him to think of his sister working that hard, but Christy laughed away his remorse. "I'd rather work outside than in. Besides, if you hadn't earned wages, you and Thos couldn't have brought us that wagonload of good things."

"We wouldn't starve without it." Fine lines had deepened at the corners of his mother's eyes. Had the wings of gray at her temples been there before? She smiled as she gave him a quick hug. "Still, it's wonderful not to have to calculate every bite and have enough to share. Wash up, dear. I'll ladle you up some stew. We'll let you feed before you tell us about your year."

He was glad of the reprieve. Bursting with his news, he was also nervous about how it would be received. What if his parents refused to attend the wedding? They loved him, yes, but hadn't they helped Jardine's runaway escape? How much would their consciences allow them to have to do with slave owners?

Still, as he relished the stew and buttered a crisp pone, Charlie had that blessedly secure feeling of being home, under his parents' roof, warmed by their fire, enjoying his mother's food. Lavish as the Jardines' table was, he'd grown up on his mother's cooking. He supposed nothing would ever quite satisfy him in the same way. He also knew that was the sort of thing he'd best not breathe to Melissa.

"The stock's wintering pretty well," Jonathan said. "There's no grain for them and not as much fodder as they need, but that sun-cured grass is just like hay. I planted wheat in October and we've had enough moisture to hope for a crop."

"Harriet Parks and Susie McHugh had little baby boys right after the first freeze when the persimmons ripened,"

Beth said. "I 'member 'cause Christy and I picked baskets of pawpaws and persimmons and took them to the new mamas. Harriet called her baby Daniel Owen, which made her mama mad, and Susie's red-headed little boy is Andrew Owen Simeon. Andy for short."

"I should hope!" Thos came in, washed sketchily, swung long legs over the bench beside Charlie, and covered a pone with butter.

"Now finish telling us about the Ex-press!" commanded Beth.

"We're racing the telegraph wires being laid from both ends." Thos grinned. He was taller, more sunburned, but he hadn't gained any weight. "There's a hundred and nineteen stations spread over almost two thousand miles of mountains, deserts, prairies, and there's Indians, Bethie. My home station's at Fort Kearny. When the Express rider comes, I'm waiting with my horse. He churns up, and tosses off his mochila . . . that's a thing that fits over the saddle and has four pouches for mail. Then he staggers off to rest. . . ."

"What happens to his horse?" Beth demanded.

"The stock tender rubs him down and waters and feeds him. I'm gone like lightning. Ten to fifteen miles later, my first horse gets to rest at the next station, but I toss the mochila on a new horse and we're off. Depending on how hard the going is, I change horses six to eight times to cover about a hundred miles."

"A hundred? That's far, far!" Beth said.

"You bet it is. So, afterwards, I loaf a day or so. Sleep, eat beans and bacon with the stationmaster and stock tender and any stagecoach drivers or travelers who've stopped by. I read quite a bit, dime novels that get left at the stations." He grinned at Charlie. "You ever read *The Indian Wife of the White Hunter* by Ann Sophia Stevens?"

63

"Can't say that I have," Charlie admitted.

"I've read it four times. Well, then the rider from the West sails in, and I'm off for the same hundred miles going the other direction." He chuckled. "I know the first names of every prairie dog and rattlesnake along the way."

"Did the Indians ever try to scalp you?" asked Beth.

"I move too fast, honey." He took half a pone at a bite and chewed reflectively. "The Indians are sure going to want to get their hands on some of the new Winchesters the Army's buying to replace muzzleloaders."

"Winchesters load through the breech," Charlie explained. "They shoot a lot faster and farther than muzzleloaders."

Thos cocked an eyebrow at Jonathan. "I suppose our Border Ruffians and jayhawkers are still using Sharpses."

"They do enough with them." Jonathan's tone was dry. "Toward the middle of November, Doc Jennison and his hotheads rounded up all the proslave settlers around Trading Post and held a sort of trial, the jury being twelve of the posse. They heard the evidence and gave everyone but Russell Hinds seven days to leave Kansas. Hinds was hanged for returning runaways to their masters. A few days later, a well-to-do old man named Sam Scott was tried by the same jury and hanged in his own yard. Jennison offered another proslave man a trial, but he somewhat naturally preferred to die fighting."

Christy said in a troubled voice: "Dan O'Brien and Owen Parks and Andy McHugh won't ride with Jennison. Colonel Montgomery would never have hanged those men, but he told Dan that Hinds was worth a great deal to hang but good for nothing else and was condemned under the sixteenth verse of Exodus, Chapter Twenty-One."

"The hangings were too much for Governor Medary,

though," Jonathan said. "He offered a reward of a thousand dollars for Jennison's arrest. Since United States marshals have never been able to catch Jennison or Montgomery, they asked for help from the military. General Harney came from Fort Leavenworth with cavalry, infantry, and even artillery. He sent two companies of infantry to Mound City under Captain Nathaniel Lyon. They scoured the countryside but never found either Jennison or Montgomery."

"Lyon may not have wanted to very much," Christy put in. "General Harney's proslavery, but Dan says Lyon is a red-headed antislavery atheist who reads political tracts, instead of playing cards. He's even said publicly that Socrates was nobler than Jesus."

"However that may be, he's back at Fort Scott now with his command." Jonathan shrugged. "Sometimes I don't see how a real war could be much worse right around here than what we've got."

"We're likely to find out." Thos slanted a questioning glance at his older brother. "I aim to fight for the Union the first chance I get. What about you, Charlie? Bishop Jardine sure wouldn't let you come calling on his daughter if you were fighting Secessionists."

Charlie gulped. And told them.

Chapter Five

Rays of winter sun shone magnified and golden through the glass panes of the conservatory where the air was sweet with roses. The parakeets' cage was covered to keep them quiet but muted grumbles punctuated Bishop Jardine's lengthy sermon and Jonathan Ware's brief one. Travis had drifted in from Nevada for Christmas, taller, heavier, his grin as ready and bold as ever. When the Wares drove up in their wagon, he'd reached Christy before her brothers could, swung her off the seat so that for a scary, uncomfortable instant he was her only support, and laughed down at her with a glint in his merry brown eyes.

"What a difference a few years make, Miss Christy! I'm glad I came home."

Did he remember ambushing her on the dogtrot the last time he'd seen her and getting his ears boxed?

"Yes, it's fortunate you arrived for your sister's wedding," she told him, and went forward with her family to be greeted by the Jardines and brought into the big white house with its long verandah.

Now Travis and Thos stood up with the couple as best men while Yvonne Benton attended her younger sister. Except for Hester Ballard, the Hayeses, and the Bentons from St. Louis, the guests were neighbors of the Jardines, and, to Christy's astonishment, the Rose Haven slaves were there, too. Dressed in their best, they spilled out into the living room, except for one frail old woman called Aunt Zillah. She was propped up on a cot beside Mrs. Jardine's wheeled chair. Her white-filmed eyes stared blindly toward the voices, but she was smiling, happier than anyone there.

Christy found it hard to smile. *At least he's not marrying someone in Santa Fé or Salt Lake City so we'd never see him.* Melissa was as generously welcoming as any bride could be on her wedding day, the bishop gruffly kind, and, in spite of a jealous pang for her mother's sake, Christy could see why Charlie so admired Mrs. Jardine. She wasn't the least bit puffed up although she was gracious as a queen. Her tenderness to old Aunt Zillah was not what Christy expected from a slave owner, and the behavior of the house servants toward the Jardines was clearly born of affection, not fear.

Yet Justus, had he been caught, would have been savagely whipped. None of these people could leave at will or choose their work. And there was Lilah, of whom Charlie had spoken, with her bronze hair and creamy skin, every bit as beautiful as the bride. She watched Travis with such longing in her green eyes that Christy made a quick, fervent prayer for her.

The wedding dinner was sumptuous. Youngsters, including Beth and the Benton children, dined in the conservatory under the sharp, if indulgent eye, of Aunt Phronie. At the table for family and close friends, Christy was placed, somewhat to her dismay, between large, slow-moving Henry Benton and Travis. The bridal pair was seated on either hand of the bishop and Jonathan and Ellen Ware were right and left of Mrs. Jardine.

Roses in crystal vases graced ivory damask tablecloths. Silver gleamed beside gold-rimmed china, cut glass sparkled, and Christy had never dreamed there could be so much food of so many kinds.

"We brought the oysters, lobster, figs, and champagne," Henry Benton informed the table at large as platters of carved ham, turkey, quail, mutton, and beef were carried around and served by Lilah and three other young women. After Christy had edged so close to Benton that Travis's arm could no longer brush hers as if by accident, what she enjoyed most was the gold-crusted rolls of fine wheat flour, fresh and hot from the kitchen, the like of which she hadn't tasted since Susie's wedding.

The tables were cleared and the top tablecloths lifted off to reveal another beneath. The bishop, Benton, and Thos went around tipping glistening champagne into glasses.

"Even if you don't drink, have just a sip to toast the young couple," urged the bishop when a Baptist neighbor demurred, as did a few strict Methodists. Resuming his place at the head of the table, the stout, ruddy man lifted his goblet. "To the bride and groom," he offered, beaming. "May you be blessed with health, children, enough of this world's goods for comfort but not sloth, and may you, in fifty years, love each other even better than you do today!"

With a chorus of good wishes, glasses were lifted high and sipped at or drained, according to the imbiber. Christy liked the bubbles although they made her want to sneeze, but thought Emil Franz's cider tasted nicer.

Henry Benton reached for a bottle and brimmed his glass again, throwing back his yellow head. "And here's to South Carolina whose leaders took only twenty-two minutes to secede from the tyrannous Union on December Twentieth! May that brave example inspire her Southern sister states to follow."

Jardine's applauding neighbors raised their glasses, but Jonathan Ware said quietly: "I cannot drink, sir, to the beginning of a tragedy that will fearfully wound, if not destroy, this republic that was birthed with such high hope and fervent prayer less than a hundred years ago."

Henry Benton stared, heavy face turning redder. The bishop crimsoned, too, but his wife's look caused him to swallow and clear his throat. "Henry," he said to his long-time son-in-law, "this is a wedding, not a political meeting. Perhaps you'll be kind enough to frame a toast we can all pledge comfortably."

Benton's eyes fell before Jardine's. "I regret, sir," he said in stiff tone, "that I cannot imagine such a proposal."

Jonathan smiled and raised his glass. "Here's to the gracious and lovely mothers of the bride and groom. May they each gain a child rather than lose one."

Other toasts were drunk with alacrity. A great crystal bowl of something that looked like vanilla pudding was placed before Mrs. Jardine who ladled it into crystal cups that were passed around the tables.

Travis pressed his hand against Christy's as he gave her a cup. "Aunt Phronie's syllabub is famous," he said. "It's far from as innocent as it looks, though it's against my interests to warn you." He flashed a white grin. "I'm hoping when we dance that you'll lose your balance and fall most charmingly into my arms."

His eyes were admiring, his young male voice full of bantering good humor, and his well-made body so close she could feel its radiated warmth. It took an effort to say austerely: "Are you afraid you'll forget how to flirt, Travis, if you don't practice at every opportunity?"

"That assumption flatters neither of us." Bowls of ice cream were being brought around. "Here, put some brandied peaches on that and see if it won't sweeten your tongue."

She closed her eyes, both to shut him out and savor the delicious creamy melting in her mouth. She'd enjoyed ice cream a few times in Illinois, but the only kind they'd had in Missouri was snow mixed with cream and molasses or honey. She accepted a small piece of the huge white-frosted wedding cake from Melissa, but was compelled by an overfull stomach to refuse plum pudding and all manner of tarts and fruit-filled dumplings.

The second cloth was carried away and almonds, figs, raisins, and mints were placed on the polished walnut table to accompany strong, rich coffee.

Melissa bent to whisper in Christy's ear: "I'll show you the way to the privy. All this drink. . . ."

Christy waited outside the white-washed little building, wondering how her sister-in-law managed with her crinoline. In spite of feeling that Charlie now belonged to his wife's family more than to his own, Christy found it impossible not to like Melissa who took her to her own room to wash and order her hair. Such a pretty room, all ivory and rose, with a velvet-covered armchair, canopied bed, and large gilt-framed mirror above a long marble-topped dresser. Roses with golden leaves twined the doors of the elaborate armoire and vases of real roses perfumed the air.

Would Charlie share this bed, tonight, after the embroidered satin coverlet was folded over its rack by servants who'd build up the fire before they withdrew? Christy put the perfumed soap — a far cry from the strong yellowish lye soap she and her mother made so laboriously — back in its porcelain dish and rinsed her hands in the flowered wash basin.

"Here." Melissa handed her a small, embroidered towel. Her dark-lashed eyes, an indefinable shade between violet and blue, looked directly into Christy's. "Let's be good friends, Christy, even if we can't agree on . . . things. Charlie loves us both."

"You, the most." Christy, to her amaze, found she could

say it without bitterness, even add, smiling, as she squeezed the other girl's soft hand: "That's the way it should be."

"It almost has to be, doesn't it?" Melissa made a face. "Papa was set on my marrying . . . well, someone he shared opinions with, but, in the end, he practically proposed for me." Her eyes danced and there was pride in her smile. "I think Papa already likes Charlie more than that suet-pudding-faced Henry Benton, and it's partly because Charlie stood up to him."

"He did?" Christy warmed to hear this. Not that she'd believed Charlie would truckle to Jardine, but he did so love this girl who would in his arms become a woman.

"Yes, and to Travis and me, too, about freeing our darkies after Papa . . . is gone."

"Charlie got all of you to agree to that?" He had told his family something of his intention, but Christy thought he was placating his parents and his conscience.

Melissa's mouth quirked. "Trav says he doesn't care what we do as long as he gets a fair income from the plantation. Papa, of course, counts on Charlie's changing his mind after he's helped manage Rose Haven a while."

"And you?"

"I don't think most of our people would leave if they could." Melissa looked up from washing her hands. "But when the time comes . . . well, after the way Charlie's talked to me, especially about Lilah, if they want to go, I guess I'd rather they did." She put down her towel and took Christy's hand. "Hear Uncle Fred's banjo and Caesar's fiddle? Let's hurry!"

Melissa and Charlie led in the Virginia Reel and Christy couldn't evade Travis by demurring: "I've never danced except at a few corn shuckings."

She had practiced with Thos before Susie's and Andy's wedding, hoping someone else would take Dan's fiddle so she could whirl and dip and circle with him, but there'd been no dancing on that day, only grief and fury over the men slaughtered on the soft spring grass above the Marais des Cygnes.

"Then we'll watch this time and dance the next." Travis drew her to the side where those not dancing watched, standing or from chairs. The temporary table had been taken away and the other set against the end of the room where an ebony-skinned man with a shock of white hair strummed a banjo while a younger, light brown man played the fiddle. *Not as well as Dan, though,* thought Christy, with a surge of longing.

The crowded space gave Travis an excuse to stand so close his breath stirred the curls above her ear. "I do believe some of the ladies have sewn grapevines into their clothes to make their skirts stand out," he whispered.

"I don't see how you can tell that," she said in her coldest tone even though she had heard two of the neighboring young women giggle about their "hoops".

"For one thing, Thisbe Shelton's trailing a vine from her skirt. Whoops! Your brother Thos just stepped on it. Good thing it cracked off clean so the rest of her framework won't be dragged out."

"You . . . you're not supposed to notice such things!"

"I'm not blind." Travis's eyes drifted over her, not insultingly, but in a way that told her he saw the pulse of her throat, the curve of her bodice. He slipped his hand beneath her arm. "The first set's finishing. Do me the honor, Miss Christy. You have full leave to tread on my toes."

She did on purpose a time or two, smiling at him to let him know it was deliberate, but then her body answered the lilting tune and her feet flew. Quadrilles were followed by polkas, schottisches, and the varsouvienne. *Put your little foot, put your little foot, put your little foot right out. . . .*

Every time Christy tried to retire to the wall, someone claimed her, brothers and fathers of the girls with the grape-vine hoops, her own brothers and father, and Ethan Hayes, but Travis most of all.

"A pity my father won't allow waltzing. Then I could get my arm around you properly." Travis shrugged. "Oh, well, for a Methodist, he's broad-minded."

"Especially for a bishop, I should think."

"*Because* he's a bishop. Since the church split over slavery in the Eighteen Forties, Southern Methodist bishops depend a lot on their own judgment. You don't think slavery's right, I guess?"

"That white Methodists own black Methodists?" Christy had resolved not to get into such arguments with her new in-laws, but wouldn't dodge a direct question. "I don't see how anyone can think it's right."

They finished the dance in silence. Christy walked off the floor without waiting for his escort, but in a moment he followed. "Miss Christy, if your parents are willing, would you allow me to call on you?"

Her jaw dropped. Probably he just couldn't stand it that she wasn't thrilled breathless at his attentions. "No," she said flatly. "I don't want you calling on me."

"Are your affections engaged?"

"They are." She couldn't resist adding: "But even if they weren't, we never could agree."

"Indeed? Now why is that?"

"You're much too full of yourself, much too high and mighty."

He eyed her with fresh interest. "Ah, but now we're

73

family, I'm sure your parents won't turn me away if I stop to inquire after their health."

"I can't prevent that, but it won't do you any good."

"I think it will."

He bowed, left her, and in the next moment smiled down at Thisbe of the draggled grapevine, inviting her to dance. Her raw-boned, red-headed brother engaged Christy, but all she could do was wish he were Dan and feel annoyed with Travis. She was glad when her father signaled that it was time to go.

Collecting Beth, the Wares embraced Charlie and Melissa. Even Jonathan had damp eyes as they wished the young pair happiness. Mrs. Jardine, in her wheeled chair, smiled up and gave her hands to Jonathan and Ellen.

"Thank you for rearing such a splendid son," she told them. "It's a blessing to know he'll cherish our daughter."

She reached up to draw Ellen and Christy down for a kiss on their cheeks, hugged Beth, and asked Lilah to bring the armful of wrapped roses she'd cut for them. "I know we're a half day distant," she said, "but you are most warmly welcome at any time. I regret that I'm unable to repay visits."

"We understand." Ellen pressed the slim white hand between her chapped ones. "Thank you for your kindness and welcome, Missus Jardine."

The bishop walked out with them to where a servant had their wagon ready. "I could wish us in better agreement." The bishop shook hands with Jonathan, bowed over Ellen's, gave Beth a kiss, and Christy a measuring nod. "Still, there is no mistaking where Charles got his integrity and wholesome nature. I thank you for that." He helped Ellen and Christy to the seat, bundled Beth between them, and waved as they drove toward the swiftly setting sun.

The Hidden Valley

★ ★ ★ ★ ★

As soon as Thos helped his father cut and split enough wood for the rest of the winter, he was off with the borrowed team to resume his hundred mile stints with the Pony Express.

"We carried the news of Lincoln's election," he said as he lifted the reins. "I sure hope we don't have to carry word that war has broken out." He looked from his father to his mother, gave Christy a long, sober look, and bent to ruffle Beth's hair. "If there's a chance, I'll come home to see you before I enlist."

"Oh, Thos!" Ellen cried.

He lifted a shoulder. "Try not to worry, Mama. Maybe it won't happen." He clucked to the mules. Just before he drove into the timber, he turned to wave. They all waved back, even after he'd passed from sight.

Tears formed slowly and ran down Ellen's cheeks. Christy would have thrown her arms around her, but her father did that first.

"My dear, my Ellen, God has protected both our boys thus far."

She nodded mutely, then said in a twisted broken way: "But, oh, Jon! Have you thought? What if they fight each other?"

Chapter Six

Didn't Melissa know how to do anything? That morning, she'd volunteered to make the mush, but hadn't sifted hulls from the meal, so now the family chewed the tough bits if they were small enough or rolled them into the corners of their mouths to dispose of discreetly.

"I'm sorry!" Melissa looked ready to cry as Beth choked and began to cough, probably from trying to swallow too big a scrap. Melissa had won her, body and soul, by giving Beth a porcelain-headed doll with real blonde hair, ivory teeth, a crinoline under an emerald velvet gown, and brocade slippers. Her own childhood favorite, she admitted, adding with a joyous look at Charlie: "Now I'm grown up, Bethie, so you must have Lynette."

After thumps on the back had cleared Beth's throat, Melissa said miserably: "I'm afraid I'm more of a nuisance than a help, Mama Ware."

"We're very glad you came, dear." Ellen's voice was kind. "It gives us a wonderful chance to get acquainted. Besides, you take the tiniest, most even stitches I've ever seen. If we finish the double wedding ring quilt before you leave, you must take it with you as our wedding gift, even though it doesn't seem quite fair that you're working on your own present."

"I'm glad I can do something." Melissa managed a wavery

smile. "I spin and weave, of course. Mama says every woman must be able to teach and supervise her s. . . ." She broke off. Had she started to say slaves or servants?

"Two of womankind's most ancient and valued skills," Jonathan put in, always the teacher, although he'd dismissed his little school — now only Luke and Mary Hayes and Beth — early in March when the ground thawed enough for plowing. "Long before Penelope foiled her unwelcome suitors by unraveling every night what she wove through the day. . . ."

"Anyone home?" called a voice at the door.

Melissa jumped up and ran to the door. "Travis!" She hustled him inside where, after bowing to the elder Wares and grinning cheekily at Christy, he went to warm himself by the fire.

"I can't believe you got up early enough to be over here at this hour!" His sister eyed him narrowly. "Mama's well? There's nothing wrong?"

"Must there be a calamity? I came to take you home, if you were getting in the way, M'liss. If you aren't, I'll stay and help a few days."

"Can you plow?" Christy didn't try to hide her skepticism.

"I can make a tolerably straight furrow, but, after swinging a pickaxe in the Comstock. . . . did you hear that Nevada was made a territory in February? . . . Colorado, too, which cuts off a good slice of Kansas . . . why, I reckon I can make pretty fair potato mounds."

Melissa turned to her mother-in-law. "Please, Mama Ware, tell me the truth! Could you manage better if I went home?"

"My dear, we hope you'll stay." Ellen pressed her hand. "It means a lot to have you and Charlie here, even if he weren't such a help with the spring work. Besides, I assure you that having your help with the quilt makes me breathe easier. I want it to keep you warm this first winter of your marriage, but Christy and I can only work on it a few hours at night." She gave Travis a pleasant smile. "Your brother's very welcome. He's been here before, you know, helping get in the winter wood."

Melissa gave her mother-in-law a swift hug and faced her slightly younger but much bigger brother with bright confidence. "That's fine then, Trav. You stay and plant potatoes or whatever Papa Ware trusts you with."

"Yes, your wifeness." He looked at Christy although he implored the room in general: "Do you suppose I could have a bite to eat? I grabbed a couple of cold biscuits when I left, but the chill's made me hungry as a springtime bear." He sniffed expectantly. "That coffee sure smells good."

One of the most appreciated things Charlie and Thos had brought was a big box of roasted Arbuckles' coffee beans. Christy rose to get Travis a mug, feeling sorry for Melissa whose fair complexion went a scalded crimson.

"I made the mush this morning, Trav, and there's . . . well, there's hulls in it. Not big ones," she added defensively.

"You made the mush?" He shook his curly brown hair while his grin spread ear to ear. "I wouldn't miss tasting it, and telling Aunt Phronie and Lilah, for all the silver I lost in Nevada."

"Lost?" echoed Melissa. "Don't you mean found?"

"Lost. Cards." He swung a long leg across the bench where Charlie had scooted over. "Bring on your mush, Sis! I hope there's plenty of milk and molasses."

The meal finished in hilarity, even Melissa laughing, although Travis must have downed most of the hulls to spare his sister's feelings. The sun was barely up when the men went out, Charlie and Jonathan hitching up the horses and oxen, Travis taking a shovel to the acre Charlie had plowed yesterday for potatoes.

Ellen watched them for a moment from the window. "Let's pray for good crops," she said. "We'd be pinched tight by now if Thos and Charlie hadn't brought that wagonload of food, and we'd have had little to share with Hester and the Hayeses."

While Beth dried dishes for Melissa, Christy skimmed cream from the covered pans on the shelf where milking things were kept in winter, and poured it into the wooden churn along with cream saved from the last few days. She worked the dasher up and down, the *swish-swash* calming her as she vented her annoyance on the innocent cream.

Travis was linked to their family now. She had to get used to that. If he chose to help his friend and brother-in-law with the planting, that placed no obligation on her. Of course, he'd really come to take Melissa home if she felt too uncomfortable at the Wares'.

Christy glanced at the slender young woman who nodded and asked appropriate questions during Beth's account of Robbie's latest defeat by a skunk. Who could blame Beth for enjoying someone's full attention? Christy was ashamed of her irritation over the hulls in the mush as it dawned on her that Melissa was as nervous about winning the approval of Charlie's family as he must have been about hers.

Melissa tossed the dish water out on the rose bushes and hung up the pan. When she turned, Christy gave her a real smile, warm as she could make it. Melissa responded with a happy laugh. "Shall I lower the quilt, Mama Ware?"

"Yes, please." Ellen finished picking over dried peas and beans, more of her sons' largesse, rinsed and poured them and dried corn into a three-legged kettle she set on the hearth over a bed of raked-out coals. "We can do a lot of stitching before dinner. Beth, crush these chinquapins as fine as you can and put them in the stew." It was an Indian dish Sarah had taught them to make, using the small, flavorsome chinquapins, thin shell and all.

Jonathan had rigged pulleys to raise and lower the quilt frame that was stored against the ceiling when not in use. Only the night before had the women finished sewing all the pieced blocks together. Ellen had started the quilt as soon as Charlie announced his engagement, gleaning her scrap basket for harmonious colors, an easier task now that they had remnants of a number of garments made from cloth Charlie had brought them.

Needles flew as Ellen and Melissa stitched through the top, the blanket batting, and the blue floral sateen back that Charlie had intended as a Christmas gift for Ellen. She and her daughter-in-law apparently had little in common except their love for Charlie, but that was powerful enough to impel them to begin forming a bond with shared work and threads of words, weft through warp running in and out like their needles, creating the pattern of what they would be to each other.

Butter was forming. Christy poured the buttermilk into crocks and the bits and chunks of butter into a big bowl. Using an oak paddle to force the remaining milk out of the pale yellow mass, she worked till the butter was ready to press into two one-pound wooden molds. It wouldn't last long with three field-hungry men to feed, but it added so much to their plain food that she didn't grudge the work.

The appetizing odor of bubbling stew made the cabin seem warmer than it was. Christy gave it a stir, replenished the coals beneath it after adding split logs to the fire, stretched to ease her shoulders, and threaded a needle.

She pulled up a stool between her mother and Melissa and started at the border, a lovely muted indigo her mother had worked hard to dye just the right color to make Christy a dress. Christy, who had stirred the cloth constantly in the smelly dye pot, not to mention having helped spin and weave it, had summoned considerable effort to bless the material's new use. She felt gratifyingly noble as she sewed it to the backing.

Melissa, to her credit, didn't prattle of her visits to St. Louis, and her only comment on the difference between her home and the Wares' was to look around with lively interest when she arrived and say: "I think I like log houses more without clapboards and whitewash. They fit the country better and look more . . . real."

This sentiment launched her visit auspiciously. Now she regaled them with stories of Charlie and how he had dived into Watt Caxton's hounds to rescue her cat. "I fell in love with him then and there." She chuckled. "That naughty Emmie, though! She still arches her back and hisses at him if he tries to pick her up when she's being cranky."

Melissa's teeth were white and pretty. Neither she nor her mother, thank goodness, used snuff. That would have been harder to endure, day to day, than conflicting political opinions. As the three quilters stitched and chatted, none of them mentioned what must be at back of all their thoughts, the inexorable slide of the nation toward war.

Kansas had been admitted to the Union as a free state late in January after years of bloody, bitter struggle. This sent a tidal wave of dread and anger crashing through the South. Slave state votes were outnumbered in Congress and would lose their Presidential ally when Buchanan stepped down. North Carolina's fiery secession late in December was followed in January by Mississippi, Florida, Alabama, Georgia, and Louisiana. After his state seceded, Jefferson Davis, a West Pointer and former Secretary of War, resigned from the Senate and had been elected President of the Confederacy.

North and South, the eyes of the shattering Union were fixed on the new island stronghold of Fort Sumter off Charleston, South Carolina, an island in more ways than one, a small Union garrison surrounded by hostile ships and militia.

It could well be the torch to set off an inferno that could not even be imagined. Thinking of her brothers, Dan, and the other young men she knew, Christy felt a cold knot form in her stomach. Strange to think that this quilt might well be in use when Fort Sumter was an echo in history books, as distant as Valley Forge was now.

Our work is slow, thought Christy, *the cutting and stitching of small pieces into a covering large enough to warm a man and woman. Slow, but the quilt may last to comfort the children gotten in that marriage bed, and even their children. Will we ever make such a quilt for Dan and me?*

Beth was at her endless chore of bringing in kindling and collecting wood chips near the chopping block when her *whoop* made the women thrust their needles into the quilt and hurry to the door.

Too early for snakes, but a vengeful black widow or rabid creature? The quilters sighed with relief, and some exasperation, as Beth tore past them to hurl herself into Dan's welcoming arms.

"Danny! You haven't been here for ages, not even on Sunday!"

"We've been taking turns with chills and fever." He smoothed her curls and kissed the tip of her snubby nose. Indeed, Dan did look thin and a little pallid. "I put in a week at plowing while Davie and Owen were in bed. Now they've taken over so I could help you folks." He glanced toward the plowmen and wrinkled his brow at Travis who was covering chunks of potato.

"Looks like I'm not needed as much as I reckoned I'd be." His tone was rueful as he straightened to his long-boned height and he looked at Christy with a hurt question in his eyes.

"Don't fear there's not work for you, if you're set on it." Ellen laughed and embraced him with a kiss on the cheek. Ever since Dan had rescued Christy from the wolves, Ellen had treated him like a son. "The old cornstalks have to be cut and burned before that field can be plowed, and there are still a few stumps to wrestle out of the land cleared year before last. Have you met my daughter-in-law? Melissa, this is Daniel O'Brien."

"I've been wanting to congratulate Charlie on his good luck . . . and you on yours, Missus Ware. Pleased to meet you." Dan bowed to Melissa.

She twinkled back, offering her hand. "I've seen you at Parkses' mill, Mister O'Brien, though we've not been introduced. Charlie's spoken of you very fondly. I declare there must be something in the wind! My brother Travis turned up this morning and behold!" She flourished her hand. "He's actually making himself useful!"

"Well, then, so must I." Dan looked more cheerful. He, of all men, would understand having a care for one's sister.

"Melissa's helping with her own wedding present," Ellen said. "I hope we can finish before she and Charlie go . . ." — she hesitated — "go home."

Dan's eyes tangled with Christy's for a moment. Would they ever lie together under such a quilt? Why, *why* not have what they could? Involuntarily she put out her hand, but either he didn't see it, or pretended not to as he took a glass of buttermilk from Beth and gazed admiringly at the quilt.

"A fine gift, cozy and beautiful at the same time. Now I'd better get to work or Mister Ware will think I came to eat his food and loll at his fire."

Beth held up a bowl of nuts and fruit. "Grab it!" she invited.

Laughing, he obeyed. "You do look after me, Bethie." He went out, munching, and the women looked at each other.

"We'll make him a pallet in this room with Travis," said Ellen. Charlie and Melissa slept in the loft on the boys' old bed. "Beth, crack up several more cups of chinquapins for the stew and add more water."

The quilters resumed their places. Ellen gave a soft laugh. "Jonathan's been worried about managing without either of the boys at home, but, look, here he has three strapping young men!"

"Charlie can always come over for planting and harvest, Mama Ware," said Melissa.

"That would greatly help, my dear, and we hope you'll come, too." Ellen didn't mention what they all knew, that Charlie could be spared because slaves did the field work at Rose Haven.

"I can chop weeds out of the corn," said Christy. She scrunched her shoulders up, then let them fall, as she remembered that summer. "I like working outside better than in, but I hope we never have to haul water for our crops again."

"We only saved a little of our tobacco," Melissa said. "Our people had all they could do to haul water for our food crops."

And your mother's roses. Christy gave herself a mental shake. She absolutely must not dwell on the contrast between the Jardines' life and the Wares', especially not with the envy that sprouted up no matter how fiercely she assured herself that even could she afford it, she'd never exist on the labor of slaves.

There was no denying the perverse allure of having someone else do the things you didn't want to, and it was easier to be righteous if you were poor than if you weren't, so long as you weren't pushed to the desperation of robbery. The thought of starving always brought Dan's fearful childhood to mind.

"Mother," she said in inspiration, "could we make Dan a quilt or blanket all of his own?"

"Why . . . yes, dear, but don't you think Lydia and Harriet and Missus Morrison . . . ?"

"I'm sure he's got covers, but probably not anything special, made just for him."

Melissa's creamy brow furrowed as if she couldn't imagine such a thing. "What makes you think that, Christy?"

"The Parkses made him part of their family, but, when you think about it, Lydia wasn't more than twelve and Susie eight when their mother died birthing David. All of a sudden they had an infant to look after as well as cooking and keeping house for their father and Owen, spinning and weaving and sewing, too. They managed, but I don't see how they had time to make anything special for Dan beyond knitting his socks and making whatever of his clothes weren't handed down from Owen."

Ellen gave her daughter a searching look. "I never thought about it, but I'm glad you did. Why don't we make him a blanket? If . . . well, if he starts moving around a lot, a blanket won't hold dirt like a quilt and there's warmth in wool, even when it's wet."

She meant that a blanket was more practical for a soldier. Christy's heart constricted. All the more reason, then, to see that he had one made for him especially, warm, comforting, and as handsome as they could contrive.

"Could we do a striped blanket?" she asked. "We have the wool already spun that came out such a lovely gold, and there's quite a bit of walnut brown."

Ellen joined in Christy's enthusiasm although stripes took more care and work than a plain blanket dyed all one color. "There may even be enough wool spun to make it, and we can dye some to get several shades of yellows and browns." She smiled at her daughter-in-law. "We'll finish your quilt first, though.

"When is Dan's birthday, Christy?"

"No one knows. Lydia just makes a cake for him and David on David's birthday, August Eighth."

"We'll have it done by then," Ellen promised. "Maybe we'll have wheat flour this year to make him his own cake."

Christy turned to give her mother a hug, heedless of acting so excited over the flour that was used every day at Jardines'. "That would be wonderful! Thank you, Mother."

None of them said what they must all have been thinking: that in August, instead of stripping green blades from the corn ears, there was no telling where their young men might be.

When the men came in, it was satisfying to see how their nostrils swelled to draw in the molasses and cinnamon smells of Indian pudding mingled with that of stew and corn pone. A handsome lot the men were as they washed up with the use of a second basin fetched by Beth. Charlie's wavy hair was browner than Jonathan's chestnut, and Travis's wild mop was the darkest. Dan's hair caught all the light there was. Christy felt a rush of happiness at seeing him come in with her father and brother, just like one of the family.

Travis stepped between them, deliberately, she thought,

and then they were all sitting down, Travis on one side of her, Dan on the other, bowing heads while her father said grace.

"Makes a world of difference, four men in the fields instead of one." Jonathan sobered as he gazed at his eldest son. "I never expected help from you, Charlie, once you took to freighting. It's good to see you working our land again." Jonathan grinned at Melissa. "Even if you are just on loan."

Our land? Well, of course, it would be part Charlie's one day, a thought that had never entered Christy's head before. She quickly thrust away the thought of her parents' death. When Christy allowed herself to dream of being married to Dan, she pictured them on a farm adjoining her parents', close enough that she and her mother could run back and forth easily. Wouldn't it be wonderful if Thos and Beth eventually settled on neighboring land? With Charlie only five miles away, the families could visit often and have holidays together? If they each had three to five children, there'd be a whole tribe of cousins. . . .

"Any news of Fort Sumter?" Travis asked Dan. "Or the inauguration of that beanpole of a lawyer from Illinois?"

"President Lincoln," stressed Dan, "according to the stage driver yesterday, said the Union is perpetual, that no state can leave simply of its own will." At Travis's derisive snort, Dan's tone deepened. "The President also said 'though passion might strain the bonds of affection, it must not break them, that the chords of memory running from every patriot grave and battlefield to every heart and hearthstone in this land will swell the chorus of union when touched by our better natures.' "

"The bonds are broken!" Travis cried. "Whatever Lincoln says, six states have seceded!"

"Seven. Much against Sam Houston's will, Texas seceded the day before the inaugural."

Caught breaths and sighs came from around the table. Texas lay southwest of Missouri with Arkansas or Indian Territory between, not far away if war came. There had been Texans along with Clarke in the infamous raid of 1856 that burned out Trading Post and dozens of Free State settlers.

"What about Fort Sumter?" Travis persisted.

Dan shrugged. "The best guess is that the President will send the garrison only food and non-military supplies."

"But Southern ships won't let Federal vessels reach Sumter." Satisfaction glinted in Travis's dark eyes as well as his voice. "The garrison can't live on air."

"If war must come, President Lincoln is probably determined not to order the first assault."

"You mean he's tricking the Confederacy into taking the blame?"

"I'd scarcely call it tricking," said Jonathan dryly. "In the end, the Confederacy will doubtless get Fort Sumter . . . and with it, a war 'the like of which men have not seen' in the words of Jefferson Davis when he resigned from the Senate."

"Hopes for peace certainly aren't helped by having an officer like that red-headed infidel, Nathaniel Lyon, trying to get the government arsenal at Saint Louis fortified."

"Captain Lyon?" Christy tried to avert an argument. "Didn't you say, Dan, that he was a great supporter of the dancing school at Fort Scott?"

"Yes, but he's famed more for other things. When forced into a duel, he named the weapons, as revolvers fired while the officers sat across a table from each other." Dan smiled. "The other officer chose to drop the quarrel."

"Any sane man would," retorted Travis. "Lyon is a maniac! Look at the way he punished a soldier by making him march around in the hot sun with a barrel over his shoulders so he couldn't brush away the flies and pests."

"He's also taken the whip away from a drover who was cruelly lashing a team and used it on the man," Dan said. "When he caught a soldier kicking a dog, he knocked him down and made him kneel to beg the dog's pardon."

"Crazy as a loon!" blurted Travis. "If he takes the part of animals like that, what would he do about a darkie getting a well-deserved lesson? Such a fanatic shouldn't be anywhere near that arsenal!"

"There are enough arms and munitions in that depot to control the state should Governor Jackson seize them." Jonathan's tone was even drier. "When he took office the last day of December, Jackson called a state convention to consider secession." He raised an eyebrow. "Isn't your father a delegate to that convention, Travis?"

"Yes. He's pro-Union like most of the delegates. He's as opposed to secession as you are, sir." He added what they all were thinking. "Provided his property rights are preserved, of course. Father's sure the convention will vote for compromise."

Jonathan said regretfully: "It may be too late for that."

"It certainly may," rejoined Travis, "with that scoundrel Doc Jennison organizing his thieving jayhawks into militia." He challenged Dan with an unspoken question.

"Jennison's been recruiting from Linn and Bourbon counties for his Mound City Rifles," Dan said. "As you say, many of them are thieves and scoundrels, which is why I haven't joined." His gray eyes locked with Travis's dark ones. "If . . . when . . . Colonel Montgomery calls for men, I'll follow him in a heartbeat."

"Montgomery?" choked Travis. "Why, he's as bad as Jennison! A slave-stealing. . . ."

"He'd call it slave freeing, his duty before God. Montgomery takes an eye for an eye, but he'll shoot a man for looting."

"You seem mightily well acquainted!"

"I rode with him after Clarke's raid, the slaughter at Marais des Cygnes, and to break prisoners out of the Fort Scott jail. Montgomery is a God-fearing man of honor."

"I'd say the same of my father." Somber for the first time, Travis stared into a future he could not predict. "What happens when honorable men can't agree on what God wills?"

"They fight all the harder and more ruthlessly, each claiming God for an ally." Ellen's voice was full of sorrow. She rose to fetch the Indian pudding. As she bent for the kettle, she brushed her eyes with her sleeve.

Chapter Seven

Christy and her mother did the washing on a rise above the creek, high enough to be safe from flooding. It was easier to fill tubs and the huge black kettle from the creek than to haul bucket by bucket from the well. Jonathan Ware had built an open stone fireplace to heat water, made wide benches for the vessels, and grooved the yard-long oak board slanted into the tub. This got clothes cleaner faster than scrubbing them out by hand, although it barked Christy's knuckles if she wasn't careful rubbing garments up and down before wringing them as dry as she could and tossing them into the rinse water. Sheets, washed first, of course, now boiled in the kettle. Ellen Ware gave them stirs between dipping things up and down in the first rinsing tub. Beth did the same with socks and smaller things, wringing them as her mother did, putting them in the second rinse where she soused them around, and at last wringing them and hanging them over bushes and fence rails. For sheets and large things, Jonathan had rigged a rope between two hickory stumps far enough away from living trees not to be stained by perching birds.

Christy straightened to rest her aching shoulders and gazed toward the nearby bottom field. She'd never seen anything so beautiful as the fresh green of the finger-length corn planted a few weeks ago at the beginning of April when shimmering cloud oceans of passenger pigeons flew back north, settling like gray-blue waves into the forests to feed on mast. Some, according to Lige Morrow, would pair off and go deeply into the timber to nest instead of flying on. Christy liked to think of them, sheltered in leafy denseness, perhaps only their red feet and eyes showing as they cooed to each other and their young.

Oddly enough, the sheep were always the first of the farm animals to regain their energy on the new grass. The dark-faced Suffolk matriarchs, Nosey, Cleo, and Mildred, *baa*ed at their descendants or benignly watched the knob-kneed lambs butt their heads together. Cavalier, the strutting rooster, had toppled over as he hailed the sun one February dawn. The Wares mourned him, but he made tasty dumpling stew, nevertheless, and his heir stalked among the hens like a new-crowned king, brilliant rose comb bobbing like the plume of a knight.

Fawn-colored heifer calves suckled Goldie, Clover, and Shadow and Maud's sides bulged. In a few more years, the herd would be back to its numbers before the drought. Spotted piglets squealed from the pen, and Heloise had presented her gander, Abelard, with five gray goslings. On the slope above the barn, a blood bay colt nuzzled at Queenie who arched her neck to admire him.

Jed wasn't getting a holiday. He pulled a shovel plow guided by Jonathan through the rows of young corn, casting the soil around the sword-like little blades to smother weeds that were growing with at least equal vigor. Around the 1st of July, the corn should be up to a man's shoulder and able to fend for itself. After last summer's drought, it was ironic to know that, if there should be so much rain that it was too wet to plow or hoe while the corn got its start, it would be choked with weeds and grass that would take arduous labor to root out if and when the field dried enough.

Farmers had to be the boldest and most intrepid of gamblers, but, after all, as Jonathan said, that was why Joseph in long ago Egypt had built granaries to store up good harvests to get the people through seven years of drought.

Seven years! It had been more than some settlers could do to last one year. Soaping one of her father's shirts, Christy gave a silent prayer for the corn, and the oats, too, planted toward the end of March, and showing bravely.

Yes, it was spring, and, along with happy manifestations, Watt Caxton would be making his rounds to buy up mules and slaves to sell to the river plantations. He was the only person Jonathan had ever ordered off the Ware farm. Caxton had actually had the nerve to stop by after he'd brought his hounds on the Ware place when he was chasing Justus.

Christy wondered where Justus was and hoped he had managed to buy his wife or somehow get her free. If war came, what would happen to the slaves? If the Union won, they might eventually be freed, but what would prepare them to build new lives? For that matter, how was anyone going to manage who was close enough to the fighting to feel its brunt?

Trying to banish the dread that was always coiled in the pit of her stomach like a growing serpent, Christy scrubbed at a stubborn spot and was rubbing on more soap when Robbie leaped up from his guardian post between master and womenfolk and raced off with his welcoming bark.

Dan strode, long-legged, into view, bent to roughhouse the dog, and swung Beth in a circle as she ran to meet him. Christy's gladness at seeing him drained away when she could read the trouble on his face.

"It's happened!" He looked from Christy to her parents. Jonathan had left patient Jed among the corn while he came to hear the news. "Fort Sumter fell, April Fourteenth, after the Confederates bombarded it for two days."

Jonathan paled around the lips. "Were many killed?"

"By a miracle, no one. Major Anderson and his garrison were allowed to leave on the Union supply ship that had been trying to reach the fort."

"Thank God!" Ellen breathed.

Dan gave a tight laugh. "Isn't it strange that not a life was lost in an affair that's setting off a war bound to kill thousands?"

"Maybe . . . ," Christy began.

Dan shook his head. "President Lincoln's calling for seventy-five thousand volunteers to serve for three months to put down what he calls an 'insurrection'." Dan appealed to Jonathan. "Do you think it could be finished that quickly, sir?"

"I'm sure the Confederates think any one of them can lick ten Northerners." Jonathan gave a grim chuckle. "If war must come, the sooner it's over the better for everyone, but I fear it's more likely to last three years than three months."

Dan looked at Christy in a way that made her heart stop. "I'll volunteer as soon as Colonel Montgomery or almost anyone except Doc Jennison starts recruiting. Talk is that General Jim Lane . . . he was elected to the Senate April Fourth . . . will ask the President for a commission so he can raise volunteers to defend Kansas."

"From what one hears of Lane, he's just as likely to ransack Missouri." Jonathan turned back toward his plow. "We appreciate your bringing the news, Dan, even though it's what we've been dreading. Stay for dinner if you can."

"Do," Ellen urged, with a shaky smile. "We'll soon be through here."

"I'll help." Dan rinsed a pair of Jonathan's trousers and wrung them hand's length by hand's length till the last drop was squeezed from them. "Davie and I don't get dinner on wash days till we've wrung out all the sheets."

"Then I'll go make the corn pone," Ellen said, drying her hands on her apron. "Beth, come along and set the table."

"Race you to the middle," Dan teased, taking one end of a coverlet. Christy fished in the tub for her end. They pressed out all the water they could, and then twisted the heavy cloth in sections as fast as they could, draping the wrung parts over their shoulders, till they squeezed out the middle together and their fingers touched.

Dan closed his hand over hers and laughed. "Call it a tie?"

Breathing hard from exertion, Christy laughed back. "I beat you by at least a whisker!" His hair tangled over his forehead, so unruly that she longed to smooth it, feel it cling to her fingers. Gazing into his eyes, the deep blue-gray of smoke or storm, she ached for the feel of his arms, the hard sweetness of his mouth.

"Oh, Dan! Please! Let's. . . ."

His hand tightened on hers, paining it. "I've told you, sweetheart. I can by no means wed you, bed you, and leave you with the worry of a babe."

"We can't stop living because there's a war!"

"Some will. Many will."

She swallowed but it still hurt to talk. "If . . . if anything happened to you, Dan, I'd want your baby more than ever. To remember you. . . ."

"But if something happens to you? God help us, there might be no one to care for the child! It could starve like my poor little sister." He dropped Christy's hand as if it seared him and took the rest of the coverlet from her.

"Dan!"

"Leave it, Christy."

"I never thought you such a coward!" His jaw dropped. She blazed on. "Of course, you'll volunteer! Shoot and be

95

shot at! No doubt you'll die bravely, if that comes. But you're afraid to live, Dan! Afraid to love me!"

She would never forget the stricken look on his face before he turned away. "Indeed, I fear to love you as much as I do, but I can't be helping that. Nor would I, if I could."

"Dan! Please. . . ."

"I'll always love you, Christy Ware, but if my way of showing it offends you, you're in no way bound to me."

Her heart hammered in her throat. "What do you mean?"

He tossed the coverlet over the line and began to peg it up. "If it's marrying itself you're set on, Travis Jardine would oblige."

She gasped. "What a hateful thing to say!"

"Most would think it no worse than your calling me a coward."

She battled angry tears as they finished the washing in silence. He helped her carry the rinse water to the budding apple trees, empty the soapy water into the grate, and carry one of the tubs to hang in the dogtrot so it would be convenient for bathing.

As they entered the cabin, Dan glanced at the blanket forming on the loom, stripes of gold and dark brown with all the shades between. "A blanket?" he inquired. "Rare pretty. Soft as a baby rabbit it looks!"

"Feel it," Ellen invited.

Cautiously he did, long brown fingers lingering on the wool. "Softer than a wee rabbit." He smiled in awe. "The lucky person wrapped in that will have good dreams for sure."

Good dreams, my love, and a safe homecoming! Tenderness surged over Christy's hurt indignation, sweeping it away. Dan was trying to protect her according to what he knew from his own cruel experience. She didn't agree, she'd gladly run the risk, but she mustn't slash at him for following his conscience. Instead, she'd work hard to help finish the gift before Dan went off so that, wherever he was, something of her love would keep him warm, would lie between him and the hard ground.

Charlie and Travis rode in at mid-morning a few days later while Christy and her father were hoeing weeds from around the potato vines. Christy froze to see they each wore two revolvers, had rifles thrust in their saddle scabbards, and Bowie knives sheathed at their belts. Bedrolls and packs were tied behind their saddles.

"We're joining the State Guard!" Travis exulted as they swung from their saddles. "Old Pap Price is recruiting so we can defend Missouri from those infernal jayhawkers and Federal troops!"

Jonathan's hands seemed to freeze on the hoe. "What . . . ?"

"Militia from Clay and Jackson Counties took the Liberty arsenal across from Kansas City and are passing out weapons," Travis said in glee.

Jonathan's face turned suddenly old. He watched his son with such grief and worry that Christy wondered how Charlie could just stand there and look glum. "Armed rebellion," Jonathan whispered.

Travis's eyes shone. "The governor, Claib Jackson, told Lincoln what he could do with his call for troops from Missouri! Told him it was illegal, unconstitutional, revolutionary, inhuman, and diabolical . . . that it couldn't be complied with!"

"Some would call it illegal for the governor of a state to defy the President of the United States," Jonathan said.

Travis stared. "They're not united any more, sir. Virginia has just seceded. North Carolina surely will, probably Ten-

97

nessee. And Missouri shouldn't be forced to fight her sister Southern states even if those lop-eared Saint Louis Dutch are willing to fill the Union quota!"

"I thought the Missouri state convention voted for compromise, not secession."

"That was before Lincoln called for troops!"

Seething, Christy tightened her grip on the hoe. "What else could he do, Travis Jardine, after the Confederacy took Fort Sumter?"

"The South has to be able to defend itself. Arms from the arsenal help, but we need to take the big Federal depot at Saint Louis. Wouldn't I love to get a shot at that little banty rooster Lyon's scruffy carrot beard!"

"I hope you won't." Jonathan spoke to Travis, but his eyes never left his son. "Lyon is a brave officer. His like is needed." A faint smile softened Jonathan's lips. "But I'd be sorry, Travis, to see harm come to you."

"We'll ride right through those Germans," Travis said cockily. "I bet I'll get a commission because of my military training."

"I didn't think you graduated from either of those academies," Christy said.

He shrugged. "I still have a sight more military training than most. One thing you can count on is that Charlie and I will stick together. Melissa made us promise."

"What does she think about this?" Christy demanded of her brother.

"She saw we had to go . . . ," Travis began, but Charlie cut him off.

"Since Travis was set on volunteering, she asked me to keep him from being too hot-headed a fool." Charlie met his father's eyes. "I hate to fight the Union, sir, but, in the pinch, I think states have a right to secede."

"That's not how Missouri's voted," Christy argued.

Travis patted a revolver. "We're going to vote like this."

"Yes!" Christy burst out. "That's how it's been along this border for years. Now it'll be that way all over the country! Oh, Charlie. . . ." Her heart sank at his closed face. She bit her tongue on bitter words. *You're the Jardines', not ours! You'll fight for what they believe, not for what you were taught at home.*

Jonathan leaned his hoe against the fence. "Come in and see your mother, Charles. Have dinner before you ride on."

Travis groaned and rubbed his stomach. "Our breakfasts aren't settled yet, sir. Aunt Phronie stuffed us like Christmas geese." His eyes sparkled and he clapped an arm around Charlie. "Anyhow, we have to hurry. No telling what's going to happen at Saint Louis!"

"Some buttermilk would taste mighty good, though," said Charlie.

He wouldn't look at Christy as he loosened his cinch, but, when Beth came pelting up, he knelt to hug her, face buried in her hair. *He doesn't want to do this,* Christy thought in sad triumph. *He still believes what we do, but he's married to a Jardine.*

Eyes blurring, she started for the well house. Adjacent to the well, the small log structure had troughs made from large hollowed logs around three sides. Every other day, water was drained from these by spigots and flowed to the maiden blush apple trees before fresh water from the well was poured in to cool the jugs and crocks.

Selecting a big crockery pitcher of gold-speckled buttermilk, Christy turned. Travis filled the door. He took the pitcher from her and set it in the trough. Before she could guess his intention, he caught her in his arms and kissed her soundly.

Something female in her responded to his strength, the warm ardor of his mouth, but this was overwhelmed by outrage. Planting her hands against his chest, she shoved him away.

"Why, Christy, sister-in-law!" His voice caressed her in mock hurt. "Surely you won't grudge a farewell kiss to a man going to fight for his country!"

"It's not *my* country, Travis, or my brother's, either."

"It is, since he married into us." Travis took her hands so urgently she didn't pull away. He still was smiling, but with an underlying earnestness she'd never known in him. "Christy, if we got married, you and I, we could save our families the aggravation of getting used to a new set of in-laws."

"*What?*"

"You heard me well enough."

She shook her head in half-amused disbelief. "That's the strangest reason I've ever heard for a marriage. It's not a very good one. I don't love you, and I don't think you love me."

He wasn't laughing now. "I may not love you, but you're the one I can't forget."

"That's because I don't swoon in your arms."

"No. It's because you're you. I think the world of Charlie. Just seems natural to love his sister."

"Travis," she chided, between sympathy and annoyance, "you think you have to ride off with some lady's favor, the way knights trailed a glove or scarf from their lances!"

"Couldn't we be engaged?"

"Of course not, you ridiculous boy! Even if I adored you, I wouldn't be engaged to a Rebel."

"Your own brother's one."

"Only because he married into your family. I'm sorry for him with all my heart . . . and just as sorry for us." She hadn't meant to upbraid Travis, but she couldn't contain her most

100

terrible fear. "What if he has to fight Thos? Maybe be on different sides in the same battle?"

"Now, Christy, that's not likely. . . ."

"All the boys and men on both sides have mothers. Most have sisters. Some even have children. Think how your mother and Melissa will mourn if you don't come back."

He was completely sober now. "They'd suffer more if I failed in honor."

"Honor! That's a man's word. Women care about life."

"This trouble's boiled and bubbled along for years. It's got to be settled once and for all." Travis's buoyant nature erupted in laughter. "Don't look so sad, sweetheart! We'll only have to whip the bluecoats roundly a few times before Lincoln sees he has to let the South go. Why, I bet the Yanks run so fast there won't be many of them killed!"

"Thos won't run. Dan O'Brien and his friends won't." Christy swallowed at tightness in her throat. "If the whole thing could just stop right now. . . ." Ducking her head, she brushed past him.

The young men stood outside to drink two mugs apiece of the tangy buttermilk. No one said much. Charlie gazed at the animals in their pens and pastures, the blooming fruit trees, the greening fields, promising and beautiful after last year's drought. Robbie pressed close to him, worshiping. What could animals think of their beloveds' comings and goings except say with mute devotion, I'd never leave you. Wherever you are is heaven.

"I always hated hoeing corn above everything." Charlie picked up Robbie and cradled him against his shoulder. "You know, I'd like right well to hoe that field. And pull fodder when the ears are grown, carry it to the barn in the light of the harvest moon."

"Oh, we'll be home in time for roasting ears!" Travis

bragged. "But first we have to go. Give us a kiss for luck, E-liz-a-*beth*."

Beth didn't shriek with glee as she usually did when Travis gave her all the syllables of her name. She kissed him solemnly. "Please don't kill Danny or Thos!"

As he stared at her, crimsoning, she threw herself on Charlie, hugging him around the waist, burying her face against his midriff. "Be careful, Charlie! Please . . . please don't get crippled or killed!"

He put down the dog and knelt to embrace his sister. "I'll be careful, Bethie. Listen, I'll tell you a nice secret." His glance swept to his parents and Christy. "About the time pawpaws and wild grapes are ripe this fall, you'll be Aunt Beth." She blinked. "I mean," he said pridefully, "that we're going to have a baby. Melissa is. So will you promise to love and help her?"

"Oh, Charlie, yes!" Her joy faded. She looked beseechingly at her parents. "We will go see the baby, won't we?"

"If we possibly can," Jonathan said, nodding.

Ellen embraced her tall oldest son. "We'll do anything we can for Melissa and the baby, dear. Be sure of that."

"I am." He kissed her and turned to Christy, blue eyes asking a question.

It wasn't the time to say the Jardines might not welcome them to Rose Haven. The only smile she was able to summon felt stiff on her lips. "I hope the baby's a boy and looks exactly like you, Charlie."

"Poor infant!"

Travis kissed Beth and Ellen, swept Christy a teasing bow, and shook hands with Jonathan. "Save some roasting ears for us, sir."

Robbie began to whimper as the young men tightened their cinches and mounted. They paused at the eastern timber edge and waved. The family waved back till the two vanished into the fresh-leafed trees. Beth ran to cuddle Robbie and be consoled in turn.

Jonathan said almost under his breath: "Instead of pulling fodder, I fear they'll be fodder of another kind. Both sides waste seed corn when our best and bravest youngsters go off to fight."

"All we can do is pray . . . that every mother's son comes home, be they for North or South." Ellen scanned Christy. "You were a long time in the well house with Travis."

"Oh, Travis!" Christy grinned and shrugged. "I should have given him my apron to flaunt from his helmet!"

They all laughed. Ellen's voice was relieved. "You . . . you don't love him, then?"

"Not a bit." Christy looked at her parents and tears filled her eyes. "It's Dan I love!" she burst out. "But he won't marry me because he's afraid he'll be killed and . . . and our baby might have as hard a time as he did."

"He's thinking of you, child," Jonathan said. "I respect him for that."

"It'd serve him right if I did marry Travis!"

Ellen looked shocked. "You won't, surely?"

"Of course, I won't! But I don't see why Dan has to be so stubborn."

"Because he's man, not a lad like Travis." Jonathan smiled and touched her cheek. "That's why you love him, Daughter."

They went back to their work. As she chopped weeds away from the growing stalks, Christy prayed for Charlie, for all the boys who would go for soldiers before they were really men.

Why was Travis still a boy while Dan, who had lived the same twenty years, was not? Travis had driven ox teams on Western trails, seen silver camps and wild life, but he hadn't endured the grief and hardship that gave Dan strength and made him so early a man. Most of all, perhaps, Travis didn't have Dan's song.

Chapter Eight

Dan's new black Army brogans pinched his left toes, but he was glad to have them. The last vestiges of his old shoes had been cut to shreds by flint rocks, shreds that melted in the sucking mud of summer rains as the hastily mustered 1st and 2nd Kansas Volunteer Infantry Regiments toiled south from Kansas City with Major Sturgis's Regulars, joined General Lyon's Regulars and the 1st Iowa Volunteer Infantry Regiment, and marched some more, building ferries and pontoon bridges to cross the swollen Grand and Osage Rivers.

Lyon was getting no chance to practice the graces he'd learned at dancing school in Fort Scott only last winter. He'd saved the St. Louis arsenal for the Union by forcing the surrender of Governor Claib Jackson's militia and chased the governor and his forces commanded by General Sterling Price out of Boonville and the capital of Jefferson City. This gave the Union control of the Missouri River and East-West travel and supply routes, vital once the Confederacy had declared war May 6th. Bitterly divided, Tennessee completed the Confederated States in June, making the fourth border state to join the seven of the deep South.

When rumors spread like prairie fire that Price was gathering men in southwest Missouri to reclaim the state and invade Kansas, Dan O'Brien, Owen Parks, Andy McHugh, and Theo Wattles left off cultivating the best corn crop they'd ever seen and rode to Leavenworth in early June to join the forming regiment. David Parks and one of the Nickel boys, begging to the last to enlist, had come along to lead back the horses.

"You're only seventeen," Owen admonished his younger brother. "Father needs you."

"Harriet and your young 'uns need *you!*" David retorted, green eyes brilliant with held-back tears of anger and disappointment.

"I'm only enlisting for three months." Owen tousled David's curly black hair. "Cheer up! When I come home, Father's agreed you can volunteer if you're still set on it."

"The war'll be over!" David blinked and added bitterly: "And by then we'll have the fodder in the barn and the corn cribbed . . . probably even have plowed under the stubble!" But he hugged his brother quick and hard as they parted, hugged Dan, too.

There'd been no uniforms and few weapons. In fact only day before yesterday, August 8th, had a wagon train of clothing finally rolled into Springfield, supplying Dan's shoes, forage cap, and dark blue fatigue blouse with yellow buttons. At Leavenworth, Dan and the other recruits were lucky to be issued Springfield rifles, haversacks, canteens, and oilcloths. Dan passed up an Army blanket to keep the soft warm striped one Christy had given him when he had told her good bye. Rolled inside the oilcloth along with his newly issued socks, the blanket comforted Dan so much that he never swore at the bedroll slung in front from left shoulder to right hip. Christy. Christy and the sweetness of her lips.

So now, partly uniformed after two months in service, marching in the darkness of what might be the last morning of his life along the Little York Road from Springfield, Dan at last felt like a soldier. Of course, on the first and second days of that sweltering month, he'd sweated and choked on dust the sixteen miles to Dug Springs where there'd been a skirmish. Price's Missouri troops broke and ran under artillery fire and cavalry pursuit. The Union volunteer companies were held in reserve while better-trained and equipped Regulars fought the Rebels. Dan's sweat had turned icy and the looseness of his bowels wasn't entirely from three weeks of eating nothing much but fresh-slaughtered beef with no salt, but the fracas had been a lot of smoke, racket, and shooting with only four Union soldiers killed and six injured. The Confederates lost a few more.

Light casualties? Total, if you were one who died. Still, the small victory lifted the spirits of Lyon's badly outnumbered army that had shrunk in even this week since Dug Springs. Three-month volunteer enlistments had run out for 3,000 of his 7,000 men, including the 1st Iowa.

They had agreed to stay for a battle, and then they were going home, glad to see the last of an army that once passed on to them a beef carcass so putrid the Regulars had turned it down. The Iowans turned their outrage into a joke, burying the beef with full military honors. Now they marched so close behind Dan that he could hear Bill Heustis's ritual lament: "I wish I'd stayed home and sent my big brother."

"How do you want us to bury you, Bill?" joked another Iowan.

"Well, see you make me a good coffin out of sycamore wood and use brass tacks to hammer on my name and. . . ." He considered a moment. "I want it to say . . . 'I am a-going to be a great big he-angel.' "

"We don't have that many tacks. Besides, Billy, you're more likely to wind up in the other place."

"Not me!" Heustis laughed. He launched into the song to which the Iowans, down through Missouri, trod on the heels of the Regulars or, when put in the lead, left them far behind. Lyon grumbled at the "damned Iowa greyhounds" and predicted that they sang too much to be good fighters.

> *The time of retribution am a-coming,*
> *For with bayonet and shell*
> *We will give the Rebels hell;*
> *And they'll never see the Happy Land of Canaan. . . .*

Slowly, then spreading with mounting gusto from back ranks to front, the Kansans joined in. They were still miles and hours out of earshot of the Confederate forces camped along Wilson's Creek where the Rebels could forage for roasting ears in bottom land fields and graze their thousands of horses and mules. Dan sang, too, but it was his mother's lullabies that sounded in his head, and the tune he'd made for Christy.

He'd left his fiddle in her care. Would he ever play for her again? What was she doing just now? He couldn't believe he'd die, but he supposed no one ever did. He was going to sleep on his feet when the order came to halt. He drowsed, leaning on his rifle, till the march resumed. They might plod only a few minutes to stop again. For what seemed hours, companies and regiments shifted around in the darkness. Caissons and artillery groaned by, blankets muting their wheels, but not Company F's commander, Captain James Totten.

"Forward that caisson, God damn you, sir!" he ordered in his soft Virginia drawl. "Mind that gun!" A profane, hard-drinking, card-playing West Point classmate of General Lyon's, the only thing Totten shared with his commander was being a tough soldier.

"Don't he cuss polite?" admired Billy Heustis. "I'd walk five miles just to listen to him."

A dark shape loomed up and paused. "This is what we came for, boys!" softly called Colonel George Washington Deitzler, the brigade commander. "Colonel Sigel and his brigade will attack from the other direction. We'll have the enemy caught between us." His horse faded away with sack-muffled hoofs.

"Caught?" growled an Iowan. "The Rebs have three to five men to our one. Be lucky if they don't just bust out like homebrew popping corks!"

Dan didn't care to think about that, so he mulled over what he knew about Deitzler. During the Border Ruffians' invasions, he'd risked his life to go to New England and bring back Sharps breechloaders for the Free State men around Lawrence. As soon as Lincoln called for volunteers, he'd organized the 1st Kansas, which along with the 2nd Kansas, 1st Iowa, and Captain Wright's Home Guards, made up the 4th Brigade.

The 2nd's own commander, Colonel Mitchell, reined in next. Dan couldn't see his face, but he'd know that genial, booming voice anywhere. "We won't be in reserve this time, lads . . . or not for long. You may not get another crack at the bushwhackers before your enlistment's up, so make it count!"

Robert Mitchell had brought his law books and hollyhock seeds to Linn County from Ohio during the worst of the border troubles. He had defeated Charles Hamelton for a seat in the territorial legislature, and, after Hamelton shot the captives at Marais des Cygnes, Mitchell had pursued with a party of neighbors.

Dan tried to wipe that day from his memory, all except Christy's scent of lilacs and blue dress, but the rest flooded back — the joy of Susie's and Andy's wedding changing to horror as men rode up with Reverend Reed whose bowels thrust out of his bloodied clothing, the ox-drawn wagon driven by a tow-headed twelve-year-old boy whose father lay dead in back while his mother tried to tend and comfort four bleeding men lying on the featherbeds while the other sun-bonneted woman cradled her terribly wounded husband.

Were some of Hamelton's bunch in Price's army? Likely. Even likelier that scores of Clarke's raiders were, unless the marauders who'd burned out the Nickels and other families were afraid to face men with guns.

What about Osawatomie? whispered a voice like Jonathan Ware's. *What of the men hacked to death with short swords, two little more than boys? What about Charlie Ware?*

Dan prayed he'd never have to fight Christy's brother. He didn't even want to fight Travis Jardine. He didn't want to fight anyone. He just couldn't stand to see his America torn apart and rotted with slavery, his new country where he had grown up with a chance in life, instead of starving.

Tramping on his right, Andy McHugh put Dan's feelings into words. "Looks like there ought to be a better way of settling things than making men kill each other who'd a sight rather not."

Ahead of Andy but close enough to hear, Owen flung over his shoulder: "I'm a Quaker, Andy, but we've got to fight if we want our children to live in a country uncursed by slavery."

"The war's not about slavery, lads," wheezed Bedad Tompkins, the oldest man in the company. Because the grizzled, stubby fifty-year-old had fought in the Mexican War, he'd been made a sergeant and put in charge of drilling the recruits. "It's about saving the Union."

"Whatever it's about," called Bill Heustis from the Iowans, "I wish I'd stayed at home and sent my big brother!"

It began to drizzle, livening the smell of earth and hay and grain fields. Some corn was shoulder high, blades whispering sibilantly, but much was heaped in shocks. The oats and wheat had been harvested. Dan treasured in his knapsack two biscuits made of flour from wheat a militia captain had bought in a field, cut with his men, and taken to a mill to be ground. How good bread tasted after nothing but tough beef, boiled, charred, or raw!

Of the supplies Lyon had been begging from the renowned Pathfinder, General John Charles Frémont, commander of the newly created Department of Missouri, only the belated issue of clothing and shoes had come. The rest, if there was more, was piled up in Rolla where the railroad ended. According to what trickled down to the soldiers, Frémont had some grand scheme to occupy the whole Mississippi Valley. He faced east, not west, and the higher-ups in the capital weren't going to worry much about what happened in southwestern Missouri after the Union defeat at Bull Run in Virginia on July 21st, when fleeing soldiers ran pell-mell into Congressmen and sight-seers who'd driven out from Washington that fine Sunday to watch their Army whip the Rebels.

"Fall out, boys," called Sergeant Bedad. "Find as dry a place as you can and sleep with your weapons. You may need 'em in a hurry."

"Here's a haystack, Dan!" called Owen.

As many as could burrowed under the fragrant hay while others sheltered by corn shocks and fence rows or other haystacks. Dan took off his waist belt on which hung his percussion cap box and scabbarded bayonet, and slipped off the cartridge box he wore slung over his left shoulder. He shoved them under the hay and unfolded his oilcloth, careful to keep it under and over his prized blanket.

Sighing with the bliss of being free of his gear, he sipped from his canteen and munched the biscuits before putting his extra socks in the haversack to use as a pillow beneath the blanket. "Still seems peculiar to be marching past fields, instead of working in them."

"Aye." Andy McHugh spoke through whatever he'd saved from his supper. "Likely the Rebels have feasted fine on fresh corn. Wish they'd left us some."

"Andy! How'd you like it if soldiers ate the corn you planted and battled weeds out of, so that Susie and your mother got none?"

"I'd purely hate it," growled Andy. "But it's what'll happen, you can bet, if we don't rearrange General Price's notions. Anyhow, Dan, Sergeant Bedad says when you're fighting across farmland like this, what one side doesn't take, the other will."

"It's stealing, nevertheless," Owen said quietly.

Andy snorted. "Susie's trying hard, Owen, but she hasn't made a Quaker out of me yet."

"I promised Mother not to do anything I'd be ashamed to tell her about," Theo said wistfully. "If I get killed tomorrow. . . ."

"None of us is going to get killed, lad," Andy said with gruff kindness. "Keep close to me and remember what Bedad's cussed into us."

"But the Rebels have almost twenty thousand men," muttered Theo. "We only have about fifty-six hundred."

"Yes, but General McCulloch doesn't have any faith in Pap Price's volunteers," countered Owen. "Calls them the Huckleberry Cavalry! Says they're great roasting ear foragers but poor soldiers. He claims his Confederate commission outranks Price's as commander of Missouri's State Guard and wouldn't help Price till Price agreed to let him run the whole shebang."

"McCulloch's fifty years old and been fighting close to

half of them," said Andy. "He was with Sam Houston when the Texans whipped the Mexicans at San Jacinto, and then, same as Price, was in the war with Mexico. Next, he was a Texas Ranger captain, and then, just during the Mormon war three years ago, he managed to talk Brigham Young and the Mormon elders into agreeing to obey the laws of the United States rather than fight an all out war."

Owen shrugged. "He may have a persuasive tongue, but neither he nor Albert Pike could talk the Cherokee chief, John Ross, into allying with the South. Pike did get promises of support from some of the Creeks, Choctaws, Chickasaws, and Seminoles."

"Choctaws!" breathed Dan. "They gave money to help feed the Irish!"

"Did they now?" Andy lifted a reddish eyebrow. "Well, it's natural they'd feel for starving folk after they were driven from the East thirty years ago like the rest of the Five Civilized Tribes."

"They've got no cause, any of them, to love the Union," said Owen. "But they've begun to prosper in the Territory. I'm bound most of them want no part of this white man's war. McCulloch has the ticklish job of keeping the Union out of Indian Territory without invading it himself. That's how come him to be in Fort Smith with his Texans and regiments from Louisiana and Arkansas."

"The Rebs have lots more cavalry than we do," Andy mused, "but we have sixteen guns to their fifteen, so that'll help."

"Bedad says cannon balls aren't so bad." Theo sounded as if he were trying to cheer up himself and his friends. "Balls kill whatever they drop on, but that's seldom more than one or two men. It's canister, grapeshot, and shrapnel shell that can kill a dozen men and wound more all at once."

113

"They do say," commented Andy, "that Henry Shrapnel invented spherical case shot during the siege of Gibraltar in the Seventeen Nineties. Wanted to get the same results as heavy musket fire but at long range. He filled a hollow cannon ball with musket balls and gunpowder and added a time fuse. Sometimes the shell exploded before it got out of the cannon, so Shrapnel hit on the notion of attaching the musket balls with resin around a tin tube of gunpowder with the fuse on top. He got his musket volley."

"Yes," grunted Owen, "except one of Major Totten's artillerymen told me some of the balls go sideways or upwards and don't hit the target."

"I hope the ones aimed at us all go sideways," Theo said so comically that they all laughed before they lay down with their rifles.

Dan longed to take off the tight new shoes and debated comfort against the extra minutes it would take to put them on if they were hurriedly ordered up. He finally compromised by loosening the laces and holding his legs up in the air for a while to let the blood drain from his swollen feet into his body the way the men often did on hard marches. Then he shifted around till he rested as easy as he was going to, and pulled Christy's blanket against him.

Did a faint trace of her lilac odor linger beneath his own and the smell of campfires and mildew? Dan didn't want to think of the coming battle. Instead, as he did every night, he thought of Christy. She might have helped her father pull fodder, or perhaps she'd churned. At this very moment, she might be spinning wool like that in his blanket, or mending, knitting, or working at the loom while her mother played the piano.

Soon now the Wares would go to bed. He stopped his thoughts there — almost. Some night, some heaven of a

114

night, would he hold Christy instead of his rifle? He huddled as much of the blanket as he could against his face and dropped into sleep.

It only seemed a minute till he roused at Sergeant Bedad's urgent voice. "Up, boys! Fall in! Don't make a sound! We want to catch the Rebs with their breeches down."

Fingers of light streaked the eastern sky, but it was still too dark to see much. Dan took a swig of water to wash down the night smell of his mouth, tightened and tied his shoe laces, and put on his accouterments before shaking hay off his blanket and oilcloth and rolling them up. As always, he tucked John Brown's New Testament into his extra shirt. How Brown would have loved to march with them! But only if he could command.

Breath seemed to thicken and clog Dan's chest. He had to strain hard to get any air. Grasping his Springfield, he took his place beside Andy. It was light enough now to make out the red bands stitched across the front of Company E's blue-gray hunting shirts.

All companies of the 1st Iowa wore different outfits. Few had traded them for Army issue when they'd finally had the chance. With a chill, Dan realized that with so many differently uniformed volunteer outfits on both sides, it might be close to impossible to tell friend from foe.

"Don't be down-hearted, boys, that we're in reserve," admonished Bedad as the troops moved into line of battle. "Before this day is over, you'll get all the fighting you want!"

"Don't the Rebs have pickets out?" Dan whispered to Andy.

A fusillade shattered the hush. The roll of drums reverberated beneath shouted commands. "Look!" Owen jerked his head. "Yonder in the oaks! See the tents?"

Then they were marching down a hollow and couldn't see

the Confederates till they reached the level and could look along Wilson's Creek and the Telegraph Road turning under the bluff below. In encampments spread farther than the eye could reach among farms and fields, men scrambled into lines or ran for their horses.

"Didn't know there was that many Rebs in the world," Bill Heustis muttered. "Oh, I wish I'd stayed at home and. . . ."

"First Kansas, forward!" yelled Colonel George Washington Deitzler. "Second Kansas, First Iowa, you and the Home Guards are in reserve till needed. Guard the wagons and pick up stragglers."

Totten's cannon roared. From across the creek thundered an answering blast. "Sigel got there." Bedad shrugged. "Maybe having his brigade over there will work out after all, 'specially since we took the Rebs by surprise." He spat a brown curl of tobacco juice on the grass. "Why on earth didn't they have pickets out?" He spat again. " 'Nother good thing is a Reb prisoner says a thousand or more of Price's volunteers don't have weapons. They're supposed to get them off dead or wounded, their men or ours. More'n likely they'll get in the way and cause a sight more trouble than they're worth."

"I didn't come all the way from Iowa to be stuck back with the wagons," grumbled Heustis. "Wish we could get the fightin' done while that nice little breeze is a-blowin'."

"Reckon the boys up ahead feel plenty warm right now," said Andy.

There was a farm cabin on their right a little way ahead. A woman stood in the door a moment as if uncertain of what to do. At the next bellow of Totten's guns, she ducked into the house and rushed out with a sack and crying baby. She grabbed a howling toddler by the hand and made for the timber where two older children could be glimpsed leading a cow and a mule.

"Doesn't seem right to be fighting all over these farms, scaring off the women and kids," said Dan.

"Where else are we going to fight?" asked Owen unhappily. He had to be thinking, as was Dan, of Harriet and Lydia, Susie and Christy, of all the women back home. "They don't mark off some big empty place a long ways from anybody and call it a battlefield."

"I still wish. . . ." Dan broke off.

"The Rebel cavalry's retreating!" hissed Andy. "There goes Colonel Deitzler with the First Kansas! Must be the First Missouri with them. Look at them go! They're chasing the Rebs right up that hill!"

"Wish we was there!" shrilled Heustis. "Our boys must be lookin' down at the whole dang' Confederate Army!"

"Their artillery's openin' up! Hark! That's Old Sacramento!" Bedad's voice thrilled with the delight of meeting an old friend, even if it was once again an enemy cannon. "She's made out of melted Mexican church bells. I was at Sacramento when we took her. She sings because silver was mixed in the metal when a crack had to be mended once."

"I've heard songs I liked better." Dan's throat was so dry he couldn't swallow. Banners flew and drums beat as a detachment of Regulars and Home Guards advanced on a cornfield on the other side of the creek where a swarm of Confederates took cover to shoot at Lyon's main force as they marched toward the Rebels who were spread out across two miles of farm land and scrub oak and hazel. Handsome roan horses galloped past, six horse teams hauling each caisson or gun as a Union battery took positions to cover the men plunging across the creek to the high green corn.

Unlimbered guns spewed grapeshot and canister over the

heads of the Union soldiers to explode among the Rebels. The 1st Iowa was ordered forward to support the battery. Then Rebel guns opened up.

An unearthly scream ripped through the din of cannon, muskets, and the cries of wounded men and horses. "That caisson's wheel horse!" cried Owen. "A cannon ball tore off his shoulder!"

Someone mercifully shot the animal. It was impossible to see much of what was going on in the high corn, but apparently the Rebels had clustered near a farmhouse. The Union battery sent two shells into the house, but there were too many of the enemy for the detachment to prevail. After what seemed forever but was perhaps an hour, the thinned Union force retreated.

Billy Heustis had no jokes as the 1st Iowa straggled back to the envious but appalled 2nd Kansas. At least a score of faces Dan had come to recognize were missing. Other men had roughly bandaged wounds. They sank down in the shade of wagons or scrub trees, drank from their canteens, and devoured any food saved from supper since no rations had been issued that morning.

"Well done, lads!" cried Bedad. "You kept the Rebs from blasting away the main army's flank."

"Yeah," drawled Heustis. "They blasted us instead. But I reckon" — some of his old grin came back — "that we're showing Lyon we can fight, even if we do sing more'n he likes."

Up in front someone yelled: "Totten's battery's blowing up a good five acres of supply wagons! Look at 'em burn! Now he's limbering the guns and making for the battle."

"Can you see the lines?" Bedad roared through cupped hands.

"Maybe, if I shinny up that big tree." In a few minutes, the same voice carried faintly to them, along with the black smoke of the burning supply wagons. "Our boys are spread out three deep for a thousand yards along the ridge. There's not more'n a few hundred yards between them and the Rebs who're headed up the hill." In another moment: "Musket smoke's drifting east, away from our line into the Rebs. Can't hardly see 'em."

"Which means they can't see our boys," grunted Bedad. " 'Course that don't keep 'em from firing. Lordy Lord! Old Sacramento sings this day! Wish she was ours."

"Aren't we ever going to get to fight?" Andy growled.

"Be sure we will," Bedad promised.

After the tumult, it grew suddenly quiet. The man in the tree shouted: "The Rebs are pulling back down the bluff to Wilson's Creek! Looks like they're reforming along the Telegraph Road."

Colonel Mitchell loomed out of the smoke. "Second Kansas!" he called, already wheeling his bay horse. "Come on! We've got our fight!"

Chapter Nine

Dan's legs didn't seem to belong to him as they tramped through the scrub at Bedad's commands. A battery clattered past and stopped to the right of Dan's company. Up the slope, beyond the unlimbering guns, Colonel Deitzler was re-grouping the 1st Kansas. What was left of the 1st Iowa was forming to the left. Beyond them, left, faintly droned the cool Virginia voice of Captain Totten, politely damning his artillerymen.

When his legs stopped at Bedad's shout, Dan looked straight at a Rebel battery, long barrels snouting up the hill. Infantry massed on either side of the guns with cavalry on the left flank and more infantry, cavalry, and guns spread out to the right, even beyond Wilson's Creek. Then Dan's bewildered gaze fixed on a rag-tag force boiling up the slope. Some wore uniforms, but more were in homespun like Missouri Home Guards, long knives belted to their sides, squirrel rifles in their hands.

"Whose side are they on?" rumbled Bedad, biting the end off a cartridge. "They're carrying the Union flag, but they've got the Confederate one, too!"

A volley from the advancing throng answered him. The battle erupted all along the line. Mitchell waved his sword and swept the 2nd Kansas over the ridge.

Dan bit the end off the paper cartridge and ordered his

hand not to shake as he poured powder down the barrel. With what was left of the paper for patching, he rammed the bullet home with the iron ramrod that was carried in a groove in the stock beneath the barrel. He eared back the hammer and put a tiny copper percussion cap on the nipple opening into the powder chamber.

"Don't aim above their knees!" Bedad shouted.

Blinding white smoke stung Dan's eyes and nostrils. Cannon fire splintered trees and sent branches and slivers flying. Squinting at a shadow dodging through the fog of dust and smoke, Dan squeezed the trigger.

The something screeched and melted into the dust.

Colonel Mitchell pitched from his saddle. Lyon took shape in the smoke. His splendid gray must have been shot from under him for he rode another horse. He swept off his hat in a flourish that revealed a bloody bandage over the wound that had bled downward to mat his wiry red beard.

"Come on, my brave boys! I'll lead you!" Then he jerked high in the saddle.

Except for a glimpse of him being carried to the rear, that was the last Dan saw of the tough little general.

Stunned, unable to believe the fiery will that had inspired and driven them was gone as well as their own colonel, the 2nd faltered in their headlong assault, but, before the Rebels could break their line, Lieutenant Colonel Charles Blair of the 2nd took command and urged them on.

Dan yelled with the others as they fought almost rifle barrel to rifle barrel. The shaggy Rebel in front of Dan raced him to load, showing strong yellow side teeth as he bit the cartridge although there were several gaps in his front teeth. He was fitting his percussion cap on the nipple when Dan pulled the trigger and lunged over the body while it was still settling to the ground.

No time to feel. No time to think. Load and fire. Load and fire. Cannon balls spat from the smoke, canister and grapeshot knocked down swaths of writhing, screaming men as a scythe mows grain. One row of Rebels dropped to their bellies to shoot from the shelter of the scrub while the next rank knelt, and the last stood, each line covering the others as they loaded and aimed.

Shooting from at least a little shelter appealed to Dan. He dropped to the ground behind a thick, dwarfed hazel, poked his Springfield through it, and fired into smoke and commotion. When he tried to reload in that position, he found that he couldn't pour the powder down the muzzle, so he compromised by kneeling. The air was thick and dust laden with bits of grass, twigs, and chipped rock. Dan, with his comrades, battled the Rebels inch by inch down the slope.

From the corner of his eye, he glimpsed Rebel cavalry plunging through heavy growth to the left. Totten waited till they were close and blew them away with a hail of canister.

The Rebel infantry retreated down the hill. Dan stopped shooting, panting as he leaned on his rifle. Blood dripped on his hand.

"You're hit!" cried Owen.

Dan wiped his arm across his temple. "Can't be much."

Owen produced a handkerchief. "Let me bandage it." As he did, he muttered: "Where's Colonel Sigel? If he'd catch the Rebels from behind. . . ."

"He must be done for," said Bedad. "I heard an artilleryman yelling that the Rebs are firing Sigel's cannon balls at us." The graying old sergeant put a bracing hand on Dan's shoulder. "Don't lose heart, boys! Haven't we held this hill against all the Rebs could throw at us?"

"One of their outfits dropped its flag," Andy noticed. It fluttered among heaps of dead 100 yards ahead. Andy was starting for it when a horseman rode out of a thicket, trotting forward.

"He wants to surrender," Bedad guessed. "Don't shoot, lads."

"Don't shoot!" Dan called up the line. Others repeated the caution till it was almost a chant.

The rider came on slowly. About twenty yards from the flag, he spurred forward, snatched up the banner, whirled his mount, and dashed for safety. No one fired. Nor did they shoot at the wounded Rebel who caught a riderless horse and hauled himself into the saddle.

As heat and the sense of danger ebbed from him, Dan never wanted to fire again. Blasted bodies were strewn up and down that scrubby hill. He almost wished for the roar of cannon to drown out the moans and pleadings.

A Rebel who looked younger than David lay half under two dead men. "Thirsty . . . ," came his weak voice. "So thirsty. . . ."

Although his own mouth was parched, Dan went to the boy. When he tried to lift him, Dan's hand dug into a pulp of blood and flesh. The yellow-haired lad didn't seem to feel it. Sickened, Dan shifted his fingers till he found a solid shoulder blade and raised the youngster, holding the canteen to his cracked lips.

The lad swallowed. His blue eyes flickered over Dan's face. He swallowed again. With great effort, he grinned. "If I meet you in hell, Yank, I'll give you a swig."

He took one more swallow. Something went out of him. The grin faded. He stared straight into the dirty white sun broiling down from the zenith through a pall of smoke.

Andy shook Dan's arm. "Back in line, Danny! That looks like Sigel's men crossing the creek, but if it isn't. . . . The devil with both sides having uniforms that look near the same!" He peered under his hand. "It must be Sigel! They're carrying the Union flag and our artillery isn't firing."

Dan wiped the boy's blood off on his pants and went back to his place. The cry of a Union skirmisher, downslope from the main force, carried on the thin breeze. "Not Sigel! Rebs!"

The Confederates opened fire all along their advancing line. From their uniforms, these were new troops, fresh and rested.

Colonel Blair shouted: "Down, men, so our guns can fire over your heads! Fire at will!"

The Union artillery withered the Rebels with shells and balls, but the attackers surged forward over the bodies of their dead and wounded. In spite of his awkward position, Dan managed to get enough powder down the muzzle to shoot. He ran out of cartridges and caps, but wormed over to a dead Iowan and got his.

A huge man in a tall black cap and duster rode up and down to encourage the Rebels. "Big as his horse!" gasped Andy. "Must be Pap Price. Look! He's bleeding from his side. Must not be too bad. He's riding on."

The sun blazed down on the sweltering men. Dan's lips cracked and bled as he bit off cartridge tails. How could the Rebels keep coming, uphill, with canister exploding amongst them like scores of muskets fired at close range?

A choked cry came from beside him. Dan looked sideways. Andy's face welled blood. His rifle and ramrod dropped from his fingers.

"Andy!" Dan cried.

No answer. The Rebels were swarming up the slope. Dan wriggled in front of Andy, and for the first time fired with real hatred, reloaded, fired again.

After what seemed eternity, the Rebels broke off the assault and retreated down the hill across the bodies of their many comrades who had fallen in the three attempts to take it.

A little scrub-grown hill in southwest Missouri.

Dan raised to stare at Andy and breathed his name. There was no answer. Andy's chest labored to rise and fall. Dan got his new socks from his bedroll and doubled one over the bleeding jaw.

"Hold that tight as you can," he told Owen who had hurried up and was cradling Andy's head and shoulders.

"There's no wound in back," said Owen. "If there's a ball, it's lodged inside."

Dan wet the other sock with his canteen and cleaned Andy's face as gently as he could. Blood mixed with clear fluid ran from Andy's nose and seeped from his ear. Freckles splotched his pale, clammy skin. He breathed, fast and shallow.

"I'm afraid the ball tore through his jaw and hit his brain," Owen whispered. "Remember that man who fell at the mill and cracked his head? Watery looking stuff ran from his nose and ears. The doctor said it came from around his brain."

"Poor laddie," Bedad sighed. "Nothing you can do for him, boys. Fall in. Major Sturgis is in command now. We're retreating to Springfield."

"But we drove the Rebs off the hill!" Dan gasped.

"Yes, but they'll be back. That flag the Rebs waved on their last charge was Sigel's. One of his sergeants rode up to say the Rebs overran him. They wore gray uniforms. Sigel thought they were the Iowans and didn't open fire till it was too late." Bedad spit tobacco at a shattered oak stump. "We're running out of ammunition."

"Maybe they are, too." Dan couldn't believe they were abandoning this hill that cost so dearly. Cost Andy.

"Maybe. But Sturgis says to march."

"I can't leave Andy." Owen's mouth trembled. "He's my brother-in-law, Sergeant. How could I tell my sister I walked away?"

"He's not got long." Bedad's tone was gruff. "If he's still alive when the surgeon's party comes around, they'll move him in a wagon."

"You go, Owen." Dan moved over to take Andy from Owen's arms. "You've got a wife and children, and now Susie's going to need you, too."

"But. . . ."

"Go on. I'll catch up."

Bedad squinted through the acrid haze. "Did I hear you say, Private O'Brien, that you're too fagged to move, but you'll be after us soon?"

"Yes, sir."

Bedad gave Owen a push. "Fall in, Private."

Owen took a few long swallows from his canteen and tossed it to Dan. "You need it more than I do. Bring it when you come."

Marching feet shuffled away to the beat of drums. Artillery rattled up the slope. Dan watched his shrunken company vanish over the ridge followed by the depleted Iowans. He had never felt so alone.

"Andy?"

Dan wet his friend's mouth and drank himself. Andy, come all the way from misty Skye to die on this hill. Why? At least Susie had his baby. She'd be helped by her family. But. . . .

Drums rolled below. Shouted commands faintly reached Dan's ears. My God! The Rebs were coming again! Up over the human wreckage that littered the hill.

Dan slumped over Andy so as not to seem a living target. The Rebels toiled past several hundred yards to the side. Dan felt the vibrations of their feet. Thousands of them.

How could so many be left? He breathed the mingled scents of grass, dust, excrement, urine, and gunpowder. A loud cheer sounded and resounded from the top of the ridge.

The Rebels had the hill without a struggle this time, the hill so many had died on. What did it matter, now that no one was fighting over it? Neither army lived here. They'd march away, the lucky ones, while the dead mulched the fields. Warily farm families would come back to trampled crops, wasted grain, ruined fences, blasted houses and barns. It wouldn't matter to them which side had done the damage for which they'd suffer through the winter.

It was high noon when the rejoicing Confederates streamed down the hill to what was left of their camps. Andy still breathed. He had never opened his eyes or spoken, but faint hope kindled in Dan. Maybe the brain wasn't affected. Maybe if Dan got him into some shade till an ambulance wagon came, Andy might live. Freeing Andy of his bedroll, haversack, and rifle, Dan left his rifle beside the pile and struggled up with Andy's limp arm gathered around his neck. Andy was lean but so was Dan. He stumbled through bodies and brush toward a blackjack oak that promised shelter although half the trunk and limbs were blown away.

Panting, Dan didn't hear the horsemen till they were almost upon him. "Look, Quantrill!" The laughing voice was disturbingly familiar. "Two Yanks for target practice!"

Dan dropped, shielding Andy beneath him, but a ball thunked into the back of Andy's neck, splattering Dan with blood as they straddled the limp body of a man in homespun. His sheathed knife was so close Dan scarcely had to move to grasp it.

He drew it from the sheath and sprang up in the same instant, ducked under the mounted Rebel's musket, seized his arm, and dragged him from the saddle. Falling on top of his foe, Dan lifted the knife, but a smashing blow from the side stabbed lightning through his head and knocked him sprawling.

Dazed, he blinked up at the smiling face above him, the hand holding the knife. That cleft chin, silver hair, blue eyes so pale they were almost colorless. A man's features now, not the boy's who'd whispered obscenities at the Wares' cabin raising.

"Lafe!" Dan gasped. "Lafe Ballard!"

The puzzlement in those chill eyes was followed by recognition. "Damned if it's not the fiddling Irisher!" Lafe glanced at the sallow young man holding the horses and the rifle he'd swung against Dan's head. A long black plume furled from his slouch black hat. His red hunting shirt was gaudy with beads and embroidery.

"This is a neighbor, Quant." Lafe grinned and narrowed his eyes. "For old times' sake, I'll just carve my initials on his cheek and let him go."

"Hell." The other shrugged. "I'll sit on him so you can do an artistic job."

Knees pinioned Dan's shoulders. Hands clamped his wrists. Groggy from the blow, he felt his head gripped between Lafe's knees who bent over him from above. Steel glinted lazily. Dan closed his eyes and set his teeth. He wouldn't scream. Wouldn't. . . .

The blade was razor sharp. It bit like ice-fire, but the trickle down Dan's cheek was warm.

"L's easy." Lafe chuckled. "It's hard to curve lines for a B, but, if I loop over the cheek bone and come down to the jaw. . . . It's bleeding too much to be sure, but I reckon it'll heal up to show who marked him."

"Bite a cartridge and rub in some gunpowder," the one

named Quantrill suggested. "Give it a little color."

Dan held his breath at the sting.

"Stay there till we're good and gone, Irisher." Lafe's knees unlocked from Dan's head. "If you move while we're in firing range, we'll both shoot."

Even if they missed once, he'd be dead before he could locate a rifle and load. Dan lay still as the horses clumped away, hoofs muffled when they struck something soft. He still lay there after the sounds faded into the groans and begging of the wounded. Andy was dead. There wasn't any hurry. In those moments when he couldn't fight while he was marked for life, something had happened to Dan's spirit. He wanted to wash away his own blood with Lafe's. He couldn't hunt him now in the midst of the Rebel Army, but soon or late, even if it was after the war, he had to kill Lafe or go through life feeling violated.

This must be how a woman felt when taken by force. The thought drove him up to his knees. Lafe and Quantrill had vanished among the horde yelling and exulting at the Union retreat. Head throbbing, Dan turned to be sure about Andy, gagged at the ruined head.

Bury him. See if there's anything Susie would want. Dan drank from Owen's canteen and sloshed a cupped hand against his cheek to wash out some of the gunpowder. He padded it with a clean sock from Andy's haversack and tied it in place with Andy's shoe strings. The wound burned like fire.

A locket with one of Susie's dark curls was around Andy's pulseless throat. Probably she'd want it left with Andy. The haversack held a crumpled letter Andy had started to Susie and half a biscuit. Dan tucked the biscuit into his own haversack. Susie must have the letter, of course. He could find nothing else for a keepsake, so he searched for a lock of unbloodied hair, found it at the nape of Andy's neck, and cut it with his pocket knife. Trimming off a piece of Andy's blouse bottom, Dan wrapped the still sweaty twist of red hair in that, along with the letter, stuffed them in Andy's other sock, and thrust it deeply in his bedroll.

The shattered tree where he'd been dragging Andy had a deep furrow plowed into its roots by a cannon ball. A bayonet might dig the hollow out enough for Andy. Dan left his friend's shoes for someone who needed them. The oilskin around Andy's blanket was bloody. Dan left it, but he put the blanket over his back. Stooping, each hand grasping one of Andy's limp ones, he half dragged Andy to the tree and dropped him on the blanket.

Earth and sky careened. Dan sank down and leaned his forehead against the tree's splintered trunk. The sapwood smelled as if it bled. Maybe everything would smell like that from now on.

When he could move, he got his bayonet from the scabbard and started digging. He wasn't going to tell Susie that Andy's grave was dug out mostly by a cannon ball.

At last there was room to nestle Andy under the roots. Dan did this as gently as he could, covered his face with his cap. Out of his own haversack, Dan took John Brown's Testament. He slipped it inside Andy's shirt, over his heart, and covered his friend with earth full of splinters from the wounded tree.

Chapter Ten

As the bullets of their troops whistled over them, Charlie, Travis, and Clay Harmon rested for a minute, panting on hands and knees behind the wet hemp bale that was only one small part of the two wings of bales that formed this peculiar breastwork protecting the attack of Pap Price's raggle-taggle army on the fortified Masonic College at Lexington which sat on a bluff overlooking the Missouri River. The Yanks were shooting back, of course, but most of their bullets and artillery fire spanged harmlessly into the thick bales.

"Might as well be a billy goat, buttin' these bales ahead of us!" Clay cupped a hand to the side of his mouth to send his voice through the roar of artillery and muskets. Bits of broken hemp, the same dull brown as his hair, stuck to the crown of his forage cap. His round freckled face was fiery red. "Wonder if it'd be easier to lever this durn bale ahead with poles like some fellas are doing?"

Charlie smeared sweat from his brow against one arm. "You'd be a better target for the Yanks."

"Yeah, and I'm not a beanpole like you!" shouted Clay. "Smart of General Harris to have us wet the bales, so shells or bullets can't set 'em afire . . . but it sure makes 'em heavy."

The bales had been found in a warehouse by the river and someone had suggested forming them into a movable barricade to shelter an advance on the Union garrison. Yesterday evening and into the night, Charlie helped push and drag the bales to the top of the bluff, facing the Union stronghold on the north and west from about 400 yards away, although in places the shaggy line bristled within 100 yards of the fortifications. As he got ready to push the bale with his head again, Charlie raised up enough to glimpse the high sod ramparts, ditches, rifle pits, and sharpened stakes that surrounded the white-pillared three-storied brick building. Giant stumps showed where Colonel James Mulligan of the Union Army had felled the splendid oaks shading the seventeen-acre campus to build the fortifications shielding his Irish brigade, a regiment of Illinois cavalry, one German regiment from Kansas City, and some Home Guards. Mulligan had plenty of time to withdraw, but he'd counted on help since several Union forces were close enough to come to his aid. Besides, according to the local citizenry, he'd buried $900,000 from the Lexington bank and the Great Seal of Missouri in the basement of the college and didn't want to lose these treasures to the Confederates.

So less than 4,000 men had been under siege since September 13th by Price's 18,000 who camped on the streets, lawns, and in the churches of the town while he waited for his ammunition wagons to catch up. Volunteers swarmed to him, including a neighboring farmer who came every morning with his dinner bucket and flintlock. From behind a big tree, he fired at any Yankee who poked his head above the earthworks, took time out for his lunch and pipe, and fired away till time to go home to his chores. The ammunition wagons creaked into the camp at the fairgrounds on the 17th. Next morning, Price opened fire with sixteen cannons, including Old Sacramento with its silver bell-like ringing.

Union guns roared back. Sniper fire from a Federal hospital building outside their ramparts struck the thin line of Rebel troops along the river. A Confederate rush took the hospital, Federals charged through the open and regained it, and Charlie, Travis, and Clay were in the company that took it back under withering fire, the "hot" fight Travis had longed for.

Now, bracing his head against the bale as Travis called — "Shove!" — Charlie thought of the poor devils inside the fortifications, and was glad that Thos wasn't there, or Dan, or anyone he knew.

Yesterday the smell of dead horses rose from the stifling heat. It was worse this morning. There were only two cisterns inside Union lines, and for a week the Federals with 700 horses to water had been cut off from the river and two good springs near the bluff. Water would be their worst need, but they must be running out of food for both men and horses. A Confederate who'd hidden in a wounded Yank's bed when the Federals took back the hospital gagged as he told his rescuers how the Yanks fought each other to drink from buckets of bloody water left from cleaning wounds. And that had been day before yesterday.

"Tree ahead!" yelled the corporal directing their section of the line.

Charlie and his team shoved their bale to the right while the soldiers on the left butted their hemp in that direction. As soon as they cleared a young oak that was badly splintered by artillery and musket fire, the men worked the bales back together and inched forward through weeds, sunflowers, goldenrod, and asters. The crushed plants gave out pungent aromas that covered some of the stench of rotting horses.

A whine, an impact that crashed in Charlie's skull, snapped his teeth together. The bale rocked, but the cannon ball hadn't torn through it.

"Good thing they don't have much canister and grape-shot," Clay muttered.

"I hear they're shooting our own cannon balls back at us."

"How much farther do we have to push these dratted things?" growled Travis.

"Why don't those damn' Yanks give up?"

"Would you?" grunted Charlie, wondering if his neck and shoulders would ever feel right again.

"No, but I'm not a bluebelly."

"That doesn't make them cowards."

"There's a white flag!" yelled the corporal. "By grannies, they've quit firing!"

"Cease fire!" sounded gladly along the ranks behind the bales. The men stood up to stretch their cramped muscles and watch Price's messenger pass through the Union lines.

He returned, looking downcast. He reported to Price and a disbelieving murmur spread through the troops. Mulligan hadn't surrendered. Without his knowing it, some officer had shown the white flag.

The firing started up again. Charlie and the others dropped to their hands and knees, set their heads against the bales, and pushed. It wasn't long, though, till Mulligan sent out a messenger under a flag of truce. Again, the firing stopped. Again, Charlie and the bale-pushers rested. The sun was well past the zenith and they'd been shoving bales since early morning.

The Union messenger hurried back to the college. Bugles and drums sounded. Soon the troops marched out and stacked their muskets, then stood in ranks as Mulligan, wounded in the arm and leg, and his officers, several of them also wounded, came to General Price to offer their swords.

The white-haired general was close enough for Charlie to hear him say: "You gentlemen have fought so bravely that it would be wrong to deprive you of your swords. You may keep your horses, side arms, and personal belongings. Parole will be arranged as soon as possible."

Then Price quirked an eyebrow at the flag still flying from the surrendered headquarters. "May I ask why, Colonel Mulligan, the Union flag is still displayed?"

Mulligan, tall and dark, with a luxuriant moustache and flowing hair, grinned like the Chicago politician he was. "It's my Irishmen, General Price. They nailed the flag to the pole before I knew what the rascals were about."

Stirring music struck up within the battlements. Price returned Mulligan's grin. "I take it, sir, that those are also your Irish marching and counter-marching around that most beautiful green and gold banner with the harp and shamrock?"

"They are, General."

One of Price's staff started to protest, but Price motioned him to silence. "They'll be along directly," he said. "Colonel Mulligan, allow me to invite you and your officers to a champagne dinner. And your charming bride who was compelled to leave the city a few days ago will be informed that you are well and she may come to you."

Accompanied by their regimental band, the Irish brigade marched into the open field and stacked their arms. Through a blur, Charlie looked at the flag they'd defended, the flag he'd revered from childhood for its promise of freedom and justice. With a heart convulsed till he could scarcely breathe, he knew it was for him the only flag. It always would be.

Charlie looked up from grating corn on a piece of tin pierced with nail holes. A farmer had invited the company to help themselves to the corn in one of his cribs, and his pretty daughters had poured cool buttermilk into eagerly proffered cups.

"Didn't think you were going to get here in time for supper, Trav."

Travis laughed and patted his stomach. "You're welcome to the corn pone, boys. I had chicken and dumplings and a hunk of apple pie."

"You . . . you hog!" Clay sputtered. "That's why you hung around that oldest gal!"

"I hung around 'cause she was pretty. Anyhow, we're all invited to a big social at the church tonight. There'll be cakes and pies and lemonade."

"*Whowee!* I'd better jump in the creek and clean up." Clay started off, then turned. "You got a clean shirt, Charlie?"

"So would you if you weren't too lazy to wash yours."

"Aw, Charlie. . . ."

"You can borrow it. But mind you don't get in a fight and tear it, and you have to wash it."

"Don't you need it yourself?" Travis asked his brother-in-law.

Charlie shook his head. "I'm going to write to Melissa tonight."

"You write her durn' near every night! How does that make me look to my folks?"

"Like what you are. Someone who'd rather play cards and yarn with the boys than write home."

"I'm trying to win us some horses or the money to buy some!"

"Seems like you'd learn something from already losing ours."

Travis sighed. "Charlie, my father's a bishop, but he's a rounder compared to you! No cards, no dice, no whiskey! Why, when those good-looking Yankee ladies came down to that spring we were guarding at Lexington, you didn't even try to swap them a drink for a kiss."

Charlie's stare made Travis blush and squirm. "Wasn't it bad enough we couldn't let them fill their buckets for their wounded?" he demanded. But he remembered with shame how he'd wondered for a second how the softly rounded girl with yellow hair would fit in a man's arms.

"Saint Charles!" derided Travis. "Don't look so fierce about it! We let them drink all they wanted themselves, didn't we?"

"It was the least we could do, when they'd risked getting shot." Charlie mixed meal with water and shaped pones to bake in corn husks in the hot ashes of the fire where their coffee steamed in tin cups that served for brewing and drinking. He looked up at his reckless, teasing brother-in-law. "I hope Melissa and Christy never have to beg soldiers for a drink of water."

The smile died on Travis's mouth. "That's a hell of a thing to think!"

"It could happen."

"Charlie, you croak worse'n any thunder pumper." That was what folks called bitterns, heron-like birds that poked their heads straight up in the air to blend with marsh grass. At breeding time, they gave a kind of hollow croak. Travis shook his curly head. "After being in the army five months, we get our first real fight and all you can do is feel sorry for the Yanks!"

Their military career hadn't been exactly glorious. They'd reached St. Louis after the surrender of Governor Jackson's militia to Lyon. Citizens had been furious over the way Union troops had killed twenty-eight people, including a baby, when they fired into a jeering, rock-throwing crowd that threatened to mob them as they marched their prisoners along the street to be shut up, overnight, in the arsenal. It hadn't helped that most of the Union volunteers were St. Louis Germans.

Joining Price's Missouri Home Guards, Charlie and Travis had toiled north to Boonville where Price had hoped to gather and train enough men to drive the Federals out of the state. Lyon had pounced. His well-equipped Regulars quickly had routed the green militia under Colonel John Marmaduke. Governor Claib Jackson had fled Jefferson City before Lyon took it and had scurried south with the militia to join Price at Wilson's Creek in southwest Missouri.

"What do you call chasing Sigel's bunch out of Carthage?" Charlie demanded. "Wasn't that a fight?"

Travis grunted. "For all the commotion and cannonading, both sides, put together, lost under fifty men. Wilson's Creek now, there was a battle. A quarter of all the fighting men killed, missing, or wounded!" He kicked a rock disgustedly. "Finally a good fracas and where were we? In camp, with trots so bad we could barely drag up our trousers before we had to yank them down."

"I'm just as glad we missed that one," Charlie admitted.

Travis stared. "Why?"

"My kid brother may have been in Lyon's army. Troops from Kansas were. More than likely some of them helped raise our cabin, like Dan O'Brien and the Parks brothers and Andy McHugh."

That silenced Travis for a minute. Then he said: "You can't afford to think like that, Charlie. Whoever they were once, the Feds are enemies! Hasn't that damned Frémont put Missouri under martial law? Ordered the slaves of Confederate sympathizers freed and any civilian bearing arms to be court-martialed and shot?"

Clay's hazel eyes burned. "I'm glad Jeff Thompson swore

138

he'd hang, draw, and quarter a Union man for every Southerner killed under Frémont's order!"

"Lincoln countermanded that fool declaration," Charlie reminded them. "Anyhow, Trav, I can't help how I feel and I sure don't want to fight Thos." Thank goodness Travis's accusing brown eyes weren't a bit like Melissa's.

After another shocked moment, Travis blurted: "Sounds like if you hadn't married my sister, you'd be on the other side!"

"But I did marry your sister." Charlie unrolled his bedding to produce a wrinkled, somewhat mildewed flannel shirt that he tossed to Clay. "Want a corn pone before you get all slicked up?"

"I live in hopes of pie, but I'll take what I can get." Clay munched a pone and glanced toward General Price's tent and the Mulligans' pitched beside it. Colonel Mulligan had refused parole so he and his pretty young bride rode in Price's carriage and camped near him at night. "Wonder what they're eating?"

"Grated cornmeal like the rest of us," said Charlie. "Pap's not just brave, always risking his life to lead his men . . . he's kind and honorable."

Travis shrugged. "Maybe too honorable. He put nearly all that nine hundred thousand dollars back in the Lexington bank when he certainly needs it for this army. He must know damned well McCulloch won't reinforce us."

"McCulloch probably won't even send Pap percussion caps for the muskets we captured at Lexington," Clay gloomed.

"General Snead's persuasive," Charlie said. "Maybe he can at least get a promise of the caps from McCulloch when he stops by Fort Smith on his way to see Jefferson Davis in Richmond."

"Snead!" Travis grinned, although he, like most of the men, liked the former journalist. "Price made him chief of ordnance when he didn't know a howitzer from a siege gun. He just about figured that out when Price made him his adjutant general."

"Looks like he's learning fast," defended Charlie.

Travis brooded. "That Confederate government in Richmond doesn't give a hoot about Missouri! Without help from McCulloch or the east, there's no way Pap could hold Lexington."

"Why, pure-dee hundreds came in wanting to join up!" Clay protested. "I hear tell there were twenty thousand men in camp a few days after we whipped the Yanks."

"Sure," scoffed Travis. "It was fun to bang away with squirrel rifles, what with Pap winning. And some really would've joined up proper, but Pap couldn't arm a lot of them so he sent them home till later."

"He was counting on an all-out uprising against the Federals," Charlie said. "Guess he still is, but I don't think it'll happen."

"Why not?" demanded Travis. "There's lots of Southern sympathizers along the Missouri River, but, after you get away from the big farms and plantations, folks lean more toward the Union till you get close to Arkansas. Even down there I'd reckon half the people favor the Union."

"We captured a power of muskets in Lexington." Clay seemed to be trying to console himself. "Three thousand of 'em! And seven cannon!"

"And over seven hundred horses, saddles, and sabers and what was left of Mulligan's supplies," added Charlie wearily. "We can make our own bullets like we did with lead from the mines at Granby on the way north, but we can't make percussion caps."

140

They considered this. After a moment, Travis hunched a shoulder. "At least there aren't so many of us to keep supplied. Men've been dropping out to go home ever since we left Lexington. I heard the sergeant say we're down to about seven thousand." He chuckled. "But we still have the Lexington brass band with us, so we've got dandy music."

Charlie said quietly: "Frémont's got forty thousand men in five divisions he's spreading across the state."

Travis whistled a derisive note. "Who's scared of Frémont? He left Lyon dangling at Springfield and didn't help Mulligan when he could have. C'mon, Clay! Let's spruce up and head for the social."

"Pie and pretty girls!" breathed Clay, and trotted off to the creek.

After they were gone, Charlie carefully sharpened his stubby pencil and built up the fire enough to see. Bedroll propped behind him, he wrote Melissa and his family. The Jardines would rejoice at the fall of Lexington, but the Wares wouldn't. And Thos . . . ? If an evil moment found him facing his brother in battle, he'd wait for Thos's bullet or bayonet. Yes, but what if Thos was too far away to recognize or the cover was too thick?

Charlie put the letters in envelopes with previous notes that he'd hand in to the postmaster. When would his regiment be in one place long enough to get letters from home? It helped to write his loved ones, but what wouldn't he give to hear from Melissa and his family!

Over by General Price's tent, the band was playing "Listen to the Mockingbird". The haunting melody made Charlie's throat hurt and his eyes sting. They had crossed the Osage two days ago, taking three days to get the whole army across. Rumor was they were heading for Neosho way down

141

in the southwest corner of the state. Their line of march couldn't be too far from home. He resolved to ask his captain for a few days' furlough. Travis might not want to come since he'd either have to lie or face the bishop's wrath over gambling away their splendid horses.

Charlie took off his shoes and rolled his pants into a pillow. Rolling up in his blanket, he concentrated on making Melissa as real as he could, imagining she was in his arms, summoning up the softness of her, the taste of her mouth and breath, the way her eyes hazed when she lay fulfilled with loving. Oh, Melissa! He ached, but it was sweet. As he drifted into sleep, a dream of her relieved his body but not his yearning. If he couldn't get leave, he'd just take off. He was almost asleep again when the foot of one of his messmates stubbed into him.

"Hey!" he yelped. Sitting up, he sniffed. "Maybe you went to a church social, but you found something stronger'n lemonade on the way home."

"Wouldn't be friendly to turn down good corn liquor." Travis almost fell beside Charlie. "Do you know what that infernal Jim Lane . . . Senator Lane, Brigadier General Lane . . . the damned jayhawking bastard . . . did two days after we took Lexington?"

"Stole some slaves out of Missouri?"

"A bunch of them! Two hundred!"

"What?"

"Lane burned Osceola to the ground except for three houses," Travis rasped. "Since he was fired at when his bunch rode into town, he held a drumhead court and shot nine men. When he marched for Kansas City, three hundred of his men were so drunk they had to be hauled in wagons."

"And he stole wagons for the three thousand sacks of flour

they looted from warehouses where Price's supplies were stored," muttered Clay. "And five hundred pounds of sugar and molasses, and fifty sacks of coffee on top of lots of powder, lead, and cartridge paper. . . ."

"And three hundred and fifty horses and mules, four hundred cattle, not to mention the fancy carriage, piano, and silk dresses he took for himself! He told his men to clean out everything 'disloyal from a Shanghai rooster to a Durham cow.'" Travis gripped Charlie's shoulder. In spite of the whiskey on his breath, he sounded stone-cold sober. "Lane looted and burned all the way to Kansas City! It was just luck he didn't go by our place."

Charlie's blood chilled at the thought of Lane's rabble carousing through Rose Haven. He had to realize fully for the first time that Melissa might face something worse than having to ask enemy soldiers for a drink. "Lane's superiors in the regular army won't let him keep on like that!"

Travis snorted. "Have they been able to stop Jennison? He and his militia jayhawked up and down western Missouri all summer! Just got through corraling all the men . . . three or four hundred of them . . . in the courthouse square in Independence along with mules, horses, and heaps of weapons, furniture, jewelry . . . even spinning wheels!"

"Surely Jennison didn't kill the prisoners?"

"Not this time. He found out which were Union men, apologized for the inconvenience, and let them collect their belongings and go home."

"Then," put in Clay morosely, "he preached the Secessionists a half-hour sermon . . . guess they had been pretty hard on Unionists . . . and finished off by saying for every Union man killed from now on, he'd see that ten important Secessionists died."

"Just like Lane at Osceola!" fumed Travis. "His gang

loaded jayhawked wagons and carriages with plunder and rol-
licked back to Kansas City with a bunch of darkies! When
they crossed into Kansas, Lane's chaplain . . . the same one
who'd robbed a church in Osceola for an altar cloth and other
things to decorate his own church . . . declared the slaves forever free in the name of God, the United States, and General
Lane! There they are, Lane and Jennison, two of the greatest
scoundrels in the country, ready to burn and plunder as soon
as Price is gone!"

"Ever since the Feds were licked at Wilson's Creek, Secessionists have been running Union people out of Missouri,"
Charlie pointed out. "Remember that eighty-year-old man
who'd fought in the Revolution? When he said it was murder
when two of his neighbors were killed for being Union men, a
gang took him away from his poor old wife and shot him. The
story about them cutting out his heart to pickle may not be
true, but for sure General McBride ordered Union men to
take the oath of loyalty to the Confederacy or be arrested or
forced to fight for the South."

"Serves them right!" Travis sank his fingers into Charlie's
shoulder. "Don't you care that Lane and Jennison and Montgomery can call themselves Union soldiers and jayhawk to
their heart's content?"

"The Home Guard. . . ."

"That's us! You know we're hearing that if the Confederacy doesn't put Price in command of forces out here, those
of us who want to go on fighting will have to join the Confederate Army and most likely fight outside the state. There
won't be any troops to protect our homes and families from
the likes of Lane and Jennison!"

"That's why Lafe Ballard asked us to join up with him,"
Clay burst in. "He's going to stay in Missouri and fight
jayhawkers along with his friend, W. C. Quantrill. You must

have noticed Quantrill charging on his black horse at Lexington. Wore a red shirt and a long black plume in his hat."

"Lafe Ballard?" Charlie whirled on Travis. "Don't you remember that row we had with him after Seth Cooley fired him for laying open an ox's back?"

"Aw, Charlie, that was a long time ago!"

"He's always been a foul-mouthed sneak. Trav, any bunch Lafe heads'll be worse than the jayhawkers."

"Can't be."

"Do you want your mother and sister to be ashamed of you?"

"Who's going to make sure they're alive to be ashamed?"

"Neither side's low enough to kill women."

"Maybe not shoot them," Travis allowed. "But is it much better to kill their men folk, burn them out, and steal everything they have?"

"The regular Union officers will get the jayhawkers under control." Charlie had to believe that. "Our families will be a lot safer with Union troops firmly in charge than if gangs like Lafe's give them a reason to go after Secessionists. Don't you see that? My God, Missouri's still one of the United States! Her citizens are under Federal protection."

"Sure," derided Clay. "Tell that to the widows in Osceola and the folks who got robbed and corralled by rifles in Independence."

"Clay," warned Charlie, "I've known Lafe Ballard since we were boys. He's poison."

"He's got enough guts to fight the damned jayhawks," Clay retorted. "I got no interest . . . not a speck . . . in fighting Yanks in Tennessee or even Arkansas. I want to fight 'em right here in Missouri! Looks like the only way to do that is to throw in with them that feels likewise." He stood up, dumpy figure silhouetted against the dull glow of the coals. "Coming, Trav?"

Charlie held his breath. He'd fight Travis if he had to, try to beat sense into his head, but he didn't want to.

"Guess I'll tag along with Pap," Travis said slowly. "Maybe Jeff Davis will put him in charge of all the Confederate forces out here."

Clay made a derisive sound.

Travis's tone grew resolute. "Pap loves Missouri as much as anybody can. Whatever he decides is best for her . . . well, I reckon that's what I'll do. How about you, Charlie?"

"I'm with you." Charlie was so relieved his rash brother-in-law wasn't turning bushwhacker that he stifled the unvoiced hope that, when their six-month enlistments ran out in November and if Price disbanded the state guard, Travis might agree to go home.

The messmates shook hands and wished each other luck. After Clay disappeared, Charlie said to Travis: "We can sign up to serve with General Price again, but first I'm going home, with a furlough or without it."

"Fine." Travis yawned, spreading his bedroll. "Listen, if you don't blab to Pa about what happened to our horses, I'll bet he'll give us new ones."

"I won't blab as long as you promise not to gamble any new ones away, but I won't lie, either."

"Saint Charles!" Travis gave him a friendly buffet. "No dancing, no drinking, no apple pie, or pretty girls! What do you let yourself enjoy?"

"Melissa," Charlie said, and hugged his pants-pillow as he settled down again.

Chapter Eleven

Just as Dan had imagined it so many times — the happy house nestled beneath the giant walnut amidst the warm glow of autumn golds and scarlets. The big white oxen and fawn-colored cows browsed in the stubble while four horses, bays and chestnuts, grazed in the pasture with the dark-faced sheep. The geese snaked their necks forward, hissing at the intruder. From down in the bottoms where two men were scything hay, Robbie dashed forward, his defender's bark changing to one of delight as he smelled Dan.

Just as in Dan's dreams, Christy stepped out, and then she was running, throwing her arms around him as he swung down from Breeze. Had she seen his scar? How could she not? What he hoped he could keep her from sensing was the darkness inside him.

"Dan! Dan! Danny!" Tears spilled down her cheeks as she laughed.

He kissed her tears and laughter. They clung together, close as they could, while Robbie tore around them in frenzied, narrowing circles. Then Christy's lips moved to the ridged mess of Dan's cheek. At least, even rubbed with gunpowder, Lafe's initials couldn't be read. The B Lafe had carved on the L had twisted into two joined, blurred circles. She kissed the scar as if she would make it vanish, then touched it with her hand. "What happened to you, Danny?"

"I'll tell you later."

Would he? Should he let her think it was a random wound? One thing sure, he wouldn't tell her that he'd been dragging Andy to shelter when Lafe or Quantrill used their friend for target practice. He hadn't even told Owen. It would make it more real by letting others know — and they might glimpse the smoldering rage in Dan, the thirst for vengeance.

Beth had hold of him now, hugging his waist, squealing his name. He stooped for a kiss and smoothed her dark curls. "Look who's growing up!"

He grinned past her at Ellen and the men coming up from the meadow, felt happy surprise at seeing Thos — Thos whose blue fatigue blouse was ragged as Dan's.

After an embrace and kiss from Ellen and handshakes with the men, Thos took over the care of Breeze while Dan was brought inside. He insisted on hearing their news before he gave them his. He wished he'd never again have to tell about Andy. Susie paled when he had told her that morning, after he and Owen rode in with a farmer who was bringing corn to the mill. Staggering as if rocked by a blow, Susie turned blindly into her sister's arms.

"My son, my laddie!" old Catriona wailed. "Was it for this you left the green isle of Skye and the hills of Cuillin? Was it for this I carried you under my heart and suckled you with your sweet cheeks dimpling as you drew in my milk? My son, my son! You shone on us . . . warmed us! And now you are gone away forever!" She keened like a banshee then, without any words.

Little Andy, a year old, almost walking, whimpered at his grandmother's weeping. He hauled himself up on his mother's skirts, burrowing his fiery red head into the folds of homespun. Daniel Owen David, also a year old, shy of the father he didn't remember, screwed his blue eyes shut and howled till Harriet picked him up.

Now, delaying the evil moment when he'd have to repeat the grievous tidings, Dan heard how the advance of Price's army had run off eighty government mules from near Fort Scott early in September. Lane's Brigade, five hastily recruited, understrength regiments, skirmished with some of Price's men, but Price marched on toward Lexington and his victory there.

"Price may never have intended to invade Kansas." Thos's dark head was level with his father's reddish-brown one and he was leaner and tougher looking than when Dan last saw him. "Or, maybe, when he found Lane's Brigade spread out along the border, he decided it wasn't worth the trouble since his real aim was to reach the Missouri River and get control of it."

"He expected the whole state to rise up against the Union." There was more sadness than triumph in Jonathan Ware's voice. "Charlie and Travis Jardine got furloughs and were here week before last. They expected to catch up with Price around Springfield."

"Price abandoned Springfield to Frémont and is down in Neosho," said Dan. "The news got to Leavenworth when Owen and I were mustering out the last of October. Seems the commander of Frémont's Hussar guard was tired of being called a Saint Louis parlor pet and craved to celebrate the anniversary of the charge of the Light Brigade at Balaclava by leading a cavalry attack on Springfield." Dan shook his head in bemusement. "Zagoni's cavalry wound up taking the town while Price withdrew."

"Balaclava was October Twenty-Fifth," reckoned Jonathan Ware. "I doubt if the boys were in Springfield yet. They were stopping to spend a few days at the Jardines'."

"Frémont's generals have joined him at Springfield, including Jim Lane," said Dan. "Someone traveling north from Fort Scott yesterday told Uncle Simeon that Price fired a hundred gun salute when the Rebel Missouri legislature convened in Neosho. They voted to secede and elected General Rains to the Confederate senate."

"So now Missouri has two legislatures and two governors, the way Kansas Territory used to." Jonathan Ware's smile was wintry. "Of course, now that Price can claim that Missouri's joined the Confederacy, he must hope to get help from McCulloch."

"He'll need it," said Thos. "Frémont has thirty thousand men." He raised an eyebrow at Dan. "Now that you're out, are you staying that way?"

Christy's hand rested in the curve of Dan's arm. He covered her tightening fingers with his own but didn't look at her for fear she'd see the festering ugliness inside him. "Not much of a time to quit, with Price holding southwest Missouri and hoping to get it all. I'm going to enlist in Colonel Montgomery's Third Kansas Regiment."

"Maybe I will, too," said Thos. "The Pony Express closed down when the coast-to-coast telegraph was finished last month. Anyhow, all I did during my enlistment was escort supply wagons. Nearest I got to a fight was when we brought General Lyon uniforms and mail at Springfield."

Dan touched his frayed sleeve. "That's where I got this, and these brogans that are falling apart. Too bad you didn't bring us some rations."

"You were at Wilson's Creek?" Thos demanded.

There was nothing for it then but to tell them about Andy and the battle, the retreat from what had been victory on the field, and the desperate families, often wives and children of Union soldiers, who trailed the army toward Rolla with whatever animals and belongings they could collect, a sight Dan would never forget.

"It was like Ireland in the starving times." The words were bitter in his mouth, painful as the saltpeter of a bitten cartridge's gunpowder on cracked lips. "That Americans should fight each other, that's terrible, but for women and children to dread men who were neighbors. . . ." He choked off.

"What happened to them?" Christy's voice was balm to his raw feelings although it couldn't reach what he'd come to think of as an inner wound, seeping poison, that could be soothed only in battle. With his brain, he knew Rebels were mostly decent, but, in the few fights he'd been in since Wilson's Creek, he wanted to kill. He wasn't so far gone that he'd shoot Charlie, or even Travis, if he could help it, but the Rebs he didn't know, they were Lafe and Quantrill.

Now, answering Christy's question about the fleeing Union families, Dan shook his head. "Some were going to relatives in other states or eastern Missouri. Others stayed around Rolla in hopes that the Confederates will be forced out of the state and they can go back to whatever's left of their homes. A few had train fare to Saint Louis where most of our troops went."

Ellen's dark eyes touched him as comfortingly as did her hand. "Dinner's ready. Come along in, Dan."

He did, Christy holding one hand, Beth hanging to the other.

"If only Charlie were here." Christy's voice was so soft he had to bow his head to hear. "If only none of you had to go away . . . if only no one did!"

"I'm here now."

She drew his head down and kissed the scar. He pulled away, cursed himself for the hurt in her eyes. "It's not you, Christy," he muttered. "I . . . I'm sorry."

During dinner — Lige Morrow had swapped a smoked

wild turkey for some corn and potatoes and there was a jar of Sarah's honey — Dan told how the 2nd Kansas was in a few skirmishes near Hannibal before arriving by train in St. Joseph in the middle of the night where they took the Rebel garrison by surprise, drove them out, and held the city till relieved by the Union troops that would stay there.

"We went on to Leavenworth by boat," Dan finished. "Mustered out the last day of October . . . and here I am. Tell me, have you had any trouble because you're for the Union?"

Jonathan shrugged. "Watt Caxton and Arly Maddux stopped by after Price took Lexington. They hinted that I might stay healthier if we moved back to Illinois. I told them this is our home."

"It's what you'd expect from Caxton." Ellen's eyes sparkled wrathfully. "But for Mister Maddux, a Baptist minister, to come on such an errand!"

"Have many of your neighbors joined either army?"

"As soon as their corn was cribbed and the wheat planted and harrowed in, Ethan and Matthew Hayes went to join Price." Jonathan sighed. "Mark . . . he's seventeen . . . begged to go, too, but Ethan told him he and Luke had to be the men of the house. I'm not holding school, but little Mary comes over when she can to study with Beth." He frowned at the strangeness of it all. "Ethan, Matt, and I shook hands when we parted. I promised to help Allie and the children any way I could."

"I thought Ethan didn't hold with slavery," puzzled Dan.

"Nor does he. But he couldn't stomach the way Lane and Jennison have rampaged through Missouri." Jonathan's tone was somber. "It's like the worst times of the border troubles, only multiplied. Both jayhawkers and bushwhackers have got into uniforms to carry out their wickedness."

Dan thought of Lafe and Quantrill and winced to know

that plenty of decent but hot-headed men like Clay would throw in with them in order to harry the Union soldiers they saw as an oppressive army of occupation.

"Emil Franz is too old to fight," said Jonathan. "Lige Morrow's got no use for Frémont's dress parade notions so he's signed on as a scout with Colonel Montgomery." He named off the other Missouri men of fighting age that Dan knew from seeing them at the mill.

"Sounds like they're split just about half and half," Dan said. "Over in Kansas, it's pretty much solid Union."

"Jennison saw to that," said Jonathan. "Will Owen stay home now? When I took our corn to the mill, young David was having fits to enlist."

"I don't think there'll be any stopping him now. Owen pretty much promised him he could have his turn after our time ran out." Ruefully Dan met Thos's gaze. "We didn't think the war would last this long."

"It's just getting started," said Thos.

Beth caught Dan's sleeve. "I don't like having wars, Danny! You and Thos and Charlie won't get killed, will you?"

"We'll try not to," he assured her. He tried not to remember children her age and younger, down to babies, trudging behind Lyon's retreating army.

"Mary cries when she comes to study because her daddy and Matt are gone." Beth stood up, gripped his face in her hands, and stared into his eyes. Hers were deep hazel. Dove's eyes. He hoped she couldn't see that abscess of hate within him. Her sweet breath, milky from the glass she'd drunk, mixed with the air he breathed. Her small hands warmed his face. "Danny, you wouldn't ever fight Matt and Mister Hayes, would you?"

"Oh, Beth, sweetheart!" Tears blinded him for a moment.

"I hope I never have to." Had it occurred to her, was it too awful to mention, that he, and even Thos, might have to fight Charlie?

Widening eyes filling with tears, she gave a stricken cry and fled outdoors. Dan felt as if he'd crushed a gentle bird, one with a heart loving and valiant for others. "I'm sorry."

"What else could you say?" Christy's voice was fierce.

Face averted, Ellen got to her feet. "Christy, why don't you and Dan see if you can find some winter grapes along the creek? Look for persimmons, too. That frost we had a few nights ago may have been enough to sweeten them."

It was, Dan knew, her way of giving them time alone. He both longed for that and feared it. He wasn't fit to be with Christy when he had such evil in his heart.

"I hope you'll play your fiddle," she said as they walked through the freshly cut meadow grass.

"I've got out of the habit of playing." He had missed it, missed it in a manner akin to the way he missed Christy.

She looked up at him. The sun brought out a hint of gold in her gray eyes, and his heart stopped with loving her. "Well, if you don't feel like playing today, you can tune up your fiddle and play tomorrow. You will come tomorrow, won't you, Dan?" She slipped her arm through his. "I want to hear your song. And maybe . . . maybe you can make one about Andy."

Not that. Oh, Christy, dearest love, you don't want to hear that. Still, a melody had been slowly forming in his head, a kind of lament, not only for Andy, but for all the young men dead in the broken corn or sprawled in the brush and scrub oaks of what was now called Bloody Hill. The song mourned, too, the maimed trees, the trampled earth gashed by caissons and cannon, blasted with iron balls. Then the song exploded into fury, a howling for blood. He couldn't play that for his Quaker foster family.

"Lydia thinks Susie and Catriona . . . well, everybody . . . will feel better if we hold a service and put up a marker for Andy down by his forge," Dan said. "I'll play then. Something. Will you come?"

"I'm sure we all will. Andy helped raise our cabin, remember? He made the nails, and, for a welcome, he gave us the hinges for the doors and shutters and made the rod and kettle hooks for the fireplace." Her breath caught. "Oh, Dan, the main reason we moved here was so Charlie and Thos could take up land close to the home place . . . so the family could stay together. But here's this awful war with Charlie on one side and Thos on the other!"

"Wars end."

"So do people."

"Christy. . . ."

She stopped and pressed her palm to his cheek. "Tell me how you got this."

When he told her, she made a strangled sound. "So Lafe still loves to hurt others!" She held up her wrist, showing a white scar Dan had noticed before but attributed to an accident while cooking or washing. "He bumped me against a hot kettle rim. Of course, he pretended it was an accident, but I saw his face."

"You never told anyone?"

"I didn't see any use in worrying my parents. Or Hester, who's been so kind." Christy held her hand against Dan's face as if she could take away the weals. "I won't tell her about this, either, unless you think I should. I don't think he's come to see her in years."

It was as if how evil a one-time neighbor could be was a secret they wanted to protect their loved ones against. Owen knew. He'd helped clean and bandage the festering cuts, but Dan had asked him not to tell the Parkses.

"You're right not to tell Lafe's mother," Dan said. "He and his friend, Quantrill, have turned bushwhacker. Maybe they won't get down this far, but I'm afraid they'll do a lot of devilment."

She buried her face against his shoulder. "Oh, Dan! Will it ever be the way it used to be?"

So dear, so troubled, so sweet she was, and he with the darkness on his soul not fit to touch her although he couldn't resist. He clasped the back of her head with one hand, working his fingers through the glossy curls that held just the faintest smell of apple cider vinegar. Like Lydia and Susie, she must use that in the rainwater with which she washed and rinsed her hair. He kissed her lightly, not daring to linger on her mouth.

"If the Union wins, sweetheart, in some ways, it'll be better. Slavery's still legal, but I'm betting it won't be by the time the war's over. Men like Justus won't be chased with dogs or sold away from their families. Watt Caxton won't come around every spring buying up Negroes the way he does mules. And there'll be an end to jayhawking and bush-whacking both."

She stepped back, holding his gaze. "Susie at least has little Andy. . . ."

Dan stepped back, too. "Don't, Christy! Not if you love me."

"That's why!"

"I'm bound no child of mine will ever starve." More, though he couldn't tell her, never would he make love to her with this corruption tainting him. He would come to her only with clean hands and a clean heart — and he thought now he might never have them again.

"Your child will have the milk of my body."

"So long as you have food. No, Christy!" He caught her arm roughly and drew her toward a tangle of vines festooning from a red oak. "Let's see if the birds and foxes have left us any grapes."

Ash lay white and ghostly in Andy's forge beside the anvil where his hammer rested. His begrimed leather apron hung from one of the poles supporting the roof of the three-walled smithy facing Timbered Mound where the victims of Marais des Cygnes were buried. A broken plowshare awaited his attention. Different sizes of horseshoes were sorted on a shelf.

Eli Snyder, the burly smith who'd stood off Hamelton over three years ago, had fashioned a wrought iron cross with a hammer and anvil at the center intertwined with Andy's initials. At Susie's wish, he pounded the bottom end into the yellowing grass beneath the huge oak that shaded cabin and smithy.

It was not a formal service, but a remembering. Eli praised Andy's skill as a smith and his courage as a man. "Why, on his wedding day, he left his bride to pursue Hamelton's gang, and he left her again, and his baby boy, to defend the Union. God rest his soul and comfort his loved ones."

Hughie Huston stepped beside the cross, gray hair fluffed around the rosy Irish face that twenty years in the West had not been able to tan. "I first laid eyes on Andrew when we were chousing after Clarke's raiders in late summer of 'Fifty-Six." The lilt of Hughie's accent pleasured Dan. He was American, would have it no other way in spite of this war, but his heart's core loved a soft misty morning and an Irish voice. "We sent Clarke's spalpeens across the line," went on Hughie, "but there was fear for John Brown and Free Staters around Osawatomie since another invading rabble had gone there. So didn't Andrew ride alone . . . when he could have met more raiders at any turn . . . to see if help was needed?"

Theo Wattles told how Andy had cheered him before Wilson's Creek. Owen said Andy had given him his only extra shirt when Owen's wore out and always had a joke or droll word to beguile the marching.

"No one . . . begging your pardon, Eli . . . could shoe a horse or mule like Andy," said big, blond Sam Nickel. He and his two oldest sons were in the 6th Kansas Cavalry and wore amazing hodge-podges of homespun and uniforms.

After the tributes, Dan played the tune that had been growing in him, determined to break off before he got to the cry for vengeance. It began shy as a fawn, quickened to a dance, hinted at the ring of blows on an anvil, the scream of artillery. Then it was a dirge, the strings wailing. Dan saw again the bullet hiss into Andy's neck, felt Lafe's blade grate on his own cheek bone. Possessed, Dan started to play a cry for retribution, full of hate and fury. Then a movement caught his almost blinded eyes.

Little red-haired Andrew Owen, stout legs braced to stand free of his mother's skirt, took a toddling step forward. "Och, now, Andy lad," Dan murmured. "Won't your boy be the spit and image of you and farm this land you claimed . . . you, who could never have owned more earth on your island than it took to bury you? Someday this laddie may even heat iron in your forge and shape it with your hammer."

The lament flowed back into the first tentative, questing notes, then swelled again into the dance. Dan stole a glance at Susie and was glad to see a smile touch his foster sister's lips although tears glistened in her eyes. Christy, beside her, was smiling, too.

Simeon called for a silent moment for each to make a private farewell to Andy. Then he led them in the Lord's Prayer.

Dan couldn't pray it. He couldn't forgive those who trespassed against him; he wanted to be led into the temptation of killing.

Susie sent her child home with Lydia and Harriet. He went without fuss at his Cousin Letty's command. At six, the chubby flaxen-haired girl bossed her small brother and cousin unmercifully, but took good care of them, too.

"We'll spend the night here, Mother Catriona and I," Susie told Dan. They needed to mourn freely with no one to hear but the sky, the earth, and the river. "Since you're leaving early tomorrow, I'll tell you good bye now." She hugged him closely and kissed him. "Be careful, Danny. We pray for you every day. Bless you for the music. Andy would have loved it."

Thank goodness the sight of her little son had kept Dan from defiling the service. From a dense hawthorn thicket, a mockingbird trilled, drawing out its notes, embellishing and repeating. Dan's jaw dropped. He stared at Susie who smiled and nodded.

"Yes, I do believe, Dan, he's trying to mimic your song. Andy always liked to have him around and put out suet for him in bad weather."

So the bird would sing to its old friend although Andy's body lay under a blasted oak on the side of Bloody Hill. Dan helped Christy into her family's wagon and mounted to follow with Thos. At the edge of the clearing, Dan heard something that tugged at deep roots.

Turning, he saw Catriona embracing the cross, face pressed against it. She was singing, an old Gaelic children's song Dan remembered from his mother.

Matthew, Mark, and Luke and John,
Hold the pony till I leap on.

Guide him safe and bring him sure,
While we fare over the misty moor.

That was the English of it, near enough. Fare safe and well and happy, lad. But if ever I get a chance at Lafe or Quantrill who shot you, when you might have lived, I'll kill them with pleasure.

Dan didn't see Christy alone again, but he left his fiddle with her after playing far into the night. "Your blanket holds off twice the wind and rain because you wove it," he told her. Leaving the fiddle was like trusting his soul to her while he went off with murder in his heart. He kissed her good bye in front of her family, aching at the hurt in her eyes. He couldn't even promise they'd be married after the war. They couldn't if the killing lust stayed in him, or if he did things for which he could never forgive himself. Like shooting a wounded man in the back of the head or carving a face.

Uncle Simeon had known something was wrong. "Shall we pray together, thee and me?" he asked gently. "If something burdens thee, Dan. . . ."

What a relief it would be to pour out his affliction! But Dan couldn't, since he couldn't forgive his enemies. The passion for revenge went deeper than will and mind. It rose in a welter of corruption from his heart and guts.

Reading Dan's answer in his silence, Simeon dropped a hand on his shoulder. "I will pray for you, my boy, just as I will for David."

"I'll watch out for Davie as much as I can," Dan assured Simeon, although his foster father hadn't asked it.

Well supplied with apples, lean bacon, and dried corn, Dan and Thos rode Queenie and her five-year-old chestnut daughter, Lass, when they left the Wares. Owen would take the mares home from the mill. Even as they said their fare-wells at the Parkses, they heard the rattle of a wagon and hurried toward the Military Road while Lydia called admonitions to her younger brother.

"Should I bundle up in Pa's overcoat so I'll look bigger?" David worried. Although wiry, he only reached Dan's chin and was delicately built.

Dan ruffled his hair. "You don't want to look like a flea in a buffalo robe, Davie. But since you're pretty young, they may make a sheepskin fiddler or straw blower out of you."

"Sheepskin fiddler?" David frowned. "What's that?"

"A drummer. And a straw blower toots a flute."

David wailed. "I don't want to beat a drum or play a silly old flute! I want to have a saber and be in the cavalry."

"So do we" — Thos grinned — "but you're welcome to the saber. Artillery makes daredevil charges plain suicide, although that idiot, Zagoni, got away with it at Springfield."

The three of them reached the Trading Post store about the same time five supply wagons rumbled up, each drawn by six long-eared mules. The escort, commanded by a young lieutenant, was far from consistently clothed but there was enough braid and gilt buttons to bring a sparkle to David's eyes.

Well, thought Dan, *let them sparkle. He'll learn soon enough. Just please, God, don't let me live if he dies.* The baby of the family, David was the light of his old father's life, and to the sisters who had raised him, he was more than a brother.

"Sure, you can ride with us to Fort Scott," the droopy-mustached lieutenant said in answer to their question. "Just pile on top of the bags and boxes."

They camped ten miles down the road and were invited to partake of Lieutenant Colby's beans, beef, coffee, and hard-tack. Of course, they had to share their good things with him, which was probably why the officer had deigned to welcome them. As he devoured bacon and two apples, he told them that Lincoln had replaced Frémont with General Hunter on the night before Frémont planned finally to march on Price.

"There were enough of our boys to whip Price, and the brigadiers warned Hunter that, if he pulled out of Springfield, the Rebs would take all southwestern Missouri." Lieutenant Colby's tobacco juice barely cleared his moustache. "It's hard to keep an army supplied that far from a railhead, and Hunter probably figgered McCulloch would join up with Price. Whyever, Hunter pulled his army back to Sedalia and Rolla, except for the troops under General Sturgis and Jim Lane. They're headed for Kansas." Colby spat again. "The Secesh may laugh at Hunter, but they won't grin at Lane. He's burning their farms and plantations and running off their darkies."

"It's hard to believe Sturgis lets him jayhawk." Dan remembered his first real taste of regular Army discipline shortly after the 2nd Kansas joined Sturgis's brigade on the way to meet General Lyon. "When the Second came through Harrisonville, a couple of our men stole vegetables out of a garden. Sturgis had them court-martialed. We were ordered to form a hollow square and the men were tied to wagon wheels and flogged." Dan grimaced. "Sturgis had cannon trained on us to keep us from cutting the fellows loose."

"Sturgis sends any darkies who try to refuge with him back to their masters and turns the air blue with ordering Lane to stop plundering." Colby chuckled. "Old Jim Lane's a favorite of Lincoln's. He promises to be a good boy but goes right on looting."

"How can he be a senator and general both?" Dan remembered that Jonathan Ware had said the U.S. Constitution prohibited such dual rôles.

"Lane's a caution!" Colby's tone was more approving than censorious. "Governor Robinson hates his guts. Said Lane's accepting a commission put him out of his Senate seat. But wouldn't you know old Jim got around that? Resigned his Kansas commission and got one from Indiana! Now he's a senator and brigadier both." The lieutenant offered David a can of evaporated milk. "Here, young 'un, try this on your hardtack and pass it around." He squinted at Dan and Thos. "You're signing up with Montgomery? Why not Jennison?"

"He's a worse pirate than Lane," said Dan.

The lieutenant laughed. "He sure put on a pious act on his way to Lawrence with the Mound City Rifle Guards last summer. A farmer offered them a pail of whiskey. Jennison thanked him and said his men didn't drink."

"Jennison doesn't drink?" hooted Dan.

"Not that day, I reckon. A lady who heard about it was so thrilled, she stitched the Rifles a flag. Jennison laid it on thick in his thank you letter. Said his boys wouldn't drink from 'the bowl of poison' and how they'd defend with their lives the banner her 'fair hands had wrought' for them. Naturally Doc sent copies to all the newspapers."

"He got someone to fancy the letter up for him," grunted Dan. "He may be a doctor, but, from the letter he wrote Uncle Simeon once when he wanted some meal on credit, he can't spell for shucks."

"He don't need to." The lieutenant shifted his cud. "He writes in blood and fire to the Secesh. They take his meaning."

The three reached Fort Scott next evening too late to be sworn in, but were welcomed by Theo Wattles and his messmates to a kettle of beans and coffee so strong it could fight back. "I was lucky enough to get in Company K of the Seventh Kansas," Theo boasted, dark eyes sparkling. "You know, John Brown's boys! John Brown, Junior's our captain! He's bringing most of the company down from Ohio, but an advance got here this week. Why don't you join us?"

Although they didn't condone the older Brown's slaughter at Osawatomie, the Wattleses had been his friends. Augustus, Theo's father, had, like Dan, been one of the party that had traveled to Virginia to rescue Brown. It was natural for Theo to thrill at the chance to serve under the martyr-monster's son. Jennison commanded the 7th and the men enlisting in the regiment were fervent Abolitionists to a man.

"My first chase after bushwhackers was with Colonel Montgomery," Dan said. "I was with him when he rode here to Fort Scott to rescue the Free-State men who were chained to the floor of the jail. I want to follow him now."

"He's a good man." Theo knelt to stir water-soaked hardtack frying in bacon grease. "Hunker down and help yourself to the skillygalee."

Eaten with beans, it tasted pretty good. If there were weevils, well, that was just part of the meat ration. One of the Ohioans at the next fire, red-haired and freckled, looked familiar to Dan. Laughing at a messmate, he said: "Sure, lads, a body needs only one spur. If one side of a nag moves, won't the other follow?"

The Irish accent had Dan on his feet. "Tim!" He squatted down by the surprised soldier. "Tim O'Donnell! Remember me? How's Peggy?"

"Danny O'Brien, as I breathe!" The brawny redhead clasped Dan in a bear hug. He had to notice the scar but, to Dan's relief, didn't mention it. "Peggy's bright and blooming with two pretty colleens at her skirts. You're looking at her husband, that great black-haired, squinty-eyed, hump-nosed lummox yonder, Harry Shepherd. I married his sister, a lovely lass in spite of his looks. Makes us closer kin than I care to be, but he's handy in a fight."

"You get us in enough of them." Harry grinned.

"How's Uncle Simeon?" Tim ran on. "Wasn't he the grand one, to take in us three Irish orphans? And how're Lydia, Owen, and Susie? I've asked for a furlough to go visit." He drew bleached eyebrows together as David hurried to them and rose to lift the boy off his feet in a swooping embrace.

"Now isn't it our Davie, all grown up? Will ye be a soldier then, boyeen?"

They were still catching up on the doings of both families since the Parkses had left the grown O'Donnells in Ohio — letters were exchanged occasionally but not often — when the fire was poked up, men gathered, voices hushed, and a willowy, long-haired officer opened a Bible.

"That's Lieutenant George Hoyt," Theo whispered. "He's a lawyer from Massachusetts. Volunteered to defend old John Brown in his trial after Harper's Ferry. Couldn't get him off, of course. Nobody could have."

Clearing his throat, Lieutenant Hoyt read in a resonant tone from a passage Dan recognized as the cry of the prophet, Joel. " 'Put ye in the sickle, for the harvest is ripe: come, get you down; for the press is full, the fats overflow; for their wickedness is great. Multitudes, multitudes, in the valley of decision: for the day of the Lord is near in the valley of decision. The sun and the moon shall be darkened, and the stars shall withdraw their shining. The Lord also shall roar out of Zion. . . .' "

When Hoyt finished, he looked around at the forty or so Ohioans. "Perhaps you don't know that men from Kansas traveled east to help John Brown escape. He refused, confident that his hanging would do more to free the slaves than could his living." Hoyt's voice sank. He raised his arms and whispered in a way that made Dan's skin prickle: "Do you swear to avenge the death of John Brown?"

"We will!" Theo's voice swelled the fervent promise. "We will!"

Dan's scalp crawled in earnest then, for, all around him, men began to sing, softly at first, then with mounting ardor.

> *John Brown's body lies a-mouldering in the grave,*
> *John Brown's body lies a-mouldering in the grave,*
> *John Brown's body lies a-mouldering in the grave,*
> *But his soul goes marching on. . . .*

The last verse swung into fast tempo.

> *Then three cheers for John Brown, Junior,*
> *Then three cheers for John Brown, Junior,*
> *Give three cheers for John Brown, Junior,*
> *As we go marching on!*

The conduct of Company K was certainly different from that of neighboring groups who loafed around their fires playing cards, yarning, and telling ribald jokes, except for those who were writing letters, using hardtack boxes for desks.

"Tattoo" sounded. While the soldiers assembled for the final roll call of the day, Dan, Thos, and David spread their bedrolls near Montgomery's 3rd Regiment. By the time "Taps" signaled quiet and candles out — for everyone but officers — Dan was almost asleep, Christy's blanket pulled over his scar.

He jumped when something touched him. "Dan?" came

David's whisper. "I . . . I'm cold."

And a little homesick, maybe a little scared? Company K was enough to scare anyone. "Haul your bedroll over here," Dan invited. "When it's really cold, Davie, we'll sleep so tight in a tent that, if one person has to turn over, he'll give the word and everybody'll switch at the same time."

"Think I'll join you," said Thos, although it was really not that chilly.

Snug between them, David was soon breathing deeply. *He's too young for war,* Dan thought with a wave of foreboding. *Raised Quaker, fussed over by his sisters. . . .*

But those sisters and an old father had let him go because they hated slavery. At least he had no brother on the other side the way that Thos did, and Christy.

Christy. He had kissed her good bye only yesterday morning. How long would it be till he saw her again? Making her as real as he could in his imagining, Dan drew her blanket closer around him and sank into sleep.

Being under eighteen, David presented Simeon's letter of permission to the rail-thin, straggly-mustached orderly sergeant who barely glanced at it before telling the three of them to raise their right hands while he administered the oath. They signed the documents pledging to serve three years or for the duration of the war. The sergeant locked the papers in a metal box and put it inside his tent.

"Now, lads," he said, straightening with a grin, "you said you want to be in the cavalry, but what we need is muleskinners to take supplies to an outpost. As soon as you hear 'Boots and Saddles', each of you get six mules from that bunch grazing yonder. Bring 'em in and string 'em out."

"Sir?" David was trying to salvage something from his dreams of glory. "My uniform. . . ."

"Go see what the quartermaster has, Private Parks, but be sure you're back here in time to harness up. Now, let's have a smart salute, if you please."

"Drat him!" muttered Thos as they hurried off. "He didn't tell us they didn't need cavalrymen till he had us sworn, signed, and sealed!"

"That's why he's a sergeant." Dan grinned at David although he himself was sorely disappointed. "Look at it this way, boys. We already know our job."

Chapter Twelve

It was hard for Christy to accept the fact that Thos and Dan would be back in the Army, and this time for who could guess how long? This war wasn't ending as quickly as either side had expected. Each night, in their evening prayers, the Wares especially remembered Andy, his wife, his son, and his mother, along with Dan, Charlie, and Thos.

The memory of how Dan had played at the funeral service for Andy filled Christy with wonder that he'd composed such powerful music. But hadn't there been a few seconds of mounting fury, something terrible indeed, before Dan had glanced at Andy's little son and then changed the notes, the tune becoming almost a lullaby? Christy knew something was wrong inside Dan, and it hurt to remember how he'd seemed almost to shun her. Yet she couldn't doubt he loved her. She had a feeling it had to do with Lafe Ballard and the death of Andy. Whatever it was had folded him in shadow.

The shadow of death? She shivered and reasoned with herself. *No, Thos had walked that valley, too, and Owen. They had changed, were older, tougher. But the chilling darkness wasn't in them.* She might have found some relief in talking to her parents about this dread, but, if they hadn't noticed it, she didn't want to trouble them with something none of them could remedy.

Jonathan had gone to see how Allie Hayes and the family

were getting along without Ethan and Matt, and he returned looking worried.

"She'll be lucky to hold Mark much longer," Jonathan predicted. "Even Luke is fancying himself a soldier." He paused and his mouth hardened in a way most unusual for him, mostly a laughing man. "Allie's heard from Missus Maddux that, after Lafe and Tom Maddux, the Baptist minister's son, mustered out last month, they decided it was better looting with one of the gangs that joins Quantrill for big raids but just ranges over the country the rest of the time. Watt Caxton joined the bunch, too, having decided apparently that it would be more profitable than selling a few slaves here and there. Missus Maddux sounds sort of proud of Tom, Allie says, but Hester wouldn't approve of Lafe's actions."

"Lafe never writes or comes to see Hester," Ellen said. "A heartache he's always been for her. I hope he keeps his devilment well away from where she'd hear of it."

Christy's spine crawled. Lafe Ballard a guerrilla, freed from any restraints of Army discipline? She looked at the wrist scar he had caused back at the cabin raising. She'd like to think he'd forgotten all about her. All the same. . . .

She voiced a thought that had been forming since Dan's visit and the certainty that this war was going to last longer than anyone had feared. "Father, why don't we see if the underground river passage has a cavern large enough to hold our animals if raiders come this way? You know, the one right across the creek from us . . . the opening we found when Justus was hiding there? We know the passage goes through Watt Caxton's land. We might be able find a big chamber beyond there."

"That could come in handy," he admitted.

"Oh, Jonathan, please do look," Ellen urged. "There might be a place where we could take refuge, too, if need be.

Certainly it can't hurt to be prepared."

Right after chores and breakfast the next morning, Christy and her father set off across the creek with torches and candles which they would use once they were beyond the light of the entrance of the cave where Justus had hid in what seemed a lifetime ago. *Where was he now? Had he ever got back for his wife, his Hildy, down in Indian Territory?* Christy wondered. The strife down there between the tribes that had joined the Confederacy and those who had declared for the Union sounded as bad as that along this border.

But soon everything but the magnificence of this expanse fled Christy's mind as she and her father held their flickering torches and gasped at the sculpturings, pinnacles, and draperies of white, yellow, and rose, the beauties hidden till light struck them. Light flashed, too, on the glide of strange pale fish that must wonder what had happened to their eternal dark.

Not far beyond the sinkhole on the Caxton farm, the passage expanded into a glittering palisaded chamber with the river murmuring through it. After awestruck moments, while their torches traced hunched formations that looked like gargoyles and fantastic beasts, her father whispered softly: "This room would hold all the cattle and horses. And there's water."

"The opening is big enough even for Moses and Pharaoh," Christy said. "Single file, the animals could make it in here."

"Yes, but it'd take a while to get them all across the creek and up the passage. Raiders likely won't give that much warning." Her father shrugged. "Still, it's good to know about it. Let's see if there's a way out on this end."

Walking cautiously, they continued on. After what seemed a long time, sun-drenched blue dazzled ahead. The river narrowed and deepened although they could still walk

171

without stooping. Blowing out the candles that had replaced their burned-out torches, they came out into a grotto. The rock floor rose on either side of the river that glistened and sang as it hurled itself down from the cave and came in sight again, sparkling through a high-grassed valley, steeply walled all around except for a narrow gorge on the other side that, through the centuries, had been cut by the river flowing to the world beyond. This was a world of its own. A hidden one.

"People lived here once," Jonathan said to his daughter, kneeling to touch a basin ground in the limestone. A stone pestle lay on the earth. He stood again, and pointed out: "Look, there are other caves in the cliffs yonder. With the only entrance being this cave . . . unless some of the others have passages to the outside . . . this is a safe, beautiful place." He laughed, admiring the tranquil meadow and many hues of trees. "I'll wager whatever others called it must have meant peace valley."

Enchanted, Christy thought sighing. "What a wonderful place to live!"

"If you didn't want to get in or out very often," her father replied thoughtfully. The sun burnished his hair into a blaze of russet. His eyes, though, turned serious. "Christy, if things turn upside down, people could live here. There's graze for animals. The silty land along the creek would grow crops. There's bound to be nut and fruit trees . . . berries. But, now, we need to get back."

They made their way out, following the path by which they had discovered this hidden valley.

Once home, they told of their discovery. Ellen was thrilled to hear of the wonderful place. They promised to show her soon.

A few evenings later, they were about to sit down to supper when a distant thunder neared enough to be recognized as galloping horses, more than just a few. Robbie set up a clamorous barking. It was warm, so the door still stood open, and Jonathan started toward it, calling Robbie inside.

Christy peered out the window at a confusion of armed men, most in the gaudy red or yellow shirts she'd heard Southern guerrillas fancied, along with broad-brimmed, plumed hats. Of the score or so, most were strangers to Christy, but in a swift fearful glance she recognized Watt Caxton and then Lafe Ballard, who was to one side of the hulking Tom Maddux, the Baptist minister's son.

"Father!" she cried. "Don't go out. Let me! They won't hurt a woman!"

"I'll see what they want," her father said as he stepped outside, calling out: "Come ahead! We just sat down for supper, but you're welcome. . . ."

Without warning, Watt Caxton charged toward Jonathan, yelling — "This is for that whelp of yours in the Union Army!" — and discharged his gun.

The shot sent Jonathan back across the threshold, arms outstretched as if still in welcome, blood pouring from his blasted chest. He breathed in labored gasps as Christy and her mother raised him up, having both rushed to his side. He tried to speak, coughed blood, and reached for his wife's hand. The life flowed out of him. Heavy he was suddenly, so very heavy in their arms.

"Next time, Watt, don't you go shootin' till I give a sign, hear?" commanded the leader, a dark young man with what looked like scalps hanging on his bridle.

"Miz Ware!" Caxton shouted, ignoring the man in charge. "Where's them Jerseys and the big white oxen?"

"Jayhawked," Christy lied.

"Funny the bays got left," Lafe Ballad put in.

"Father . . . father had driven them to the mill that day."

Reining his horse between the house and Caxton and Ballard, the leader ordered: "Let the ladies be. Don't bother the house. Leave these folks some corn and bacon and ham!" he shouted to the men who were already hitching Queenie and Jed to the wagon. "And hustle! Quantrill expects us at Black Jack day after tomorrow."

Christy and her mother somehow carried Jonathan inside.

"Hold Robbie, Beth," Christy choked. "We don't want him getting hurt out there."

Could this be happening? It had to be a nightmare. Yet her father's blood soaked the bed where they had placed him.

Ellen fell on her knees beside her husband. Her silence was worse than screams. She stroked his hair and held his hand to her cheek.

From outside came volleys of shots, wild yells and laughter, the squeals of dying pigs and blatting of terrified sheep. Christy started to run out, but Beth caught her around the knees.

"Christy! Don't! Don't go out! They might kill you, too!"

Trembling, weeping at the piteous sounds of the animals she knew like friends, Christy remembered that they had been keeping the cows up in the woods, along with the oxen and Lass and Laddie, too. Had Christy been alone, if her mother and Beth wouldn't suffer for her actions, she'd have run out anyway, grabbed a hoe or anything handy, and attacked the devils shooting Patches' and Evalina's offspring and using the black-faced flock for target practice.

Beth had crept close to her mother but was not touching her, as if she were afraid this wasn't the woman she knew. Christy dropped beside her, huddled against their father's knee that splayed near the edge of the bed. Beth held to her as if scared she might change, too.

Christy had changed. She would never, ever be the same.

174

But she hugged Beth as they murmured the psalms and prayers they knew by heart. " 'Yea, though I walk through the valley of the shadow of death, I will fear no evil. . . .' "

I do, though, Christy thought, *and it's out there. Hear it, oh, God, no, don't hear.*

After what seemed an eternity, the tumult outside was over, although from a distance the creak of the wagon sounded along with gusts of laughter and yells of triumph.

"Bethie," Christy whispered, "I want to see if I can help any . . . any of the animals. You stay here with Mother. Bring her a drink, honey. While I'm out, I'll bring in the cows. It's past time and they'll be needing to let down their milk."

Outside, twilight hazed the barnyard, stable, and pens, thick with the smell of gunpowder. Pale heaps piled inside the sheeps' fence. There wasn't a moving animal inside. At least, none was crying with pain. The marauders had been thorough. From the best count she could make in the growing darkness, all thirty sheep were dead, left where they fell. Poor Nosey and Cleo and Mildred, who had walked the long way from Illinois, their neat-hoofed black-faced family! Through tears, Christy peered at the opulent black and white bodies of Patches and Evalina. Deemed old and tough, they'd been left, but the carcasses of the younger pigs had been taken. Succulent meals they'd make, spitted over a fire.

At first Christy thought all the chickens had been stolen, but nervous *cluck*s came from the trees where some had found refuge. Heloise and Abelard — no telling goose from gander, they were so ripped with bullets — lay by the sheep pen. *Poor creatures, what had they to do with North and South? What kind of men could take pleasure in this?* Christy told herself that Jed and Queenie were valuable horses. That the mounts of the guerrillas looked well cared for.

A plaintive lowing floated from the timber. The Jerseys

and oxen couldn't understand why they had to stay in the woods by day. Christy gave herself a shake. Lady Jane, Guinevere, and Maud would have ordinarily been milked before supper, but, in these harrowing times, her father had begun bringing them in as night fell, when no intruders were likely to come. He milked them then and again in the morning before turning them back into the woods.

Christy trudged toward the forest. No use wasting the meat of the sheep and Patches and Evalina although she didn't think she could eat such old friends. Tomorrow she'd ride Lass to the mill so it could be arranged for the Parkses to come and get the carcasses to butcher. Maybe Lydia Parks could stay with them a few days. . . .

The cows came to meet her, and she stroked the bump on each of their heads, the one between their black-rimmed ears. "I'm glad you don't know what people can do," she told them, hot tears scalding her face. But they seemed to understand, at least to a degree. Although the pig and sheep pens were a little distance from the barn, the cows appeared nervous.

When she was done milking, she carried the buckets to the well house, which she found emptied of butter and cheese. Several jugs lay wantonly smashed. It was as she washed the pails that she noticed the drying blood on her dress. *Now we must somehow bury Father.*

Back in the house, Ellen, as if in a trance, was bathing Jonathan's ghastly wound. Christy helped without a word. What could she say? They brought lifeless hands and arms through the sleeves of a clean shirt, and finally wrapped him in the treasured quilt the neighbor women, including Nora Caxton, had stitched under the great tree the day the house was raised. How long ago that seemed, and not just in years!

"The ground's softest and sweetest in the garden or fields

where the rocks have been cleared," Ellen said as if rousing from a dream. "The edge of the cornfield will be easy to dig. Jonathan would like it there, where he worked the most. It was always something with the corn . . . plowing, planting, cultivating, pulling fodder, cribbing, plowing stubble under, but he said young corn was one of the prettiest sights on earth."

"Do . . . do you want a piece of his hair?" Christy asked as she touched her father's head.

Her mother flinched. "No, oh, no. Let it stay on his dear head. But I'll cut off some of mine for him. He did love my hair."

"All of you," Christy said.

"All of us!" Beth cried, pushing in to bury her face against their mother. "Mama, Mama, put on a clean dress! You're all bloody! Christy, you change, too!"

So they washed, put on clean dresses, set the stained ones and the sheets to soak. Cloth was too precious to discard. Then Ellen and Christy dug the grave in the rich-smelling earth while Beth fished rocks from the soil. They lined the hole with yellow stalks of goldenrod that still flourished and then brought Jonathan, wrapped in the beautiful quilt. More goldenrod covered the quilt. They threw in the first handfuls of sod, then gently filled the oblong, heaping the dirt into a mound.

Kneeling, arms around each other, they repeated the Shepherd's Psalm, but then they sobbed and wept before, at last, going back up to the house. Ellen sank into her rocker. Christy lit the lamp on the table by the forgotten supper. She didn't think she'd ever be hungry again, but she knew they must all eat something, and sleep if they could. She poked up the coals and poured the stew back in the kettle to heat while the teakettle nestled at the edge of the hearth.

Ellen managed a few bites at Christy's urging, but mostly she sipped her tea, letting her hand rest on Robbie's head who sat near her. Christy was too exhausted to do their few dishes so put them to soak while she and Beth made their parents' bed. Christy thought she had cleaned up the blood but found a few more spots that left stains no matter how hard she scrubbed. Maybe black walnut in some butter would cover the places.

"I think we should sleep with Mother," she murmured to Beth. "And keep Robbie close to the bed, too."

Beth nodded. "That way it won't . . . won't be so lonesome. But . . . what'll we do, Christy?"

"Right now, you brush Mother's hair and put it in a plait while I take off her shoes and rub her feet with some of her lavender ointment."

When weariness set in, Christy helped her mother into her nightgown and led her to the bed. Once settled, Ellen sighed and pressed her face into the pillow. Beth got in to warm her back, and, as soon as Christy had banked the coals and blown out the lamp, she put on her gown and lay at her mother's other side. Robbie stayed by the side of the bed where she could touch him. He gave her hand a comforting lick, followed by a soft whimper. *How much does he understand about Father's death?* Christy wondered, and scratched behind his ears.

The next thing she knew it was morning although she hadn't believed she would sleep at all. She roused, a weight on her even before she remembered, waiting for the pain as if it were a stalking beast wakefulness could bring upon her. To her surprise, it didn't seize her at once. She lay still, by her mother, like hiding prey, and rested her tired body. But the beast sensed her consciousness. It padded toward her on clawed feet, sank in its fangs. She fought it off by rising from her parents' bed, trying not to wake Beth, who slept curled in a ball around Lambie, thumb in her mouth, eyes red and puffy. Let her sleep as long as she could. If you slept eight hours of twenty-four, that was a third of the time you didn't have to remember.

Christy planned out the day as she got ready. The cows needed milking and hiding, and then she'd go to the Parkses. Maybe seeing them would help bring her mother out of her numbed stillness.

After she had poured the milk into pans for the cream to form and washed and rinsed the buckets, Christy and Robbie escorted the cattle across their old pasture. Pharaoh, Moses, and the dry cows waited at the gate and lowed to welcome their companions. Lad and Lass grazed in plain sight on a grassy slope.

It might be possible to hide a few animals, but with this many it was just a matter of time till all of them would be stolen. Peace Valley would be the safest place, but Guinevere, Maud, and Lady Jane had to be milked twice a day. Their spring calves still suckled, but were almost weaned. Christy caught Lass with an old halter and led her to the barn. The saddles were gone, but the thieves had left an ancient bridle and a few faded saddle blankets. She tied these around Lass with some strips of canvas hoarded from their covered wagon. She left the mare by the house and went to tell her mother and Beth where she was going.

Ellen had changed from her nightgown, but her hair still hung in the single braid. "What, dear?" she asked, turning to Christy.

Christy repeated herself. "I won't be gone long." She bent to kiss her mother who placed cold fingers on her wrist. "Have you had breakfast?"

"Bread and milk," Christy said. "Beth, will you make new

179

mush for you and Mother? I'll fry what's left of the old to go with supper."

She never passed a soul till she neared the mill, and was glad. She didn't want to talk to anyone, except to trusted friends. After she told them what had happened, Simeon and Lydia Parks wept with her, prayed with her, and then made her join them for corn chowder before they followed her back with the wagon in which they would haul away the dead animals.

Simeon gave Christy a serviceable saddle someone had left at the mill as payment for meal, so the ride back home was more comfortable. The Parkses tried to persuade Ellen to come stay at the comparative safety of the mill, across the border, but she said: "My daughter-in-law's expecting a baby soon. I'd like to be there when he's born."

He? Then Christy understood. Her mother hoped to see in Charlie's son an infant Jonathan, his smile, some of his features and nature living on. Well, that might be the best for now, for her mother and Beth to stay with the Jardines. Lavinia and Melissa would welcome them lovingly, and the bishop knew his duty.

The Parkses, at Ellen's request, would come back to take her piano, the heirloom rocking chair, silver, and china, and keep them till safer times. Lydia, angular and strong as a man, told Christy she and Simeon would load the pigs and sheep. "I know they were your friends," she said, giving Christy a quick hug. "Go fetch your milk cows while we clear away. You say you have a safe place to take them?" At Christy's nod, she held up a hand. "Don't tell us. Better it's a secret, so there'll be no slips."

Christy was on her way back with the cows when Hester Ballard came up from the creek like a shadow. "Yesterday, at nooning, someone who looked like Lafe . . . but wasn't . . . hanged Emil," she said. "Killed Lottie when she got in the way of bullet."

Hester explained how she had been gathering nuts and had heard the uproar. She had hidden, and, when the gang left, she'd cut Emil down, dug out a grave for him and Lottie in the orchard, dragged a log over it so the beasts couldn't get at them. She couldn't remember much after that. She woke this morning where she must have fallen asleep in a shallow cave. When she heard a man groaning, she'd thought she was remembering the raid, but after a while the sound had come again.

"He's down there by the creek. Too heavy for me to carry and burning up with fever," she said in conclusion.

"Do you know him?" Christy asked.

Hester shook her head. "From the stink of the wound in his shoulder, he was shot several days ago. Will you help get him to your house?"

"A gang rode up last evening," Christy told her. "Watt Caxton shot Father down . . . right in the doorway. If that man you found is one of them. . . ."

"Your father?" Hester broke in. "Jonathan?"

Christy nodded.

Hester's anguish came out in a frightening way, with no sound, just a contorted face and heaving shoulders. "God rest that lovely man," she choked at last. "I'll come to your mother as soon as I do what I can for this man . . . whoever he is. All I know, honey girl, is that's he's young and hurt bad and will die if he's not seen to." She turned away, seeming very old.

"Wait!" Christy said. "I'll bring Lady Jane down and we'll see if we can get him slung over her." While she got the Jersey, she thought about what Hester had said. If the same group that had attacked her family had attacked the Franzes, and she knew it had to have been, then Lafe had been among the group. Hester had seen her son take part in this horrible act. But she couldn't let herself acknowledge it.

"Let's take him in the other cabin, put him on Beth's and my bed," Christy instructed Hester, meaning the cabin connected by the dogtrot to the larger cabin. "Mother wants to go to Jardines', so maybe she won't know he's here."

"I'll see to him," Hester promised. "And then I'll go speak to your poor mother. Oh, Lordy Lord!"

They dragged more than carried the strange man to the bed. His calico shirt was in tatters and his curly black hair was plastered to his comely browned face that had a hawk nose and imperious brows.

Christy led Lady Jane back to the barn, saw to the milking, and went in to find Hester frying the old mush while Beth set the table. With maple syrup and cream, the mush made an easy supper.

As they ate — Ellen with only a bit of an appetite — Christy said: "Mother, if you want to go to Jardines', let's do it tomorrow. Then, unless you can think of a better place to hide them, I'll take all our animals, except the milk cows, along the underground river to the hidden valley."

"Peace Valley, your father called it," Ellen said. "He said it was a beautiful place. Remember, you two were going to take me to see it."

"I'll take you when you come back from Jardines'," Christy assured her, then changed the subject. "I wonder if Melissa's going to have a girl or little boy."

"I wish she'd have one of each!" Beth brightened at the prospect. Her smooth brow furrowed. "You know, Christy, you don't have to hide Lass from any bad men. They don't steal crippled horses."

182

Had Beth taken leave of her senses? Christy studied her sister with concern. "Lass isn't crippled."

Beth gave her impish grin for the first time since the horror. "She can act that way, though."

"What?"

"Remember when Lad kicked her when they were playing and she limped for so long?" The other three nodded. "Well," Beth triumphed, "to make her feel all better, I took her apples and turnips and roasting ears and corn pone dipped in molasses. She's so funny and smart! After her leg was fine, she'd limp when she saw me coming, 'specially when I held my hand like I had something in it."

"So you kept sneaking goodies to her," Christy chided.

"Didn't have to sneak," retorted a virtuous Beth. "Mostly, everyone's too busy to notice what I do, as long as I don't get in their way."

Christy exchanged guilty looks with her mother. Beth was the baby and often indulged, but she had no playmate, save Robbie, and was often admonished not to pester.

"I trained Lass," Beth went on loftily. "It was fun to have a secret." She sighed at its loss.

"Being able to keep Lass around will be a big help," Christy praised. "She can pull the cultivator, though we'll have to fetch Lad when we need a team for plowing."

"Plowing?" Ellen looked stricken. "Surely this awful war will be over by spring."

"From what Dan and Thos said, it sounds as if the armies will go into winter quarters, and there won't be much fighting till spring." Christy hated to distress her mother, but there was no use in encouraging hopes that were almost sure to prove false. "Beth should go with you, of course, Mother. Hester and I can look after things here."

"But if more guerrillas come. . . ."

"You know how they brag that they never hurt women."
What Christy didn't want to say to her mother, for fear of it
sounding like reproach, was that she didn't want to abandon
their farm, the garden and fields, the orchards just starting
to yield bountifully, the well witched by old John Brown, the
home by the giant walnut that had held so much love, life,
and laughter. Christy needed to believe it would be the
happy house again. To show that faith, she felt she had to
stay.

Beth jumped up from the table. "Come on, Christy! I'll
show you how to get Lass to act lame!"

As the neared the Jardine plantation, Christy first thought
the odor of smoke came from the many fireplaces of Rose
Haven.

"Unless they really want me to stay, I'll go back with you,"
her mother said as she stared off into the distance. "We'll just
visit and leave the baby things we've knitted."

"They'll want you and Beth to stay," Christy reassured
her. "Melissa loves you, and Missus Jardine's a sweet lady,
even if they do have slaves."

"Slaves," repeated Ellen, as if she'd forgotten. She looked
distraught. "Oh, dear! Your father wouldn't approve. . . ."

"These aren't ordinary times," Christy said to calm her
down. "He'd want you to do whatever helps. Being with Melissa will do that."

"I shouldn't leave you. . . ."

"I want to stay at the house. Besides, Hester'll be with
me."

"Hester is demented."

"Just about Lafe, Mother. I guess it's the only way she can
stand what he did . . . believing it really wasn't him."

"Poor Hester!" Ellen's voice shook. "It's better to mourn

a good man than know a little boy you raised and loved has grown into a monster."

He always was a monster, Christy thought to herself, growing cold at the memory of his pale eyes and parted lips when her father was shot. The leader of the guerrillas had kept his men from robbing the house or offending the women, but Lafe could come back alone. Christy glanced at the crescent on her wrist. Dread surged through her, sweeping away her resolve to protect the happy house as much as she could. *If Lafe caught me alone. . . .* She fought off the terror. He was only a man. He could die. But how she wished Dan or Thos or Charlie was home!

As Lad and Lass left the woods for the cleared lands of Rose Haven, Christy thought they had followed the wrong trail until her brain had to recognize what her eyes saw.

The sprawling two-storied white house with its pillared verandah was gone. Blackened chimneys, tumbled fireplaces, rose from heaps of ashes and charred logs. Smoked, shattered glass was all that was left of the rose room, that and the smell of scorched feathers mixed with the odor of burned wood, fabric, and rotting meat. This last came from the remains of several carelessly slaughtered cattle and hogs from which vultures rose sluggishly at the riders' approach. The rest of the livestock and all the fine horses had vanished. The wagons and carriage had either been stolen or burned. Barns, stables, outbuildings had been fired, but the slave cabins were spared, although no one seemed to be there. Apart from the vultures that returned to their feast, no living creature stirred.

Beth gave a strangled sob and buried her face against Christy's back.

"Dear God!" prayed Ellen. "Oh, dear God. . . ."

Then a shriek cleft the air.

Hair rose at the back of Christy's neck. Did ghosts scream?

There was another cry, then a murmur of voices. Christy noticed for the first time that smoke curled from the chimneys of Aunt Phronie's double cabin behind the ruins of the big house.

As another scream resounded, Ellen said: "It's not time for Melissa's baby, but *someone's* birthing."

Nudging Lad and Lass forward, Christy and her mother halted outside the cabin. Ellen helped her younger daughter off, before Christy slid down. As they tethered the horses, a double-barreled shotgun poked out the door, and then a wrinkled yellow face showed behind it.

"Land's sakes!" A relieved smile plumped out the lines in Aunt Phronie's face. "Master Charlie's mama and sisters!" The smile faded. "Reckon you hear Miss Melissa. She tried hard not to holler and upset Miss Vinnie, but that baby's givin' her a sight of misery. Maybe it'll be big and strong enough to live, even it be a good month or more early. Terrible doin's, Miz Ware, terrible!" Face crumpling, Phronie blindly leaned the shotgun against the wall by the door, but she didn't forget the proprieties. "Miss Beth, you run along into the other cabin . . . or, no, go down to that first cabin yonder. Some hens got away and been roostin' there. Maybe you can find a couple of nice eggs. Miss Christy, bein' as you're not married. . . ."

Christy moved past Phronie. "Maybe I can help," she said.

What had happened here was clear enough. It didn't seem to matter much at the moment which side had done this.

Holding Melissa's hands, Lilah bent over Charlie's wife as her knees drew up as her sheeted belly heaved. Lilah, too, was big with child. Her dark eyes looked bruised in her pale gold face that was as sweaty as Melissa's even though wind came through the chinks of the wall, chilling the whole cabin except for directly in front of the fire.

Lavinia Jardine, wrapped in the violet shawl her old nurse had made for her, sat in her invalid chair. Emmie, the gray cat Charlie had rescued, curled up at her feet. Seemingly unaware of her daughter's pain, she threw an unseen shuttle, worked an invisible treadle, and crooned an old song.

> *For I have dreamed a deadly dream,*
> *I fear it may bode sorrow.*
> *I dreamed I pulled the rowan green*
> *With my true love on Yarrow. . . .*

"She wheel her chair in front of Master Mord when he was tryin' to keep them jayhawks from smashin' her rose room," lamented Phronie.

Ellen threw off her cloak and went to speak kindly, encouragingly, to Melissa as Phronie went on.

"One of 'em . . . hope he fries in hell . . . clubs her alongside her head. She go limp and I get her outside . . . the house already blazin'. Jayhawks shoot Master Mord a whole lot, bang away after his head's nigh shot off. They strangle Miss Vinnie's birds and toss 'em on top of the master."

"When was this?" Christy asked.

"When?" Phronie rubbed a welt on her skinny arm and thought. "Must've been towards sundown day before yesterday. They had a flag. Some wore uniforms . . . claimed they was Union cavalry and needed supplies. Their captain said he'd give the bishop a chit so he could collect from the Union gov'ment, providin' he could prove he was loyal. Wasn't much the bishop and the overseer, Mister Blake, could do, but, when some of the gang started in on the rose room, Master Mord couldn't stand it and he tried to fight them off. Mister Blake, he just disappeared."

187

"Where are all the other people?"

"That bluecoat captain, he asks don' they want to be free and come along with him to Kansas. Say they can take anything his gang left. I reckon some would rather have stayed and got along the best they could helpin' Miss Vinnie and Miss Melissa, but that captain said, if Confederates came through, they'd think the colored folks was in cahoots with the jayhawks and most likely would kill 'em or at least break up families and maybe sell 'em away down south."

"So there's just you and Lilah left?"

Phronie nodded. "We got Miss Vinnie in here quick as we could. Zillah, she drag herself out of bed and guard the door . . . she call down all kinds of devils on any jayhawks who peek in till their captain, he say leave us alone, they not fightin' old women or them in the family way."

"Where is Zillah now?"

"When the jayhawks leave off pesterin', she creep over and hug Miss Vinnie, then she lay her head against Miss Vinnie and her poor old heart, it stops. We buried her with what was left of Master Mord. By then, Miss Melissa, she starts her pains." Phronie glared suddenly at her granddaughter, the one Charlie had said was only an eighth colored. Christy remembered uneasily how Lilah had watched Travis with such longing — Travis who'd been chagrined when Christy refused his proposal.

"Don't you even think about having your baby till things straighten out a little!" Phronie admonished Lilah before she glanced at her mistress. "Though I declare I don't see how they ever be straight with Miss Vinnie like she is, shut up some place in her mind. Maybe that's a mercy. She don't know Master Mord be dead."

"Aunt Phronie, will you come here?" Ellen called out. She added in a whisper the gasping Melissa couldn't hear: "I'm afraid the baby isn't turned right."

Phronie lifted the sheet. Her jaw clamped till the bone showed through withered skin. "Lord help us . . . its little rump is comin' first!" Her eyes closed. When they opened, she spoke briskly: "Lilah, you fetch more of the blue cohosh tea. It'll urge her along. Poor lamb goin' to need it. Miss Christy, let her keep ahold of your hands. Miz Ware, be ready to help."

Melissa stared up at Christy, her blue eyes glistening as she blinked back her tears. "Oh, Christy, I'm glad you and Mama Ware came! But I wish Charlie were here!"

"He wishes it, too, dear, be sure of that." Christy tried to speak cheeringly even though her lips were stiff. She raised Melissa so she could sip from the cup Lilah held. *Why bring babies into a world where men like Father were shot down on their thresholds, or killed like Andy, or mutilated like Dan?* Christy thought as she bent to kiss her sister-in-law's pretty well-kept hands. "Just think how happy and proud Charlie will be!"

"Yes!" panted Melissa before her eyes squeezed shut. Pain wracked her. She cried out: "Charlie! Charlie!"

Christy's back was to her mother and Phronie, so she couldn't see what they were doing. Her hands ached, the knuckles ground together, as Melissa grasped them with frantic strength. A scream, a spasm, that seemed to last forever. Melissa went limp. Her fingers drooped from Christy's grasp. Christy caught Melissa's shoulders in a shake, but it was a tremulous wail that opened Melissa's eyes.

"He . . . he's here?" she said weakly.

"Indeed he is!" Ellen gave a sobbing laugh. "A beautiful baby boy! He looks just like Charlie did when he was born." She held the baby while Phronie tied the pulsing cord in two places and cut between them. Phronie washed him with warm

water Lilah had brought, and she snuggled the small red creature into Melissa's arms while Ellen took care of the liverish-
looking afterbirth and directed Christy and Lilah as they
eased the bloody cloths and sheets from under Melissa,
bathed her swollen, torn parts, and put a clean sheet beneath
her.

"He be good-sized and husky, even if he came early,"
Phronie praised. "Look, he's already huntin' his dinner."

Melissa turned and helped the tiny questing mouth find
her breast. "Will I have milk, Aunt Phronie?"

"Your real milk won't come in for a few days, honey."
Phronie smoothed Melissa's damp curls back from her forehead. "But you'll have a sort of thin yellowish juice he'll like
real well and get strong on."

Melissa wonderingly touched the eyelash-fine dark hair
thatching the skull with its throbbing soft spot. "Oh, I wish
Charlie could see him!" Tears filled her eyes. "I wish Charlie
were here!"

"Of course you do!" Tears glinted in Ellen's eyes, too, as
she kissed her daughter-in-law's forehead. "Of course you
do."

"I have to call the baby Charles," Melissa said, and gave
her mother-in-law a look of appeal. "I . . . I hope you and Father Ware understand if I give him Daddy's name . . . not
Mordecai . . . that's so awful! But his middle name, Joel."

Ellen nodded.

Christy was sure she didn't speak because she couldn't.
How, in all this tragedy, were they going to tell of their own?
What a bitter trick of fate that they'd come here for solace and
found nightmare.

"Soon's Miss Melissa can travel, I reckon we'd ought to
come stay with you, Miz Ware," ventured Phronie. "No men
folk here . . . Miss Vinnie fuddled so bad . . . and Lilah havin'

190

her baby soon . . . well, that just leaves me to look after everybody."

"Aunt Phronie," said Ellen, straightening. "Come over here a moment. You, too, Christy."

When Phronie heard the terrible news, she stifled a groan. "Oh, my dear Lord," she whispered. "Oh, sweet Jesus! Mister Ware, he was a good, good man! Best not tell Miss Melissa for a while. Might curdle or stop her milk. She thought an awful lot of her daddy-in-law." Phronie buried her face in her hands and her frail shoulders convulsed. "Ever since this happen, I been thinkin' we'd go to you folks till we could figger a way to get to Saint Louis and Miss Yvonne, or send word to the young masters out in Oregon and California, though Lordy knows how we'd do that! Oh, Miz Ware, what we goin' to do?"

Ellen took Phronie's hands. "Be grateful you helped birth a baby who probably would have died without your skill. Be glad Melissa, thanks to you, should be all right."

"Bless the good Lord for that," wept Phronie. "But . . . but. . . ."

Even if they had a wagon or carriage, it was a long perilous way to St. Louis where Lavinia's daughter, Yvonne, lived with her complacent husband, Henry Benton.

"The Parkses would help if we went to them," Christy suggested.

"There's too many of us." Ellen looked weary to the bone. "If only there were a cabin in your father's Peace Valley!"

Christy closed her eyes and saw again the broad valley, encircled by cliffs, with the river sparkling through. She saw the mortar in the limestone, a glimpse of women grinding corn, or perhaps weaving, calling gaily to each other from cave to cave as their children played.

"There's no cabin," she said. "But, Mother, there are

caves where people used to live. If we find a good big dry one and wall up most of the front, it could be warmer than a house."

"Lord have mercy!" Phronie shuddered. "Live in a cave like an old bear? Best stay here in a decent cabin!"

"Do you think the next jayhawks or bushwhackers will let it stand?" Ellen demanded. "Phronie, it's better to be safe than civilized. Peace Valley is the only close place we know of that won't be found by raiders."

Phronie's jaw clenched again. After a moment, she sighed. "Then we better get ourselves there quick as Miss Melissa's able."

"We'll bring our cattle to the valley," said Ellen. "And all the chickens we can catch. Did the jayhawks leave any food?" she asked Phronie.

"Might be a little in the cabins. They emptied the corncribs and smokehouses and root cellars. What turnips and cabbages their horses didn't eat, they squashed into the ground by ridin' over 'em. What molasses they didn't steal, they poured in the dirt. Stirred it in with a stick so we can't skim any off."

Such waste of food was almost as shocking as murder. They were all glad when Beth edged in with a carefully held-up skirt.

"I found four eggs! And there was some hominy in a box and a little piece of candle . . . and an apple. It was sort of shrivelly, so I ate it!"

"Bless the child!" Phronie took the eggs as if they were gold, then shot Ellen a pleading glance. "Is it all right, Miz Ware, if I scramble these for Miss Vinnie and Miss Melissa?"

"They need them," Ellen agreed. "But Melissa's asleep." She went to look down tenderly at the young mother and the baby, who was sleeping, too. "She needs her rest, poor lamb."

Phronie put another log on the fire. "I'll fix the eggs when she wakes up. Lilah girl, take a basket and start goin' through the cabins for anything we can use."

Lilah slipped on a cloak and went out, moving heavily. Her time could not be far away. It must hurt her, that her child would not be welcomed like Melissa's, and that no matter how white it was, it would be a slave. Still, in the hidden valley, slave would be an empty word. There would just be women and children who'd have to help each other to survive. *We'll love Lilah's baby and look after it like we will little Charlie,* Christy thought.

"Beth," said Ellen, "why don't you help Lilah hunt for food and any useful things? Christy, you'd better go home and tell Hester what's happened."

"I can bring Lady Jane here this afternoon, so there'll be milk," Christy offered. "Then, if Hester's afraid to stay alone, I can be home before dark."

Her mother nodded and embraced her. "Be careful, darling. Oh, I still can't believe. . . ." They clung to each other.

Why, I'm taller than Mother, Christy thought. *And she feels like her bones are light as a bird's. She needs to eat more.* Strange to worry about her mother who always looked out for everybody else, but, as Christy kissed her and went out, she realized that she now would have to do a lot of the looking after, a lot of the watching over and taking care, even though these terrible happenings at the plantation seemed to have roused her mother from her bewildered reveries.

If only Dan were here. . . . If only he's safe, she amended. As she rode away from the ashes of Rose Haven, his song resonated through her as if he played for her and smiled. From this, she took courage for what she must do now, for all the days ahead.

Chapter Thirteen

When Hester recovered a little after being told about the destroyed plantation, she wiped her eyes. "There's food at my place. I'll fetch a load of it, if you'll keep an eye on the lad yonder. Give him willow tea, if he wakes up, and try to get a little soup down him."

His wound seemed to be too old to have been inflicted at Emil's or the Wares', but who knew who and what he was? Christy, none to eager to handle him, nodded reluctantly. "All right, but I want to take a cow to Jardines' today. If you'd like for me to be back here by nightfall. . . ."

"No use in that." Hester's hazel eyes were clear. She had combed her curly, light brown hair and looked more like her old self, not the wraith that had come up from the shadows three nights ago. "Why, child, haven't I lived alone these years since Lafe went off?"

"Yes, but that was before the war."

"I saw Emil hung and Lottie die. And Jonathan's . . ." — Hester swallowed — "reckon nothing worse than that's going to happen." She touched Christy's cheek. "Don't fret about me, honey. You're needed at Jardines' a lot more than here." She lowered her voice even though the man in the other cabin was probably sunk in fevered sleep. "Fancy that hidden valley! Sounds like heaven in the middle of all this woe. Now we'll put everything we can scrape up together, and share and share alike. More than likely there's provender at the Franzes' the guerrillas didn't bother with, and Sarah, I'm bound, would spare us some honey."

"Sarah!" Stabbed with remorse, Christy caught Hester's arm. "How could I forget about her? And Allie Hayes?"

"Sarah's all right," Hester soothed. "Any bad men come along, she'd just fade into the timber."

"But if they took her food . . . ?"

"Bless you, but Sarah can find things to eat in the wilds that even I don't know about."

"Still, maybe she'd like to go to the valley," Christy persisted.

"Maybe she would, since Lige is off being a scout for the Army, but she'd do it more to help the others than for her own sake." Hester laughed; it was good to hear. "That Sarah, she's always been a wild child. Lige never wanted to settle her down." Hester paused at the door. "I'll stop by the tannery and see how Allie and the young 'uns are. Don't forget to eat yourself, dear. I'll be back in plenty of time for you to get the cow to Jardines' before dark."

Hester vanished into the trees, where red-brown leaves of blackjack oak, the green of cedar, and white of sycamore trunks lent color to skeleton trunks and limbs. *If she ever let herself know Lafe had helped hang Emil, would it drive her mad?* Christy shivered at the memory of his eyes, burning like the iron he'd shoved her wrist against. *If he hadn't been under the command of a man who respected women the other day. . . .* The thought was so terrifying that Christy forced it away. Hester wasn't, thank goodness, totally cut off from reality like Lavinia. With her knowledge of plants and healing, Hester would be a powerful help.

Christy wanted to visit her father's grave, but first she looked in on the wounded man. In his hard-angled fashion,

195

he was the handsomest man she'd ever seen, even with dark stubble covering his jaws and chin. He was tall and well made, but so helpless right now a child could plunge a knife into one of the fluttering arteries in his throat and in seconds he'd be as dead as Christy's father, as dead as Emil and Lottie. Horrified at a flash of desire to do exactly that to a helpless person who might well be innocent of any sort of crime, Christy pulled on her cloak and ran to the edge of the cornfield.

It was plowed under and waiting for spring seed, but never again would Jonathan Ware plant and husband the crop. Husband. That meant to take care of. He had done that, not only with his farm and family, but with his students and neighbors, with Justus and other runaways the Wares had helped.

Father! You can't be dead! We'll wake up from this bad dream and you'll be with us. . . . But it wasn't a bad dream. Christy fell to her knees by the patch of raw earth. He'd never again guide Moses and Pharaoh along the furrows, feast on juicy roasting ears, carry sweet-smelling fodder to the barn by the light of the harvest moon. He wouldn't, with strong, gentle hands, help a scared heifer birth her first calf, or smile at the fine sight of the bay and chestnut horses grazing on the slope. He wouldn't finish teaching Beth and Mary Hayes their multiplication tables or get Luke Hayes straightened out on the difference between verbs and adverbs before beguiling them with *Don Quixote, The Song of Roland,* or *Sohrab and Rustum.* He couldn't delight in the brilliant flash orioles and tanagers in the giant chestnut, or the spring serenade of whip-poor-wills and chuck-will's-widows.

Father, if you can hear me, let me know it. Let me feel your spirit. She waited. What came instead of a sense of communion was a powerful image of him coming toward the house,

196

laughing, head thrown back. *Thank God!* she thought even as she wondered if there was one. Thank God, she hadn't seen his face at the moment of the blast outside the doorway, arms outflung in a strange obeisance of welcome. That had to be his gift to her, to remember him happy and strong. *Thank you,* she told him, touching the cold earth, rising. *Help me, Father. Help us all.*

She decided she should look for food that might tempt Lavinia or build Melissa's strength. In the kitchen, Hester had pressed fresh-churned butter into molds. Indian pudding, flavored with dried persimmons, was the best Christy could think of by way of a delicacy. Potato onion soup should please everyone. When these were simmering, she made willow tea and took it and a bowl of soup to the other cabin.

The man moved a little as she entered the room. "Sir? Are you awake?"

His eyes opened slowly. "Josie!"

"I'm Christy Ware," she corrected him. "Let me prop you up so you can sip some tea."

He drank the brew, grimacing, then smiled at Christy as if his conscience was clear as a newborn's. "You sure look like my kid sister. Her name's Josephine." Appraising eyes were made bluer by black lashes and eyebrows. "She's quite a bit younger than you, though. Just turned twelve. I've got two other sisters, but Josie's my pet."

Christy couldn't chat with a man who might be a guerrilla even though she was sure he couldn't have been present at her father's murder. "She'll be glad to see you again, I'm sure. Now try some soup, please. You've been too feverish to eat."

Although Hester's herbs gave it an enticing smell, he curled his lip at the soup. "What I'd relish is a slab of fried ham," he said.

"You'd better have soup and the like for a few more days. I'm making Indian pudding, and you may have a bowl, after you eat your soup."

He made a face but let her feed him. "I don't remember much after I got shot out of my saddle by someone hid in the timber."

"Hester . . . the woman who's been tending you . . . found you by the creek yesterday morning. We brought you to my family's home."

His eyelids drooped before he finished all the soup, and he drowsed half propped on the pillows. She hurried to stir the pudding and collect food to take back to Jardines' — she couldn't call the place Rose Haven any more. The Parkses had insisted on trading a winter's supply of wheat flour and cornmeal for the slaughtered hogs and sheep, and had left it when they had come for her mother's things. Christy put about five pounds of flour and fifteen of meal into pillowcases inside tow sacks. A pound of the fresh butter, a jug of molasses, a hunk of ham and bacon, bags of beans, hominy, and dried fruit, and candles.

Surveying the growing pile, she knew she'd have to rig some kind of panniers to balance the supplies on Lass. How long would it be till Melissa could travel? Christy prayed that Lilah's baby would wait to be born till they were safe in the valley. Their refuge must be a complete secret. Even Lige Morrow had never mentioned it.

Taking the pudding off the heat to cool, Christy ladled some into a bowl for the dark young man to have later. Thought the world of his sister, didn't he? Why was it when men had mothers, sisters, wives, and daughters they loved and wanted to spare grief, they went off to kill the brothers, sons, husbands, and fathers of other women? *Father! Would it ever stop hurting?* The pain, a presence she could almost see, kept its distance till she exposed herself for a second. Then it seized and mauled her till it tired and dropped her like a cat losing interest in a dead thing.

When the spasm of grief eased enough for her to move, Christy put on a shawl and went out to the root cellar. She'd take a bag of potatoes and big sweet onions that came from sets Emil had given them, and some apples gathered from his maiden blush tree. *God rest him,* she thought. *And Lottie.* . . . Emil had come from another country at sixteen. He had limped the rest of his life from a musket ball taken in the War of 1812. He'd lost his only son in the war with Mexico. Who could call him a Dutchman after that? At first it had seemed wrong that the trees and vines he'd cherished could outlive him, but, when Christy remembered Emil's delight in his orchard and vineyard, she had to believe his spirit would rejoice in spring blossoms and ripening fruit, even on the tree where he had been hanged.

A trundling sound brought up Christy from her knees. Why, here came two wheelbarrows, one pushed by Hester, bright as a tiger lily in her store-bought calico, and the other by Sarah Morrow, Lige's hounds streaming around her. Christy ran to meet them, only now admitting that she'd been nervous there, alone, except for the wounded man.

Sarah dropped the handles and held out her arms. Christy flew into her embrace. Some of the strength of Sarah's lithe body passed into her own. "I'm here to help every way I can. Lige dried lots of venison for me before he went off to scout, and I've got bushels of nuts and dried persimmons." Sarah's blue-green eyes were startling against skin the color of sassafras tea with cream and her black hair caught back with a scarlet ribbon. "Of course, I've brought honey and some maple syrup."

"Best thing is you've brought yourself!" Christy turned to

Hester. "Is Allie all right?"

Hester nodded. "One of the guerrillas is a friend of theirs, so that gang they didn't bother her."

"But the jayhawkers . . . ?"

"Mark and Luke heard them coming in time to drive the cows and mules into the woods. Not even jayhawks will yank stinking hides out of tanning vats, and I expect they figgered they'd get all the plunder they could carry at the Jardines'. The captain made Allie cook them a big meal, but that was all the bother they were."

"Is she going to stay there?"

"Says so." Hester shrugged. "She thinks the war'll be over soon and Ethan and Matthew will come home. She wants to keep the tannery going. Mark's well nigh man-size and does a lot of work."

"Yes, and he's going to cut loose any day and join the Army." Sarah's tone was sad.

Christy turned to her. "How did the guerrillas happen to miss you?"

"They knew who had anything worth stealing. We don't have livestock or corn or much else worth their time. Watt Caxton must have guided them."

And Lafe, Christy thought but couldn't say it out loud in front of Hester.

"So Rose Haven was cleaned out by jayhawkers?" Sarah went on as she and Hester pushed the wheelbarrows forward. "Never had much use for the bishop, but he died like a man. Fancy you finding that valley, Christy, when, for all his ridge running, Lige didn't know about it! Of course, he was never one for caves."

"The underground river is the only way into the valley, except for a steep, narrow chasm where the river flows out through the cliffs on the other side."

The Hidden Valley

"I want to go to that valley," Sarah declared. "I'll bet I can find a bee tree or two, and next summer I'll fix a bee gum so whoever's living there will have their own honey."

"You probably can tell them more than I can about wild foods and what roots and bark make good tea," said Hester. "But I'll help put in a garden and plant a little corn."

"I hope everyone's out of there by summer!" Christy blurted, unable to imagine this kind of raiding and daily fear going on for long. "I hope the war's over and. . . ." She broke off, realizing that things couldn't, not ever, be the way they were. *Father is dead. So is Andy. So is Bishop Jardine, and Lavinia will probably never regain her right mind.*

"I've got to be getting along to Jardines'," she said with a glance at the westering sun.

"I'll go with you," Sarah volunteered. "The hounds'll keep off anything short of an army. Lige told old Sam and Blue Boy to look after me, and Chita, that young red bone, I hand-fed when her mama died." Then she patted the fullness of her skirt. "There's a sheathed knife in my pocket. I always sew in great big ones that hold all kinds of stuff. Come in handy."

Swiftly they added provisions from the wheelbarrows to Christy's piles, did them up in two sheets, and tied them across Lass' back. The young mare eyed the bundles with suspicion but was mollified with a wrinkled apple. Hester took the wheelbarrows to the house.

Escorted by the hounds, hurrying all they could, the young women reached Jardines' by sundown. Ellen held Christy a long time. "Thank God you're safely here! And how good to see Sarah's all right."

They put together a good meal from the supplies Lass had carried, but Lavinia scarcely ate in spite of Phronie's coaxing.

Better received were the old nurse's exhortations to Melissa to eat so she could feed her baby. No one felt like talking. They were all tired. As soon as dishes were done, they wrapped up close to each other for warmth. Christy dropped at once into heavy slumber.

The waiting beast had no chance to savage her next morning for she woke to Phronie's wails.

"Oh, my poor lady! She gone. She gone away."

Death had come gently for Lavinia. She was smiling, with a look of expectation.

Everyone wept, especially Phronie, but Christy's sorrow was mixed with relief. Getting a wheelchair through the cavern would have been near impossible. In fact, Christy and Sarah had been planning to take it apart, for easier carrying, and bringing Lavinia in on an improvised litter. But they would have been moving a shell. When he had been placed in her arms, Lavinia had held Joely — as the women found themselves calling him — but she hadn't seemed to know or care that he was her grandson. That blow on the head had destroyed the essence of a lovely, loving woman. Huddled in old Zillah's shawl, she had sung and woven her invisible patterns, a ghost of Rose Haven, a ghost of what had been.

Melissa insisted that her mother be buried in the violet shawl even though Phronie warned that all their wool and the looms had burned with the house. "The livin' need warm things more'n the dead," Phronie said. "Miss Vinnie would be the first to say so."

"We don't have a single rose for her," said Melissa, pale but determined. "She won't have a coffin. She's going to have the shawl."

The ground wasn't frozen beneath a thin crust. With the shovel and pickaxe, Phronie and Lilah had salvaged to bury the bishop, Sarah and Christy dug a grave between him and

Zillah, grateful that the bitter cold kept the corpses from stinking. They lined the narrow place with cedar boughs and, with Phronie's and Lilah's help, eased Lavinia into her resting place.

What's happening to me? thought Christy in horrified contrition as her mother led them in the Shepherd's Psalm. *Here I am glad that we don't have to go to a lot of fuss to get Missus Jardine to the valley.* Christy would have felt differently had Lavinia's mind been clear, but she still felt guilty as her mother praised Lavinia's sweet nature, courage in her invalidism, and the way she had tried to protect her husband.

"He tried to save her rose garden and birds. She tried to save him. Their love was great. Melissa, my dear daughter, you were born of that love. It will be part of you as long as you live, and your parents will live on in your son."

"Let's sing Miss Vinnie's favorite hymn," Phronie suggested as her quavering voice steadied as it soared into "Amazing Grace". After the Lord's Prayer, Melissa dropped the first of the waiting boughs over her mother, then sobbed and let Lilah take her inside while the others finished their sorrowful work and dragged burned rails over the three mounds to keep out scavengers.

"This redbud was a pet of Miss Vinnie's," Phronie said, fingering the leaves of a rosebush near the graves. "It'll bloom over her this spring, every spring, till this trouble's over and the young folks raise a proper stone over their parents. Zillah deserves one, too."

"She'll get it," Christy vowed. Till then, it was better not to mark the graves. She'd heard of guerrillas and jayhawkers digging up new graves in hopes gold or valuables were concealed inside them.

Five anxious days later, Melissa was able to travel with

little Charles Joel Jonathan. If men kept getting killed, every new baby boy would carry a string of memorial names — a heavy load for them, to try to fill the places of two or three men, dead, in their families.

After Lady Jane was milked and wood carried each morning at the Jardines, Christy and Sarah had been going to the Wares'. Then, after checking with Hester to be sure her patient was still in bed, they led an animal apiece through the cavern, across the creek, the gentler ones laden with supplies.

"You don't want to take too many critters through at once," Hester warned. "Too much commotion or noise can play peculiar tricks in caves. I remember hearing about a hunter who followed a bobcat into a cave. He shot at the cat, and the roof caved in on him. Best you keep quiet, step careful, and take your time."

Moses and Pharaoh were so big that, in a few places, they could barely get through, and Lad's head had to be held down so he wouldn't bump the lower-hanging stalactites, but, by the day Melissa was ready to go, all the animals, except the milk cows and Lad and Lass, were in Peace Valley and supplies had been heaped inside the cave entrance from the valley.

As soon as it was light enough to move around that morning, the company set out with Sarah's hounds — Sam, Blue Boy, and Chita — keeping close, while Phronie and Melissa rode the horses. Melissa cradled Joely, and, in front of her, Phronie held Emmie cat, tied up in a pillowcase. Walking beside Lilah, to whom she'd taken a great fancy, Beth carried Lambie and the Lynette doll Melissa had given her, along with her clothes. Lilah balanced her awkward body with the help of a hickory staff.

If the child she carried wouldn't be born to freedom, what was the use of all of the killing and all the pain? Christy

204

thrilled neither to the idea of the Union's supremacy or the Confederacy's states' rights. What she cared about was rights of everyone. If it took war to get them, standing on her father's grave, she'd say it was worth it. Her eyes blurred. The chickens, in the covered basket she carried, squawked at the jounce they got when she tripped on a rock. The surviving Jardine chickens clucked nervously from the willow chest her mother and Sarah held between them. Her mother's remaining Silver Laced Wyandottes would join them as soon as a pen was made. So would the other cows, except for Guinevere. They feared the wounded man was likely to notice a sudden absence of milk and butter.

Hester had been warned to make sure that he didn't look out the door or window that morning. Through the leafless trees and bushes, anyone standing in the doorway could look across the creek in the general direction of the hidden cave entrance. It wouldn't do for a stranger to see this singular caravan disappear into the bluff.

"Are you going to stay in the valley?" Sarah asked Christy over her shoulder.

"I don't know," Christy admitted. The tranquil serenity drew her, yet abandoning the happy house was like abandoning her family's hopes and dreams. "Hester wants to go to the valley to help out, so I don't know how bad I'll be needed."

Ellen glanced back as she and Sarah switched sides on the heavy chest. "Of course, you'll stay in the valley, child! I couldn't draw an easy breath if you were out here alone."

"I'll stay with Christy," Sarah promised Ellen. She jerked her head toward the flow of hounds, blue ticks, and red bones, sniffing and exploring ahead. "What with the dogs, no one can sneak up on us. There's no stock or food left to steal, and you've sent your best things over to Parkses'."

"That could make thieves so angry that they'd burn down the buildings," Ellen worried aloud. "They might even hurt you."

Sarah shrugged. "The devils on both sides claim they don't kill women."

"They killed Lottie Franz."

"Hester said she got in front of a bullet."

"So might you."

"I doubt it." Sarah grinned hardily. "I've already taken my cooking stuff, bedding, and tools to the valley. Guess I'll move my bee gums over to your house, Christy, if you and I stay there."

"But . . . ," Ellen began.

Christy shifted her basket to just one hand long enough to press her mother's shoulder. "It's really not far away, Mother. We can go back and forth. . . ."

"I hate caves!" Ellen blurted out. "Once I get to that valley, I may never come back."

"When Charlie and Thos come home, we'll put a blindfold on you and lead you out," teased Christy.

"Oh, if I could see my boys, I'd walk through hell!"

They didn't speak again until everyone had gotten across the creek by taking turns on the horses. Praying the recovering man would stay in bed, Christy handed candles to everyone except Beth, who she adjured to stay between her mother and Lilah.

"Don't talk," Christy reminded them. "Move quietly as you can and try not to let the animals brush into anything."

Sarah led with Lady Jane. The cow, considerably smaller than the oxen, could pass through with her panniers. Melissa followed with the baby, tagged by Phronie. To keep Lilah's staff from making noise, Christy shredded the bottom of it with a knife. Ellen carried Emmie over her shoulder, still curled in her pillowcase. Christy brought up the rear with Lad. They'd have to make another trip for the chickens. Lad had worn his shoes down, so they barely made a sound except where silty dust gave way to stone. These chinkings, Lady Jane's shuffle, muted feet scuffs, and muffled clinks of tools and cookware were the only sounds except for indrawn breaths when light danced off crystalline rose or gold formations.

The river, sometimes hidden, sometimes murmuring like a fluid mirror, reflecting the glow of candles and sculpturings of roof and walls, now and then yielded glimpses of weird white swimming things. Scorpion-like creatures pursued quarry too small to be seen in the gloom. A pale lizard scuttled from a rock near Lad. Startled, he reared his head into a low-hanging swag before Christy could control him. The end of the swag crashed down, striking Lad's shoulder. The impact brought down a hail of fragments and whole stalactites. Scared, drubbed, and smarting, Christy urged Lad forward. The candles ahead halted at the racket. Fortunately Christy was far enough behind that the mineral downpour hadn't struck anyone else.

"Are you all right?" her mother whispered.

Christy wiped blood out of her eyes, explored the cut on her forehead, and then felt along Lad, searching for any injuries. "I'm fine," she whispered back. "Lad has a gash on the shoulder, but it's not bleeding much."

"I hate caves!" Ellen breathed.

It seemed forever, but, at last, the heaven of blue sky shone ahead. One by one, they blew out candles in the big open chamber. As they waited for their day vision to return, a figure rose from beside the ancient mortar.

"Animals are welcome here." The voice had a husky, unused quality, like the rustle of cornstalks. Beyond her, in the valley, they saw the cattle grazing. "But if humans mean to stay, as it seems you do . . ." — she indicated their belongings with a sweep of a leather-clad arm — "I must ask why you've come and who you are."

Author's Note

As shown in the first volume of this trilogy, *The Underground River*, there had been war along the Kansas-Missouri border since 1854 with brutal massacres by both Free-State and proslavery forces. Soldiers on both sides were overwhelmingly from farms. Those who used fence rails for campfires had split plenty of them and knew the labor involved. When they turned their horses into a cornfield, they knew how the owners had worked to raise it. When they heaped curtains, clothing, and coverlets on a bed and set them afire, they knew from having watched their mothers and sisters how much patient work they destroyed.

Next to Virginia, Missouri had the highest number of Civil War engagements, although most of these were skirmishes. Indians fought on both sides, and black soldiers served for the first time in Missouri. Throughout most of the war, Union troops controlled St. Louis and sizeable towns, but the countryside was ravaged by regular and irregular forces of both persuasions. Still, there were gleams of humanity. There really was one house along the border that was spared because the mistress nursed the wounded of both sides. There really was a soldier who ran to the man he'd mortally wounded, promised to stay and pray with him till he died, and was himself killed.

Ferocity increased as North and South declared war, and

the Indians south of Kansas in Indian Territory were drawn into the struggle, fighting on both sides. The Indian rôle in the war is depicted in Annie Heloise Abel's *The American Indian as Slaveholder and Secessionist*; *Between Two Fires* by Laurence M. Hauptman; *Stand Watie* by Kenny A. Franks; and *The Civil War in the Indian Territory* by Donald A. Rampp and Lary C. Rampp. Chronicles of the border war that I used most were William E. Connolly's classic, *Quantrill and the Border Wars*; Carolyn M. Bartels's *The Civil War in Missouri Day by Day 1861-1865* and *Civil War Stories of Missouri*; Joanne Chiles Eakin's *The Little Gods: Union Provost Marshals in Missouri 1861-1865*, and *Order Number 11*; and Thomas Goodrich's *Black Flag*. *Gray Ghosts of the Confederacy* by Richard S. Brownlee has a list of all known members of Quantrill's, as well as other, guerrillas with notations of their fate. Very few survived the war. *Bushwhackers of the Border* by Patrick Brophy presents a strongly pro-Southern view and has a map showing the dividing line between prairies and the woodlands that created such a haven for guerrillas. *Three Years With Quantrill as told by John McCorkle to O.S. Barton* gives the guerrilla side of things from the standpoint of a man whose sister was killed in the collapse of the women's prison in Kansas City. *General Sterling Price and the Civil War in the West* by Albert Castel shows Price as a kindly, honorable man who valued Missouri above the Confederacy, but who, through vanity or ineptitude, bungled several good chances to expel Union forces from Missouri. The account of Wilson's Creek is mostly gleaned from *Bloody Hill* by William Riley Brooksher.

I found much of value in Henry Steele Commager's monumental *The Blue and the Gray*, which covers every angle of the war from the writings of participants. Other excellent sources were *Soldiers Blue and Gray* by James L. Robertson,

Jr.; *Army Life in a Black Regiment* by Thomas Wentworth Higginson; and Bell Irvin Wiley's wonderfully readable *The Life of Billy Yank* and *The Life of Johnny Reb*. These reveal the life of the common soldier. An engaging and detailed memoir of the Union Army is *Hardtack and Coffee or the Unwritten Story of Army Life* by John D. Billings. *Doctors in Gray* by H. H. Cunningham shows some of the terrible difficulties of caring for the wounded or sick. Excellent information on uniforms and equipment are in these volumes of the Osprey Men-at-Arms series: *American Civil War Armies, Union; American Civil War Armies, Confederate;* and *American Civil War Armies, Volunteer Militia,* all written by Philip Katcher and illustrated by Ron Volstad.

An excellent overview of the border troubles is in *The Civil War in the American West* by Alvin M. Josephy, Jr. Jay Monaghan's *Civil War on the Western Border 1854–1865* is lively reading that captures the human essence of the conflict, although events are sometimes telescoped as is inevitable in a work covering so many complicated situations.

Soldiers have always sung, and the war had spirited tunes on both sides. I listened often, with great enjoyment, to Bobby Horton sing *Homespun Songs of the Confederacy, Volumes 1 through 6* and *Homespun Songs of the Union Army, Volumes 1 through 4*. From the humorous "Goober Peas" to the cantering lilt of "Riding a Raid", the fervor of "Maryland, My Maryland" or "The Battle Hymn of the Republic" to the melancholy "Lorena", these evoke the dreams, fears, courage, and laughter of those young men.

The Ozarks have many extensive caverns, some with underground rivers. I like to think that, while war raged all around, there was a valley of peace for all creatures.

Jeanne Williams
Cave Creek Canyon

About the Author

Jeanne Williams was borne in Elkhart, Kansas, a small town along the Santa Fe Trail. In 1952 she enrolled at the University of Oklahoma where she majored in history and attended Foster-Harris's writing classes. Her writing career began as a contributor to pulp magazines in which she eventually published more than seventy Western, fantasy, and women's stories. Over the same period, she produced thirteen novels set in the West for the young adult audience, including *The Horsetalker* (1961) and *Freedom Trail* (1973), both of which won the Spur Award from the Western Writers of America. Her first Western historical romance, *A Lady Bought with Rifles* (1976), was published in 1976 and sold 600,000 copies in mass merchandise paperback editions. Her historical novels display a wide variety of settings and solidly researched historical backgrounds such as the proslavery forces in Kansas in *Daughter of the Sword* (1979), or the history of Arizona from the 1840s through contemporary times in her Arizona trilogy — *The Valiant Women* (1980), which won a Spur Award, *Harvest of Fury* (1981), and *The Mating of Hawks* (1982). Her heroines are various: a traveling seamstress in *Lady of No Man's Land* (1988), a schoolteacher in *No Roof but Heaven* (1990), a young girl heading up a family of four orphans in *Home Mountain* (1990) which won the Spur Award for Best Novel of the West for that year. She was also the recipient of the Levi Straus Saddleman Award. The authentic historical level of her writing distinguishes her among her peers, and her works have set standards for those who follow in her path. *The Trampled Fields*, the final book in her *Beneath the Burning Ground* trilogy, will be her next Five Star Western.

lem was similarly out of focus. We were saying quite openly that French unwillingness to characterize the war as a Western response to Communist infiltration rendered impossible the active support of "other" free world nations. But quite contrary to this policy, we continued to dole out economic and military aid in support of France's plainly weak political position in Indochina. No sharper indication of this contradictory approach toward Indochina was available than in Washington's predictable reaction to the July 3 declaration. Two months previously, on May 13, 1953, the State Department had written Senator John F. Kennedy concerning official thinking with respect to French policy. By the accords of 1949 and 1950, the letter stated in unusually emphatic language, France "had granted such a full measure of control to the 3 states over their own affairs that the point of no return to their former colonial or semicolonial status had been amply passed and these 3 countries became sovereign states." [34] It was hence not surprising when, on September 30, the United States and France reaffirmed the declaration and announced an additional $385,000,000 loan to Paris [35]—despite the Administration's supposed opposition to just the kind of evasive language contained in the declaration, which must surely have been recognized as a temporizing measure to prolong France's hold on the Indochinese states. The Secretary of State also shunted aside temporarily the fear of becoming identified with French colonialism. At a news conference on July 14, he referred to the July 3 declaration as "a very clear and unequivocal offer of full independence and sovereignty to the states" of Indochina.[36]

While the President may therefore have felt, and quite correctly, that the French cause was inextricably linked to white colonialism, it is probable that the United States, by virtue of its continued support of France and its acceptance of French promises, likewise became attached in Vietnamese minds to imperialist ambitions.[37] The DRV's campaign to control popular opinion, which had expanded perceptibly as the winter 1953 began, may not have been successful entirely because of fervent nationalism; [38] but that majority control resided in the Communist camp is incontestable. And it is difficult to believe that peasant hostility, or at least apathy, was directed only toward France and not, after 1950, toward her American counterpart. In point of fact, Communist propaganda, beginning with the first appearance of American aid, turned upon the United States as the number one supporter of, and eventual replacement for, French rule.[39]

What reasoning lay behind the Administration's willingness to accept at face value French assurances of further concessions to the Associated States? Certainly the United States was fully aware, as Ambassador Heath has testified,[40] that the war "was not merely a military struggle . . . but a political one as well, and that French-Viet efforts to combat the communist forces would be greatly helped by an outright French engagement to grant absolute sovereignty to the Associated States." But the over-riding fear in Washington was that, if pressured too much by the United States, the French Parliament would be provoked into voting for a pullout of the Corps. France was in the struggle for the preservation of French interests; if these had to be compromised by American demands, the way was opened for an eventual U.S. "takeover." Seeing the French depart was precisely what Washington did not want, for that would have meant either abandoning Indochina or taking the single irrevocable step the Administration was determined at all costs to avoid: the dispatch of ground forces to another Asian war. The Administration's dilemma is clear: It could make intimations to the French, but could not give orders; it could urge the Vietnamese to be patient, but could give them few assurances; [41] because it needed French forces in Indochina, it cared little that Paris regarded them as protectors of French interests instead of barriers against the Communist conquest of Southeast Asia. And as

EDC came to have top priority in American security planning for Western Europe, it was doubly vital that the National Assembly not be antagonized by American criticism of France's approach to Indochina.[42] The American position had consequently undergone only slight change since 1950, when Hanson W. Baldwin, military editor of the *New York Times*, was informed both by Ambassador Heath in Saigon and by Washington officials "that our policy toward Indochina had to be essentially a French policy, that we were aiding France, that they were running the war, not we, and that we could not possibly take an independent position." [43]

The same fear of a French withdrawal once the United States pushed hard for meaningful concessions to the Associated States prevented Congressmen concerned about the political situation there from legislating greater leverage for the American aid program. Senator Barry Goldwater, Republican of Arizona, had proposed an amendment to the MSA (Mutual Security Act) bill on July 1 that would have prohibited offering appropriated funds to France until "satisfactory assurance" was given the President that a target date would be set for the "complete independence" of the Associated States.[44] The strong language in the amendment led Senator Kennedy to offer a substitute. Kennedy proposed that U.S. aid "be administered in such a way as to encourage through all available means the freedom and independence desired by the peoples of the Associated States, including the intensification of the military training of the Vietnamese." Although the new amendment removed the tone of an ultimatum and did not propose that aid be conditioned upon a French grant of independence, it was roundly defeated.[45] The Government, supported by a Congress not yet fully engrossed in events in Indochina, prepared to go along with the French military effort and keep key political problems in the background. Rejecting change, Washington found safety in "holding the line," a policy which it believed all the more warranted upon presentation of a new military strategy by General Navarre.

While Western and American security factors pressured the French to stay on in Indochina despite the political handicaps inherent in our support of a colonial power, the French prepared to make what proved a final stand against growing Vietminh resistance. Having gained an important and heartening victory at Lang Son in the northeast corner of Vietnam on July 17, General Navarre submitted a broad plan of action to the Committee of National Defense at Paris. The plan called for increasing the size of French Union forces from 200,000 to 250,000 and of native troops from 200,000 to 300,000. By the end of 1954, it was expected that the 550,000 goal would be attained, that total strength would then exceed estimates of Vietminh manpower by 150,000, and that victory would be accomplished in a dramatic offensive during 1954 and 1955.[46] According to Navarre,[47] the plan further envisaged a relaxation of France's attitude toward Indochinese independence. Inasmuch as a buildup of native forces was contemplated, genuine Indochinese support for the war was required. But the general's hope that France would renounce its colonial ambitions and join with the United States in guaranteeing Indochinese independence was deflated by the lack of support at home.

The Navarre Plan received a far warmer reception in Washington than in Paris. American policy planners were pleased that complete victory would be realized within two years at the most, and their contentment was part of the reasoning behind the $385,000,000 loan of September 30. Premier Laniel, however, considered the plan a halfway measure. Only three days after it was presented to the Committee on National Defense (July 24), the Panmunjom armistice agreement was signed. The Laniel Government had hopes of following the example of the United States and negotiating with the DRV for a *cessez-de-feu*.[48] This viewpoint, backed by a number of cabinet members and notably by Anthony Eden as well,[49] was made more explicit during September and October. Speaking at the Eighth Session of the General Assembly on September 25, the head of the French delegation, Maurice Schumann (who was also Deputy Minister for Foreign Affairs), suggested using the ongoing Panmunjom Political Conference to negotiate the Indochina issue.[50] Of greater significance was a major address before the National Assembly by Laniel himself on October 27. In the course of a full-scale debate on the government's Indochina policy, Laniel backed the Navarre Plan [51] but added that peace had always been France's "supreme objective" in the war. If it were necessary that Communist China be a party to peacemaking, that could not be excluded. Citing statements by Soviet Premier Georgi Malenkov and China's Chou En-lai, and then latching on to Dulles' September 2 pronouncement that "the return of peace in Indochina" was conceivable "if Communist China desired it," Laniel went on:

Which of us would object to the idea of negotiations on the international plane for the reestablishment of peace in Indochina? . . . My Government now stands ready to avail itself of every opportunity to make peace, whether it is to be found in Indochina or on the international level. . . . We shall make every effort to bring this war that was imposed on France to a just and honorable conclusion. . . .[52]

France, he reiterated, was no more interested in a military solution than the United States had been in Korea; his government "would be happy to welcome a diplomatic solution of the conflict" if an "honorable solution were in view. . . ."

Laniel's statement carried the day in the Assembly, which revealed its own strong leanings toward a settlement the next day when it returned a vote of confidence of 330–260.[53] With French public opinion equally desirous of ending the seemingly interminable and costly struggle in the rice paddies,[54] Washington clearly had cause for concern. The American reaction was not long in coming. Vice President Richard M. Nixon, on a tour of the war front in November, made the brash statement that the United States would never approve a peace that "would place people who want independence under a foreign bondage." In an evident rebuttal of the Laniel position, Nixon added that "It is impossible to lay down arms until victory is completely won." [55] Far stronger than a "feeler" of Paris' attitude, the Vice President's comments were completely in keeping with American policy, which had as its prime object the maintenance of French Union forces in the thick of things. As the *New York Times* noted editorially, "From the United States view the biggest single problem in Asia now is to keep the long-growing French disillusionment with the seven-year campaign from exploding into an indefinite truce of the Korean type." [56] As later developments made clear, signs of dissatisfaction with the war and a penchant for acceptance of a truce began to place both London and Paris in direct counterpoint to the American objective of ousting the Communists from Indochina.

The probability that adverse developments at the front would cause the movement for talks with the Communists to mushroom pushed Washington into further compromising its opposition to the French view on independence for Vietnam. Ho Chi Minh's peace offer in November, which was probably designed to encourage that movement, likely also affected the decision of the three allies to meet in Bermuda in early December. As a result of this high-level conference—attended by Eisenhower, Churchill, and Foreign Minister Georges Bidault in place of the ailing Laniel—the "vital importance" of the French war effort "to the defence of the free world" was recognized.[57] Reports from the scene of the meeting indicated additional, though unpublicized, agreements: a promise from Bidault to press ahead with the war and not take up Ho's proposals for negotiations; unanimity on the preconditions to acceptance of a Soviet-proposed Big Five (including the CPR) meeting, among which was a genuine desire by the Communists to break the Korean peace talk deadlock.[58] For the French, this latter point had the advantage of linking the Korean settlement to the Indochina war, thereby assuring continued American support. Washington may have been calmed, in return, by French acknowledgment of the war's connection with the overall anti-communist struggle. Also, Bidault's promise probably allayed fears that negotiations would be considered, prompting the fall of the Laniel cabinet and propelling a march to the conference table from a position of military weakness. Once again, however, Washington had sacrificed in principle in order to insure an uninterrupted military effort; it had left unsettled the problem of independence which, as one Vietnamese put it, "must be recognized, not only as a deep national aspiration of the Indochinese people, but also as a weapon, the most important one, to win the war." [59]

The Western position was hence only superficially harmonious. While the July 3 declaration had promised to "complete" the construction of three independent states from Indochina, while new monetary subsidies had been granted the Navarre Plan, and while renewed encouragement had been voiced at Bermuda, all these tended to obfuscate the divisive tendencies that underlay allied policy on Indochina. In London and Paris, a sizable body of official as well as public opinion already held for negotiating with the Communists on a truce in the Southeast Asia region. It was a feeling that, as Laniel's speech unveiled, was not confined to the opposition parties but reached into the highest echelons. If Indochina really was to be kept out of Communist hands, a radical departure from existing policies was desperately needed to alter the course of the war for France and save American policy from defeat by association.

Yet the implications of the resurgent Vietminh military and political campaigns of late 1953 had not produced any fundamental changes in American policy. While cognizant of the essentially political nature of Vietminh growth, the Administration was apparently not as familiar with the factors that accounted for French decline. Washington's thinking seems instead to have rigidified around the belief that the Navarre Plan would ultimately reverse the tide of battle and somehow eliminate the need to rehash the volatile colonialist question. Considerable optimism in fact pervaded the Western camp.

In May, General Raoul Salan (Navarre's predecessor) had predicted a "shift" in the war to France's advantage within three years; [60] and in August, Navarre himself said that within one year his forces would have command of the situation and would be able to carry the war to the enemy.[61] Now, in December, Secretary Dulles, questioned about these prognostications in light of the Vietminh invasion of Laos, denied that Indochina had been cut in half. His basic confidence in "the timetable of General Navarre's plan" had not diminished; the war would, he agreed, be over in one year.[62] The motivation of Dulles' statement, so precise in prediction and devoid of qualifications, seems to have run deeper than the boosting of morale or reassurance of the public. Like others to follow, the remark was apparently in line with actual judgments of the war situation held at the time in Washington.*

As the new year opened, prospects for the Navarre Plan took a sharp turn for the worse, gradually cracking the facade of optimism. The general had intended that Dienbienphu serve as a bottleneck to plug up Vietminh access into Laos and the Red River delta. What is not generally realized is that the chiefs of MAAG, first Major General Thomas J. H. Trapnell and later (in February 1954) Lieutenant General John W. ("Iron Mike") O'Daniel, concurred in the Dienbienphu opera-

---

* Had Dulles been hesitant about the Navarre Plan at this date, it would seem that a less clear-cut statement could have been offered to the press. He might, for instance, have said that he thought the plan would work *if* greater mobility on the field could be attained and *if* military operations were coupled with strengthened political measures.

tion.[63] General Giap evidently spotted the weaknesses in the plan. Having given every sign of marching to Savannakhet and Luang Prabang, Giap reversed his tracks in the afterphase of a classic feinting operation and returned to Vietnamese territory. French intelligence, on the basis of interceptions of Giap's orders, notified Navarre that there was the strong possibility four Vietminh divisions would arrive at Dienbienphu by December 28. Downgrading Vietminh tactical capabilities, and believing that Giap could not for long maintain 40,000 men so far from their natural bases, Navarre dismissed the report as part of the "noise" of intelligence.[64]

In reality, Giap's decision was precisely what Navarre had originally hoped for—an opportunity to pit his 12,000 élite troops against the core of the Vietminh in conventional battle, and thus to break the back of the VPA. On January 1, 1954, however, Navarre wrote secretly to the French Government.[65] Two weeks before, he observed, he would have estimated his chances for success at one hundred percent. Now, he could make no such guarantee. The Indochina theatre had become "above all an air battle"; if that battle were lost, it might mean the end of the entire French effort. The fate of his garrison hinged on whether the Vietminh "succeed[ed] at employing their heavy weapons [received from China] . . ." Navarre requested air power reinforcement, apparently to interdict Vietminh supply lines to the CPR border. He also announced his intention to take a "chance" by remaining at Dienbienphu although, on the same day, he ordered that a secret study be undertaken (Operation XENOPHON) in the event the fortress had to be abandoned.[66] Once certain of his plan's feasibility, Navarre was now unsure; yet he would stake the entire French presence in northern Vietnam and upper Laos on the defense of Dienbienphu.

Further working against the plan was the growth of the Vietminh. By late 1953 the VPA, though outnumbered by the French, was "capable of deploying in divisional strength," especially in the northern delta region where Navarre vowed to make a stand.[67] A Central Intelligence Agency report on December 30, 1953 confirmed this finding: Vietminh troops were attacking at 10,000-man strength.[68] With Chinese aid on the increase and Vietminh attacks at the level of conventional armies, the Administration was being cornered into making a difficult choice, one that only months before would have been deemed unlikely. Complete abandonment of the French and strategically vital Indochina was unthinkable. Washington would therefore have to decide between continuing to rely upon existing policies and gingerly going beyond previous statements. In the "New Look" lay one key to the unfolding drama of 1954, and it is therefore essential that the steps leading toward that strategic renovation be traced.

4. STRATEGY: THE NEW LOOK AND "MASSIVE RETALIATION"

PROGRAMMING FOR THE LONG HAUL

The basis for the vital policy decision to depart from the Truman security program rested on a critical examination not only of the Korean experience but of the entire containment era. A clear majority within the Eisenhower Administration, as well as a vocal public sector, considered Democratic foreign policy anywhere from "soft" to near-treason and urged a "tougher" approach to the communists. On the other hand, some wanted a reduction in commitments, both military and monetary, charging that containment implied in the end an impossible attempt to stop communist power plays along the entire Euro-Asian front. The New Look emerged as the end product of these contradictory forces.

John Foster Dulles, who had by May 1952 clearly spelled out a bold alternative to containment,[1] took the lead in pacifying the first sector. His influence was strongly felt in the New Look's reorientation of the defense establishment toward greater reliance than before upon American air power superiority. This shift delved with Eisenhower's concern about the overwhelming monetary and manpower burdens allegedly imposed upon the country under the wartime and postwar Truman budgets. Eisenhower insisted upon developing maximum strength at minimum cost, building national security on the twin pillars of economic and military strength, strictly correlating economy and defense requirements, and avoiding the mistake of generating inflation through vast outlays of money for the military. As a consequence of these conflicting pressures for a powerful as well as a frugal United States, all the services would feel a pinch in allocations, with the Army the hardest hit. Whereas the Truman people had advance plans for utilizing the armed forces in a variety of war situations, "Eisenhower cleared away some of this underbrush by ordering the Pentagon to assume that if we got into war it would be fought with nuclear weapons," [2] tactical as well as strategic.[3]

The aim of the New Look strategy was clearly to avoid a repetition of Korea, that is, of a large-scale commitment of ground forces abroad without decisive results. National Security Council (NSC) paper 162/2, approved by the President on October 30, 1953, specifically incorporated this aim.[4] On December 9 the final New Look document was handed to Defense Secretary Charles E. Wilson by the Joint Chiefs.[5] It closely followed the formats of NSC 162/2 and a previous study made by the Chiefs immediately upon taking office. Both general and limited wars were recognized; but in both cases, nuclear weapons were to be relied on either for deterrence or actual combat. A ready and mobile strategic reserve based at home and strengthened by a redeployment of forces overseas was asked. In line with Dulles' contention that the West could best insure its vital security interests by utilizing native forces in conflicts abroad,[6] the document stipulated that ground troops in limited conflicts were expected to come from allies. Mobile ground, sea, and air power would be provided by the United States, but only in an ancillary capacity. The Administration's apparent unity of mind on the budget-military relationship by December 1953 thus paved the way for what basically amounted to a substitution of more technical weapons, air power, and continental defenses for the large numbers of ground troops that dominated the military as a consequence of the Korean War.

The final defense program that emerged in late 1953 immediately became the subject of heated controversy. The debate divided generally between those who saw a "stretch-out" of defense spending as incompatible with international realities and those who believed with equal conviction that across-the-board reductions in manpower and allocations would not vitiate national security. To the first group belonged a number of key military leaders under Truman, notably Eisenhower's choice as Army Chief of Staff, General Matthew B. Ridgway. Once the Army was cut from twenty to eighteen divisions, Ridgway registered his strong objections to the New Look line even though he had consented to the final paper of December 9.[7] In words which would become significant during the spring 1954 crisis over Indochina, Ridgway testified that the ground soldier was still "the ultimate key to victory" and would "remain so in the foreseeable future."[8] But proponents of air power were equally at variance with the New Look despite the fact that the Air Force was the chief beneficiary of the program over the long run. Some in the military could not understand the seeming disregard of NSC 68, the strategy paper of the Truman Administration which had forecast Soviet achievement of a dangerous level of nuclear response or launch capability by 1954.[9] Considerable debate over Soviet nuclear strength and potential came into the open in budget hearings. The Administration sought to calm the dissenters from both Army and Air Force. To the former, Admiral Arthur W. Radford, JCS Chairman, gave assurances that the New Look planned "force levels which provide us [with] versatile, combat forces in readiness, and an adequate mobilization base."[10] To the latter, the President insisted that the defense program recognized "the great importance of air power" by allocating "60 cents out of every defense dollar for air power."[11] But the controversy continued well into 1955.

The arguments for and against the New Look clearly reflected vastly different reactions to the Korean experience. The outgoing Joint Chiefs, and Ridgway, revealed in their testimony a reluctance again to demobilize and risk the same kind of unpreparedness uncovered in June 1950. The limited war decision in Korea had capped a postwar period in which American inability to mold events or meet small-scale crises with only its nuclear monopoly had been starkly spotlighted. The Chiefs therefore argued that 1953–1954 were years of maximum danger which required a buildup of forces rather than a stretch-out. Economizing during those years carried a distinct element of risk; ground troops as well as a nuclear deterrent capacity were vital to a credible defense posture. Against these views, the Eisenhower Administration postulated the thesis that an emphasis on air power would deter aggression and avoid the economic risks of a major peaking of forces. Limited wars and large-scale troop deployments overseas were verboten; nuclear weapons were now so sophisticated that their use was feasible in all types of wars. By relying on such weapons, ground troops could be gradually "replaced" and indigenous forces trained to do the job of American GI's in brushfire conflicts; but in case of major aggression, the United States would not again refrain from using its massive nuclear power. What remained to be seen was whether the New Look's reputed strategic advantages could meet the challenge posed by indirect aggression in Indochina. We shall want to pursue, therefore, the extent to which the New Look impinged upon policy-making on Indochina, upon diplomacy with our allies, and upon the Communist orbit's strategy in the war.

THE JANUARY 12 SPEECH AND ITS IMPACT ON THE WEST

Unfulfilled French optimism in the field and growing distaste for the war at home, Vietminh victories in the northern delta and increasing Chinese assistance to Giap, American disturbance at the danger to its Far East security coupled with the CPR's disregard of its warnings, and uncertainties at home over the wisdom of the new military planning—all these forces converged with a climactic policy announcement from the State Department. On January 12, 1954, John Foster Dulles went before the Council on Foreign Relations with a statement of Administration purposes and principles in implementing the New Look.

Secretary Dulles began by explaining that behind the New Look and the contemplated withdrawal of two divisions from Korea (announced in the President's Budget Message of January 21) was an attempt to avoid the wholesale commitment of American fighting men to every brushfire conflict on the Sino-Soviet periphery. Soviet policy, he said, was to lure the United States into overextending itself, thereby creating, as Lenin had predicted, "practical bankruptcy" of the West's financial and manpower resources. "It is not sound military strategy," said Dulles, "permanently to commit United States land forces to Asia to a degree that gives us no strategic reserves." The alternative he offered was "community deterrent power," "a maximum deterrent at a bearable cost," "a great capacity to retaliate instantly, by means and at places of our choosing." "Local defense will always be important," Dulles stated. But strict adherence to the containment thesis operated solely to the benefit of the Communist bloc in the long run, and he therefore proposed to reinforce that concept "by the further deterrent of massive retaliatory power." [12]

The timing of Dulles' speech makes it difficult to establish whether or not events abroad prompted it; but the available evidence suggests that it was intended to confirm the Administration's changes in the military establishment, not to rattle American air power over areas in dispute with the Communists.[13] Dulles later denied that the January 12 speech bore any connection to "present conditions" (early 1954) in Indochina.[14] And the address itself made only passing reference to the Indochina situation. Nevertheless, certain other aspects of the speech—particularly the phrase "massive retaliatory power"—quickly became the focus of attention. The editor of *Foreign Affairs*, Hamilton Fish Armstrong, in asking Dulles to expand upon the speech, pointed out that "doubts remain in some minds both as to your meaning at some points and as to probable consequences at others. I have been hearing questions vigorously asked in private by people of far from negligible importance, and certainly they will soon be asked in public. . . ." [15]

In ensuing weeks qualifications and redefinitions, supplied primarily by Dulles himself, sought to clear up this great residue of uncertainty. In the first place, Dulles definitely did not mean that retaliation in case of armed attack would be instant, automatic, and nuclear. Atomic bombs and tactical nuclear weapons were intended to be but one part of the defense arsenal; they would be *stressed* in case of *major* aggression but would not be used indiscriminately.[16] At least theoretically, the Administration retained the right to choose from several crisis responses, including the wide-scale deployment of ground forces.[17] In fact, "Close associates of Dulles have confirmed, in interviews, that what he had in mind was a whole spectrum of possible degrees of retaliation." [18]

Furthermore, retaliation would never be automatic. What the Administration intended was that the enemy recognize our *capacity* to wreak swift devastation, not our *necessity* to do so. Dulles pointed out that the possession of a massive, instant strike capability was essential; but he added that such a capacity "does not impose the necessity of using it in every instance of attack. It is not our intention to turn every local war into a general war." [19] What some critics missed was the Secretary's admission that limited "setbacks to the cause of freedom" were to be expected, especially since "massive atomic and thermonuclear retaliation is not the kind of power which could most usefully be evoked under all circumstances." [20] A final disturbing element in the speech concerned the meaning of "our choosing" in case of attack. Dulles assured those who read into the speech a qualification of collective defense that prior consultations with our allies would be forthcoming before a retaliatory blow were struck.[21]

These clarifications during early 1954 were mainly necessary for the dissipation of domestic rumors and accusations. Abroad, the January 12 speech seems to have raised few eyebrows. Although the reactions of high officials in London and Paris have not been disclosed, commentaries in the leading newspapers may be indicative. *The Times* of London and the *Manchester Guardian Weekly*, close followers of American foreign policy developments, paid scant attention to the speech. The *Guardian* did not immediately comment on it at all, while *The Times* only carried the text. The French were similarly disposed to treating the speech lightly. Aside from reporting it, for instance, *Le Monde* refrained from editorializing. It would be legitimate to suppose that if the speech was suspect of having application to specific foreign policy problems of the moment (such as Indochina), London and Paris had adopted a wait-and-see attitude.

That Dulles emphatically rejected various constructions of the address, and that neither allied capital evinced any noticeable uneasiness, to a certain extent obfuscated one point which would later become highly disruptive of a common Indochina policy. In the event of an enemy attack upon some area of free world value, Dulles had said that "an aggressor must not be able to count upon a sanctuary status for those resources which he does not use in committing aggression." [22] The Secretary further stated explicitly that atomic weapons would be considered "conventional" when retaliating and should (he felt) be used in both the general or local war "whenever and wherever it would be of advantage to do so, taking account of all relevant factors." [23] Placed beside Dulles' previous assertions, this strategy, applied to Europe as well as to Asia, implied that atomic weapons might be used as both first- and second-strike weapons. Clearly, however, the use of "conventional" atomic weapons to meet a Soviet land attack in Europe might be extended to the case of a Chinese ground march into Vietnam. As the Korean conflict demonstrated, the primary interest of European allies lay in keeping small wars from becoming larger ones for fear of ultimately shifting the theatre from Asia to Europe. It was precisely on this point—the implications of American strategy for war in Asia—that allied debate over Indochina in the coming months would rest. When unity was required, the basis was already laid for wide disagreement on fundamental strategic issues as well as political policies.

AMERICAN STRATEGY AND ITS IMPACT ON THE COMMUNIST CAMP

Whatever effect the January 12 address had upon the Communist world cannot be considered apart from either the evolution in Communist world strategy that occurred during 1953 or the different values attached to "national liberation movements" of the Indochina type by Moscow and Peking. Both aspects became of primary significance as Washington fulminated against China between mid-1953 and January 1954.

The View from Moscow. Uncertainty in Soviet politics in the immediate aftermath of Josef Stalin's death lent itself to a calmer international outlook. Repetitions of the blatant probings of Western strengths and weaknesses exhibited during the 1946–1952 period were generally avoided; the post-Stalin period marked at least a temporary lull in Soviet thrusts and a search for détente pending a consolidation of Party power. By late 1953 there were already signs of division within the Soviet leadership. Premier Malenkov, Chairman of the Council of Ministers, headed a "New Course" in domestic policy linked to the potentiality for international peace. Throughout the remainder of 1953 and into early 1954,

Malenkov in substance rejected Lenin's formulation of war as the inescapable by-product of capitalism, became convinced that the United States feared the consequences of and would therefore not initiate nuclear war, and postulated that the receding of world tensions was achievable. In a major address before the Supreme Soviet on August 8, 1953,[24] Malenkov highlighted the significance attached by the Kremlin leadership to the peace offensive. Although his eyes were open to "the fact that there are forces which are working against the policy of relaxing international tension . . . ," Malenkov seemed especially concerned with dramatizing Soviet interest in peace. He reported that the international situation showed "clear improvement," and he sensed "a certain relaxation in the international atmosphere . . . for the first time in the postwar years." Perhaps speaking with self-assurance of Soviet deterrent power—the announcement of a hydrogen device was made August 12—Malenkov asserted flatly: "We consider that there is no objective basis for conflict between the United States of America and the Soviet Union."

Malenkov's views on deterrence and war [25] were rivaled by those of a faction led by Nikita Khrushchev, then ranking member of the Central Committee Secretariat of the Communist Party (CPSU).[26] The position taken by Stalin and propounded by Khrushchev stressed the inevitability of war during the lifetime of the capitalist system. It was held that despite possession by both the Soviet Union and the United States of atomic bombs, nuclear world war was still possible and Russia had to be prepared for that eventuality. The United States was charged with "conducting a mad arms race" [27] and "intensive preparations for a new war" that made it "the basic threat to the cause of peace." [28]

Thus, at the very time that criticism of the New Look was at a peak, the Malenkov government was undergoing a similar attack; and, in both cases, the dispute was grounded in a protest over the in-group's assessment of the international situation and the military posture to be assumed accordingly.

It is not surprising that Moscow waited until late March before issuing a full reply to Dulles' speech; the speech had caught the Kremlin leadership at a moment of acute discord which would not be resolved for two months. The inner debate is left at this juncture; but its threads will be picked up later, for it became crucial as events in Indochina reached crisis proportions.

The View from Peking. The thesis of Liu Shao-ch'i's speech of November 1949, which had posited the Chinese revolution as a model for underdeveloped nations, underwent delicate revision during succeeding years. By the time of the 1954 Geneva Conference, the CPR had changed considerably its world perspective and calculations of the international balance of power, manifesting a certain appreciation for trends which it previously denigrated or overlooked.

First, and perhaps primary, among the significant signs that a recalculation of the world power balance had taken place in Peking was the disposition toward recognizing the existence of a "third force" in international politics, that of the nonaligned state.[29] A second shift was away from direct encouragement of, or participation in, wars of "national liberation." The *People's Daily* in early 1953 continued to advocate "waging resolute and unyielding struggle against" colonial powers as the only means of throwing off "the yoke of imperialism";[30] but Peking was hesitant to make a more specific commitment.

One consideration behind these subtle but emphatic changes in viewpoint was the costliness of the Korean War for the Chinese economy. Barring some fresh threat to its security, military adventures were not in order. China's professed desire by late 1952 was to settle the Korean War firmly and get on with the task of "socialist reconstruction" at home, a desire reinforced by the regime's announcement in 1953 of its first Five Year Plan. Secondly, setbacks to "wars of liberation" in

Korea and Malaya evidently led Peking to adjust its methods of promoting pro-Chinese sentiment. Beginning with the Peace Conference of the Asian and Pacific Regions in September 1952, Peking made known its desire for peaceful coexistence with all nations regardless of their political systems.[31]

Failures in Korea and Malaya and a need for economic acceleration at home provide only a partial explanation for the regime's adoption of a peace tack. The death of Premier Stalin and the ensuing search for détente in Europe by Malenkov undoubtedly also had an impact upon Peking. Malenkov's statements expressing a hopeful outlook for the improvement of Soviet-American relations were at this time generally upheld by the Chinese.[32] Nevertheless, despite tangible as well as polemical signs of genuine closeness between the two Communist powers,[33] Peking appeared to hold back from a blanket endorsement of Malenkov's international outlook. For the Chinese, although the international situation had "somewhat eased," American obstructionist tactics proved that the United States was "unwilling to bring about a further easing of international tension." [34] In fact, the United States "has not abandoned its desperate attempt to turn Asia into the hotbed of a new world war." [35] The *People's Daily*, in an editorial of January 4, 1954, pointed out that "wide and irreconcilable discrepancies exist between the peace gestures and the policy practiced by the U.S. ruling circles." [36] In sum, Chinese analyses suggested that the outlook was less propitious than Malenkov imagined, and implied that Moscow's optimism over American intentions had little in common with reality.

The real point of disagreement, one that is important for our analysis with respect to events in Indochina, seems to have rested on the respective perceptions of United States policy in the Far East. During Malenkov's tenure as the leading spokesman of Soviet foreign policy, aspects of American "aggressiveness" in the Far East were discussed, but without the same sense of urgency characteristic of Chinese statements.

For instance, at a dinner welcoming the North Korean Prime Minister, Malenkov referred to the United States-Republic of Korea Treaty of Mutual Defense as a "military springboard" for future American operations. But he added that "all peace-loving forces . . . can and must make the Korean truce a starting point for new efforts aimed at further relaxation of international tension throughout the world, including the [Far] East." [37] To the contrary, the Chinese showed concern over the Administration's Far East military activities. The *People's Daily*,[38] beginning in February 1953, dealt on almost a daily basis with topics such as the President's State of the Union Message and its implications for Chiang Kaishek's future military moves; United States exploratory discussions with Pakistan over a military pact; American bases in Japan; the organization of a United States "bloc" in the Far East; and the general American aim of fomenting war in the Pacific. The regime seemed unimpressed by Eisenhower's order of a cutback in troops for the Far East. *World Culture*, attuned to the thinking of the Ministry of Foreign Affairs, reasoned that disengagement was actually a policy of substituting Asian soldiers for GI's in order to carry out expansion of war under an Asian front.[39] Where the Kremlin saw the danger of war receding, Peking saw no end in sight to the peril.

Chinese regard for the course of American action in Asia was reflected even more clearly once the New Look took shape. The essence of the New Look, as seen by NCNA in January 1954, was a worldwide effort on Washington's part to substitute native forces for American soldiers, and "strong air power equipped with atomic and other new weapons" for ground and naval forces. The United States ambition remained "to keep up its long-term war preparation" even though "faced with the two-fold difficulties of manpower shortage and financial pressure. . . ." [40] A more detailed account appeared in *World Culture* following the President's State of the

Union Message for 1954 and Dulles' January 12 speech. The article interpreted the Administration's decision to give added emphasis to air power as follows:

> This is to say that the United States will expand the production of atomic weapons, will not take note of the opposition of all the people of the world but will use the air force to drop atomic bombs, and moreover will, in unison with America's dependencies, use tactical atomic weapons.[41]

By "means of our choosing," according to the same article, Dulles meant atomic weapons. Nevertheless, the author ridiculed the application of those weapons to "places of our choosing." The Korean War *had* been a place of America's choosing; American abstention from use of the bomb was because "the United States had already early lost an atomic weapons monopoly, and moreover atomic weapons indeed cannot serve any purpose in deciding victory or defeat in war. . . ."[42]

With a view toward the shifting tides of Chinese and Soviet thinking, it now rests to determine (or conjecture about) the position occupied by the Indochina crisis in the Communist panoply. Unlike the CPR, the Soviet Union had taken little interest in early developments in communist Vietnam.[43] Soviet aloofness from events there was no better demonstrated than in the difference in timing between Soviet and Chinese recognition of the DRV, and in the formation of the friendship associations. By 1952, in fact, prior Soviet dissent to Chinese claims that Maoism constituted a unique contribution to Communist theory on revolution in Asia had been reversed.[44] From the onset of China's involvement in the Vietminh struggle, the CPR's primacy in Indochina was tacitly accepted by Moscow.

The Russians, of course, contributed to the Vietminh cause. Soviet advisers, for example, were known to be aiding the DRV;[45] and arms shipments to China for use in the Indochina war have already been touched upon. But the main thrust of Soviet involvement was tendentiousness. Press statements revealed that Moscow's design was to undermine the Franco-American alliance, not so much for the sake of the communist struggle over Indochina as for the purpose of blocking a Franco-German entente in EDC. The rearming of Germany, which EDC would facilitate, was deemed a threat directed at Moscow; impugning Washington's aims in Indochina (as by charging that the United States desired to take Indochina over for itself) would, if properly executed, subvert Western unity, cast doubts in Paris over American motives in rearming Germany, and encourage a French reaction that would destroy all hopes for EDC.[46]

The obvious value a settlement in Indochina would have for Russian policy toward EDC, together with Malenkov's forecast of brighter relations with the United States and policy differences within the Kremlin, suggests that the Russian aim in Indochina was to avoid a showdown with the United States, especially over an area outside direct Soviet control. Accordingly, the official army organ *Red Star* proposed ending the Indochina war in a statement days after the Panmunjom armistice.[47] Ho Chi Minh's later offer of a negotiated settlement received similar support from *Pravda* and the government daily, *Izvestia*.[48]

Chinese backing of negotiations, first proclaimed September 2, 1953,[49] fitted conveniently into the reshaped pattern of CPR foreign policy. As the Korean War wore on, Peking's discouragement with a *coup nul* and decision to discuss peace seem to have been prompted by a serious re-evaluation of the tactics in the absorption strategy. There appeared no reason why gains could not be achieved piecemeal (the familiar "two steps forward, one step back" approach) without the risk of incurring disastrous setbacks. As subsequent Chinese diplomatic initiatives would testify, the peace tactic was to be applied more to long-term, *revolutionary* goals, while militant methods remained the chief tactic for high priority, *national* goals. Indochina was, as has been remarked previously, a composite picture: a revolutionary goal, because the war was a Communist struggle against "Western imperialism," nurtured and fought along typically Maoist lines; a national goal, because the area was historically part of China's sphere of influence. The adoption of a peace offensive coincident with the Soviet drive consequently masked China's continued encouragement of struggles such as Ho Chi Minh's.

While it would be premature to attempt a full assessment of the place occupied by American statements in China's strategy in Indochina, some initial comments seem desirable. The January 12 address, coming after months of public discussion in the United States of a "New Look" in defense, does seem to have given both Moscow and Peking cause for renewed attention to, if not anxiety over, American ambitions in the Far East. Viewed in its distorted form from Communist capitals as a potentially dangerous new component of the American foreign policy program, the speech held out with greater clarity than before the possibility of atomic attack on Communist Chinese or even Russian territory. Yet for Peking, considerable room for militant behavior short of armed intervention was apparently still available notwithstanding the Dulles address and the alleged danger of a new world war. The Vietminh, with a favorable wind at their backs, seemed on the brink of major victories that promised achievement of a vital Chinese foreign policy goal, consolidation of control of a border area under a communist power. As far as the Communist Chinese were concerned, then, the January 12 speech left unaltered basic policy directions even as it stimulated renewed caution. The events of February would go a long way toward validating this course while magnifying differences in the West.

5. THE ROAD TO DIENBIENPHU: DIPLOMACY AND STRATEGY, FEBRUARY–MARCH 1954

JANUARY–FEBRUARY: ERECTION OF A DEADLINE

Communist reaction to Dulles' momentous speech of January 12 showed that increased American concern over the fate of the French war effort was not being lightly regarded, particularly in Peking. In ensuing weeks, the Administration's main policy line focused, in the short range, on bolstering the French military position and, in the long view, on impressing upon the Communist camp its solid commitment to Indochina. But while the Chinese devoted greater attention to the Administration's activities, they remained glued to their previous position in support of the Vietminh morally and materially. The fact that deepening concern by Washington was not translated into concrete action could only have confirmed the Communists in their course.

On January 25 General Giap suddenly abandoned his encirclement of Dienbienphu (on the very night the first major assault was expected) and headed his main force for Luang Prabang. Finding the Laotian capital well fortified, he returned to Dienbienphu without attacking.[1] On January 30 came the first report of heavy fighting around the fortress, with aircraft and artillery involved. "Dien Bien Phu can be compared to an aircraft-carrier on land, anchored in the middle of a sea of mountains where the enemy troops are hidden," ran one Saigon broadcast.[2]

The deterioration of the cork-in-the-bottle defense under which Navarre operated did not diminish French optimism. Whatever sobering impression Navarre's secret letter of January 1 made in Paris was offset to a considerable extent by a report on the third from the Commissioner General of Indochina, Maurice Dejean. Not only did Dejean express renewed confidence in victory at Dienbienphu; he cast doubts that a battle would even take place.[3] With the monsoon season only a few months away, with French logistical superiority seemingly assured, and with Giap's decision taken to avoid Luang Prabang, exhilaration again swept the French command. The Vietminh offensive in Laos had been blocked, and any attack by Giap on Dienbienphu would be stymied. *Le Monde's* frontline correspondent, Robert Guillain, wrote critically: "We are carried away, as always, by an unwarranted optimism which unceasingly underestimates the power and courage of our adversary." [4]

Whether because Washington saw an imminent danger to the garrison or because it went along with French optimism, the announcement was made February 6 that forty B-26 bombers and two hundred technicians to help service them would be sent to Indochina.[5] Despite assurances that the technicians would be withdrawn by June 12,[6] the announcement provoked instantaneous outcries that the action would be the forerunner of American participation in the war. Pressed on the question whether the killing of an Air Force technician might bring about United States intervention, the President declared at his February 10 news conference: ". . . no one could be more bitterly opposed to ever getting involved in a hot war in that region than I am. . . ." [7] This flat rejection of intervention, coming over three months after Vice President Nixon's trial balloon suggesting the necessity for a military victory, confused rather than mollified Congressmen. What particularly rankled legislators was the failure of the Administration to inform anyone on the Armed Services or Foreign Relations Committees of either House that bombers or technicians were being dispatched. The impression of intervention without forewarning was daily becoming more ingrained, and accompanying that impression was the recollection of Truman's "police action" in Korea. Disturbance mounted higher when, later in February, the State Department proclaimed that it had taken under consideration the offer by Korea's President Syngman Rhee to use one Republic of Korea division in the Indochina war.[8] The fact that Paris, not Washington, was the first to reject the offer did not pass unnoticed.[9]

The Administration meanwhile was behind several military undertakings in the Far East. At sea, the United States conducted naval maneuvers in early January off the Formosa coast. Late in January an American ship for the first time participated in large-scale maneuvers with the Royal Thai Navy.[10] During mid-February, the United States, Great Britain, and France held joint maneuvers for ten days in the South China Sea.[11] At the same time, the commander of the United States East Atlantic and Mediterranean Fleet, Vice Admiral Jerrauld Wright, paid an informal visit to Burma and India.[12] To accent American air power, General Otto P. Weyland, United States Far East Air Force commander, toured bases on Taiwan in mid-January.[13] To what extent these events departed from normal procedures is unknown; but, as we shall see, the Chinese took notice of them all.

The importance of Indochina was re-emphasized. From Paris came René Pleven who, as defense minister, was one of the highest ranking French officials to visit the area in many years. His visit coincided with a trip by Harold Stassen, head of the Foreign Operations Administration. On returning to Washington, Stassen recommended increased support and commented that the war had received a bad press.[14] His remarks followed by just a few days a broadcast from Dalat, southern Vietnam, that described a Communist encirclement of Dienbienphu.[15]

The future of Indochina had meanwhile shifted to the diplomatic arena as the foreign ministers of the Big Four (the United States, the USSR, Great Britain, and France) met in Berlin in late January. The Berlin Conference had first been proposed in mid-1953 without any intention on the West's part of bringing the Far East situation up for discussion. Quite to the contrary, the Western Big Three strongly resisted Soviet attempts to have Communist China included in a Big Five parley on the whole purview of international problem areas. However, when the Russians finally consented to the original Allied agenda—Big Four talks on the two East-West sore points in Europe, Germany and Austria—they retained for themselves the right at some future date to call for the convening of a five-power roundtable.[16]

From the opening bell the West was put on notice that Moscow considered the German and Austrian questions subordinate to the "threat" of EDC and proper recognition of Communist China's role in international relations through the vehicle of a wide-ranging Big Five conference. V. M. Molotov, the chief Soviet delegate, spent half of his lengthy opening address (January 25) dealing with a five-power conference, the one topic none of the Western representatives had come to discuss.[17]

Initial remarks from the Western side deceptively indicated a solid lineup against the Soviet position. In speeches on January 25 and 26, Dulles lashed out at Communist China's foreign and domestic policies, which he said disqualified Peking for accreditation in international circles. "Nothing that has happened up to date," said Dulles, "enables us to say that Communist China is willing to collaborate in efforts to bring about a solution on an acceptable basis of the Korean or Indo-China questions, or for that matter of any other Asian problem." Dismissing the matter of a five-power conference, Dulles insisted that the delegates return to the issues for which they had met.[18] In these views, the Secretary of State received firm, if only slightly less forceful, backing from Eden and Bidault; both argued that Communist China had shown no sign of a willingness to settle outstanding Asian problems.[19]

The end result of the Berlin Conference belied the inauspicious beginning. In adjourning February 18, the conferees reached the decision to place Indochina and Korea on the agenda of a meeting at Geneva scheduled for April 26. Communist China would be invited to join the Big Four. The attachment during 1953 of preconditions to such a meeting, one of which was concrete steps by the Communists to end the Indochina war,[20] had been retracted, as had all previous indications from Washington that truce talks on Indochina would not be considered while the Communist forces were of threatening proportions.

The reasons behind the sudden about-face at Berlin that had left the German and Austrian problems in suspension and taken up the heart of Soviet proposals were not far to seek. Despite Bidault's verbal steadfastness, the French delegation had clearly been under mounting pressure from Paris to bring back a substantive sign of the government's interest in ending the war. Laniel's reiteration of his "keep fighting-seek talking" platform on January 8 had begun to lose its magic with the Parliament.[21]

Beyond Paris lay the hand of Moscow and the debate over EDC. It was precisely because of French interest in an Indochina settlement that EDC, despite Dulles' naked threat of an "agonizing reappraisal" in the event of Assembly disapproval,[22] could not be rubber-stamped. As perceived from the Quai d'Orsay, the Kremlin held the key to a sincere Communist approach to negotiations on the war. The obvious quid pro quo was French procrastination on (and eventual rejection of) EDC in return for Russian pressure on Communist China and the DRV. No matter how hard Washington fought to convince Paris that EDC was the only answer to lessoning Franco-German hostility and providing for a sound West European defense, a settlement in Asia occupied a higher place in French minds. The French, after all, were at war in Asia; in Europe, where the threat of conflict had once seemed so close in 1950, the need for EDC had substantially diminished with the death of Stalin, the adoption of a far less belligerent program under Malenkov, and the conclusion of a Korean armistice.[23] Paris would therefore have agreed with Hanson Baldwin's observation that the United States was "putting a tremendous amount of weight on EDC which was probably unjustified." [24]

Dulles' acceptance of an international conference at which Communist China would be represented became the target of sharp criticism from both sides of the political aisle on his return from Berlin. But the Secretary was prepared to rebuff his critics; and his ammunition was potent. On the sudden decision to face Peking across the bargaining table for the second time in two years, Dulles retorted quite correctly that negotiations with the Chinese were unavoidable because of French insistence. Bidault had reportedly brought Dulles around to accepting talks with the persuasive argument that China, being the real power behind the Vietminh, could no longer be ignored.[25] And if the United States did not acquiesce on this point, Bidault warned, EDC would doubtless be scuttled.[26] What Bidault probably did not mention was that it was in French interests to *delay* action on EDC until after Geneva so as not to antagonize the Soviets. Yet signs of French determination to end the war through bargaining were too abundant to have been missed in Washington. Premier Laniel, addressing the National Assembly on March 5, once again pleaded the case for a peaceful settlement, and went so far as to offer cease-fire conditions which included ceding northern Vietnam to the Communists.[27] Washington's concern about approaching Geneva from a position of strength must have given way to real anxiety, for it was now abundantly clear that, come what may at Dienbienphu, the French were prepared to throw in the towel on reasonable terms.

Dulles could further contend that diplomatic concessions were wrung from the Soviets in return—a passage in the final communique acknowledging that American recognition of the CPR would not be read into the Geneva Conference; [28] and restriction of the Geneva agenda to Korea and Indochina rather than its extension to topics of no concern to the CPR. But these gains were comparatively minor when contrasted with those of the East. In the first place, the agreement to an international conference enhanced the repeated claims by the Communist camp that no outstanding international issue could be solved without China's participation. Notwithstanding Dulles' denials, the Soviet Union hailed the placement of Indochina on the Geneva agenda as "virtual recognition of the Chinese People's Republic as a great power" which would further world peace despite obstacles imposed by "U.S. aggressive circles." [29] For the CPR, which had persistently held out for a five-power conference, the prospect of again confronting the United States was received on a similar note of triumph.[30]

This significant propaganda victory was coupled with another development of far greater consequence. By agreeing to a high-level conference on Indochina in the first place, the Western delegates inadvertently contributed to the inauguration of a crucial period during which the CPR increased its arms deliveries and encouraged the Vietminh to drive for a spectacular victory. The Chinese Communists had, according to French sources, upped the supply rate even as the Berlin Conference was under way.[31] With an international meeting on Indochina assured, the Communists were provided with a deadline; if they could meet it, they would present the West with a fait accompli and measurably strengthen their bargaining position. The same tactic had already been demonstrated with Giap's drive on Luang Prabang as deliberations began at Berlin. Dulles later related that he had informed Bidault the Vietminh would intensify their activities in advance of the Geneva Conference. The French countered that they could hold Dienbienphu; a victorious stand there would symbolize a revitalized war effort. "The French military people knew what was likely to happen and felt they were able to cope with the situation," [32] said Dulles.

For Washington, French assurances were sufficient. True, the Berlin Conference decision was a major blow to American hopes for negotiating on Indochina from a position of diplomatic strength. In yielding to French pressure for talks with the Communists much sooner than desired, the United States became aware of what Molotov already knew—that the French wanted out of the war on honorable terms. If it was a secret before, it was now public knowledge, and with that the West was diplomatically handicapped well before the start of the Geneva Conference.

Nevertheless, officials continued to take comfort in the military picture. No one at the highest echelons in Paris or Washington was yet prepared to retreat from predictions of success on the battlefield. The French Chief of Staff, General Paul Ély, and Defense Minister Pleven had completed a tour of the front (February 7–28) which found cause for considerable optimism about Navarre's chances.[33] Navarre was unmoved by the Vietminh surrounding him. Two American missions had agreed with his command's sanguine evaluation of Vietminh artillery capabilities and vulnerability.[34] In a news conference announcement of February 19, Navarre said: "The Vietminh offensive is slack, or about at its peak . . . ," and, less equivocally, "Giap's offensive is blocked." [35]

Washington's outlook reflected, and even went beyond, French confidence. During the Berlin Conference, the President cabled Dulles: "General O'Daniel's most recent report is more encouraging than given to you through French sources." [36] And on Capitol Hill only days later, Admiral Radford and Under Secretary Smith reaffirmed the ambitions of the Navarre Plan. Following their testimony before a House Foreign Relations subcommittee meeting, Representative Walter Judd issued a statement based on the closed-door presentation. Although the Vietminh had become "increasingly powerful because of Chinese Communist assistance, Communist prospects of achieving any decisive immediate success are slight, while their prospects of ultimate victory are non-existent." The Navarre Plan, Radford told the subcommittee, was "a broad strategic concept which within a few months should insure a favorable turn in the course of the war." [37] In short, none doubted that the Vietminh would throw all their weight behind seeking a military victory at Dienbienphu that could be cashed in for political dividends; but all gained strength from French estimations that the Vietminh were treading on thin ice. The United States had to give ground diplomatically at Berlin; but prevailing official opinion was that the Communists could be faced at Geneva from a militarily sound position which, in Radford's words, was only "a few months" away.

MARCH: PLANS FOR ACTION

March saw the beginning of intensive diplomatic activity among the three allied capitals as the military situation in Indochina bordered on collapse. Before the end of the month the bankruptcy of the Navarre Plan would finally be recognized and, in reaction to the siege of Dienbienphu, efforts made on Washington's initiative to save the region through collective action.

The conventional warfare size and deployment of the Vietminh during the first two months of 1954 did little, as has been seen, to alter outward confidence in either Paris or Washington. Until the last week in March, the story was much the same. Writing in a weekly armed forces magazine, General Navarre declared that the Vietminh northern campaign had failed utterly and opened the way for a French offensive soon.[38] Two weeks thereafter, Harold Stassen proclaimed that mounting American aid, to which the Administration had decided to add military items originally slated for Korea amounting to $250,000,000–350,000,000, was aimed at military victory. The war, he reported, was going favorably. "I returned from the Far East with the strong conviction that the forces of freedom are growing stronger and that the Communist position is weakening. This is true," he added, "in both an economic and a military sense." [39] Secretary Dulles, at a March 23 news conference, was once more put into the position of having to defend his optimism about the Navarre Plan. And he refused to revise his December analysis; the Plan would, he asserted, bring about "at least decisive military results . . . roughly a year from now." The Plan, explained Dulles, was based upon "no serious military reversals" in the period of the French Union offensive; as he saw it, none were in sight. Closing the matter, the Secretary strongly intimated that the United States would continue to press for a military victory, since the prospect of a political settlement rested squarely on the readiness of the Chinese "to cut off military assistance, and thereby demonstrate that they are not still aggressors in spirit. . . ." [40]

But military realities tended to fly in the face of these enthusiastic pronouncements. Although the Navarre Plan had achieved greater mobility, French Union tactics showed a distinct failure to concentrate forces at the moment of battle. As a result the French remained, as before, numerically inferior in any given battle. Navarre's effort to break the defensive psychosis that had long characterized the army's activity thus ran afoul of an important military rule.[41] The United States recognized this weak point and, without fanfare, pressured the French to accept an army training mission which would replace certain French officers and attempt to revitalize the native forces. The appointment of General O'Daniel to replace Major General Trapnell as head of MAAG was a clear indication, despite the President's denial,[42] that Washington was dissatisfied with the French training program. Washington may have had the move under wraps for almost a year, for O'Daniel had covered Indochina and conferred with French officials in Saigon on a trip through the Far East in the spring 1953.[43] In any event, the French again revealed their displeasure at the prospect of an American "takeover." On the basis of experience and other factors, they held that the United States program would not succeed in Indochina as it had in Korea;[44] General Navarre publicly rejected an American training mission as soon as he heard of it.[45] The training program episode demonstrated anew that Paris wanted to run the war her own way, with a helping, not a directing, hand the only acceptable form of assistance from Washington.

Adverse developments at the front pressed President Eisenhower to deny for a second time that American involvement was imminent, although he qualified his statement of the previous month to mean involvement without a Congressional declaration of war. To a conference of newsmen on March 10 he stated tersely: "I will say this: there is going to be no involvement of America in war unless it is a result of the constitutional process that is placed upon Congress to declare it. Now, let us have that clear; and that is the answer."[46] But on March 13 the VPA, under the personal direction of General Giap, began the investment of Dienbienphu and its surrounded defenders. This long-awaited siege set into motion a concatenation of events that would destroy the last remnants of hope that the French could win alone and cause top officials in Washington to ponder carefully direct intervention.

On March 20 General Ély arrived in Washington. The Ély mission, made in response to an invitation extended to the French Defense Council by Admiral Radford, had several objectives: to inform Radford of the actual military situation in Indochina; to obtain American assurance of air interdiction if the Chinese intervened by air; to sift out the probable American reaction to increased Chinese aid and to the actual dispatch of "volunteers"; and finally, to request increased American assistance for building up the Vietnamese army.[47] The aims were therefore, according to Ély, in keeping with French policy: No drastic American military adventures would be permitted to interfere with prospects for a negotiated settlement; a stronger indigenous army would assure negotiations conducted from a strong military base; formal guarantees against possible Chinese intervention would be sought.[48] But by the time of Ély's arrival, two important points at Dienbienphu had already fallen to the Vietminh, and General Navarre had sent telegrams requesting air and parachute support to defend against the onslaught.[49] The moderate demands of the Ély mission were being tested even before his conversations with the Americans.

Ély found the leading American officials, from the President on down, far more concerned about Dienbienphu than Paris. In the course of discussions, which lasted from the twenty-first to the twenty-fifth, the President instructed Radford, in Ély's presence, to put at France's disposal all means to save the fortress.[50] Ély was at the outset interested mainly in gaining American assurance of an immediate response if the Chinese intervened with air power since, without direct U.S. participation, the Navarre Plan would be shattered by a sudden loss of air power supremacy.

Ély's request was met on the twenty-fifth through an agreement signed with Radford which provided for United States air power to counter Chinese air intervention.[51] From the American side, however, came more far-reaching plans. Asked by Radford to remain an additional twenty-four hours, Ély was confronted on the same day with a proposition for a nighttime raid against the perimeter of Dienbienphu by the U.S. Air Force and Navy. The plan, conceived by joint American-French military staffs in Vietnam and named *Opération Vautour* (VULTURE),[52] called for about sixty B-29 heavy bombers to take off from Clark Field near Manila under escort of 150 fighters of the Seventh Fleet, conduct one or several raids about the garrison, and eliminate Vietminh troop, communications, and artillery installations. VULTURE would be justified as simply another phase of the American aid program, and as an answer to continued Chinese assistance. But the limited nature of the raid in point of time and area would, Radford believed, give no cause for China's direct intervention.[53] Radford made it clear, nonetheless, that *the raid was an offer and no more;* Paris would have to approve it, and even then, the United States would only be prepared to examine it further inasmuch as it constituted entry into the war.[54]

On the twenty-seventh Ély thus flew home with much more than he had bargained for. His plea for an American guarantee against Chinese air attack had been met, as had a request for more aerial assistance with a promise of twenty-five B-26's.[55] Renewed American insistence upon acceptance of a training mission for indigenous forces, which took the form of an offer by Radford to send twenty-five or thirty officers, had been successfully bypassed by a promise to transmit the offer to Paris.[56] The attainment of important pre-discussion objectives was overshadowed, however, by a plan which, if accepted in Paris and Washington, would place American combat personnel into the fighting for the first time. Eisenhower's statement of March 24 that Indochina and the south Pacific were "of the most transcendent importance" to the United States [57] clarified orally what VULTURE indicated as fact: United States preparedness to consider that the stakes in Indochina might require direct involvement.

The Berlin Conference had an important impact upon Dulles' thinking. First, the Secretary anticipated, and warned

Bidault about, intensified Communist activity. That expectancy was fulfilled not only by the attack upon Dienbienphu on March 13 but also by a decided pickup in Chinese assistance. By the latter end of March, according to State Department information, Chinese aid was "approaching a peak of 4,000 tons a month," not including nearly 2,000 tons of food being delivered monthly "despite widespread starvation in China." [58] Secondly, the conference confirmed to Dulles that some kind of regional defense in Southeast Asia would be the strongest way of buttressing the French.[59] In talks with Ély, Dulles broached the concept of a collective security arrangement which, if signed or at least adhered to by certain other nations, might compel the CPR to recalculate the risks of continued aid and thus preclude a new American commitment not only at Dienbienphu but throughout Southeast Asia.[60] On March 29 this concept was elucidated in the broadest statement yet presented of American determination not to see Indochina succumb to the Vietminh.

Speaking before the Overseas Press Club,[61] Dulles now supplemented the implied threat of air attack made September 2, called for a "united" approach to the Indochina situation, and in effect rejected widening Anglo-French preference for a negotiated settlement and partition. The Secretary began by pinpointing Communist assistance to the Vietminh: training and equipping of the rebels in China; deliveries of artillery and ammunition; transporting of munitions from the Czech Skoda works to China for use in the war. In addition, 2000 Chinese soldiers were giving military and technical guidance "in staff sections of the high command, at the division level and in the specialized units such as signal, engineering, artillery and transportation." The threat to Indochina was therefore evident:

If the Communist forces were to win uncontested control over Indo-China *or any substantial part thereof,* they would surely resume the same pattern of aggression against the other free peoples in that area.

The propagandists of Red China and of Soviet Russia make it perfectly apparent that the purpose is to dominate all of Southeast Asia.
Now Southeast Asia is an important part of the world. It is the so-called "rice bowl" . . . It is an area that is rich in many raw materials . . .
And in addition to these tremendous economic values, the area has great strategic value. . . . Communist control of Southeast Asia would carry a grave threat to the Philippines, Australia and New Zealand . . . The entire western Pacific area, including the so-called "offshore island chain," would be strategically endangered.

The Secretary then called to mind previous policy statements, which were "designed to impress upon potential aggressors that aggression might lead to action in places and by means of the free world's choosing, so that aggression would surely cost more than it would gain." The Chinese Communists, while not directly using their own armies, "have, however, largely stepped up their support of the aggression which I have described in that area. And, indeed, they promote that aggression by all means short of open invasion." The facts demanded new measures:

Under the conditions of today the imposition on Southeast Asia of the political system of Communist Russia and its Communist Chinese ally, *by whatever means*, would be a grave threat to the whole free community. The United States feels that that possibility should not be passively accepted, but should be met by *united action.*

Dulles' speech seemed to represent a distinct departure from previous American policy. First, the United States was broadening its warning to encompass not simply the possibility of blatant Chinese intervention but de facto Communist hegemony over Vietnam. The CPR's brand of aggression fell just "short of open invasion," but stood as "a grave threat to the whole free community" all the same because it might eventually result in the communization of all or part of Indochina. For the first time, Communist control over "any substantial part" of Indochina was in itself considered dangerous. Secondly, the renewed call for "united action" seemed designed to quell Anglo-French fears of American action without their knowledge and Congressional disquietude over involvement without its sanction as much as to supplement the dark hints of massive attack.

Moreover, the March 29 address plainly indicated two major developments: first, the American conviction that the Navarre Plan could not win in Vietnam; second, a willingness to take unprecedented steps to pull Indochina out of the fire. In reinforcing American determination to stand firm behind France, the speech also aimed at preparing Congress and the public for the possibility of intervention. Should involvement prove necessary, the President's news conference remark of March 31 hinted that American participation would be through air-naval rather than ground attack (i.e., VULTURE). For although the President did not absolutely exclude the dispatch of troops, he made it clear that they would be reserved except as a last-ditch contingency. United action, as he defined it, was a responsibility primarily to be undertaken by the people under threat of attack.[62]

United action, however, proposed to go beyond the local threat posed at Dienbienphu and deal directly with the general threat of increasing Chinese aid. The Indochina crisis, Washington now believed, demanded action by coalition, a return to the thesis broached initially in the spring of 1953 and forwarded in talks with Ély. If Peking could be persuaded, by a multi-nation warning underwritten by several free world partners, that the West meant business, assistance to the Vietminh could be stopped. And if Communist Chinese aid persisted, subscribers to the joint declaration would be prepared to take military action.[63] As Dulles explained to the British Ambassador, Sir Roger Makins:

. . . we possessed a military superiority in the area now which we might not have in a few years' time. So if a warning was not heeded, we should now be in a position to put our threats into effect. Military action involved risks, but the risk of letting Indo-China go was greater. The United States was thinking in terms of a joint warning, by several countries, of naval and air action against the China coast; it would not threaten the landing of American troops.[64]

Where the United States had previously indicated tacit acceptance of surreptitious Chinese assistance, it was now saying that Chinese aid constituted the single greatest menace to Vietnam's safety and could no longer be ignored.

The urgency with which Washington regarded the crisis, and the means of dealing with it, were appreciated only in Paris. There, on March 29, the French received and acted upon Ély's report. A thirteen-man Committee of War, which included Premier Laniel, President Reynaud, Bidault, Pleven, and Ély, convened that day and determined that no final decision would be reached on VULTURE until General Navarre's evaluation had been obtained. One Colonel Raymond Brohon, from Ély's General Staff, was chosen to approach Navarre on the plan.[65] Despite these proceedings, the United States and France were in reality moving in divergent directions. For as Ély noticed during his talks in Washington, the Americans were bent on establishing a general security framework for all Southeast Asia, whereas the French, although perfectly willing to adhere to a limited tactical plan for rescuing a given military target, were also concerned about any broader action which would threaten the Geneva Conference, dissolve chances for an Indochina peace,[66] and transform the war from a unilateral to a multilateral effort. The persistent fear of United States "domination" of a French war came into play once again. United action, as Admiral Radford has admitted, was political dynamite, for it proposed internationalizing the war at a time when Paris considered victory under the Expeditionary Corps' leadership still possible.[67]

Although apprised of the ramifications of united action,

neither France nor England had indicated approval; in fact, every indication pointed toward dissent. In actuality, then, the call for a united approach had been made on the *assumption* of a favorable response abroad. The question was whether this tactic would outflank the strong "peace factions" in London and Paris or accentuate differences over Indochina policy. And if the latter occurred, the United States in general and the Secretary of State in particular were diplomatically defenseless.

The Communist camp, perplexed over massive retaliation and its implications for American policy in Indochina, pondered the qualifications of and additions to Administration phrase-making during February and March. For with the speech of March 29, Dulles had thrown into play a new element: the prospect that the United States might not await actual Chinese entry before joining with its allies in direct intervention.

The Chinese attitude in those two months, as expressed through the news media, was consistently defensive. Having obtained the right to bargain directly with the United States at Geneva, the CPR quietly augmented aid shipments to the Vietminh and simultaneously remained highly cautious over changing American policies toward Indochina. The Chinese stuck almost exclusively to portraying themselves as the potential target of American military "maneuvers" in the Far East, military pacts, inspection tours, the training of native armies, and assistance to Indochina and her neighbors. The press offered as the rationale behind these multi-faceted American activities the explanation that the United States was becoming more and more troubled by the situation in Indochina. Yet articles demonstrated that the regime was itself unsure about the real role of American aid, or about the precise amounts being sent, an uncertainty born, it might be added, of the arbitrary use of American sources, which varied widely over what the sundry kinds of assistance portended.

Just what the Chinese Communists perceived, or said they perceived, going on around them deserves attention. In early February NCNA asserted that "Forty additional B-26 bombers" were being sent by the United States to Indochina, as well as two hundred men to supplement an alleged detachment of 400 Americans already stationed there.[68] (Actually, American military personnel on duty in Indochina at the time numbered 325 technicians, not including about forty civilian pilots attached to Civil Air Transport of Taiwan.) Before the end of the month, NCNA further charged that the United States planned direct involvement in the war through air support flights manned by Americans. Civilian volunteers and Japanese would be permitted to fly in Indochina also. Other plans were being considered, noted another broadcast: the use of indigenous troops, the sealing of the Sino-Indochinese border with American forces, a naval blockade of Vietnamese ports under DRV control, and the delivery of more planes.[69] Naval maneuvers and various tours by civilian and military personnel were carefully observed; all were termed part and parcel of the American scheme to step up its intervention under the New Look's "power policy."[70] The Americans were considered to have devised a two-stage program for wresting control of the war from the French. The first step would be to pressure Paris to continue the war; the second, to take over command of native troops and ultimately conduct the war alone (citing the visit of General O'Daniel).[71]

Outside Indochina proper the appraisal differed little from this odd mixture of truth and nonsense. Through the training of Asian troops, the supplying of important modern war matériel, and the conclusion of military pacts with China's neighbors, the United States was said to be encircling the CPR with the purpose of invasion clearly in sight. Particular attention was paid to the alleged forward movement of jet aircraft and bombers to bases within striking distance of the mainland,[72] and to unusual military activity in Thailand.[73] Perhaps significantly, Peking offered no disparaging remarks about the American nuclear threat when it reported on United States hydrogen bomb tests over the Marshall Islands on March 1 and 26.[74] Concomitantly, the news media reacted uncertainly to various Administration statements on the crisis. In the President's remark of March 10 that Congress would have to sanction American involvement in Indochina, Peking saw the germ of active American participation. Eisenhower really meant "that the U.S. Government may use the killing of any American Air Force personnel now taking part in the Indochina war as a pretext for obtaining Congressional approval for formal participation in the war."[75] Yet the subsequent call for united action on March 29, which sparked a long front-page editorial in the *People's Daily*, did not provoke so serious a picture. United action was designed "to create a tense situation and in preparation for extending the Indochina war in order to make a profit for American monopoly capitalists."[76]

That the publicity attending every American move in the Far East did not accurately reflect Chinese concern over an "extension" of the war in Indochina may be derived from the nature of Peking's responses to alleged American "provocations." While the regime proceeded to change the *characterization* of the threat, it studiously avoided a *commitment* to any course of action to deflect the threat. Between February and late March, Peking maintained a tone of concerned aloofness: The United States "will undoubtedly meet with still greater failures" if it persists in its policy course (February 22);[77] American "adventurous activities will not be able to escape judgment by just world opinion" (March 21).[78] But verbal gymnastics dropped by the wayside on March 25 when Peking spoke for the first time of "the military encirclement of China," in which Indochina was the center of the American "military crescent." The United States had not learned the lesson of Korea. "But it is a true old saying that those who refuse to learn their lessons will have to pay the penalty." [79] And on March 30 an unusually long article, the first to ascribe a "grave threat" to the chain of United States bases, depicted them as "clearly directed against the Soviet Union, the Chinese People's Republic, and the other People's Democracies." [80] Yet in changing the direction of the threat from one against the "Asian people" to one against the CPR and the socialist bloc, Peking abstained from any allusion either to a possible rebuff from the bloc or even to the bloc's capacity to deal with a potential aggressor. Moreover, although the comment that the United States "will have to pay the penalty" indicated a shift upward in the "intensity level" of Peking's warnings, the CPR still failed to specify what the "penalty" might be or what action might trigger a retaliatory response. The explanation of this hesitation may lie in Peking's already-quoted reaction to the March 29 address, which avoided an opinion on Dulles' rejection of passivity in the face of the Vietminh threat. By returning to the earlier theme that "the forces of peace" would "undoubtedly" work toward relaxing tensions, Peking may have indicated continuing uncertainty over American policy rather than real alarm.

The CPR's close observance of American military activities, its portrayal of them as a threat to itself and the Soviet Union, but its hesitation to become committed either unilaterally or otherwise through some precipitate act or word, may at bottom have reflected continued irresolution in Moscow over the deterrence issue. By March Malenkov's conviction that the time was ripe for attempting a lasting solution to cold war differences was being vigorously assailed by the Khrushchev group. Arguing for continued military expansion with particular attention to the air arm, Khrushchev and his supporters warned often against viewing the West's military production as defense-oriented.[81] Responding to the opposition, Malenkov on March 12 acknowledged the existence of "aggressive circles" but declared that peace remained a viable alternative to cold war and "fresh world carnage"; and he repeated his contention that nuclear war would mean "the ruin of world civilization." [82] Soviet armed forces thus needed to be prepared; but possession of both atomic and hydrogen warheads, as Anastas Mikoyan (the Minister of Trade) averred, lessened the danger of war [83] and hence the need of a rapid buildup in the military.

The climactic beleaguerment of Dienbienphu consequently occurred amidst moments of clear indecision on the part of the CPSU over vital defense problems. And American policy statements in early 1954 did little to "prove" the correctness of either faction. Eisenhower's press conference remark of March 10 was construed by the *Pravda* correspondent to betoken greater American involvement.[84] The writer presumably experienced the same difficulty as the Chinese in deciding whether the massive retaliation doctrine was now applicable in the event of military action. This misinterpretation was carried over into *Pravda*'s late commentary on the January 12 address. Whereas Dulles had by no means stated that the United States would react with nuclear weapons to every local crisis, this was precisely the meaning attributed to him by the official Party organ. Basically, however, the analysis was mild in tone; the Party seemed unsure as to the purport of Dulles' message. "It also seems very likely," Herbert Dinerstein has commented, "that the editorial was written with the purpose of smoking out some further American reaction which would give the Russians some clues as to what was meant." [85]

The inner Soviet debate had thus floundered over American intentions to use nuclear weapons in local as well as general war, and this lent itself to similar uncertainty over American policy in Indochina. When it is recalled that the CPR had been emphatic on America's readiness to use strategic and tactical nuclear weapons, and had expressed a decidedly pessimistic view of the future, there is reason to suppose that the question of "taking sides" in the Soviet debate had been decided as March passed into April. Yet even if this conclusion is accurate, it should further be observed that the Chinese made no public effort to take the final plunge on the salient question in the dispute: whether or not the immediate future warranted military expansion. No Chinese comments have been found which indicated a set position on this score; although supposedly threatened with the full force of American air-atomic might, the Chinese issued no call for a buildup in the Communist camp (as Khrushchev did). The inference that might be made from this contentment to sit tight on the deterrence problem is that Peking, despite the alleged danger to her borders, was not panic-stricken. Had the CPR been "running scared," in other words, we might expect to have found consistent boasting about the Soviet deterrent capability in the face of American retaliatory power.

Prospects of important propaganda gains at Geneva seem also to have persuaded Peking of the importunity in warning the United States and perhaps setting off the kind of united action China would have wanted most to avoid. Throughout the pre-Geneva period (February 18–April 26) the Chinese jumped on any sign that the United States was pessimistic about prospects for the conference. In early March the *People's Daily* castigated the United States and Great Britain for seeking to subvert the conference through obstructionist tactics.[86] In belittling the probable results of the conference, commented NCNA, the United States was looking toward a continuation of the war rather than a satisfaction of the demands of the world's peoples for peace. The United States should recognize that its policy of non-recognition had been proved bankrupt, and that it could no longer afford to ignore either the People's Republic or "the aspirations of the Asian people for peace and freedom." [87] Geneva would therefore be a turning point since, with China's participation, there "will be a new stage in the development of international relations and . . . favorable conditions for the settlement of pressing international questions as well as the easing of tension in Asia and the whole world." [88] The Chinese line here was clear: By closely aligning the conference with the interests of the Asian peoples, the CPR was making every effort to reap propaganda value from the contention that China welcomed talks while the United States backtracked. Secondly, by calling attention to the danger that the United States *would* pull out and continue the war on its own terms, the CPR seemed desirous of mobilizing opinion to insure American attendance. The CPR determined not to miss a major opportunity to inflict a serious diplomatic setback on the West. Conferring with the United States, especially at a time when the American military seemed to be "moving up" its power to within striking distance, would serve the dual purpose of diverting attention from the battlefield and avenging American snubbing of China's place in Asian affairs. But at that moment, the attention of Washington policy-makers was riveted on Indochina as plans for intervention moved into high gear.

6. THE PROBLEM OF INTERVENTION: APRIL 1954

APRIL 1–14: QUEST FOR SANCTION

The twenty-six days following Dulles' March 29 address stand as the limited period during which the Administration sought to solve the deteriorating Indochina situation with direct American help. With allied approval and Congressional backing of a united approach, the Administration envisaged possession of an effective counter both to the Chinese-supported Vietminh assaults on Dienbienphu and to the general dilemma posed by mounting Chinese arms deliveries.

On April 2 Colonel Brohon met with Navarre at Hanoi, outlined Operation VULTURE, and returned to Paris with the general's decision on April 4. To Ély's surprise, Navarre was no longer four-square behind relief of his position with airpower. As Brohon explained, Navarre found no fault with the operation, but was distraught at the risks of Chinese air retaliation. But on the same day a telegram from Saigon revealed a change of heart. Perhaps as a result of a meeting with Maurice Dejean, the Commissioner General, Navarre had decided that VULTURE could "have a decisive effect" if engineered at the latest before April 11.[1]

Navarre's acceptance of an American air strike where previously he had rejected so much as a training mission was based upon a drastic turn of events at Dienbienphu. Both the

General and Premier Laniel assumed the inability of the Chinese to deliver heavy artillery or anti-aircraft guns to the VPA, a conviction sustained by the failure of the Vietminh to attack en masse as expected in late January. Although postponement of the siege until March 13 may have been due to the lack of munitions supplies and the incompleteness of heavy artillery placements,[2] the French command wrongly supposed that artillery would not reach VPA in time to count, if at all. Pursuing this train of thought, it was believed that Dienbienphu would finally enable French Union forces to bring their superior firepower to bear against the Vietminh in a pitched battle that would extinguish the enemy's core.

Loss of the garrison was thus foreshadowed by prospects which the French command had discounted: the ability of the Chinese to get through shipments of heavy artillery, and their directives in the placement of those weapons.[3] The Communists knew that a dramatic military success would give their side a preponderant bargaining edge in the Geneva negotiations. The means for such a success were at hand as April opened, for by then the balance of power in Vietnam had, without French awareness,[4] swung to the Communist side. Seizing Dienbienphu was therefore compatible equally with Communist political aims and the objective military situation. If the CPR leadership did not direct that Dienbienphu be taken, its active support indicated concurrence with Giap that the time for meeting the French in a set-piece battle had arrived. The Vietminh tactical advantage in occupying the hillsides ringing the garrison, and in possessing a numerical superiority, cleared the way for an all-out drive.

The daily undercutting of Navarre's position intensified American determination to act decisively. The Congress, which had reacted to Dulles' March 29 address with the expression of a wide variety of opinions on whether to intervene,[5] still sought in vain for a clear-cut declaration of Administration policy. Senator Hubert Humphrey expressed the views of several colleagues when he said on March 31: ". . . it has disturbed me that there seems to be a reluctance on the part of the executive branch of the Government, in the present critical situation, to fully inform the responsible committees of the Congress." [6] The perplexed attitude in Washington during early April was summarized by James Reston:

. . . neither Governments nor Senators on Capitol Hill like to feel that decisions which might involve peace or war are being taken in haste or that they are being cornered into accepting United States policies with which they disagree.

Even . . . Mr. Dulles' supporters in the State Department . . . don't know whether he is bluffing the Reds or getting the United States ready for military action in Indo-China and, after all the casual talk about "massive retaliation," they don't particularly like either course.[7]

Congressional support was absolutely vital, in the President's mind, if the United States was to be party to war. Moreover, by the first week of April the fighting at Dienbienphu had reached major proportions as Chinese-supplied Vietminh artillery zeroed in on French compounds and drove the Corps steadily backward.[8] This circumstance apparently pushed immediate implementation of VULTURE into a position of top priority; time did not allow Washington to go through the laborious process of sounding out every allied capital on an American-engineered strike against the Vietminh.

On April 3 Eisenhower therefore called a secret meeting, at which he was reportedly not present, to inform a representative body of leading Congressmen of the critical situation confronting the nation in Indochina. Admiral Radford was the chief speaker and VULTURE the topic. Radford told the assemblage that Dienbienphu could be rescued with a single air strike using 200 planes, which would take off from the aircraft carriers *Essex* and *Boxer* stationed on "maneuvers" in the South China Sea. Additional air support from bases in the Philippines was planned. He agreed that such action would mean war, and that an unsuccessful strike would be followed by another.[9] It has further been averred that the planes on board the carriers were armed with atomic weapons meant for Chinese Communist staging areas and other militarily vital points.[10] If so, the warheads were reserved for the contingency of a massive Chinese intervention.[11]

Apparently, neither Radford nor Dulles solved the poignant problems raised by the startling presentation: Would land forces be sent in if a second air strike failed? (Radford could not be definite,* though Dulles made it plain that any ground support would have to be supplied by allies.[12]) Would our allies support the proposal? (Dulles said no other nations had yet been consulted.[13]) Would the Chinese intervene and thereby create a second Korea of more mammoth proportions? (Dulles believed they would back down before a show of force.[14]) And with regard to the position of the other Joint Chiefs, Radford was forced to admit that he was the only one who favored the attack plan.[15] The result was that Dulles, who had looked toward a joint Congressional resolution authorizing Presidential use of air-naval power in Indochina, came away from the meeting without vital support. The Congressmen—three Republicans and five Democrats— agreed that the United States should not support France alone.[16] Instead, they laid down three conditions for their support: formation of a coalition force, a declaration of French intent "to accelerate their independence program," and French agreement to maintain the Corps in Indochina.[17] The meaning of this hesitation to back the Secretary and his top military advisor was patent: The most influential men on the Hill

---

* According to Radford (interview with the author), ground forces were never discounted, but were not viewed as an immediate requirement. In the aftermath of an air strike, United States troops might have been needed, but the point of seeing a requirement for them had not been reached. Air-naval power was the chief French need. It was precisely on this score that General Ridgway would register his strong dissent to intervention (see chapter 7).

would not condone unilateral intervention in behalf of a colonialist cause. Having sounded out Congressional sentiment and having met with stubborn resistance, the Administration took the first steps toward acquiring the support necessary to making any Indochina venture a collective one. In an evening conference at the White House April 4, the President, meeting with Dulles and Radford, reached the decision to intervene only upon satisfaction of the three conditions outlined by the eight Congressmen.[18] On the same day, the President spelled out his views on the meaning of united action in a letter to Prime Minister Churchill. Although noting Paris' desire for a cease-fire and his personal "fear that the French cannot alone see the thing through," Eisenhower dismissed a negotiated settlement and proposed formation "of a new, ad hoc grouping or coalition composed of nations which have a vital concern in the checking of Communist expansion in the [Far East] area." Within the grouping, the United States "would expect to play its full part"; yet the President did "not envisage the need of any appreciable ground forces on your [Britain's] or our part." As Dulles had already explained, the President saw united action as workable against the Communist war effort provided the coalition was "strong and . . . willing to join the fight if necessary." He therefore enumerated the members: the Western Big Three, the Associated States, Australia, New Zealand, Thailand, and the Philippines.[19] But the plan, which later materialized as the Southeast Asia Treaty Organization (SEATO), still had underlying vaguenesses about it. What was the precise role of United States military power to be? And what were the limits to which the United States was prepared to go if full-scale entry into the fighting were unavoidable? The President's personal effort to sway Churchill did not plug up the loopholes that were already very much in the minds of the London leadership.

Eisenhower's reassertion of the Administration's desire for

the support of other states in any Indochina undertaking temporarily shelved VULTURE. Yet the unwary French were moving as though VULTURE remained the dominant motif of any American intervention. The decision was reached on April 4 by a fourteen-member War Committee to go ahead with VULTURE in the conviction that the operation "would not provoke extension of the war." American Ambassador Douglas Dillon was summoned by the committee and asked to convey the decision to Washington. Dillon reminded Laniel and Bidault that Congress would need to be informed before any action could be undertaken, but promised to transmit the request.[20] Probably sometime later in the same day, however, French Ambassador Henri Bonnet was given an explanation by Dulles of American planning quite different from what the French had been led to believe. The Secretary, obviously reflecting the policy decision arrived at April 4, spoke of the necessity to form immediately a coalition of states in order to make clear to the Communists, in advance of the Geneva deliberations, that they could not hope for victory. The coalition should, Dulles elaborated, be capable of swift action and be willing, moreover, to draw the line for Peking by a joint declaration similar in structure to the sixteen-nation warning of July 27, 1953.[21]

With Dulles' explanation to Bonnet, the French were made aware that, by "united action," the United States meant not VULTURE's provision for joint United States-French operations but the establishment of a military force within a broad political framework of Western and Asian states. The secret session with Congressmen brought home to the Administration that VULTURE could only be implemented within an allied framework, and that any attempt to divorce the operation from plans for a united front against Peking would run afoul of Congressional opinion. On April 5 the changed American approach was made official when Bidault was informed, through Ambassador Dillon, that United States involvement would be predicated upon Congressional approval and the accord of other states besides France. The notification indicated that these two requirements had been confirmed "at the highest level," that is, by the President. Until a coalition to include Britain could be formed, and until the constitutional issue could be satisfied, the United States would continue to aid by all measures short of direct intervention.[22] To the French, this fusion of VULTURE to "united action" meant certain, perhaps irreparable, delay when time was of the essence.[23]

As the French pondered the implication of Washington's proposals, particularly as they affected prospects at Geneva, the Administration made renewed efforts to swing public, Congressional, and allied support behind further steps in Indochina. In a striking presentation on April 5 before the House Committee on Foreign Affairs, Dulles offered conclusive evidence that Chinese support of the Vietminh effort at Dienbienphu had reached new heights. In testimony fully corroborated by General Navarre's own intelligence, Dulles pointed out that the VPA surrounding the garrison included a Chinese general serving with Giap as quartermaster general; under the general were "about twenty" Chinese technical military advisors, with "a number of others" serving in various VPA divisions; Chinese were responsible for the installation, maintenance, and operation of special telephone lines; Chinese army personnel had been and continued to be behind the wheels of some 1000 supply trucks, most of which had been delivered since March 1; the CPR had furnished all artillery, munitions, and equipment for prosecution of the seige; and Chinese gunners were operating 37mm anti-aircraft guns at the front.[24] For the first time, Dulles acknowledged not simply that Chinese army personnel were at the front, but that they were active participants in the war. Yet, almost incredibly, he refused to admit that French planning had gone awry. "There is no reason to question the inherent soundness of the Navarre

Plan," he said. "Nothing has happened to change the basic estimate of relative military power for 1955. On the contrary, the Communists are now expending recklessly their military assets in Indochina." The Chinese were at Dienbienphu to assure its demise; but France still held Indochina.

The Secretary coupled the dramatic announcement of Chinese involvement with a reaffirmation of the pledge implicit in his March 29 address—that the United States would not stand idly by while the Communist overran Indochina. He stated again that the situation was "fraught with danger, not only to the immediate area but to the security of the United States and its allies in the Pacific area." The Communists' purpose was "to dominate all of Southeast Asia," an aim that represented a "grave threat" (his phrase of March 29) to the whole southern Pacific region. The Secretary held that France and the Associated States "ought not to feel that they stand apart in an hour of supreme trial"; they should know that the West would refuse to accept Communist domination "by a unity of will, and, if need be, unity of action."

In toto, the phrases dittoed those of the previous week; the United States, if it could gain the cooperation of its allies, vowed to join in the French effort rather than witness the subversion of Indochina and, potentially, of the entire southern Pacific area. Underlining this projection of events, the President, at his April 7 news conference, once more spoke of the perilous circumstances in Indochina. For the first time enunciating the "falling domino" principle, he alluded to Indochina as perhaps the first victim of "a disintegration that would have the most profound influences." Because a Communist conquest of Indochina would pose a threat to all other areas south of the peninsula, "the possible consequences of [its] loss are just incalculable to the free world." [25]

The Secretary's disclosure of a Chinese presence in the front lines at Dienbienphu and the President's dramatization of Indochina's importance went for naught. On April 6 the

French war committee rejected an international formula for dealing with Indochina on the ground that the plan would prejudice the chances for concluding an acceptable armistice at Geneva. Formation of a coalition force and the issuance of a declaration aimed at China should be final steps, taken after learning of China's attitude. Paris would also want to know further details on the nature and scope of the coalition's membership. The rejection notice, of which these points were the substance, was handed to Dulles April 8.[26] Sandwiched in between was a brief letter received by the President from Churchill on the seventh that pointedly indicated British coolness to the plan. Churchill desired to speak personally with Dulles.[27] There could be no mistaking the threat to the very existence of the united action proposal.

By the time of Dulles' flight to London on April 10, word had reached Washington through official and unofficial channels to the effect that the British were strongly opposed to the American proposal. Eden summarized his views on united action:

The United States proposal assumes that the threat of retaliation against China would cause her to withdraw aid from the Vietminh. This seems to me a fundamental weakness. There is a distinction between warning China that some specified further action will entail retaliation, which might be an effective deterrent, and calling upon her to desist from action in which she is already engaged. I cannot see what threat would be sufficiently potent to make China swallow so humiliating a rebuff as the abandonment of the Vietminh without any facesaving concession in return.[28]

Coming more and more to accept the prospect of a negotiated settlement and partition, the British were open to suggestions of a *post*-settlement warning to Peking that would, in effect, guarantee an Indochina agreement. But the long-range possibility of an armed conflict with the CPR weighed heavily in Eden's mind, for it did not seem to him that the Americans had "yet formed any clear conception of the military operations which they propose should be conducted . . . if threats fail to produce the desired result." [29]

The London press similarly downgraded the value of a joint warning only two weeks prior to the opening session at Geneva. *The Times*, closely attuned to thinking at 10 Downing Street, wrote: "His [Dulles'] sudden decision to try to secure agreement to a hurried declaration was probably taken almost without thought of its possible effect on Geneva, but with the intention of doing something quickly to discourage the Chinese Government from taking any irrevocable step before the rains come [to Vietnam]." [30]

The strength of British opinion behind proceeding to the Geneva Conference with an open hand apparently was significant in Dulles' recantation of the joint warning concept. By April 7 Dulles had come around to the view that united action should consist simply in an expression of common purpose which would by itself be sufficient to deter Communist ambitions in Southeast Asia. [31] At the air terminal prior to taking off for London Dulles announced that Thailand was prepared to join such an alliance. If other states whose interests were threatened could be brought in, "then the threat can be ended." [32] The Secretary, in dropping the joint warning from the American propositions, had returned to the bare essentials of the April 4 decision. Nevertheless, opinion abroad could not be changed overnight. The publicity attending the Secretary's trip, therefore, made it evident that a rebuff in allied capitals would leave the United States without recourse but to accept a decision at Geneva, and simultaneously demonstrate a serious polarization of opinion within the allied camp.

Not surprisingly, Dulles found the British stubborn and intransigent when it came to selling united action. In talks held April 11–13 Dulles brought across the main points of the crisis as perceived in Washington: the French on the verge of collapse, the exposure of Southeast Asia should Indochina fall, and the military plan backed by Radford which had already resulted in the movement of "some aircraft-carriers . . . from Manila towards the Indo-China coast." Aside from French willingness "to grant the Associated States real independence within the French Union," Dulles further desired British backing of an ad hoc coalition in Southeast Asia. "He thought," wrote Eden later, "that this in itself would deter China from further interference in Indo-China, and would strengthen our position at Geneva by giving evidence of our solidarity." [33] Eden was not convinced. He argued that, pending consideration of Communist intentions at Geneva, warnings were not in order, although the British would agree to preliminary discussions of a regional security arrangement. Secondly, India should, Eden felt, be offered the opportunity to join the coalition. Finally, if intervention in Indochina proved imperative, the British military doubted the effectiveness of air-naval power alone.[34] Yet the United States had already made clear its firm intention to avoid the dispatch of land forces. The British had three potent arguments for awaiting developments at Geneva.

The two allies were clearly wedded to totally incompatible positions. Their joint communiqué of April 13 mirrored this fact. Both governments deplored the Communist advance into the Associated States and recognized that Communist infiltration endangered "the peace and security of the entire area of Southeast Asia. . . ." But the manifest failure of Dulles' mission came through in the reference to united action; an agreement could only be reached to examine "the possibility of" a collective defense arrangement.[35]

The rebuff in London was duplicated in Paris. Like the Britons, the French were skeptical of the value of forming a coalition force. Because it was directed at Peking, a united front could not help but subvert the upcoming peace talks. As Eden argued, such an alignment gave the Chinese little maneuvering room. Ély wrote in this connection: "Viewed from the angle of negotiations, to demand for example of China that she cease all aid to the Vietminh while menacing her with a Southeast Asia pact would have been to have her lose more face than by inflicting a tactical defeat upon Vietminh forces by a direct military action against Dienbienphu."[36] The French would have accepted VULTURE, which by its limited nature was calculated not to carry the threat of a widened war; but united action, which held out the grave risk of bringing in the Chinese, could not be underwritten.

At bottom the attitude in Paris stemmed from the cumulative effects of the faltering war effort upon public opinion and troop morale. The Laniel government was in its most precarious position, under strong pressure to resist the temptation of American involvement. A war that would ultimately cost the Republic 65,000 men killed and 82,000 wounded was impinging upon Paris' determination to end the fighting at the bargaining table. *Le Monde*'s Washington correspondent accused the American press of having underestimated the French public's desire for peace and of having incorrectly touted French backing for united action. This misinformation extended to higher circles:

The offices of the State Department have perhaps undervalued the intensity of French public opinion in favor of a negotiated solution of the Indochina conflict. Some people were asking themselves if Mr. Foster Dulles had not been imprudent in proposing united action without having proceeded first toward a more serious sounding of the intentions of the European allies. . . .[37]

At the front the courageous defense of Dienbienphu could not completely blot out a distinct morale problem, especially among the Vietnamese troops. For them, reported a French writer, "national sentiment is still insufficiently developed . . . and they seem, in general, to fight more by obligation than by profound conviction."[38]

On April 9, these facets of the Indochina dilemma and rumors of American intervention schemes prompted an infrequent appearance by Premier Laniel before the National Assembly. In a full account of French policy, Laniel reiterated that the government remained in accord with the American goal not to permit the Communist conquest of Southeast Asia. But resistance at Dienbienphu would not be allowed to impede the search for an honorable peace at Geneva:

> Our line of conduct is as follows: first, to make all preparation for resisting victoriously at Dienbienphu and to maintain, with American material aid, our military effort; secondly, to approach the negotiations at Geneva in complete liberty, with the willingness to neglect no opportunity that they meet the sought for result: peace with respect to the fundamental rights and the liberty of the peoples concerned.[39]

Laniel's statement reaffirmed the fundamental dichotomy that had, since October 1953, been the hallmark of French policy—fighting on in Indochina, but keeping the door open to an honorable solution. By siding completely with neither the pro-war nor pro-peace advocates, Laniel could justify acceptance of a limited United States air attack against Dienbienphu but rejected united action as incompatible with a total effort at obtaining a negotiated settlement.[40]

The French had consequently chosen the middle road between the Americans, who were pushing hard for united action, and the British, who would have none of it. On April 15 the final Franco-American communiqué duplicated the one issued from London; [41] like the British, the French would make no binding commitment to united action. The trip abroad which Dulles had called, prior to his departure, a "mission of peace through strength" [42] had ended with the United States still alone in its drive for a united front to prevent the fall of Indochina. For the second time, a public call for action by Washington had been unanswered. Both London and Paris were now as one in belief that formation of a united front would injudiciously hamper the ability of the Geneva negotiators to hammer out a satisfactory truce.

APRIL 15–24: COLLAPSE

The state of American diplomacy as Dulles returned home was unenviable. The British had emphatically rejected united action in the belief that it ultimately invited a head-on collision with the CPR. But Eden's alternative, which was to listen to what the Communists had to offer at Geneva, smacked of abandonment of Indochina to the Communists. The French had, from the first, made a subtle distinction between ending the war peacefully and accepting limited American assistance toward winning the war. With the virtual withdrawal of the offer to Ély, the French veered away from entanglement in American plans with dangerous overtones. Both European powers entertained serious doubts as to the effectiveness of uniting to compel Peking to cease and desist from aiding the VPA. A coalition was a form of blackmail which would antagonize, not deter. The American intention was therefore worthy; but the timing was fraught with danger. The Administration had suffered a serious setback, and Dulles a personal rebuff; our two foremost allies had turned their backs on a plan which promised to thwart the Communists. A crisis of confidence had occurred which, in the final days of Dienbienphu, would prove costly.

Complicating British adamancy and French resolution for talks was the symbolic value of Dienbienphu. As the United States saw it, the military value of the fortress had been magnified beyond reality. Washington viewed this development with extreme regret because it knew that the French, from every objective standpoint, could sustain the loss of the garrison and continue fighting. A mere fraction of total French Union strength was involved in the battle. On the other hand, it was also clear to the Administration that the extinction of the garrison and its defenders would make French determination to pull out of Indochina and accept a cease-fire insurmountable. Dulles revealed the frustration inherent in discussing the Dienbienphu situation with the French when he wrote the President: "There is, of course, no military or logical reason why loss of Dien Bien Phu should lead to collapse of French will . . . Dien Bien Phu has become a symbol out of all proportion to its military importance." [43]

The Administration's growing disturbance with the various obstacles strewn in the path of intervention apparently provided the backdrop for another trial balloon on unilateral action. The Vice President, who previously had sent aloft an indication that the United States could not accept less than victory in Indochina, bluntly stated that the United States could not afford another retreat in Asia. The remark, coming in some "off-the-record" comments to the American Society of Newspaper Editors on April 17, was quickly leaked. If the French were to pull out, said Nixon, the situation would become desperate (although it already *was*); the Vietnamese would not be able to repel the Communists, who would gain control of the entire country within a month. America hopefully would not have to send troops; but, Nixon concluded, the Administration might find it necessary to face the facts and dispatch forces to the region.[44]

Startled Congressmen and newspapermen anxiously inquired whether Nixon's statement reflected a policy change under which the United States would act regardless of allied backing. On the day of the statement, the Department of State upheld Nixon's statement, saying "he was stating a course of possible action which he was personally prepared to support under a highly unlikely hypothesis." [45] And Dulles later denied the implications; Nixon's comment, he said, was a perfectly legitimate and personal one, and the Vice President had every right to say as he pleased.[46] From the timing of the remarks, there is reason to believe that the Administration was simply engaging in another test of wind direction, both public and allied, soon after the letdown of Dulles' trip.[47] Nevertheless, Nixon's comments and the reactions to them pointed up not only continued uncertainty outside the official circle on American involvement, but also dissonance within the Administration's top ranks between proponents of immediate action and those who demanded allied sanction as the precondition to action.

Dulles, meanwhile, was under the impression that while the British had rejected immediate action on Indochina, they had agreed through the communiqué of April 13 to discuss the setup of an ad hoc, preliminary defense body for the Southeast Asia region.[48] Once back in the Capital, the Secretary called for a meeting on April 20 to begin work on a draft. But on the eighteenth, perhaps in response to Nixon's off-the-record comments, London ordered the British ambassador, Sir Roger Makins, not to attend the April 20 session. The rebuttal was, in Dulles' viewpoint, due to the personal interposition of India's Prime Minister Nehru, who protested to London that a show of strength prior to Geneva would nullify hopes for peace. * But the action was certainly further prompted by Eden's own fear that Dulles would construe British attendance as an assent to united action.[49] Once again pushed into an awkward position, Dulles revamped the conference to deal only with Korea (the second item on the Geneva agenda). On April 19

* Chalmers H. Roberts, "The Day We Didn't Go to War," *The Reporter*, XI (September 14, 1954), p. 34. The influence of Prime Minister Nehru upon the British position deserves further comment. Indians sympathized with the Vietminh because they saw in the movement an anti-colonial struggle for independence led by the most popular man in Vietnam, Ho Chi Minh. Charges that the Vietminh were Communist-dominated were deemed irrelevant, particularly since the Vietminh enjoyed widespread popular support. Until March 1954, Nehru said virtually nothing in public about the war; but Dulles' speech of the twenty-ninth seems to have been the catalyst for the Indian leader's involvement, for he sensed that the world hovered close to all-out war in Indochina. A definitive account of the Indian viewpoint is contained in Vidya Prakash Dutt and Vishal Singh, *Indian Policy and Attitudes Towards Indo-China and S.E.A.T.O.* (New York, 1954); see especially pp. 7–9.

he silenced rumors of unilateral action with a statement that it was "unlikely" troops would become involved in the Far East and, for the second time in ten days, hopped a plane for Paris on the twentieth.[50] Every indication pointed to an end to intervention plans just six days before the opening session at Geneva.

But as the military situation at Dienbienphu reduced to a day-by-day wait for collapse, French desperation to act bordered on panic. Following a NATO meeting of foreign ministers in Paris on the twenty-third, Bidault asked Dulles point-blank for an American Air Force strike employing B-29 bombers operating from United States bases outside Indochina proper, that is, for a reactivation of VULTURE. The French foreign minister showed Dulles a telegram from Navarre which called for a massive air strike around Dienbienphu as the only alternative to a cease-fire.[51] The Secretary answered that "the judgment of U.S. intelligence was that Dienbienphu was doomed, but Bidault insisted that U.S. intervention could save it." [52] Dulles promised that he would discuss the matter, and immediately cabled Eisenhower of the request.[53]

The Administration decision of April 4 that intervention would require a united front demanded that British opinion once more be sought. This policy was confirmed by a telephone call from the President to Under Secretary Smith.[54] At a dinner the evening of April 23, word was relayed to Eden that, in the absence of an American air strike, Dienbienphu was seventy-two hours away from capitulation. The British general staff was given details of the attack plan. Although still uncertain of the value of an air strike at this late hour, Dulles told Eden of his preparedness, with a British go-ahead, "to recommend the President to ask Congress for 'war powers' [Eden's paraphrase]." [55] Dulles was apparently banking on swaying Eden with the presentation of a decisive plan of action during a moment of overwhelming urgency. But Eden would not be moved. His government would discuss only a guarantee of Thailand's safety, to which Dulles for the time being acquiesced.[56]

The twenty-fourth was a day of intensive diplomatic exchanges. Admiral Radford, a vigorous proponent of intervention, arrived from Washington to join the Paris deliberations. Premier Laniel conveyed a plan for placing an American force under French command as a direct response to the presence of Chinese artillery gunners.[57] This latest addition, so clearly borne of utter desperation, was apparently brushed aside. The Americans pressed Eden instead to back an attack plan; although Dienbienphu could no longer be saved, the French effort would be sustainable if the allies acted decisively.[58] One word from Eden, said Dulles, and the President could go before Congress on the twenty-sixth; air intervention would take place on the twenty-eighth. The State Department had already prepared a statement of intentions (presumably including a joint declaration to Peking), he added. (In the Capital, Ambassador Bonnet was briefed on this sequence by Under Secretary Smith.[59]) But the Foreign Secretary remained firm: He again questioned the military feasibility of an air strike; he reminded the Americans of the Sino-Soviet Treaty of 1950, which he felt would be implemented since the Chinese would intervene; and he voiced genuine fears that a new war might be touched off, one of global dimensions. Radford's effort to quiet these fears by doubting that the Chinese would intervene proved unsuccessful; indeed, he must have nourished hesitancy by expressing confidence in allied ability to knock out Chinese airfields.[60] With all this, the decision to intervene contemplated war, a decision which Eden had no authority to make. He therefore proposed to return to London and confront his chief, Churchill, with the final choice.[61]

As far as Dulles was concerned, the problem of intervention had been resolved, in the negative, with Eden's departure. On the afternoon of the twenty-fourth the Secretary and members of his State Department staff struck off a letter to

Bidault explaining American inability to aid the French cause further. The letter reiterated the necessity of a united Southeast Asia coalition in order to comply with Congressional sentiment. In addition, it was observed that the military situation at Dienbienphu could no longer be salvaged even with a massive air raid on the order proposed by the French. Dienbienphu need not be regarded as the key to continued defense of Indochina, the letter went on; the hope was expressed that the French would in fact sustain their interest in organizing a collective defense for the region and "will surmount this temporary ordeal. . . ." [62] Bidault's response, made the same day, asserted that French military experts were convinced that a massive aerial attack could save the garrison because Vietminh men and matériel were heavily concentrated about the rim of the blockhouse. Coupled with the oncoming rainy season, a massive blow by American air power might well knock the Vietminh out of commission.[63] But even if Bidault's assessment were allowed, Eden's demurrer clinched the American decision to go to Geneva with the fall of the garrison behind the Western negotiators. On April 24 plans for a VULTURE-like operation were unceremoniously buried a second time.

APRIL 25–MAY 8: TAKING THE MIDDLE ROAD

Eden's personal opposition to the second go-round of American intervention proposals received full support from Churchill. At an unusual Sunday session at 10 Downing Street on the twenty-fifth, the two leaders met with the service ministers, the chiefs of staff, and the cabinet members.[64] This meeting probably was the first at which the British mapped out policy with a complete awareness of the gravity of the military situation at Dienbienphu; as The Times (London) pointed out, previous British calculations had counted on the monsoon season to halt serious fighting and permit the French time to improve the Vietnamese army.[65]

But a reaffirmation of previous objections was the outcome anyway. In summary, the British cited the insufficiency of an air strike, the grave damage that would accrue to the West if a strike were attempted, and the broader political problems deeply imbedded in the Indochina imbroglio that military action would leave untouched.[66] Looking toward Geneva, the British were also unwilling to sacrifice the chances for a settlement to the winds of unpredictable military adventures. Finally, Eden was acutely sensitive to the position taken by Great Britain's Commonwealth partners. The prime ministers of India, Ceylon, and Pakistan, as well as of Indonesia and Burma, had convened the Colombo Conference on April 27 to bring their influence to bear on the Geneva conferees in favor of "direct negotiations between the parties principally concerned." [67] Eden, who later said he had been "able to keep in constant contact with them [the Asian Commonwealth members] at every stage of our work," felt that the Colombo powers would be vital in the supervision or guaranteeing of a peace settlement, or to the success of a regional defense organization.[68] Joining in a united action would thus have severely undercut Britain's hopes of cooperation from her nonaligned allies. The final decision was consequently as Dulles had anticipated: Great Britain would not join the United States in a journey to the brink of war.

The British, in the way of a positive proposal, seem to have been quickly reconciled to the partition of Vietnam. Reports of favor shown the concept of ceding the Vietminh part of Vietnam filtered out of London several days before the Paris meetings.[69] Some British officials even admitted to the press that a scheme for dividing Vietnam under international agreement was being studied.[70] A dispatch published in *Le Monde* detailed three conditions of the British plan forwarded at Paris: a "cease-fire" accord; an actual territorial division (which the French insisted should take place only in Vietnam and be along clearly demarcated French-Vietminh zones); and a joint declaration by potential SEATO partners guaranteeing the new frontiers against further aggression.[71] What the British arrangements indicate is how far apart British-American thinking really was at the very time Dulles and Radford were peddling intervention plans and involvement in war.

With the British formally committed to awaiting the results of the Geneva talks, the Administration reversed gears and began to move closer to the British position. Speaking before the United States Chamber of Commerce on April 26, the President termed the struggle in Indochina "one of the testing places between a free form of government and dictatorship. Its outcome is going to have the greatest significance for us, and possibly for a long time into the future." Strategically, Indochina was likened to a "cork in the bottle, the bottle being the great area that includes Indonesia, Burma, Thailand, all of the surrounding areas of Asia. . . ." These phrases all seemed to harken back to the earliest warnings sent out after the Korean War; but the President shied away from a direct threat to Peking. Instead, he said that at Geneva the concerned parties were trying to reach a modus vivendi, and implied that this was one alternative to a reliance upon war or the threat of war to settle disputes. Perhaps intentionally, he followed talk of accommodation with the observation that the conference was in session at a time when atomic weapons were so awesome that "we sometimes visualize in a single destructive and surprise attack, almost a decisive act in the event of an outbreak of hostilities." [72] Out of context, the sentence might have been considered a veiled threat of instant retaliation; in context, however, the President seemed to be saying that the Communists would do well to bring the war to an end; if they choose to continue hostilities and reject negotiations, the United States might think twice about employing atomic weapons. The presentation was precisely in line with British thinking: forestalling action against Peking until after the failure of talks. More broadly, the speech resembled the Administration's previous use of the atomic threat in Korea, where the President chose to withhold actual employment of atomic weapons pending an assessment of Chinese sincerity in concluding an armistice.

The President's preparedness to follow British policy rather than heed counsels of unilateralism was manifested again the same day. Meeting with Congressmen at the White House, Eisenhower reported on the failure to obtain French or British backing for united action. As Sherman Adams has told it:

Eisenhower repeated that we were not going to "carry the rest of the world on our back" and that he had no intention of sending in American ground forces independently, but warned once more that there might be tremendous consequences ahead and that the leaders should keep in mind the possibility that some U.S. units might become involved. But the free world must understand that our most effective role did not lie in furnishing ground troops, he added.

Later in the discussion, the President also observed: "The French have asked us to send planes to Dienbienphu, but we are not going to be involved alone in a power move against the Russians." [73] The policy decision of April 4 would not be disturbed.

Two days after Churchill's announcement before Commons that Britain would definitely not undertake military action in Indochina,[74] the President was asked at a press conference (April 29) to reveal what he had meant about searching for a modus vivendi. He replied that between the unacceptable (Communist conquest of the entire region) and the unattainable (a firm, stable relationship with the Communists) lay a practical middle path.

The most you can work out [said Eisenhower] is a practical way of getting along.

Now, whether or not even that is possible, I don't know; but when you come down to it, that is what we have been doing in Europe—the whole situation from Berlin all the way through Germany is really on a practical basis of getting along one with the other, no more.[75]

As Chief Executive, Eisenhower went on, he had done about all he properly could do in Indochina without exceeding his constitutional authority. While he refused to endorse any specific method of achieving that "practical way of getting along," the President appeared to be preparing the American people for a negotiated settlement not detrimental to American security interests. If the Communists would accept *some part* of Indochina rather than continue to fight for the whole, the United States would be amenable. Like London and Paris, Washington was now disposed to dealing with the Communists across the bargaining table.

But any appearance of Western unity at Geneva was ludicrous. Beneath the surface, the allied camp was now riven by recriminations over the failure of united action as it had been previously over whether to intervene. Both Paris and Washington regarded the British as the main obstacle to intervention. One report told of French anger at London's refusal to provide even token aircraft to an attack force consisting mainly of American air power.[76] Dulles was equally distraught with British inflexibility. At Geneva, he privately inveighed against Eden, accusing London of refusing to back *any* American action in Indochina. He told Eden he had merely wanted British moral support; but when the Foreign Secretary asked precisely what action the United States wanted to take, Dulles was said to have replied that no action "had . . . yet been decided."[77] The outward concordance of positions within the Western camp at Geneva overshadowed the strong feeling prevalent in official Paris and Washington that the British had been the chief roadblock to the implementation of American attack plans and the rescue of Indochina from communism.

On May 3 Secretary Dulles, in accordance with plan, turned the American delegation over to Under Secretary Smith. Two days later Dulles returned to the United States prepared to inform Congress that Dienbienphu could not be saved but that the feasibility of a collective defense system for the western Pacific area remained. On the battlefield the Vietminh accomplished the inevitable when, on May 7, after a seige of fifty-five days, they overran Dienbienphu's last defenders. A major Communist victory, planned since the winter of 1953 and hastened by the Berlin Conference, had been achieved in the midst of Western inaction. A posture of confusion, indecision, disunity, and mutual recriminations characterized the Western camp and exposed "American leadership to its worst diplomatic defeat since the fall of Continental China." [78] The Communist victory at Dienbienphu for all practical purposes sealed shut the Indochina case. The scene shifted from the battlefield to the negotiating table as, on May 8, discussions on Indochina opened at Geneva.

7. TOWARD A SETTLEMENT

By the time of the opening session at Geneva, friction among the Western allies was matched against a closing of the Soviet ranks and a strong determination on China's part to bring the Indochina war to a halt. In late April Premier Malenkov retreated from his original stand on deterrence. He held on April 26 that World War III "would inevitably lead to the collapse of the capitalist social system," a statement that represented a near-capitulation to the Khrushchevites.[1] The shift in the Premier's stand presaged a more total turnabout. The Soviet press reported an increasing belief abroad in American intervention in Indochina whether or not the French requested it. Such bits of hearsay were grist for the Khrushchev mill; they provided "unmistakable" evidence that the United States, far from preparing for a permanent accommodation on East-West issues, was convinced of its nuclear power superiority and would not hesitate to widen a crisis even to encompass the Soviet heartland.[2]

The swing of the pendulum Khrushchev's way, if influential upon Chinese policy on the eve of Geneva, would probably have had the effect of excluding senseless risk-taking. The Soviet theme of "anything is possible," after all, saw the United States as building up its military bases abroad (as the Chinese "observed") and as being capable of an irrational pre-emptive blow that the Soviets might not be able to deflect. Continued maneuvering for position within the Kremlin leadership contributed to a policy of caution. While neither the Soviets nor the Chinese would have countenanced a permanently stabilized situation, careless miscalculations were equally impermissible. If the Chinese had been attuned to the Soviet inner controversy, the Khrushchev position would have been overwhelmingly (though reticently) supported. Alice Hsieh has written in support of this contention:

. . . Khrushchev's insistence on a war-fighting posture [in his speech of March 6] implied that the Soviet Union would seek to develop some kind of military superiority over the United States, thus opening the way for a more aggressive bloc military posture. . . . With a view to forwarding their own objectives, the Chinese could hope to exploit both politically and psychologically a Soviet military superiority over the United States. . . . It is thus possible that Khrushchev's visit to Peking in September–October 1954 . . . only solidified a choice that the Chinese had already made between the contending Soviet positions.[3]

The relative concordance of Sino-Soviet strategy as Geneva opened was no more clearly demonstrated than in the response to the United States-Japan Mutual Defense Assistance Agreement signed March 8, 1953. In a joint declaration, the USSR and the CPR declared their policy of peaceful coexistence, spoke of promoting broader cultural and economic ties with Japan, and expressed a willingness "to take steps to normalize relations with Japan. . . ."[4] On her own the CPR revitalized the diplomatic offensive that had lain practically dormant since the end of the Korean War. On April 29 the Chinese signed an important agreement with India in settlement of differences over Tibet. In the preamble to the agreement, China for the first time introduced the now well-known "five principles" that it vowed to follow in interstate relations if other countries reciprocated.[5]

All the while, however, Peking continued to observe American activities in the Far East; for if Khrushchev was right, the United States was fully capable of initiating large-scale war over Indochina. Secretary Dulles' disclosures before the House Committee on Foreign Affairs (April 5) were deemed attempts "to create pretexts for starting another Korean war. . . . This will in turn pave the way for invading China." [6] Military maneuvers were duly noted, and the appearance in the South China Sea of the carriers *Essex* and *Boxer* provoked the most strongly worded *People's Daily* editorial of the crisis. The editorial warned: "We do not commit aggression against others and are firmly opposed to aggressive action by anyone else. . . . We advocate peace and oppose war. But we certainly will not take it lying down if someone else's armed aggression is directed against us." [7] Still evident, however, was the defensive tone of Peking's responses. Even while vehemently ranting about provocatory American activities in the Far East, *World Culture* expressed the "deep friendship for the American people" felt by all Chinese, and hoped for "peaceful coexistence with the American people." [8] Once again the Foreign Ministry had rejected an explicit warning that might upset the carefully laid plans for consolidating battlefield gains at Geneva.

News of the fall of Dienbienphu was greeted with unusual cautiousness. The victory was hailed by the *People's Daily*, but with the comment that "the time is . . . ripe for ending the war in Indo-China. . . ." [9] Chou En-lai, who headed the China delegation, followed up the "go-slow" approach when he remarked at the May 12 session that Korea had set an example for the settlement of disputes through negotiations. Noting the CPR's concern over "the danger of the war's expanding," he said: "The Chinese people consider that: the Korean War was stopped; now, the Indochina war should be stopped in the same way." [10] As in previous months, Chou's aim was two-fold: to align support for talks and shift the spotlight away from the military sphere, and to affirm Chinese willingness to abide by time-honored diplomatic methods. But at the same time, Chou further revealed the same general uneasiness over what the United States might do if the Geneva talks bogged down. These fundamental considerations—the long-range importance of peace in Indochina versus the slim but ever-present possibility of war—would be decisive in guiding the Communist hand at Geneva.

PREVENTING A STAMPEDE: THE WESTERN POSITION

The unproductiveness of Dulles' trip abroad made him, as might have been expected, vulnerable to bipartisan criticism upon his return. Specifically, the Secretary was taken to task for having failed to consult with a number of Congressional leaders before considering the French request for intervention; for having consulted with Congressmen only after having talked with the British and French and after having announced "united action"; and for having gambled and lost on the chance that our allies would support united action.[11] To these charges, the Administration was prepared to reply that little had been lost in the end, that the West's security interests could still be maintained in Southeast Asia, and that with the meeting of certain conditions the United States remained as always ready to act in a war not yet lost. It was around these three points that American diplomacy worked in the months after the fall of Dienbienphu in a final bid to avert diplomatic catastrophe at Geneva, as well as to lay the groundwork for a graceful exit from the entire affair.

The President was first to respond to critics of Dulles. Addressing himself to the problem of united action, Eisenhower said on May 5 that advance notice of the policy had been given our allies. The policy was, he insisted, "not a new one"; it merely reaffirmed the collective security principle. Of the failure to implement united action, he added: "Obviously, it was never expected that this collective security arrangement would spring into existence overnight." Nevertheless, he revealed that the Administration had not given up on united action. "The fact that such an organization is in process of formation," he said, "could have an important bearing upon what happens at Geneva during the Indochina phase of the Conference." [12] The implication was that Washington would stick to a policy of "watchful waiting," putting the gun in the holster but keeping a finger on the trigger.

Secretary Dulles was next to speak in defense of Administration policies. In a nationwide radio and television address on May 7, he stated that present conditions in Indochina did not warrant participation by American forces. Turning instead to the conditions of a settlement, he hoped that peace would be concluded at Geneva "on terms which do not endanger the freedom of the people of Vietnam." "But," he warned, "we would be gravely concerned if an armistice or cease-fire were reached at Geneva which would provide a road to a Communist take-over and further Communist aggression." In that case, "or if hostilities continue, then the need will be more urgent to create the condition for a united action in defense of the area." [13] Within one year, the United States had come full circle, for Dulles' speech was closely akin to Eisenhower's first observation on April 16, 1953, that any armistice in Korea which freed the Chinese for action elsewhere would be "a fraud." The Secretary's remarks were a clear admission, too, that the work of five weeks at obtaining a united front had been unsuccessful but would continue.

With the fall of Dienbienphu behind it, Washington pressed ahead on the implementation of united action. As it did so, a completely different security framework began to evolve. No longer was Indochina deemed absolutely essential to free world security, as had once been the case. Instead, the argument advanced was that even if the entire peninsula should be lost—which was still a strong possibility if the Communists pressed their attack—the rest of Southeast Asia could be held. This first compromise of the "domino principle" came from Secretary Dulles when he said on May 11:

What we are trying to do is create a situation in Southeast Asia where the domino situation will not apply. And while I see it might be said that I felt that Southeast Asia could be secured even without perhaps Vietnam, Laos, and Cambodia, I do not want for a minute to underestimate the importance of these countries. . . . But I do not want to give the impression either that if events that we could not control, and which we do not anticipate, should lead to their being lost that we would consider the whole situation hopeless and we would give up in despair. . . .[14]

Asked to amplify the statement that Indochina's loss would not be the prelude to the loss of Southeast Asia, the Secretary said that a collective security arrangement would seek to save "essential parts" of Southeast Asia if not the whole. But what parts were "essential"? Laos and Cambodia were not, he said. "They are important but by no means essential. Laos and Cambodia are relatively poor and thinly-settled areas. I would say 90 percent of the total population approximately of Indochina is in Viet-Nam. . . ." [15] Significantly, the press conference transcript distributed by the State Department deleted these latter remarks.[16] And with good reason, for the remarks not only stirred comment in diplomatic circles but seemed literally to have pulled the rug out from under the whole basis for American involvement in Indochina—the fear that the fall of the peninsula would inexorably lead to the fall of neighboring free countries.

The dramatic turnabout in strategic thinking over Indochina was minimized by the Administration. Speaking on the same day as Dulles (May 11), Eisenhower concluded that the falling domino principle would be offset once nations joined together in collective defense. Preparing the way for what now seemed imminent, he went on to say that even if all the Associated States, or any one of them, fell by the wayside, collective security would make the defense task more difficult but not irretrievable. The United States was engaged in trying "to create a situation in Southeast Asia where the domino situation will not apply." [17] Through united action, the United States was seeking to build a row of dominoes strong enough to withstand the fall of one, he added the following day.[18] But while the Administration was protesting it was not writing off Indochina, the evidence suggested that such was the case. In the process of dissociating itself from responsibility for events in Indochina, the Administration was fostering the notion that loss of the peninsula under the impact of renewed hostilities would not really be as dangerous to international security as had previously been thought. Through a collective defense organization, Eisenhower and Dulles were saying, the threat to the safety of the entire Pacific, once considered bound up with the fall of Indochina, was now neutralized. Within a week of the tragedy at Dienbienphu, the Government had beaten a full-fledged retreat from the original hypotheses advanced in support of intervention. For united action had been advanced on March 29 specifically to save all or part of Indochina; by May 11, united action was still being sought, but Indochina was being counted expendable.

Throughout the remainder of May and June Washington became more and more reconciled to a settlement. Although Chinese assistance continued to pour in,[19] leading the Vietminh to push the French farther south, the Government refused to be pressured into involvement in what it must have recognized as a lost cause. On May 15, for example, the State Department indicated that the conditions for American involvement were: full independence to the Associated States; a vigorous program to strengthen the Vietnamese National Army (VNA), preferably through an American training mission; and moral support of the United Nations following political concessions from Paris.[20] Where the French had been stymied before by British recalcitrance, they were now being shunted aside by renewed State Department insistence upon the realization of past political pledges, as well as by the sudden injection of the United Nations into the crisis. And since the Laniel government had barely managed to survive a vote of confidence, it was clear to Washington that the French public still held fast to a policy favoring peace at any price.[21]

The Administration's backwatering into calmer seas came in the midst of pessimistic reports on the war situation. Defense Secretary Wilson returned from a three-week tour of the Far East with a forbidding picture of French retreat.[22] General Van Fleet, in the United States following a similar trip as the President's personal representative with the rank of ambassador, gave closed-door testimony before two Senate committees on June 3 and spoke with the President and Radford on June 7. According to a news commentary by Chalmers M. Roberts, Van Fleet informed Eisenhower that the United States, with South Korean and Formosan troop assistance but without Great Britain, "should be prepared to enter the Indochina war . . ." [23] The general's suggestion came as representatives of Britain, France, and the ANZUS powers met in Washington to consider the military outlook.[24] Once more, Eisenhower was under pressure to act.

The President refused to rush headlong into a commitment in Indochina; he firmly stood by his and Dulles' statements of the previous month. The Secretary of State lent substance to this conclusion with a series of important comments immediately following upon the Wilson and Van Fleet reports. At his news conference of June 8, Dulles repeated that the United States would not become involved in the Southeast Asian crisis "unless the whole nature" of aggression by Communist China changed.[25] On the West Coast, he again brought up the question of collective defense, which he said still required that France "make good" on its July 3 pledge. Because Communist China had committed neither "open invasion" nor "open military aggression," the United States could not intervene unless certain moral, legal, and political conditions were met. The United States, in short, was prepared; but, Dulles said, "The future depends largely on decisions awaited at Paris, London, and Geneva." [26]

Dulles' stated conviction that American incapacity to act boldly in defense of Indochina was caused by inertia abroad could only with great difficulty be squared with facts. First, by again insisting upon French fulfillment of the July 3 declaration, and by declaring that American hands were tied until the Associated States received what Dulles called "complete independence," the Administration masked the fact that the Secretary on several occasions privately expressed the opinion that the French had made adequate strides forward toward political sovereignty for their dependencies. It will be recalled that less than two weeks after having been issued, the July 3 declaration was assessed by the Secretary as "a very clear and unequivocal offer of full independence and sovereignty" to the Associated States. During May 1954 Dulles told a Senate hearing that the promises of that declaration had been "pretty well implemented." ". . . the French have really carried out their declaration of independence. This seems to be accepted pretty much by the representatives of the Associated States with whom I have talked. . . ." [27] And in early June the Secretary was even more emphatic. Personal talks with representatives of other governments, and reports from American diplomatic officers in Saigon, had led him to conclude that there seemed "to be rather complete satisfaction with the degree of independence which has now been made available by the French." Complete independence would prove premature and even disastrous for "people who have had no experience in exercising it, and developing political institutions." [28]

The contradiction of Dulles' public statements by his private views makes it clear that, at least so far as the Department of State was concerned, France had really done all it could

on the Indochina political front. But if American reluctance
to become involved, either alone or in unison, was decidedly
not explainable in terms of French temporization on the independence issue, what of the "decisions" Dulles awaited in
London? Here too, the opposition lay not abroad but at
home. For in contending that VULTURE or any multilateral
move directed at Peking would eventually bring about the
need for a ground troop commitment to Indochina, the British
had American company in General Ridgway. Concerned about
the prospect of intervention, the Army Chief of Staff sent a
team of expert "engineers, signal and communications special-
ists, medical officers, and experienced combat leaders who knew
how to evaluate terrain in terms of battle tactics." [29] A firm
believer in the continued value of ground troops regardless
of technological changes in the military establishment, Ridgway was out to prove that sudden involvement in war—
which London saw the Americans drifting toward—would
compel the utilization of U.S. forces, precisely what the
President indicated on several occasions he wished most to
avoid.

It appears that the report reached Ridgway's, and eventually
the President's desk, prior to the fall of Dienbienphu (May
7).[30] The report proved conclusively that the United States,
had it decided upon involvement, would have faced a major
military commitment with anticipated losses on a scale far
greater than had been incurred in Korea. The investigating
team determined that

the [Indochina] area . . . was practically devoid of those facilities
which modern forces such as ours find essential to the waging of
war. Its telecommunications, highways, railways . . . were almost
non-existent. Its port facilities and airfields were totally inadequate,
and to provide the facilities we would need would require a tremendous engineering and logistical effort.

Because the terrain was most suitable for guerrilla warfare,
the United States would have needed a ground force with

the capacity to sustain "heavy casualties" under conditions strikingly similar to those encountered by the Allied Pacific forces in World War II.[31] At the outset, a minimum of five divisions was deemed imperative, and a maximum of ten once the war was in full swing.[32] In view of the New Look's de-emphasis of the Army, leaving only six divisions available (though not combat-ready) for movement to trouble spots at mid-year,[33] the invasion force could not have been battle-ready until December 1954 or January 1955, and would for some time have had to rely for supplies upon distant bases.[34]

The Ridgway Report, brought before the National Security Council, "played a considerable, perhaps a decisive, part in persuading our government not to embark on that adventure." [35] It was a jolting rejoinder to Administration advocates of military action, and at the same time a confirmation of British suspicions about American unpreparedness to deal with the military demands of involvement in Indochina. While Dulles may have objected to the report, and while Radford paid it short shrift,[36] there is no question that the President was strongly moved by the persuasive military conclusions. In summary, the French failure to accede to Indochinese demands was recognized and accepted by Dulles, while the reasons behind British failure to join in united action were firmly supported by the Administration's own Army Chief of Staff.

COMING TO TERMS

The resignation of Laniel's cabinet in Paris on June 12, paving the way for the accession of Pierre Mendès-France on a pledge to end the war by July 20 or resign, made evident the superfluousness of further talk about a united action. Indeed, the Communist victory at Dienbienphu put into sharp relief not only the futility of working to save northern Vietnam but also the probability that the best offer the West would receive from the Communists was a divided Vietnam.

For the United States, which had sought and failed to attain national unity in Korea, the prospect of agreeing to the partition of Vietnam could not have been pleasant, especially as the Administration had long since made known its mistrust of the concept. But although Washington found partition repugnant, and although the deputy chief of the Saigon embassy (Robert M. McClintock) urged Dulles to reject it,[37] clearly no better alternative was available.[38]

Communist China's support at the conference table for Vietminh hopes of national unity made sound propaganda but poor policy. By late June the riskiness of supporting a VPA drive south to attain national unity became obvious with the issuance of a joint statement from Washington by Eisenhower and Churchill. The long-awaited agreement to "press forward with plans for collective defense" in Southeast Asia had been concluded. The outcome at Geneva would not affect such plans; but impossible demands made upon Paris by the Communist side, it was decided, would tend "seriously" to aggravate "the international situation. . . ."[39] For the Chinese, the implications of the Eisenhower-Churchill accord were clear: Vietnamese unity, hardly a priority item anyway, would have to be put off. Chou En-lai's meeting with Ho on the DRV-CPR border between July 3–5 may, in this light, have been prompted by a need to thwart Vietminh ambitions with the promise of later Chinese support.[40]

China's awareness of the pivotal position of Great Britain in American intervention plans may also have prompted positive steps by Chou En-lai to assure Eden of the CPR's good intentions. On June 16, Chou informed the Foreign Secretary that the Vietminh had been persuaded to withdraw from Laos and Cambodia. Interestingly, the Communist concession occurred at a time when newspapers were alive with rumors of American pressure upon the British and French to pull out of the conference.[41] But the shift also coincided with an affirmative Chinese response, awaited for four years by Downing Street, to Britain's offer to exchange diplomatic representatives.[42] Peking, anxious to assure that Britain remained free from Dulles' clutches, was quite willing to use both the Vietminh and diplomacy as bargaining devices. Equally at stake for the Chinese in settling the Indochina dispute by negotiations was the continued effectiveness of their diplomatic offensive in Asia. On June 28 the five principles had been reaffirmed with India in New Delhi. A joint statement issued by Chou and Prime Minister Nehru revealed that Indochina had been a primary topic of discussion. The hope was expressed for an early settlement of the war in conformity with the five principles.[43] In talks with Prime Minister U Nu of Burma the next day, the principles were incorporated into an agreement patterned after the April 29 Sino-Indian text.[44] A *People's Daily* editorial placed these diplomatic gains in a larger perspective by contrasting China's firm steps toward peace in Asia with American-dominated schemes for new military alignments both in Europe and the Far East.[45] Peking was apparently convinced that the diplomatic gains from an Indochina settlement were well worth the price of temporarily sacrificing Ho Chi Minh's personal designs upon southern Vietnam.

As even the French became disgusted with the lack of results at Geneva, the Communists were squarely faced with a possible breakdown of discussions and a victory for American intervention hopes. Prior to departing for Geneva, Premier Mendès-France confessed before the National Assembly "the possibility of failure" in the negotiations. As a consequence, the new French leader considered it might prove necessary to conscript soldiers for the protection of the retreating Expeditionary Corps.[46] The willingness of Paris to take the unprecedented step of drafting recruits for Indochina duty might well have clinched the Sino-Soviet case for concluding the war. By mid-July, coincident with the return of Secretary Dulles to Paris, NCNA reported from Geneva: "Chinese delegation circles see no reason whatsoever why the Geneva Conference should play up to the U.S. policy [of obstruction] and make no efforts towards achieving an agreement which is acceptable and satisfactory to all parties concerned and which is honorable for the two belligerent sides." [47] The stage was thus set for an end to the war.

On July 21, after seventy-five days, the Geneva conferees reached a consensus on the Indochina problem.[48] Three separate cease-fire agreements were signed with a representative of the DRV; the French Commander-in-Chief signed for Laos and Vietnam. The governments of Laos and Cambodia issued declarations of nearly identical wording in which they pledged to adopt basically neutral foreign policies; in accordance with the Final Declaration of the Conference, general elections were to be held in both countries during 1955. Vietnam, on the other hand, was divided into Communist and non-Communist zones at roughly the seventeenth parallel; but the West succeeded at postponing for two years elections looking toward reunification. Ho Chi Minh, who could still look forward with some confidence to a legal ballot box victory in 1956, assured his people that the demarcation line "is a temporary and transitional measure . . . [which] does not mean by [sic] any way a partition of our country nor a division of powers." He promised that "our country will surely be unified and our compatriots throughout the country will certainly be emancipated." [49] But inwardly the Vietminh leadership considered partition an undeserved setback. Some Vietminh officials privately expressed annoyance at the pressure from Chou and Molotov which had forced acceptance of less than satisfactory terms. Given another month of fighting, these officials contended, the VPA could have improved its military position to the point of holding down nearly the entire country and bringing Laos and Cambodia within Vietnam's sphere of influence.[50] Whispered dismay was about all the Vietminh dared voice, for the Chinese still held the tangible keys to future military efforts.

On the other hand, the United States readily revealed its distaste for the Geneva agreements by refusing to support the Final Declaration. (The Republic of Vietnam also refrained from adhering to the document.) At the final session Under Secretary Smith read a position paper which declared that the Government "takes note" of the agreements, would not violate them by forceful acts, but "would view any renewal of the aggression in violation of the aforesaid Agreements with grave concern and as seriously threatening international peace and security." Smith lent support to the Republic of Vietnam's hope for national unity; but in accepting partition, the Administration had reconciled itself to a solution which it regarded as ephemeral and which the Vietnamese considered objectionable.

To Dulles, the agreement to slice Vietnam in half had at least one saving facet. "We have a clean base there now without a taint of colonialism," he is reputed to have said. "Dienbienphu was a blessing in disguise." [51] But to others, a settlement for one-half of Vietnam where the United States had presented itself as willing to fight rather than accept that outcome represented a distinct failure to achieve an important objective. The partition of Vietnam did indeed result in part from the influence of a potential united action upon China. But the Geneva accords also pointed up the shortcomings of Western strength matched against Communist tactical flexibility both on the battlefield and at the conference table. In the following chapter we shall want to examine the extent of America's failure in Indochina and highlight Chinese Communist strategy.

8. THE CRISIS IN VIETNAM

THE AMERICAN FAILURE

The American approach to the Vietnam crisis employed a complex mixture of risky, unclear proposals and concrete policy decisions.* Taken together, these revealed that the Government, while cognizant of the long-range threat posed by Communism in Southeast Asia, treaded a far less certain path when dealing with the war crisis itself and with those allies whose acquiescence was requisite to action. At bottom, the chief stumbling block of both proposals and policy lay

* The distinction made here between "proposals" and "policy" is more semantic than real, the aim being to facilitate analysis. The American military and diplomatic proposals did constitute "policy" in the sense that they must certainly have been advanced by the Secretary of State or the Chairman of the Joint Chiefs of Staff with the full knowledge of the President on the understanding, moreover, that fulfillment of certain preconditions would result in favorable Presidential action. It is difficult to believe that approaches to allies and Congressmen were made without explicit Presidential authority. And in view of the formidable, at times dominant, place of Dulles in the formulation of American foreign policy, together with Eisenhower's great confidence in his Secretary, it seems quite likely that a recommendation from Dulles for intervention would have obtained the President's approval provided Dulles could acquire the support of key allies. Dulles was given considerable leeway toward seeking to sway allies and Congressmen; but the President, by his insistence on at least allied sanction of American involvement, never had to make a "policy" (yes or no) decision on the proposals. In this light, the American plans were not Administration "policy" but overtures, since they were ultimately subject to Presidential "veto."

in an underestimation of the fundamental political problems posed by the Indochina war. The breaking point of the United States reaction to the crisis was our consideration that French choice of primarily military over political means was logically justifiable, diplomatically unopposable, and therefore worthy of material support. It was a consideration which deepened our involvement and eventually left us without allied backing.

The Proposals. The problem of, and American military plans for, intervention would not have arisen had French optimism been well-grounded. Early suppositions of the non-necessity of direct American involvement in Indochina were tied inextricably to a strong belief that the French eventually would overwhelm the Vietminh. Based on that projection, which had been one of the "assumptions" for Joint Chiefs of Staff approval of NSC 162/2, Washington deemed economic and military assistance adequate to insure victory. But the hoped-for series of battlefield successes and victory by 1955 never came about. Consistently favorable reports made by American as well as French observers and visitors at the front obscured the ever increasing threat posed by the Vietminh. Until late March 1954 the White House held to the belief that the French could win in Indochina so long as the Chinese were kept out, a confidence that had long been part of the rationale behind warnings to Peking, dramatizations of Indochina's security value to the West, and conditioning of direct American involvement on overt Chinese intervention.

The initial willingness to "let things ride" in Indochina seems explainable as a product of inaccurate reporting from the front lines, and overoptimism in certain sectors of the American decision-making apparatus. Put another way, intervention did not become a problem for Washington until so late because of the existence of a very real intelligence gap, the product of a "French" policy toward Indochina. Hanson Baldwin pinpointed the sources of gross exaggeration of French chances:

Our assessments of the prospects in Indo-China have been perennially overoptimistic—partly because of a Francophile influence in the State Department (which has viewed Indo-China largely through the eyes of its French desk), partly because our representatives in Paris urged restraint and caution in Indo-China lest France refuse to ratify the European Defense Community treaty, and partly because of a question of competence on the part of our own diplomatic and military representatives in Indo-China.[1]

The foundations of overoptimism lay in the relationship between Saigon's intelligence network and Washington's policy. In Saigon, assessments of the military situation were based primarily on French intelligence sources. While it is true that military reports sent on to Washington emanated from American channels—the Embassy itself, the military mission (MAAG), and our armed forces attachés [2]—the fact is that few Americans made independent, on-the-spot evaluations.[3] And those who did were, unfortunately, not in a position to get their views to the top.[4] The reason for these occurrences has already been intimated: The leading American representatives in Indochina, Ambassador Heath and Generals Trapnell and O'Daniel, were following a policy formulated in Washington, and that policy, beginning in 1950, called for only the most discreet involvement in French activities. The policy required that the French receive complete American cooperation; any attempt at going over the heads of French authorities, as by establishing a completely independent intelligence or evaluation network in Indochina, might be construed as "intervention" and decisively undercut Franco-American relations.

It also appears that the intelligence problem in Saigon was complicated by a lack of full cooperation between the Embassy and O'Daniel's MAAG. Ambassador Heath has admitted to "some divergence of viewpoints between the political and military representatives of the U.S. in Indochina. While the Embassy was supposed to be kept in touch with the military estimates of the military mission it is possible that some of their reports, oral and written, escaped our attention." [5] O'Daniel's "own past experience and his own personality," it has been alleged, made him ill-suited for the job of chief military advisor in an unconventional Asian war.[6] The picture of inadequate American intelligence from the front, an Indochina policy compromised by consideration of an ally, and differences within our own politico-military team helps to explain why it was possible for high-ranking Administration officials to continue to predict victory under the Navarre Plan until the latter days of March 1954. The same factors would also account for the stark contrasts between the troubled findings of survey teams of congressmen, who were independent observers, and the glowing reports of Stassen, Trapnell, and O'Daniel, who were influenced by loyalty to Administration policies. The Navarre Plan did not fail simply because of "the declining will of the French people and the French Parliament to see the struggle continued . . . ,"[7] or because of French politicians who rejected a callup of reserves.[8] Every indication is that the plan's collapse, notably over the decision to stand at Dienbienphu, rested equally on fundamental military and political weaknesses discounted by the confident French and accepted by an inadequately informed and overly cooperative American advisory mission. Subsequently, the bases for American adoption of a "pro-French" policy shall be examined; for now, it is necessary to evaluate the American reaction to the discovery that the Navarre Plan had failed.

By the spring of 1954, the Indochina war matched neither of the patterns the Eisenhower Administration had been prepared to cope with: The war was not one the French could win, even with massive United States assistance; nor was it one which could be classified as a "major" aggression demanding "massive" retaliation. As a result, the attempt to frustrate the Vietminh offensive went awry. Washington claimed British recalcitrance and French dalliance; Paris, which had invited VULTURE but rejected united action, finally joined the Americans in pinning the blame on Britain; and London alluded to American acceptance of the consequences of a widened war. It now rests to examine the American proposals in the light of these accusations.

The sudden offer of American planes and flyers to Ély on March 25, the first united action formula presented to London and Paris in the wake of decisions reached by Congressmen April 3 and by the White House April 4, and the final plan hastily coordinated three days prior to the first Geneva session all contained a common intangible thread: They betrayed Washington's conviction that an exclusive reliance on military means would somehow eradicate the Vietminh threat. Quite aside from the significance of this omission of political measures, which will be discussed below, the three propositions were subject to considerable debate on their military merits alone.

From the British standpoint, the American plans with respect to VULTURE were ultimately infeasible. Dulles and Radford were originally convinced that a single air strike could, as Bidault believed to the end, knock out the main cog of the VPA and virtually end the fighting in France's favor. Put another way, it was felt initially that air power would shift the balance of power on the ground even though, in a guerrilla war, that balance was born of political rather than military advantages. As the British pointed out consistently, the American plans made no immediate provision for removing the basis of Vietminh strength—popular support. Nor did the plans take account of the need to eliminate the Vietminh supply lines, which would have involved the fruitless task of flying sorties against coolie lines, underground fortresses, and trench communications networks.[9]

A third drawback to VULTURE centered about Radford's intention to relieve Dienbienphu with air power while not annihilating the defenders of the fortress. As we have seen,

Dulles was not at all certain by late April whether the maneuver could be executed; yet his doubts did not prevent him from proposing the raid to Eden. It was left to Eisenhower to nullify VULTURE. Said the President years after the event:

Well, I couldn't think of anything probably less effective than in a great big jungle area and with a besieged fortress, trying to relieve it with air force. I just can't see how this could have been done unless you were willing to use weapons that could have destroyed the jungles all around the area for miles and that would have probably destroyed Dienbienphu itself, and that would have been that.[10]

Since allied sanction of VULTURE meant war, the British, aware of the operation's grave deficiencies, feared that the war would necessarily spread into CPR territory when local attacks proved indecisive. As we shall explain subsequently, Radford was probably correct to have depreciated the probability of Chinese intervention under air attack confined to Dienbienphu; but his accuracy was highly questionable on the effectiveness of VULTURE itself. For at the heart of British cynicism over VULTURE was the conviction that, far from turning the tide in Vietnam, the operation would inevitably create the need for ground forces (principally American) and a repetition of the Korean conflict.

The Ridgway Report bolstered the British objections at the same time that it exposed the flaws in the New Look defense program: the optimistic reliance for ground support on Asian troops;[11] the creation of a "mobile reserve" which, in March 1954, consisted of one combat-ready division;[12] and the replacement of manpower by "new weapons" which were still in the planning stage.[13] British suspicions proved correct; the United States not only had vastly overrated the ability of an air strike to do the job at Dienbienphu, but had not counted at all upon the need for GI's and at least a partial mobilization.[14] From the military angle, to sum up, Indochina demonstrated not a case where the United States stayed out of war when it should have intervened,[15] but a case where the debate on intervention almost resulted in a disastrous decision based upon faulty analysis and "wishful thinking." [16]

Aside from overoptimism and the basic military drawbacks of American planning, the manner in which the Administration conducted diplomacy during the hectic months prior to the fall of Dienbienphu also revealed a lack of circumspection. Statements of American officials during mid-1953 hinted at our hope for the future deterrence of Communist aggression in Asia through some form of collective defense. Yet the Administration, from the available evidence, did not follow up on this until the conclusion of the Berlin Conference in mid-February 1954, when Dulles recognized the depths of the Vietminh threat to Dienbienphu.

The switch from thinking about an informal defense mechanism for Southeast Asia to belatedly pushing for its implementation, represented by Dulles' Overseas Press Club speech on March 29, was ill-timed. Although regarded from allied capitals as a proposal worthy of future study, united action nevertheless revealed that the Administration had miscalculated the impact upon our allies of the decision to convene an international conference at Geneva. Made without thorough soundings in either Paris or London, united action implicitly assumed that both allies would fall in line behind a united front against Peking. But to the French, action in unity not only with Washington but a host of other nations aroused the old fear that singular control of Indochina would gradually be eroded by a coalition. Related to that belief was the French attitude toward negotiations. Laniel's allusions between November 1953 and April 1954 to an honorable peace were tacit admissions that the eight-year struggle in Indochina would have to result in much less than total French victory. Ever mindful that full-scale American entry into the fighting would considerably reduce France's opportunity to salvage economic, political, and cultural influence in the region, Paris adopted a different interpretation of the agreed aim to negotiate from a position of strength. While the Americans, determined to contain communism at the China border, wanted complete military victory before again engaging in a diplomatic tête-à-tête with the Communists, the French were satisfied to find an "honorable settlement" as prosecution of the war proceeded. The Administration grossly underestimated the power and purpose of the "peace faction" in Paris. The highest circles of French officialdom were firmly behind talking peace at the first reasonable opportunity; any united action courted war with China at worst and the collapse of hopes for an Indochina settlement at best. Thus, the possibility in late 1953 that different war aims might lead to different tactical thinking and different views on the timing of negotiations became a reality in the spring of 1954.

To the British, Dulles' request for united action appeared as an attempt to dictate policy. In London as in Paris, the Administration had incorrectly gauged official opinion; far from leaning toward action in Indochina, the British, well in advance of Dulles' trip of April 11, were committed to giving the Chinese a hearing at Geneva. Aside from a constant, stubborn determination not to get involved in Asia again, the British were terribly disturbed by the lack of clear American military aims under united action. Until April 7, when Dulles publicly discarded thoughts of an air-naval attack upon the CPR if a joint warning were disregarded, the United States had evinced a readiness to engage in full-scale war with Peking. Thereafter, perhaps to meet British objections, Dulles proposed an ad hoc defense body which would, he believed, be sufficient to deter Chinese aid. Despite the shift, the British were certain that the coalition would be ignored by the CPR and the West's bluff called. On at least one point London considered a warning and a coalition synonymous; both entailed the risk of internationalizing the war with Geneva days away.

In this light, the decision to meet at Geneva not only provided the Communists with a deadline but the British with a strong argument for avoiding provocative action.

Policy. The military and diplomatic pitfalls in the Administration's approach to the crisis provide, however, only a surface picture of the American dilemma over intervention. For neither British backing, French steadfastness, Congressional support, nor Asian contributions could have altered the unsolved political crisis in Indochina which was at the heart of the Vietminh's successful challenge to French rule. The primary weakness which permeated the Administration's policy lay not in having failed to acquire the support necessary to intervene but in having yielded on French political concessions as the precondition to any further American involvement. Administration conduct brought into the open not only that it thought less of association with colonialism than it was willing to admit, but equally that it viewed the Indochina problem as essentially solvable through military rather than political action. Until the laying of the seige of Dienbienphu (March 13), a grant of independence had been the object of considerable Administration attention under the argument, advanced also in on-the-spot Congressional surveys, that French political initiatives could do more to defeat the Vietminh than hard-won military victories. With the first indications that the Vietminh meant to throw everything they had into taking Dienbienphu, the Administration leap-frogged over the political problems facing Paris. Immediate military needs came to predominate over long-standing political difficulties; the Administration tended to subordinate the independence issue pending a military victory. The prerequisite of full sovereignty to the Associated States, although part of the discussions with Ély, the April 4 White House policy decision, and the Dulles-Eden talks April 11–13, was never pressed upon Paris.

The public call for political concessions from France resurfaced only after the battle had been decided. What seems to have occurred in Washington was a transformation of the colonialist problem from one which required immediate French attention to one solvable through internationalization of the war. As Eisenhower has written, formation of a coalition force with units representing both Asian and Western nations "would lend real moral standing to a venture that otherwise could be made to appear as a brutal example of imperialism." [17] Organization of a regional defense body within the meaning of Article 51 of the UN Charter would, it was apparently believed, remove from France the stigma of fighting solely to retain its colonies, clothe any allied intervention in legality, and demonstrate that the war aimed at countering Communist aggression.

Postponement in this manner of meeting Vietnamese demands ignored the possibility that early French consent to a grant of full sovereignty by a specific date might have gone a long way toward easing the war burden. By removing the taint of colonialism which Communist propaganda had successfully attached to the anti-Vietminh effort, by undermining the basic appeal which had been behind growing Vietminh strength, and by giving the Vietnamese a stake in the war worth fighting for, the French might themselves have borne the nationalist standard. There is reason to believe, also, that French forces would not have been ordered to leave an independent Vietnam, although satisfaction of Vietnamese demands would likely have permitted a gradual reduction in French troops in favor of a revitalized VNA.[18]

By failing to give the Vietnamese an unequivocal promise that independence awaited them at a particular date, the French lost whatever hope of victory existed. From the American side, the failure rested in not having demanded, diplomatically but firmly, that Paris either revise its conception of the Franco-Indochinese relationship or face discontinuation of American assistance in vital war material. Despite almost certain French antagonism, it was essential that a positive American position on Indochina be taken before we became irrevocably committed. The French should have been informed that, from America's standpoint, the aid program constituted unacceptable de facto support of the anti-nationalist side in the war; that the Vietminh would continue to gain ground until France relaxed its grip on political power in Vietnam; and that aid in and of itself was only prolonging inevitable defeat. It was therefore of the utmost urgency that France set a specific target date, perhaps two, three, or five years, before which time the Vietnamese could expect a gradual turnover of economic and political controls with French administrative training, and after which Vietnam would have complete independence. With unqualified independence would go the right of choice on membership in the French Union. Treaties concluded by both sides April 28, 1954,[19] like others before them, failed to permit Vietnam such a choice and thereby made a mockery of Vietnamese "independence." An attempt might have been made to convince the French that their influence had greater likelihood of being preserved where independence was voluntarily granted than where it was attained under force of Vietminh arms. A French concession of the Vietnamese prerogative to accept or reject Union status, for instance, might have altered Vietnam's attitude toward the Union; as it was, Vietnam rejected membership following its attainment of independence under the Geneva accords.

As a third step, the United States might have gone further toward demonstrating its confidence in the future of the Associated States and its desire for their independence. The stationing of ambassadors in each of the three nations was one possibility. Finally, when it became crystal-clear that the planned buildup of a native army was running afoul under French auspices, Washington should have done more than complain. The Administration voiced regrets about French unwillingness to accept an American training mission, to begin organizing a guerrilla force of its own, or to conscript soldiers for service in Indochina [20]—but without daring to push the French on these matters. Nor were measures taken to alleviate the strained relations between American and French military staffs in Indochina over Gallic reluctance to divulge more information on strategic planning.[21] Again, the intelligence gap was allowed to persist out of a wish to avoid offending French authorities.

Administration officials had many arguments for refusing to adopt an alternative course of action. They contended that to pressure France would harm relations with an important NATO ally and practically destroy chances for ratification of EDC; that interfering with French decision-making would provoke calls for withdrawal of the Corps; and that the United States would then be faced with the unenviable choice of replacing the Corps with GI's or seeing Indochina fall into Communist hands. Moreover, as Dulles' private thoughts disclosed, political concessions to the Associated States were not only deemed nonessential but also inherently dangerous because the Indochinese were unprepared for self-government. At the last, the Administration could always point out that the time for pressure had passed; any move to use our aid leverage should have occurred when the program began under Truman.

The tenability of Administration arguments is open to serious doubts. First, our concern over EDC was matched by concern over the fate of Indochina; but the relationship between these two problems was overlooked in our desire to solve both of them. As we have seen, France placed a lesser priority on EDC than did we; an integrated army was, as Paris perceived it, neither an immediate necessity nor, in view of the great French fear of a revitalized *Wehrmacht*, a political desirability. Moreover, to have ratified EDC would have meant the elimination of hopes for a lenient war settlement with Soviet help. Even if France had wanted EDC adopted, American insistence on winning in Indochina actually forestalled that prospect. Our aid in support of the Navarre Plan, by enabling France to commit more officers and men to the war, in fact prohibited France from contributing effectively to a multi-national force so as to offset German contributions. The American effort to convince Paris that quick ratification of EDC would indicate Western unity and better French chances at Geneva was thus short-circuited by weightier considerations in Paris and our own shortsightedness. Yet Washington persisted in the belief that EDC could be approved *and* the Indochina war won; we ended with the realization of neither. Had the Administration accepted the fact that the two ambitions were mutually exclusive, it could have devoted its energies to forcing France's hand on the Indochina independence issue without being restrained by concern over EDC.

Secondly, the strong possibility that the Laniel government would have been forced under parliamentary pressure to withdraw the Corps once the United States "interfered" was beside the point. The ever-present French threat was tied to, and played on, the widespread fear of Communism that was so influential on American diplomacy and domestic life in the early 1950s. Maintenance of our aid program was described by the President as "almost compulsory . . . unless we were to abandon Southeast Asia." [22] Pressure upon France was impossible unless we were prepared to see the start of a Communist avalanche that would eventually topple every government within China's lengthy reach. It was this fear of a domino reaction that led Washington to over-react to the collapse of the Navarre Plan by hastily formulating its own military plans at a time when thoughtful, calm judgments of the Indochina situation were in order. Had Indochina been treated as a unique foreign policy problem rather than as simply another thrust outward of Communist Chinese expansionism, the conclusion might have been reached that prevailing political conditions in the Associated States made some kind of Communist victory a virtual certainty and any kind of strictly military response a delaying measure only. The real issue was not what the fate of Indochina would be if Frenchmen were to depart, but rather what long-range effects alignment against the forces of nationalism there were having and would continue to have upon American political and security interests throughout the Far East. Granted the strategic importance of Indochina, was not our anti-colonial image worth preserving and drastic responses to deep-seated political problems worth avoiding? Were there not differences, in short, between the Korean and Indochinese conflicts that required different American reactions? Only after our proposals had been aired and rejected did the Government answer these questions affirmatively.

In conclusion, it would appear that the virtual surrender by the United States of the considerable influence it possessed through its massive aid commitment to Indochina was a grievous mistake. That the Administration chose not to apply the leverage it could have exercised may in large measure be attributed to the long-held conviction, born of inadequate intelligence, that France could win militarily. Believing that neutrality toward France's Indochina policy was in the best interests of Franco-American relations, EDC, and the containment of Communist ambitions, the Government refused to change the Truman policy. The end results—the allied rebuttals of united action, the partition of Vietnam, and the defeat of EDC—showed clearly the fallacy of having forfeited our rightful role in an area to which we were deeply committed by word and deed.

Flaws in perceptions, proposals, and policies, which might have given way to a decision to intervene, did not push the United States over the brink. The signal American achievement of the Indochina episode must surely stand as the President's determination against involvement despite the pressures, military and emotional, from within as well as without the Administration, which came into play days before the tragic end at Dienbienphu. And that determination must in large part be attributed to Eisenhower's steadfastness on the major ground rule for intervention decided upon on April 4: action in unison with our free world partners, both Asian and European.

The President's handling of the crisis further revealed the respect he attached to Congressional opinion. Until Eisenhower's announcement of the dispatch of Air Force technicians in February 1954, Congressional debate on Indochina was negligible. And limited debating was mainly a reflection of limited information; as Senator Mansfield said as late as April 14, "the only information I get is what I read in the newspapers or what I happen to hear." [23] Throughout the crisis period, congressmen were confused about, and critical of, Administration shifts of position, equivocations, and failures to confide in the appropriate committees of Congress. Whether because of or in spite of these shortcomings on the Executive's part, it is a fact that an overwhelming number of Senators and Representatives took a firm stand against unilateral intervention, while a still greater number declared against American involvement under any circumstances.* Of no less interest is

---

* A survey of all statements in Congress on Indochina from June 1953 through July 1954 revealed thirty-five speeches or insertions into the *Record* that took a position on intervention. The positions were as follows:

House and Party	In Favor	Unreservedly Opposed	Opposed to Unilateral Intervention
Senate (Dem.)	1	2	10
Senate (Rep.)	0	1	4
Senate (Ind.)	0	1	0
House (Dem.)	0	6	1
House (Rep.)	2	7	0
Totals	3	17	15

Cf. Joseph C. Harsch's report in the *Christian Science Monitor* (April 29, 1954, p. 1): "The Administration's poll takers on Capitol Hill reported . . . that there were no more than five men at the most to be found in all of Congress who were positive and unequivocal in their approval of quick and decisive action."

the finding that the quality of Congressional discussion, particularly on the implications of French colonialism for American policy, ran high. The ability of Congressmen to grasp the key issue in the crisis forecast difficulty for the President in leading and, if necessary, persuading Congress when intervention loomed as a possibility. The sharp Congressional reaction against VULTURE was a pointed illustration of how Executive leadership of foreign policy could be undercut by a hesitation to confide in congressmen or precisely to define Administration policy for them.

To the President's credit, he was as deeply opposed as Congress to making a major American commitment first and receiving sanction afterwards. The significance he attached to Congressional sentiment became evident with the policy decision of April 4, which was framed about Congressional rather than State Department or JCS opinion. When Eisenhower felt the tremors of anxiety and opposition on the Hill, he stuck by his intention not to repeat the "police action" tactic employed by Truman, even though it is conceivable that a personal appearance before Congress could have swung a majority into Eisenhower's corner. The President was not going to apply or risk the great prestige of his office for the sake of a war unwanted by our allies, the Congress, the public, and the Chief Executive himself.

The President's exercise of what Emmet John Hughes has called a "presidential veto upon military intervention in Indochina" [24] also reflected his eventual reaction against the military proposals themselves. A military man, Eisenhower must have been persuaded by the Ridgway Report, which held out the danger of involvement in another costly Asian war where air-naval superiority would be indecisive. And decisiveness was an important criterion of American action, as Eisenhower has since commented.[25] On the opposite side of the scale had to be balanced the security value of Indochina, United States prestige, the probability of a partitioned Vietnam, and pressures from Laniel, Dulles, Nixon, and Radford. In short, Eisenhower found himself confronted with an intolerable alternative to proceeding on to Geneva: If he wanted involvement, it would have to be unilateral, beside a colonial power, under highly risky military operations, and with costs comparable to those in Korea. As James Reston put it, the President simply was not convinced "that United States interests in the Orient [then were] worth a war." [26] Indochina was one of those limited setbacks to freedom Dulles had anticipated.

In standing opposed to intervention, the President sharply qualified the rationale behind American interest in Indochina at the outset of the crisis and thereby changed the distorted perspective of the Chinese threat in Southeast Asia. Statements during May and June 1954 belittling the "essentiality" of the Indochinese states for Western security overturned previous prophesies of doom for Southeast Asia's free communities if communism triumphed anywhere in Indochina. The so-called "falling domino principle," which had dominated Administration policy statements on Indochina prior to the fall of Dienbienphu, was designed in part to convince the Communists that the United States would not tolerate the conquest of Indochina. But exposition of the domino thesis in private discussions (e.g., at the April 3 session with congressmen and during Dulles' talks with Eden) elucidated the Administration's sincere belief in the doctrine's validity. Consequently, the loss of northern Vietnam had a cathartic effect: It removed a verbal strait jacket, an adherence to a doctrine of inevitability surrounding the fall of Indochina, that had bound the Administration to large-scale support of a losing cause upon which it could only exert negligible influence.

CHINA'S PERCEPTION OF THE VIETNAM CRISIS

The collapse of American plans for involvement in Indochina at the eleventh hour provided a sharp contrast to the success of Communist China's trial run in the strategy of indirect aggression. Throughout the conflict, the Chinese seem to have followed a remarkably consistent and rational course designed to obtain important gains at minimal risks. In assuming the role of an active sanctuary, and then in pushing for negotiations at the moment of maximum advantage, Peking demonstrated that its fundamental re-evaluation of the world situation in the latter phases of the Korean War very definitely applied to Indochina.

Although, in the broadest sense, China's strategy in the Indochina war was guided by the overall shift to perception of a third, nonaligned world, and consequently to appreciation of the tactical uses of diplomacy, several immediate considerations were influential and deserve mention. Primarily, the maintenance of an active sanctuary status was dictated by the obvious fact that at no time after 1952 was the Vietminh in need of Chinese troop support. China's military assessment all along seems to have been that so long as American forces stayed out of the fighting the Vietminh guerrillas, technologically inferior but tactically superior, could win a hit-and-run war of attrition on the basis of Chinese advice and logistical support alone. Dulles was undoubtedly correct when he spoke of the deterrent effect of American warnings; [27] but he omitted the essential point that the CPR, while doubtless impressed with United States preparedness to back its threats with deeds in the event of overt Chinese intervention, recognized the illogic attending direct involvement. As the Assistant Secretary for Far Eastern Affairs, Everett F. Drumright, observed in a marginal comment on a Dulles speech:

Note: The Viet Minh have been doing well without Chinese troops. It is doubtful that Chinese would send their troops in when they are not needed.
                                        FE-EFD [28]

And, of course, fear of another in a long series of invasions from the north would, from the Vietminh side, also have mitigated against a large Chinese presence in Vietnam. Ho's success in 1954 may have been his ability to have imported Chinese Communism but not the Chinese. How Ho would have reacted if on the verge of collapse is another problem; but the question of Chinese forces on Vietnamese territory never arose. While these practical considerations doubtless confirmed to Peking the sensibleness of remaining the assistant in the Vietminh corner, the fact that the CPR hinted at a willingness to negotiate as early as September 1953 would indicate a more general set of guiding principles. Peking had gone on to back Ho Chi Minh's peace feelers in November and had expressed complete satisfaction with the Berlin agreement to hold a Geneva Conference on Korea and Indochina. What had prompted Peking to support negotiations? In the Korean War, Communist interest in a cease-fire and armistice (first expressed by Jacob Malik, the Soviet representative to the Security Council, in his well-known address of June 23, 1951) came on the heels of the blunting of the North Korean-Chinese spring offensive. To the contrary, both Soviet and Chinese interests in talks on Indochina arose at a time of Communist military strength. Although the winter, 1953 "general counteroffensive" of the Vietminh had not yet begun, Moscow and Peking were likely convinced of Vietminh military supremacy. Strong French peace signals may also have been influential. The Laniel government was obviously under considerable pressure to accept Ho's bid for talks; one proof lay in the premier's November 1953 speech to the National Assembly in which an "honorable settlement" was declared an important component of French policy.

Confidence in Vietminh strength and the sense that France was ripe for negotiations formed, however, only part of the rationale behind working toward a settlement. The prospect of a diplomatic confrontation with the leading Western powers, guaranteed at Berlin, could not help but meet China's demands for a major role in ironing out Asian problems and bolster

China's claims to great-power status. Coming at a time of significant changes in Peking's approach to international relations, participation in a second major war-ending conference would enhance China's prestige, particularly among Asian nations, provide a forum from which to assail the United States, and appear to sustain Peking's sincerity about "peaceful coexistence."

China's interest in peace was further dictated by domestic considerations. As has been pointed out, the Panmunjom armistice permitted the regime an opportunity to devote itself to the pressing task of "socialist reconstruction" under the First Five Year Plan (1953–1957). Being particularly concerned with industrialization, which had been heavily taxed by military demands during the Korean War, the regime could not afford another direct involvement in war. Furthermore, the Chinese knew that escalation of the Indochina crisis into a major war was not desired by the Soviets, whose support was essential to the Five Year Plan.[29] The Berlin decision to bring the war to the bargaining table therefore went a long way toward assuring Peking that the economic sacrifices sustained during Korea would not be repeated.

Long-range political and domestic factors moved China toward the negotiating arena; but because Indochina represented a high priority or national interest of the CPR, the augmentation of assistance to the Dienbienphu front was deemed consistent with the search for a peaceful settlement. Indeed, Dienbienphu mirrored the closeness of the military and political idioms in Chinese thinking. In recognizing the great value of a victory at Dienbienphu upon negotiations at Geneva, China also looked toward the attainment of a major objective, certain control of the border area by a communist power. The limited exploitation of military power in coordination with diplomacy was not peculiar to China's "pre-Bandung" tactics; it was revealed by the Chinese Communists as early as 1940. Mao wrote then:

After we have repulsed the attack . . . and before . . . a new
one [begins], we should stop at the proper moment and bring
that particular fight to a close. . . . Then we should on our own
initiative seek unity with the [enemy] and, upon [his] consent,
conclude a peace agreement with [him]. . . . Herein lies the
temporary nature of every particular struggle.[30]

It was in the military sphere that Communist China's pre-
Geneva strategy was most vulnerable and hence by no means
"fail-safe." For in perceiving a French bent for discussions
under the weight of mounting costs and frustrations, Peking
may have been led to underestimate the possibility that the
United States would depart from its declared intention to aid
the French by all means short of direct intervention. The
People's Daily's muted commentary on Dulles' March 29 speech
may have been indicative of the doubts which suddenly seized
Peking's strategists. Unknown to Peking, Dulles' thinking had
turned toward denying the Vietminh a sanctuary in southern
China; if China's surreptitious assistance continued, Dulles
acknowledged to the British his preparedness to warn Peking
and follow up with concrete action if the warning were
ignored. Although Peking knew from published statements
and press clippings of Eisenhower's opposition to the use of
United States ground forces and of strong British and French
sentiment against a united action, there could not have been
equal certainty about unilateral American action. Pro-Khrush-
chev analyses, with which the Chinese were in general agreement, did not exclude the possibility that the United States,
in some irrational gesture, might launch a surprise attack and
instigate a world war. And the presence of two United States
aircraft carriers in the South China Sea on April 10 evoked
Peking's most vigorous press reaction of the crisis. It was
British and French reluctance to accept either a joint warning
or a united front, and not the infallibility of Chinese strategy,
which prevented China's indirect involvement from becoming
a casus belli rather than the key to Vietminh victory at Dien-

bienphu. Peking might have overplayed its hand; but it did apparently calculate correctly that the capture of Dienbienphu was worth risks which it considered minimal.

The culmination of the crisis with the signing of the Geneva agreements did not, in spite of all pre-conference indications, result in the cession of the whole Indochina peninsula or even all Vietnam to the Communists. Although the West came to the conference divided, weakened by the fall of Dienbienphu, and wholly prepared for Chinese demands that the French concede the Vietminh the entire peninsula,[31] the final terms were clearly better than had been foreseen by many of the participants. What had motivated the Chinese to depart from support of Vietminh demands for a unified nation and to settle for half a loaf rather than the whole?

The primary factor accounting for Chinese agreement to a settlement far short of a "victor's peace" seems to have been their sustained conviction that the diplomatic offensive inaugurated at Panmunjom and revitalized in late 1953 constituted the "correct" line of foreign policy in the Far East. The conclusion of an Indochina peace neither humiliating to the French nor totally at odds with Ho Chi Minh's hopes for national unity was probably regarded by Peking as an important step on the road toward leadership of the economically underdeveloped community of Asian states. A war-ending agreement at Geneva would forcefully demonstrate that the "five principles" in fact would be followed by the CPR as promised in the Sino-Indian declaration of June 28. In short, Peking had found that active pursuance of the peace line could gain more friends for China than interminable prolongation of talks amid continued fighting.

The coincidence of the signing of a final Indochina accord with the peak of China's diplomatic offensive should not obscure the influential role played by the Soviet Union at the Conference. The Russians were as aware as the Chinese that Ho Chi Minh's forces possessed the momentum to overrun the better part of Vietnam. But Moscow was concerned, perhaps to a greater degree than Peking, about the potential explosiveness of the Indochina situation in the event talks failed to produce results. Molotov in fact agreed with Eden in private conversations during the Conference that the Soviet Union and Great Britain would have to play moderating roles in inducing their respective allies to come to terms. Both delegates foresaw a Sino-American collision if talks broke down.[32] The Kremlin leadership may therefore have become convinced that the price of a new military venture southward by the Vietminh was clearly too high: setting the spark to an anti-Communist movement throughout Southeast Asia, with the United States at the head. For Moscow, the replacement of Laniel by Pierre Mendès-France in mid-June 1954 provided a splendid opportunity to conclude an armistice that would simultaneously work against the dreaded EDC. Mendès-France, a well-known opponent of EDC, was committed to concluding an honorable truce. A proposition not excessively costly to Paris would credit the Russian peace line and push Paris away from EDC. As far as Moscow was concerned, Indochina was hardly as important as the threat of a rearmed Germany. By extracting far less than the Communists were in a position to demand, Moscow gambled that France, freed from her Indochina manpower commitments, would again have sufficient ground power to offset German contributions to, and thereby the need for, an EDC.[33] The tactic paid off when EDC was defeated by a single vote on August 30, 1954.

Obviously, the Soviets could not use their interests in seeing EDC dissolved as a strong lever against any Chinese ambitions. The lever used may have been the aforementioned Soviet aid which, as revealed by Khrushchev's trip to Peking and the subsequent treaties signed on October 12, was vital to the CPR's First Five Year Plan.[34] Although announced in January 1953, the plan required two years and a series of Soviet aid agreements (of which the October treaties were the last) to get started in February 1955. The Soviets may therefore have urged upon the CPR at Geneva, were the Chinese not already convinced (which, as indicated, seems unlikely), the importance of stopping Ho Chi Minh from provoking American intervention. Had the Chinese refused to do so, or had they failed, the price would have been the diversion of Soviet rubles away from Peking.[35]

The recourse to serious diplomatic bargaining under the impetus of China's revised world outlook and Soviet urgings of mild terms for France was also linked to military realities and assessments. In the short run the Chinese probably argued in meetings with the Vietminh delegation against the resumption of a sustained drive south. Since the Vietminh's principal supply and communications complex existed near the China frontier, a vast follow-up assault would have hazarded over-extension of the supply line and have encountered unprecedented problems of logistics and telecommunications. Having gained the decisive revolutionary objective where success was certain, the CPR apparently chose not to extend the battle line and introduce the element of doubt. In Peking's projection, control of the Indochinese states, the national goal, was postponable, the more so as the Vietminh had long since indicated designs upon the area which would have run contrary to Chinese ambitions.[36] In return for acquiescing in China's veto of a renewed offensive, the Vietminh may have received the assurance of future Chinese support for unification.[37]

In the long run, however, the move toward a settlement of the crisis was, from the military angle, probably keyed to China's assessment of the risks further Vietminh advances carried *for Peking*. Although the preponderance of American military power in the Far East seems to have had the greatest impact upon the Soviet position at Geneva, it has been shown that the new attention of the Eisenhower Administration to Asian affairs, its touted reliance upon air-atomic power, and its talk of nuclear weapons even at the tactical level, coming at a time of growing Chinese awareness of atomic power,[38] attracted considerable attention in Peking. The fifty-five day siege of Dienbienphu had been conducted with Chinese heavy artillery and advisors present, but apparently under a calculation of costs and gains far different from that which Peking applied to the problem of military action with the Geneva Conference in progress. Peking must surely have been aware that the British would remain averse to American intervention plans only so long as the Communists showed a genuine willingness to compromise at Geneva. Renewed fighting amidst intransigence and stalling at the conference table might throw the British in with the Americans and revitalize united action. As has been suggested, the CPR delegation was aware of American pressure upon their allies to walk out of the conference; with the conclusion of United States-United Kingdom talks on collective defense in Southeast Asia and the return of Dulles to Paris, Chou En-lai had voiced concern to Eden about the proposed pact. The United States was not in a position, as during the impasse at Panmunjom over the prisoners-of-war exchange, to issue strong signals threatening to widen the scope of the war unless the Chinese changed their attitude. But while the American nuclear potential did not take on the aura of an immediate threat to Peking, it probably provided a further reason for the Chinese to consider a drive to unify Vietnam unduly risky of gains already made, and to deem the time propitious for reaping the credit of having brought the war to an end. In this respect, the partition of Vietnam was the best outcome the West could have hoped for, but also the most the Chinese thought politically expedient or militarily sound to demand.

9. EPILOGUE: THE INDOCHINA LEGACY

Policy results, A. Whitney Griswold has observed, can only be measured in terms of objectives. From this standpoint, the cession of northern Vietnam to the Communists where partition had been deemed inadmissible by both the United States and France represents the obvious disparity between objective and result in Indochina. But the purpose here has not been simply to explore *what* happened, but also *how* and *why* it happened. The *crisis reactions* of East and West over Vietnam are most important. Historically, those reactions revealed rather sharply the changing Chinese approach to international relations and made it imperative that the Americans took stock of strategy in Southeast Asia; for the present, these reactions serve as relevant sources of reference in the continuing Sino-American confrontation. In this concluding chapter, the aim will be at illuminating those aspects of the crisis which, from the perspective of today, retain a peculiar value for America's Far Eastern policy.

Without ever approaching the brink of war, the United States suffered a sharp reversal in Indochina that transcended a significant but limited loss of "prestige." In its handling of the crisis from the diplomatic end, the Administration betrayed an insecure sense of direction and lack of foresight that placed American political goals and military proposals in direct opposition to those of our allies.

In viewing the diplomacy of the 1953–1954 period, a serious question of principle, one with long-range implications, arises over the Administration's determination that "holding the line" (i.e., continuing the Truman approach to the Indochina war) constituted the only real choice of American policy. For by re-instituting a pro-French policy in Saigon, Washington in effect assured that the underlying weaknesses of the French position would remain intact. There are, of course, weighty arguments against the contention that acceptance of American aid should automatically entail acceptance of American advice and the imposition of American policy. But in the Indochina case—where American security was said to be directly involved, where American aid was a significant component of the peninsula's defense, and where the sovereignty of three nations was severely compromised by colonial rule —certain prerequisites already noted should clearly have been stipulated prior to and even during United States involvement. Should basically the same kind of emergency that overtook Indochina recur, the United States, as a major contributor to a war situation, must guard against being relegated to the role of silent partner; the end result could again be attachment to allies who suspect and disrupt our purpose, to policies with which we disagree, and to consequences which we want desperately to avoid.

On the other hand, American involvement must not evolve into domination. The futile French attempt to win a military victory while effectively controlling the Vietnamese government and army should serve as a firm warning against the future corruption of our primary role as assistants in countering aggression or subversion. Where "support" becomes de facto control, not only is the motivation behind assistance undermined, but the major task of rallying the moral and physical resources of the native population is seriously hampered if not fundamentally destroyed. If the United States is to appear as the champion of freedom-loving peoples, it must not fall victim to the same "colonialism" that crippled the French cause. Where an American commitment is deemed necessary, it must be guided by alignment with the forces of nationalism that will work to promote freedom, and further by a willingness that the manner in which freedom shall be promoted will, while consistent with our own values, ultimately be determined by our ally. To defend independence we must respect it not only as a concept of territorial sovereignty but further as a condition of governmental sovereignty.

Working with allies and congressmen proved equally as difficult as working with the French. The Indochina case demonstrated emphatically the inherent dangers of what James Reston then referred to as "sudden diplomacy"—diplomacy so secretive and so changeable as to confound allies and congressmen alike. Effective diplomacy must surely be that which has as its lowest common denominator an outward sense of consistency to parallel a supposed inner sense of direction. The elements of that consistency must be a full awareness by our allies of our policy and we of theirs; and it must further mean Executive confidence, expressed through periodic meetings, in members of the Congress concerned with all aspects of the impending or ongoing crisis. When an ally's long-standing policy is discounted, when American policy publicly takes a direction counter to that revealed privately, or when a leading Senator finds a newspaper his best source of information on national policy, diplomacy stands ready for improvement.

The crisis also underlined the weaknesses of the overall American defense program. The New Look had decided upon inaugurating certain changes in military tactics and weaponry; but Vietnam caught the Administration shorthanded, lacking possession of the kind of power appropriate to war in Asia. The distinction that the White House did not make until too late, but that the Chinese in effect recognized, was between the value of nuclear intimidation and a superior air arm as *deterrents*, as opposed to their infeasibility as instruments of *defense*. Since the beginning of the war the *chief* military problem lay not in deterring Chinese volunteers (although the post-Korean atmosphere necessitated the warnings that ensued) but in finding a winning formula for defending against and ultimately gaining a military advantage over the Vietminh operating from within.

As a result, the Indochina experience dictated the need for review of the methods for dealing with "national revolutionary wars" supported indirectly by Peking. The dissents voiced often during 1953 against reducing ground troop strength called for renewed attention. Indochina bolstered the post-Korean arguments centered about American unpreparedness for war with political, topographical, geopolitical, and other limitations. Prohibitions against future large-scale commitments of United States manpower to Asia might have to be lifted under certain circumstances despite dogmatic assertions after the Korean conflict of "never again."

Moreover, because the Vietminh proved that Maoist guerrilla doctrine was just as sound in 1954 as in the thirties and forties, forces prepared for coping with guerrilla soldiers on guerrilla terms would have to be organized, with the emphasis away from heavy armaments and air power and toward lightness and mobility.[1] Diplomacy would, in Asia no less than in Europe, need to be backed by credible military power. As General Ridgway has written, ". . . if military power is to be an instrument of diplomacy it must be real, and apparent to all concerned, and it must be capable of being applied promptly, selectively and with the degree of violence appropriate to the occasion."[2] And basic to the effectiveness of such power would have to be an intelligence network in the war theatre having access to independent sources, but being guided by cooperation with our diplomatic and military arms. The direct relationship between an intelligence gap at the front and ill-timed diplomatic and military moves in Washington was no more clearly demonstrated than in the Indochina war.

What the crisis did not elucidate was the type of situation that could be classified as the "appropriate occasion" for United States action. The Administration's rush to establish SEATO was premised on the notion that American security could doubtless withstand the shock of seeing Indochina go under so long as the new organization proved an effective counterweight to further Communist expansion. The subsequent shattering of Dulles' dream posed anew the issue of Indochina's, and especially Vietnam's, security value.

The Administration's consistent contention that Indochina held the key to control of the entire Western Pacific seems, regardless of time context, highly unreasonable. Far too much power was credited to Communist China; far too little attention was paid either geographical considerations, historical peculiarities, or the diverse developments of Marxism of the nations in that area. Intervention was so seriously considered because perception of the nature of the enemy was so distorted. By linking the Korean conflict to the Indochina war, the Administration revealed not only that it was plagued by the fear of a domino reaction but also that it was convinced of the ultimate sameness of the Communist threat wherever it appeared in Asia. Coming on the heels of the Communist guerrilla threat in Malaya, the traumatic Communist conquest of mainland China, the Korean conflict, and tension in Thailand, the Indochina crisis elicited an American response understandable only as a product of the times.

Perception of Southeast Asia in terms of the Chinese Communist threat has also had effects upon the official American attitude toward Peking extending into the present. Communist China has long been America's bête noire in the Far East. That Peking may espouse, advocate, and support revolution has been taken in Washington to mean that Peking foments such revolutions. "Liberation war" is invariably Chinese sponsored; and the response has frequently resembled the Dulles approach, to cut or weaken China's accesses south so as to disable the primary antagonist of American policy. When we recall the initial observations about the development of the Vietminh, it becomes evident that the American view of Communist China's aims in Indochina has long lacked objectivity. For it was not Communist China which prompted the Vietnamese Communist movement and gave it a broad national appeal. Peking proved adept, rather, at utilizing the Vietminh in furtherance of Chinese goals. Despite the CPR's active assistance of Vietnamese Communist military thrusts then and since, it has been the Hanoi leadership which, judging from its own background, has posed the major threat to a stable Indochina. In seeking to understand the present Vietnam dilemma, we should differentiate between Peking's underwriting and its authorship of insurrection. So doing, the focus of our Vietnam policy should be on North Vietnam's national interests and historic ambitions in Vietnam and Indochina, factors that place Hanoi apart from, and conceivably in conflict with, Peking's aims in the region.

As this study has sought to demonstrate, no problem in Indochina demanded more immediate efforts at solution, yet received less searching treatment, than the political, social, and economic causes of peasant discontent. Perhaps the single most important lesson of the war was that military measures divorced from political guidance and socio-economic reform are infeasible against an enemy which utilizes latent hostility toward Westerners, economic backwardness, a "scientific" vision of the future society, and a Communist-oriented program hitched to the bandwagon of strong nationalistic feelings. The real crisis in Indochina was not one of military exigency. Rather, the crisis centered on the failure of the West to respond to the broad spectrum of challenges underlying a popular surge of nationalistic, anti-colonialist sentiment that had been very evident and powerful in Indochina since 1945. The inadequacies of land reform, the huge gap separating the Saigon leaders from the rural led, the corruption and inefficiency of a powerless native elite, instability of the currency, inequities in the legal system, press controls, the inability to provide security for peasant villages, the absence of a counter-appeal to Communist propaganda—all these, and many more, went far toward explaining French collapse and Vietminh strength.

Since the end of the First Indochina War, it has often been said, and still bears repeating, that guerrilla war is not only military war. The strongest point brought home by the crisis was the multifaceted nature of guerrilla war: the technical, psychological, financial, agricultural, organizational, and even terroristic aspects of the struggle that demand a total commitment by the threatened country. And without that commitment, military strength is ephemeral and American involvement purposeless. The Vietnam crisis left to some future time, therefore, the provision of effective responses to some major questions: how, and in what proportion, to bring superior military power to bear upon an enemy which draws strength from an essentially political appeal; how to instill in the government we support a firm sense of direction and a measure of effective administration adequate to successfully prosecuting the war while satisfying legitimate popular demands for political freedoms; how to coordinate in realistic fashion a meaningful social revolution in the countryside with programs aimed at governmental stability and military effectiveness; how to counteract the inherent weaknesses of a white man's democracy in areas in which democracy is unknown objectively and linked to colonialism subjectively. No clear answers emerged from the war; yet, by revealing the nonmilitary causes behind a military threat, the Indochina crisis served the equally important function of pinpointing the questions.

The United States could find much to learn, too, from Chinese Communist conduct during the war and at the conference table. Geneva had provided the Chinese with their first opportunity to sit as equals with the delegates of other nations at a high-level diplomatic conference. The CPR's prominent role at the conference enhanced its prestige to the extent that it "loomed as the colossus of the East in the eyes of many Asians. . . . Peking's demonstrated power now convinced many Asians that neutralism and accommodation with Communist China were necessary and desirable. . . ." [3] By making use of the conference table as an extension of the battle front and of diplomacy as the handmaiden of protracted struggle, the CPR accelerated the trend in Asia toward neutrality and pro-Chinese sentiment. In sum, the gains acquired in July 1954 represented a dynamic synthesis of aggressiveness and diplomacy in the CPR's world outlook: The Korean conflict was paralleled by the Panmunjom armistice, the Indochina war by the Geneva Conference, and the subsequent Taiwan Strait crisis by the Bandung Conference.

While playing the role of silent partner to the maximum advantage of its own interests, Peking inadvertently added some insight into the conditions under which it would again risk overt involvement in war. With reference both to Indochina and Korea, it appears that the most likely contingencies for the CPR's active and massive involvement in war would be: direct attack upon the mainland; United States involvement in a land action carrying close to the China border and appearing (to Peking) to threaten Chinese security; and the threat of extinction, and hence occupation by an enemy power, of an already existing Communist state on the China border. With its growing respect for American power already evident as early as 1954, it is proposed that Peking—influenced also by a determination to preserve economic and military assets, and by a strategy of relying where possible upon local Communist forces—will grow less willing over time to invite retaliation, and more cautious in responding to real and imagined "provocations."

Negotiating with the Chinese Communists at Panmunjom and Geneva has been the only formal, prolonged, and direct United States-CPR contact. Noteworthy are the facts that serious peace talks in both cases began only when the Communists clearly foresaw: (1) that further military advances were either impossible or too risky and (2) that a negotiated settlement was the most practical way of securing their long-range interests. If such are the circumstances, forcing a conflictual situation to the conference table requires complementary Western positions: (1) negotiating only from a position of military strength on the battlefield, and from a credible defense posture in the immediate Far East area and (2) providing the Communists with viable alternatives, face-saving "outs" to continued warfare.

As to the first point, the stalemated war in the spring of 1953 in Korea, and the risks apparent to Moscow and Peking in pursuing military ambitions in August of 1954 in Vietnam, provided sound military reasons for sincere Communist approaches to negotiations. Beyond these factors lay the economic burdens of further hostilities in Korea and, in Indochina, the international political goals and domestic economic plans of Peking, all of which were responsible for compelling subordination of territorial ambitions to practical, long-term considerations.

Providing alternate avenues for Chinese Communism poses a challenge to imaginative diplomacy on a par with the challenge to the military in establishing an appropriate strategic and tactical framework for meeting local wars in Asia. For if inconclusive agreements of the Korean and Indochinese types are not to recur, it seems clear that new initiatives must be attempted toward Communist China. The fundamentals of Sino-American conflict must be attacked as earnestly as the individual points of tension under contest. Fullest consideration should be given to major policy innovations, innovations which take into account the following elements basic to Peking's motivations in 1954 and since: the CPR's search for economic and technical assistance, concern over international identity, obsession with the large-scale American armed presence in areas ringing the mainland, and subtle differences with North Vietnam over Indochina.

The problem of reaching an accommodation consistent with our security interests and defense commitments is undeniably enormous, and perhaps on this count a final judgment of the Eisenhower Administration's policies must be held in abeyance. The potentially explosive legacy of two powers more prone to tests of strength than to negotiations has been bequeathed through four successive administrations; yet the haunting difficulties of the First Indochina War are no closer to solution in the second. And while this is so, the familiar pattern of Chinese-backed limited warfare will doubtless remain the dominant form of Sino-American confrontation in Southeast Asia.

NOTES

1. THE SINO-VIETNAMESE RELATIONSHIP

1. Harold C. Hinton, *China's Relations with Burma and Vietnam* (New York, 1958), p. 11.

2. Bernard B. Fall, "A 'Straight Zigzag': The Road to Socialism in North Viet-Nam," in A. Doak Barnett, ed., *Communist Strategies in Asia* (New York, 1963), p. 201.

3. Fall, in the Introduction to Truong Chinh, *Primer for Revolt* (New York, 1963), p. xi. Truong is presently Chairman of the Standing Committee of North Vietnam's National Assembly.

4. Hsiao Yang, *Chieh-fang chung ti Yüeh-nan* [Vietnam in Liberation] (Shanghai, 1951), p. 65.

5. Wu Chih-ying, ed., *Hu Chih-ming ch'uan* [Biography of Ho Chi Minh] (Shanghai, 1951), p. 13.

6. Fall, in Barnett, ed., *Communist Strategies*, pp. 202–3; Hinton, pp. 11–12.

7. Fall, in Barnett, ed., *Communist Strategies*, pp. 203–4.

8. See Ho Chi Minh, *Selected Works* (Hanoi, 1961), III, 17–21. All subsequent references will be to Vol. III.

9. Philippe Devillers, "Vietnamese Nationalism and French Politics," in William L. Holland, ed., *Asian Nationalism and the West* (New York, 1953), p. 214.

10. Chinese domination of present-day Vietnam began in 111 B.C. and lasted continuously for over ten centuries. The details are in Joseph Buttinger, *The Smaller Dragon* (New York, 1958), pp. 95–130. The deplorable conduct of Chinese occupation troops in northern Vietnam in the post-Japanese surrender period reinforced Vietnamese hostility toward the Chinese; see Hinton,

p. 14. Evidence of the mutuality of Chinese and Vietnamese feelings on this latter episode may be seen in the contents of a chronicle of the Indochina war published by Peking in 1954. The chronology omitted mention of Chinese Nationalist troop *activities* even as it is stated that troops were in Indochina during 1945 and 1946. "A Chronicle of Principal Events Relating to the Indo-China Question (1940–1954)," in American Consulate General, Hong Kong, *Current Background* (hereafter cited as *CB*), No. 286 (May 5, 1954).

11. Truong, *Primer for Revolt*, p. 55.

12. *Ibid.*, p. 106.

13. Hoang Van Chi, *From Colonialism to Communism* (New York, 1964), p. 44. Hoang Van Chi was for ten years a bureaucrat with the Vietminh.

14. Nguyen Duy Thanh, "My Four Years with the Viet Minh" (Bombay, n.d.), p. 15. The author was special envoy of the southern government to India in 1950.

15. Devillers, in Holland, p. 214.

16. Quoted by I. Milton Sacks, "Marxism in Viet Nam," in Frank N. Trager, ed., *Marxism in Southeast Asia* (Stanford, 1959), p. 160.

17. In New China News Agency (hereafter cited as NCNA), Weekly Bulletin No. 143, February 28, 1950, pp. 5–6. All statements of NCNA originated in Peking unless otherwise noted.

18. Lu Ting-yi, "The World Significance of the Chinese United Democratic Front of China" (July 5, 1951), in DeVere E. Pentony, ed., *China, the Emerging Red Giant* (San Francisco, 1962), p. 15.

19. Cited in A. M. Halpern, "The Foreign Policy Uses of the Chinese Revolutionary Model," *The China Quarterly*, No. 7 (July–September, 1961), p. 5.

20. "On the People's Democratic Dictatorship" (June 30, 1949), in Mao Tse-tung, *Selected Works* (New York, 1956), V, 416.

21. NCNA, Weekly Bulletin No. 130, November 29, 1949, p. 6.

22. NCNA, November 23, 1949, quoted in Bureau of Intelligence and Research, *Chinese Communist World Outlook* (Washington, D.C., Department of State Publication 7379, 1962), p. 112; Allan B. Cole, ed., *Conflict in Indo-China and International Repercussions* (Ithaca, 1956), p. 87.

23. Buu Loc, "Aspects of the Vietnamese Problem," *Pacific Affairs*, XXV, No. 3 (September, 1952), 239.

24. Ho, *Selected Works*, p. 184.

25. Viet Nam News Agency [DRV] broadcast of January 16, 1950. See also NCNA, January 18–19, 1950, in *Weekly Bulletin* No. 138, January 24, 1950, p. 2.

26. *Shih-chieh chih-shih shou-ts'e 1954 nien* [Handbook of World Knowledge, 1954] (Peking, 1954), p. 184.

27. Voice of Nambo broadcast, October 1, 1950.

28. *CB*, No. 311 (February 1, 1955), pp. 8–9; *Jen-min shou-ts'e 1952* [People's Handbook, 1952](Tientsin, 1952), p. 191. A sketch of Hoang (*Jen-min shou-ts'e 1952*, p. 192) credited him with knowledge of Chinese and involvement throughout the Vietminh movement's formative years.

29. *Jen-min shou-ts'e 1955*, pp. 290–91; NCNA, September 1, 1954.

30. Voice of Vietnam [DRV] broadcast, March 13, 1951.

31. Chi, p. 71.

32. Shen-Yu Dai has written in this connection: "These pronouncements [in the Manifesto], it seems quite evident, are almost amazingly Maoist in character. Those who read their Chinese translation would perhaps tend to suspect that some Chinese Communist or one who is thoroughly reared in the tradition of Chinese Communism must have had a hand in their drafting." Shen-Yu Dai, *Peking, Moscow, and the Communist Parties of Colonial Asia* (Cambridge, Mass., 1954), p. 122.

33. The document is given in a Viet Nam News Agency broadcast of March 13, 1951, and in Robert V. Daniels, ed., *A Documentary History of Communism* (New York, 1962), II, 379–82.

34. Chi, pp. 109–12.

35. Ho proclaimed September 17, 1945 the start of "Gold Week," during which time North Vietnamese "were compelled to give their gold for the 'purchase' of weapons from the Chinese. . . ." See Fall, in Barnett, ed., *Communist Strategies*, p. 205; and Ho, p. 27.

36. George K. Tanham, *Communist Revolutionary Warfare* (New York, 1961), p. 68. A Communist source lists munitions and heavy weapons (bazookas, trench mortars, and howitzers) among the items put together in homemade factories; Leo Figuères et al., *Yüeh-nan ti chieh-fang yün-tung ho ti-kuo chu-i ti ch'in-lüeh* [Vietnam's Liberation Movement and Imperialism's Aggression], trans. from the French by Sung Kuei-huang (Shanghai and Peking, 1951), p. 6.

37. Bernard B. Fall, *Street without Joy* (Harrisburg, Pa., 1963), p. 29.

38. Chi, p. 63.

39. Wu Chih-ying, p. 48.

40. *New York Times*, February 23, 1950, pp. 1, 12.

41. *Ibid.*, March 1, 1950, pp. 1, 24.

42. Fall, *Street without Joy*, p. 29.

43. *New York Times*, March 1, 1950, p. 24.

44. Viet Nam News Agency broadcast of October 13, 1950. On the campaign, see Fall, *The Two Viet-Nams*, p. 109.

45. Fall, *The Two Viet-Nams*, pp. 110–11.

46. Robert Guillain, *La Fin des illusions* (Paris, 1954), p. 39.

47. Dwight D. Eisenhower, *The White House Years; Mandate for Change: 1953–1956* (Garden City, N.Y., 1963), p. 338.

48. Hinton, p. 18.

49. *New York Times*, August 6, 1953, p. 3.

50. *Ibid.*, August 30, 1953, p. 5.

51. Testimony of Harold E. Stassen, Director of the Foreign Operations Administration, in U.S. Congress, Senate, Committee on Foreign Relations, *Hearing on the Mutual Defense Assistance Control Act of 1951*, Vol. 11, 83d Cong., 2d Sess., April 9, 1954, p. 13.

52. The figures vary somewhat, although the upward trend is evident. George K. Tanham, in his study for The RAND Corporation (*Communist Revolutionary Warfare*, pp. 68–69), has asserted that the monthly average flow of aid was 10–20 tons in 1951, but 250 tons at the close of 1952, and 400–600 tons in 1953. The State Department's calculations, however, showed about 400 tons being shipped monthly by China in 1952 and about 750 tons the following year; draft dated March 24, 1954, of Overseas Press Club speech (delivered by Secretary of State Dulles March 29), p. 5, in John Foster Dulles Papers (Princeton University, Princeton, N.J.) [File I.B.]. Hereafter cited as Dulles Papers.

53. Guillain, *La Fin des illusions*, p. 39.

54. *Ibid.*

55. Hsiao, p. 71.

56. *Ibid.*

57. E. L. Katzenbach, Jr., "Time, Space, and Will: The Politico-Military Views of Mao Tse-tung," in Lt. Col. T. N. Greene, ed., *The Guerrilla—and How to Fight Him* (New York, 1962), p. 20.

58. See *People's War People's Army* (New York, 1962).

59. Hsiao, p. 71. Both *On the New Stage* and *On the Protracted War* were written during the Sino-Japanese War. The first, dated October 1938, consists of Mao's report to the Sixth Enlarged Session of the National People's Congress. The second is a series of lectures delivered during May and June 1938 at the Chinese Communist base at Yenan.

60. Truong, *Primer for Revolt*, p. 117 and *passim*. Emphasis is Truong's.

61. Some of these programs to gain peasant support are highlighted in Ho, *Selected Works*, pp. 329, 378.

62. See Joseph Starobin, *Eyewitness in Indo-China* (New York, 1954), a product in part of a visit to the VPA lines, p. 82.

63. These political "mistakes" are described by Ho, pp. 254, 266. It may well have been the lackluster performance of the party cadres that prompted the dispatch, in December 1952, of Chinese political workers to northern Vietnam. The workers were youths sent by the so-called Political Department of the General Headquarters of the Chinese People's Volunteers to Help Vietnam. A captured "top secret" handbook, the only written evidence of direct Chinese participation in the war, ordered that the workers organize the overseas Chinese communities to fight alongside the VPA. The workers were further directed toward intelligence-gathering, propaganda, and actual fighting. (The handbook appears in Cole, pp. 125–30; cf. also *New York Times*, May 13, 1954, p. 4.) No evidence exists, however, that these "volunteers" made any impact on the war.

Tactically, VPA commanders were often guilty of "adventurism"—undue haste in switching from guerrilla warfare to conventional attack and the "general counter-offensive." See, for instance, Truong Chinh's criticism of Giap's carelessness in 1945 and 1946 (Truong, *Primer for Revolt*, p. 116), and Ho's speech on avoiding "precipitation, rashness and impatience," February 1951, in Ho, p. 253.

64. Dr. Phan Quang Dan, "The War in Indochina: A Comparative Study of the Vietminh and the French Union Forces" (N.p., 1954), p. 14.

65. For a discussion of French strategy, see Major Lamar McFadden Prosser, "The Bloody Lessons of Indochina," *The Army Combat Forces Journal*, V, No. 11 (June, 1955), 26.

66. Ho, pp. 408–9; Peter V. Curl, ed., *Documents on American*

Foreign Relations 1953 (New York, 1954), p. 162. Hereafter cited as *DAFR* [*year*].

67. *New York Times*, December 14, 1953, p. 5.

68. Ho, p. 431; *New York Times*, December 18, 1953, p. 4.

69. Jean Renald, *L'Enfer de Dien Bien Phu* (Paris, 1955), p. 31.

70. The Vietminh interest in Laos was supposedly based on so-called Khmer (Cambodian) and Pathet Lao people's governments established soon after Ho seized power in Hanoi. On March 11, 1951 a conference of the "National United Fronts" of each such government adopted a resolution of merger to form a Viet Nam-Khmer-Pathet Lao People's Alliance Committee. (See the "Chronicle of Events" in *CB*, No. 286 [May 5, 1954], p. 35.) However, Giap's winter invasion of Laos seemed to be dictated by military rather than political considerations; he was more interested in widening Vietminh-held territory, it appears, than in helping the Laotian Communist leader, Prince Souphanavong, attain an independent importance.

71. *New York Times*, March 6, 1953, p. 4; *ibid.*, March 7, 1953, p. 9; *ibid.*, March 20, 1953, pp. 1, 3.

2. OUT ONE DOOR AND IN ANOTHER: THE AMERICAN COMMITMENT

1. See, for example, U.S. Department of State, *Foreign Relations of the United States; Diplomatic Papers: The Conference of Berlin (the Potsdam Conference) 1945* (Washington, D.C., 1960), I, 917.

2. U.S. Department of State, *Foreign Relations of the United States; Diplomatic Papers: The Conferences at Malta and Yalta 1945* (Washington, D.C., 1955), p. 770. Roosevelt wrote Secretary of State Cordell Hull (January 24, 1944) that he had told the British Ambassador, Lord Halifax, that "Indo-China should not go back to France but that it should be administered by an international trusteeship." The people "are worse off than they were" when France first took possession, the President wrote. "France has milked it for 100 years." Quoted in James Reston, "The 'Agonizing Reappraisal' Has Already Begun," *New York Times*, IV, May 2, 1954, p. 8.

3. Discussion of United States policy toward Indochina between 1945 and 1950 may be found in "L'Amérique et l'Indochine du Débarquement japonais de 1940 à Dien Bien Phu," *Chronique de*

Politique Étrangère, VII, Nos. 4, 5 (July–September, 1954), 492–95; Bernard B. Fall, "La Politique américaine au Viet-Nam," *Chronique de Politique Étrangère,* XX, No. 3 (July, 1955), 315.

4. Ellen J. Hammer, *The Struggle for Indochina* (Stanford, 1954), p. 232. The Franco-Vietnamese political dilemma is detailed in chapter 3, below.

5. Quoted in Paul Mus, *Le Destin de l'Union Française* (Paris, 1954), p. 61.

6. Hammer, p. 234. Vietnam became an Associated State in March 1949; Laos and Cambodia entered under similar conditions later that year.

7. The United States sought to influence favorable French Parliamentary action by sending a special ambassador, Philip C. Jessup, to deliver a message of congratulations to Bao Dai (January 27, 1950). The message expressed the hope of "establishing a closer relationship" with the Vietnam government, obviously after French ratification; U.S. Department of State, *The Department of State Bulletin* (hereafter cited as *DSB*), XXII, No. 554 (February 13, 1950), 244.

8. *Ibid.*

9. *Ibid.,* No. 555 (February 20, 1950), 291.

10. *Ibid.*

11. The President said: "Americans have looked with sympathy upon the desires of the people of Vietnam, Laos and Cambodia for self-government within the French Union." However, he closed by expressing the hope that "the Associated States within the French Union *may take their place* among the other free nations of the world." *New York Times,* August 14, 1950, p. 5, emphasis supplied.

12. *Ibid.,* March 13, 1950, p. 13; *ibid.,* April 13, 1950, p. 3.

13. Interview with Donald R. Heath, New York, New York, June 28, 1965. Mr. Heath was appointed United States Minister to the Associated States in June 1950. From June 1952 through 1954 he served as American Ambassador to Cambodia and Vietnam.

14. See *New York Times,* September 24, 1951, p. 5. Blum's methods were appreciated by neither the French nor the Americans (see chapter 3). Indeed, according to Ellen Hammer, he "had even been described by French colonial administrators in Viet Nam as 'the most dangerous man in Indochina'" (Hammer, p. 315).

15. U.S. Congress, Senate, Committee on Foreign Relations, *Indochina: Report of Senator Mike Mansfield on a Study Mission*

to *the Associated States of Indochina,* 83d Cong., 1st Sess., October 27, 1953, pp. 4–5. Hereafter cited as *Mansfield Report 1953.*

16. *New York Times,* July 5, 1954, p. 1.

17. Dan, p. 5.

18. *New York Times,* July 5, 1954, p. 1.

19. Dulles, *War or Peace* (New York, 1950), p. 231.

20. *New York Times,* January 28, 1953, p. 2.

21. U.S. Congress, House, Committee on Foreign Affairs, *Report of the Special Study Mission to Pakistan, India, Thailand, and Indochina, pursuant to H. Res. 113,* H. Rpt. No. 412, 83d Cong., 1st Sess., May 6, 1953, p. 53; emphasis supplied. Hereafter cited as *House Special Study Mission Report 1953.*

22. NCNA (Kunming), January 10, 1953, in American Consulate General, Hong Kong, *Survey of China Mainland Press* (hereafter cited as *SCMP*), No. 489 (January 10–12, 1953), p. 35.

23. See *China and the Asian-African Conference (Documents)* (Peking, 1955), p. 26.

24. The CPR expressed growing concern in this period over the alleged oppression of overseas Chinese in Thailand and the Philippines. Cf. NCNA broadcast of January 19, 1953.

25. *House Special Study Mission Report 1953,* p. 48.

26. Lorna Morley, "Menaced Laos," *Editorial Research Reports,* II, No. 12 (September 23, 1959), 721.

27. *House Special Study Mission Report 1953,* p. 47.

28. In addition, a mutual defense agreement with Korea was initialed by Secretary Dulles and President Rhee on August 8, 1953. The treaty was signed October 1 and was in force in November 1954.

29. *New York Times,* February 3, 1953, p. 14.

30. Remarks at the White House Conference for the Advertising Council, March 24, 1953, p. 8, in Dulles Papers [File I.B.1].

31. Secretary Acheson had been the first to link the two wars. On June 18, 1952, following a trip to Indochina, he issued a communiqué jointly with Jean Letourneau, Minister of the Associated States for France, that characterized Indochina as "an integral part of the worldwide resistance by the Free Nations to Communist attempts at conquest and subversion."*DSB,* XXVI, No. 670 (June 30, 1952), 1009–10.

32. *New York Times,* March 29, 1953, p. 12. Both governments further agreed that the Korean and Indochinese conflicts were "parts of the same pattern," and therefore that "the prosecution

of these operations cannot be successfully carried out without full recognition of their interdependence." Department of State Press Release No. 160, March 28, 1953, in Dulles Papers [File I.B.1].

33. *New York Times,* April 17, 1953, p. 4.

34. Address before the American Society of Newspaper Editors, April 18, 1953, Department of State Press Release No. 200, same date, in Dulles Papers [File I.B.1].

35. Laotian Home Service (Vientiane) broadcast, April 21, 1953. This invasion, like others that followed, was a Vietminh show; the Pathet Lao troops with Giap were supposed to clothe the invasion in legitimacy as a national liberation force.

36. *New York Times,* May 3, 1953, p. 1; *ibid.,* May 10, 1953, p. 4.

37. *Ibid.,* May 6, 1953, p. 16.

38. *Ibid.,* May 10, 1953, p. 4.

39. *DAFR 1953,* p. 214.

40. *New York Times,* July 28, 1953, p. 6.

41. The sixteen-nation declaration of July 27 stated that a resumption of the fighting in Korea would be resisted in such a way that, "in all probability, it would not be possible to confine hostilities within the frontiers of Korea." With obvious reference to the CPR-Indochina relationship, the declaration concluded: "Finally, we are of the opinion that the armistice must not result in jeopardizing the restoration or the safeguarding of peace in any other part of Asia." *DAFR 1953,* p. 433.

42. General Navarre registered his agreement when he offered that direct Chinese involvement would touch off a UN and United States response that would risk a third World War. *New York Times,* August 6, 1953, p. 3.

43. *Ibid.,* August 5, 1953, p. 10.

44. *Ibid.,* September 3, 1953, p. 4.

45. *Ibid.*

46. *Ibid.,* September 6, 1953, p. 17.

47. Admiral Arthur W. Radford, then Chairman of the Joint Chiefs of Staff, has told this writer that the intelligence community was nearly unanimous in believing that the Chinese would not repeat their Korean aggression, either with "volunteers" or planes. It was held in Washington that the logistical problems faced by the Chinese in Southeast Asia were far graver than in Korea. Consequently, the Administration's attention to the Asian theatre in 1953 and 1954 was related to the general policy of containing communism, not to preparation for an imminent Chinese thrust

southward. Interview with Admiral Radford, Washington, D.C., July 13, 1965.

Radford's opinion has been seconded by Everett F. Drumright, Deputy Assistant Secretary of State for Far Eastern Affairs beginning in November 1953. Drumright has written: "I do not believe that [Dulles] or other high officials of State or the Pentagon seriously entertained the idea there would be direct Chinese intervention. Sometimes statements are made for political rather than realistic reasons." Letter to the author, Poway, California, July 15, 1965.

48. This decision was placed in the final defense program position paper of December 9, discussed in chapter 4. As paraphrased, the paper said: "An attack on such an area [Indochina] would be met either locally or by strategic attacks against the centers of the aggressor's power." Glenn H. Snyder, "The 'New Look' of 1953," in Warner R. Schilling, Paul Y. Hammond, and Glenn H. Snyder, *Strategy, Politics, and Defense Budgets* (New York, 1962), p. 453.

49. *Mansfield Report 1953,* p. 5. Ambassador Heath has written to the author: ". . . we made it clear [to the French] that we would not use American forces to aid the French-Vietnamese military effort, and it was clear that we would not use or threaten the use of the first absolute weapon in history, the atom bomb, of which we still held the practical monopoly." Statement by Ambassador Heath of July 5, 1965.

3. WASHINGTON AND PARIS: THE POLITICAL TANGLE

1. For a brief discussion of the constitutional issue, see Mus, pp. 24–25.

2. Harold Callender, "Indo-China Showdown Clarifies Paris Policy," *New York Times,* IV, November 1, 1953, p. 4.

3. Buu, pp. 240–42.

4. Information on French domestic policy in Vietnam comes from two articles by Thomas E. Ennis, a former Washington official concerned with Indochinese affairs. See his "The French Empire I: In Asia," *Current History,* XXVIII, No. 165 (May, 1955), 283–84; and "Indo-China at the Crossroads," *Current History,* XXV, No. 147 (November, 1953), 301–3.

5. Buu, p. 247.

6. *House Special Study Mission Report 1953,* p. 51.

7. U.S. *Congressional Record* (hereafter cited as *Cong. Rec.*), 83d Cong., 2d Sess., 1954, C, Pt. 4, 4679.

8. *New York Times,* June 8, 1953, p. 1.

9. Dalat Regional Service broadcast, June 20, 1953.

10. This single Vietnamese had, however, spent most of his life in France; he consequently spoke and understood very little Vietnamese. *Mansfield Report 1953,* p. 43.

11. Dan, p. 23.

12. *DAFR 1953,* p. 348.

13. *New York Times,* November 15, 1953, p. 2.

14. *Ibid.,* November 16, 1953, p. 24.

15. *DAFR 1953,* p. 349.

16. See *New York Times,* October 23, 1953, pp. 1, 8.

17. The 1953 agreements released control of the Cambodian police and judiciary, and a large measure of control of the armed forces. In February 1954 economic and technical services were transferred into Cambodian hands. David J. Steinberg et al., *Cambodia* (New Haven, 1957), pp. 149–50.

18. Callender, p. 4.

19. As an example of this feeling, the French insisted that the Kingdom of Laos present any appeal for UN condemnation of Vietminh aggression—such as one prepared during the invasion of April 1953—through Paris rather than directly to the Organization. See *New York Times,* April 16, 1953, pp. 1, 3.

20. Eisenhower, *Mandate for Change,* p. 336.

21. U.S. Congress, Senate, Committee on Foreign Relations, *Report on Indochina: Report of Senator Mike Mansfield on a Study Mission to Vietnam, Cambodia, Laos,* 83d Cong., 2d Sess., October 15, 1954, pp. 4–5 (hereafter cited as *Mansfield Report 1954*); James Reston, "Uninspiring Bao Dai Regime Held Weak for War on Reds," *New York Times,* July 17, 1953, p. 3; U.S. Congress, House, Committee on Foreign Affairs, *Special Study Mission to Southeast Asia and the Pacific,* 83d Cong., 2d Sess., January 29, 1954, p. 47 (hereafter cited as *House Special Study Mission Report 1954*).

22. *DAFR 1953,* pp. 241–42.

23. *House Special Study Mission Report 1953,* p. 58.

24. U.S. Congress, House, Committee on Foreign Affairs, *Report on H.R. 5710 a Bill to Amend Further the Mutual Security Act of 1951,* H. Rpt. No. 569, 83d Cong., 1st Sess., June 16, 1953, pp. 36–37.

25. *Mansfield Report 1953*, p. 3.

26. U.S. Congress, Senate, Subcommittee on the Far East of the Committee on Foreign Relations, *The Far East and South Asia: Report of Senator H. Alexander Smith*, 83d Cong., 2d Sess., January 25, 1954, p. 14. The survey was made in November and early December 1953; Vietnam and Cambodia, but not Laos, were visited. See also *House Special Study Mission Report 1954*, p. 47.

27. Eisenhower, *Mandate for Change*, pp. 337–38.

28. William B. Dunn, "How West Could Win Vietnam's Support," *Foreign Policy Bulletin*, XXXIII, No. 17 (May 15, 1954), 1. Notably, the same outlook was reportedly not present in Laos or Cambodia, where the Vietminh were strongly resented. See, in this connection, two articles by Richard Adloff and Virginia Thomson: "Laos: Background of Invasion," *Far Eastern Survey*, XXII, No. 6 (May, 1953), 62; and "Cambodia Moves Toward Independence," *Far Eastern Survey*, XXII, No. 9 (August, 1953), 105–11.

29. Eisenhower, *Mandate for Change*, p. 336.

30. Interview between Eisenhower and Walter Cronkite, Columbia Broadcasting System (Television), November 23, 1961.

31. Citing "a most reliable American observer," one writer reported: ". . . technicians attached to the American aid mission were barred in many instances from direct contact with the Vietnamese, except in the most innocuous assistance fields. It is also interesting to note that American technical assistance in the field of public administration was prohibited by the French until 1954, and even then the American public administration advisor had orders to work through the French every step of the way." Robert J. MacAlister, "The Great Gamble" (unpublished Master's essay, University of Chicago, 1958), p. 31.

32. Henri Navarre, *Agonie de l'Indochine (1953–1954)* (Paris, 1956), p. 33.

33. *Ibid.*, p. 71, n. 1, a memorandum to the French government written in July 1953. Navarre also criticized American aid for having been ill-suited to unconventional warfare. *Ibid.*, p. 27.

34. *Cong. Rec.*, XCIX, Pt. 6, 7624.

35. *DAFR 1953*, p. 350.

36. Press conference, July 14, 1953, transcript, p. 1, in Dulles Papers [File I.B.1].

37. One newspaperman's report of a conversation with a "small

farmer near Saigon" may have been illustrative of the actual American position:

> Through my interpreter I asked him [the farmer] to tell me what he thought of the Americans [MAAG] coming to Indochina. He said: "White men help white men. You give guns to help the French kill my people. We want to be rid of all foreigners and the Viet Minh . . . was slowly putting out the French."
> I said: "Don't you know there is a white man behind the Viet Minh? Don't you know that Ho Chi Minh takes Russian orders?"
> He said: "In Saigon I have seen Americans. I have seen Frenchmen. I have never heard of any white men being with the Viet Minh."

Chicago Daily News, September 30, 1950, quoted in Hans Morgenthau, *Politics Among Nations* (New York, 1955), p. 317.

38. In 1953 as in 1946, the Vietminh resorted also to violence, terror, and assassination to compel adherence. As Theodor Arnold has pointed out, for example, the Vietminh intimidated random members of various social, economic, and political groups in order psychologically to produce fear of reprisal within the whole of those groups. "Rich inhabitants of French-occupied cities, including even Saigon," Arnold has written, "received nocturnal visits during which Vietminh representatives confronted them with the alternative of paying the 'war tax' imposed on the whole of the country by Ho Chi Minh's 'government' or of facing reprisals. The murder of one such businessman, who had not necessarily been hunted by the Communists, resulted in the payment of large sums to the Vietminh. . . ." Theodor Arnold, "The Technique of Revolutionary War," in Pentony, ed., pp. 175–76. In this context, see also the foreword by Roger Hilsman to Giap, pp. xx, xxiii.

39. Liang-t'ien, *Yüeh-nan Lao-chua ho Chien-pu-chai ti min-tsu chieh-fang yün-tung* [The National Liberation Movement in Vietnam, Laos, and Cambodia] (Peking, 1951), pp. 74–75.

40. Statement by Mr. Heath.

41. In an interview cited previously, former Ambassador Heath noted that on several occasions he tried to persuade influential Vietnamese that they would eventually get their independence, that independence was inevitable. But he cautioned them that independence would have to await an end to hostilities, arguing that an immediate concession from France would provoke an outcry in Paris for the removal of the Expeditionary Corps. Undoubtedly, the Vietnamese were not satisfied, for the paramount question—

exactly when after the war would independence be granted—remained unanswered.

42. EDC was, in fact, another consideration behind the $385,-000,000 grant. Sherman Adams, *Firsthand Report* (New York, 1961), p. 121.

43. Interview with Hanson W. Baldwin, New York, N.Y., July 14, 1965.

44. *Cong. Rec.*, XCIX, Pt. 6, 7779.

45. *Ibid.*, pp. 7787, 7789.

46. Joseph Laniel, *Le Drame indochinois* (Paris, 1957), pp. 16–17.

47. Navarre, pp. 70–71.

48. Laniel, pp. 16–17.

49. Anthony Eden, *Full Circle* (Boston, 1960), p. 91.

50. Ambassade de France, Service de Presse et d'Information, Speeches and Press Conferences (New York), Doc. No. 13, p. 4.

51. Laniel said in connection with the plan: "The primary condition of an honorable peace" was an increase in the French Union army's strength. In fact, "Our military potential there is increasing in both men and matériel, while the time when the Vietminh was at the peak of its power now seems to have passed." *Ibid.*, Doc. No. 15, p. 1.

52. *Ibid.*, p. 2. Excerpts from the speech may also be found in Hammer, pp. 311–12.

53. *New York Times*, October 28, 1953, p. 2.

54. *Ibid.*, November 13, 1953, pp. 1, 8. A survey of French public opinion taken by the periodical *Sondages* in May 1953 disclosed that 65% of those who responded favored ending the war. Forty-six percent supported negotiations, while 19% desired withdrawal of troops and abandonment. See "La Guerre d'Indochine," *Sondages* (1953), No. 3, 5.

55. *New York Times*, November 5, 1953, p. 8.

56. *Ibid.*, November 28, 1953, p. 28.

57. *DAFR 1953*, p. 214.

58. *New York Times*, December 9, 1953, p. 4.

59. Dan, p. 47.

60. Paris broadcast, May 30, 1953.

61. *New York Times*, August 6, 1953, p. 3.

62. Memorandum of press and radio news conference, p. 2, Department of State Press Release No. 678, December 29, 1953, in Dulles Papers [File I.B.1].

63. Interview with, and statement by, Mr. Heath. Heath recalled

having been "rather flabbergasted" by the Dienbienphu operation and by "a rather surprising belief among our military personnel in the chances for [its] success . . ."

64. Jules Roy, *The Battle of Dienbienphu*, trans. from the French by Robert Baldick (New York, 1965), pp. 58–60.

65. Parts of the secret report are in Navarre, pp. 208–9. Roy (p. 100) gives a similar account, and claims to have seen a copy of Navarre's communication.

66. J.-R. Tournoux, *Secrets d'État* (Paris, 1960), pp. 36–37; Roy, p. 96.

67. *Mansfield Report 1953*, p. 1. In approximately the same period the French and Vietnamese forces also increased, partially fulfilling the goals of the Navarre Plan. By January 1954 French forces totalled 252,000 (including 110,000 Vietnamese in French units); the VNA and ancillary local forces added 255,000 for a combined total of 507,000. Raymond Aron, "Indo-China: A Way Out of the Wood," *Réalités*, No. 40 (March, 1954), pp. 10, 12.

68. Eisenhower, *Mandate for Change*, p. 339.

4. STRATEGY: THE NEW LOOK AND "MASSIVE RE-TALIATION"

1. Dulles, "A Policy of Boldness," *Life*, May 19, 1952, p. 151. The well-known speech of January 12, 1954 was patterned after the ideas expressed in the *Life* article.

2. Adams, p. 398.

3. Snyder, in Schilling, Hammond, and Snyder, pp. 436–37.

4. *Ibid.*

5. *Ibid.*, pp. 451–53.

6. *New York Times*, February 19, 1953, pp. 1, 3.

7. Ridgway later declared that his consent to the paper had been dependent upon the correctness of several assumptions that underlay approval by the Joint Chiefs of Staff of NSC 162/2. These assumptions generally foresaw "no further deterioration in international political conditions," which meant, with regard to Indochina, a stabilization and end of the war. Snyder, in Schilling, Hammond, and Snyder, pp. 442, 443.

8. U.S. Congress, Senate, Subcommittee of the Committee on Appropriations, *Hearings on H.R. 8873 Making Appropriations*

for the Department of Defense, Vol. 89, 83d Cong., 2d Sess., March 15–26, 1954, p. 59.

9. See Snyder, in Schilling, Hammond, and Snyder, pp. 402–3.

10. Address before the National Press Club, December 14, 1953, in *DAFR 1953,* p. 64.

11. *New York Times,* June 11, 1953, p. 20.

12. *Ibid.,* January 13, 1954, p. 2.

13. From the Dulles Papers, we know that the speech was conceived of before December 28 (when Thakhek was taken). On that day, Dulles telephoned his brother, Allen, and inquired about using the Council on Foreign Relations as a forum for "a major address" to follow up on the President's State of the Union message. (Note on telephone conversation with Allen Dulles, December 28, 1953 [File I.B.1]) But further background information is lacking.

14. U.S. Congress, Senate, Committee on Foreign Relations, *Hearing on Foreign Policy and Its Relation to Military Programs,* Vol. 11, 83d Cong., 2d Sess., March 19, 1954, p. 25. Hereafter cited as *Senate Foreign Policy Hearing 1954.*

15. Armstrong to Dulles, February 5, 1954, in Dulles Papers [File I.D.].

16. *Senate Foreign Policy Hearing 1954,* p. 30. Elsewhere Dulles said: "It [the free world] must have the mobility and flexibility to bring collective power to bear against an enemy on a selective or massive basis as conditions may require. For this purpose its arsenal must include a wide range of air, sea, and land power based on both conventional and atomic weapons. . . ." *Ibid.,* p. 4. See also Dulles, "Policy for Security and Peace," *Foreign Affairs,* XXXII, No. 3 (April, 1954), 358.

17. "Interview with Admiral Arthur W. Radford: Strong U.S. Defense for the 'Long Pull,' " *US News & World Report,* March 5, 1954, p. 49.

18. Snyder, in Schilling, Hammond, and Snyder, p. 467, n. 26.

19. *Senate Foreign Policy Hearing 1954,* p. 4.

20. Dulles, *Foreign Affairs,* XXXII, p. 356.

21. News conference of March 16, 1954, Department of State Press Release No. 142, same date, pp. 4–5, in Dulles Papers [File I.B.1].

22. U.S. Department of State, *American Foreign Policy 1950–1955* (Washington, D.C., 1957) (hereafter cited as *AFP*), I, 91–92.

23. "Proposed 'Talking Paper' for Use in Clarifying United

States Position Regarding Atomic and Hydrogen Weapons During Course of NATO Meeting in Paris on 23 April 1954," April 22, 1954 (originally marked "Top Secret"), pp. 6–7, in Dulles Papers [File IX].

24. *Pravda* and *Izvestia*, August 9, 1953, in *The Current Digest of the Soviet Press* (hereafter cited as *CDSP*), V, No. 30 (September 5, 1953), 10–12.

25. The outline here follows the more detailed discussion in Herbert Dinerstein, *War and the Soviet Union* (New York, 1962), pp. 66–69.

26. The Khrushchev "wing" included K. E. Voroshilov, Chairman of the Presidium of the Supreme Soviet and titular head of state; M. M. Kaganovich, a First Deputy Minister; Nikolai Bulganin, Minister of Defense; and V. M. Molotov, Minister of Foreign Affairs.

27. *Pravda*, February 14, 1953, in *CDSP*, V, No. 7 (March 28, 1953), 15.

28. *Pravda*, February 23, 1953, in *CDSP*, V, No. 8 (April 4, 1953), 30.

29. See Halpern, p. 5.

30. NCNA broadcast, February 21, 1953.

31. See, for instance, Liu Ning-i, "On the Eve of the Peace Conference of the Asian and Pacific Regions," *People's China*, No. 19 (September 1, 1952), p. 7; Chang T'o-jo, "New China's Peaceful Foreign Policy," *Shih-chieh chih-shih* [World Culture] No. 39 (October 4, 1952), pp. 5–6; Kuo Mo-jo, "The Korean Armistice and World Peace," *People's China*, No. 16 (August 16, 1953), p. 6.

32. See, for instance, the NCNA broadcast of January 4, 1954 quoting a *People's Daily* editorial.

33. On December 31, 1952 the Soviet Union transferred all rights to the Changchun Railroad to China without compensation, as well as the financial and administrative powers of the Soviet Insurance Organization in northeast China. *Pravda* and *Izvestia*, January 1, 1953, in *CDSP*, V, No. 1 (February 14, 1953), 20; *Pravda*, January 12, and *Izvestia*, January 13, in *CDSP*, V, No. 2 (February 21, 1953), 23. As will be recounted subsequently, other agreements of this nature were concluded in late 1954.

34. *People's Daily*, quoted by NCNA, November 18, 1953, in *SCMP*, No. 691 (November 19, 1953), p. 19.

35. *People's Daily*, quoted by NCNA, October 9, 1953, in *SCMP*, No. 666 (October 10–13, 1953), p. 17.

36. NCNA broadcast, January 4, 1954.

37. *Pravda* and *Izvestia*, September 20, 1953, in *CDSP*, V, No. 38 (October 31, 1953), 19.

38. Based on a survey of foreign affairs articles in the daily issues for January–February, June–July, and November–December 1953.

39. NCNA broadcast, March 21, 1953.

40. *Ibid.*, January 12, 1953.

41. Cheng Wan, "On America's So-Called 'New Look' Foreign Policy," *Shih-chieh chih-shih*, No. 4 (February 20, 1954), p. 8.

42. *Ibid.*

43. See Max Beloff, *Soviet Policy in the Far East 1944–1951* (London, 1953), pp. 224–27.

44. The changed Soviet position may be seen in entirely different viewpoints expressed by Ye. Zhukov, head of the USSR's Oriental Institute of the Academy of Sciences and an expert on Asian affairs. Prior to 1952, Zhukov had said "it would be risky to regard the Chinese revolution as some kind of 'stereotype' for people's democratic revolutions in other countries of Asia." (Quoted in Donald S. Zagoria, "Some Comparisons Between the Russian and Chinese Models," in Barnett, ed., *Communist Strategies in Asia*, p. 18.) In what Zagoria has termed the "compromise" of 1952, Zhukov wrote of China's "unusually great revolutionary influence upon other nations of the East . . ." in an unusual article said by the editors to have been "written in response to the invitation of" *World Culture*. Zhukov further stated: "The victory of the Chinese revolution and the example set by the leadership of the glorious Chinese Communist Party and its leader, Comrade Mao Tse-tung, have enriched the treasury of experience in carrying out revolutions of national liberation . . ." "China's Revolutionary Victory and Its Influence on the Liberation Movements of the Various Asian Peoples," *Shih-chieh chih-shih*, No. 38, (September 27, 1952), pp. 7–8.

45. See a statement by Senator Mansfield in *New York Times*, February 21, 1953, pp. 1–2. In a report later in the year, Mansfield stated: "There is no evidence of Soviet Russian personnel within Indochina but there are reports of such personnel operating across the border in southern China." However, he made no attempt to

elaborate on what was meant by "personnel." *Mansfield Report 1953*, p. 2.

46. See, for example, *Pravda*, July 27, 1953, in *CDSP*, V, No. 30 (September 5, 1953), 19; *Pravda*, August 31, 1953, in *CDSP*, V, No. 35 (October 10, 1953), 22.

47. *New York Times*, August 2, 1953, p. 3.

48. *Pravda* and *Izvestia*, in *CDSP*, V, No. 49 (January 20, 1954), 39.

49. NCNA, September 2, 1953, in *SCMP*, No. 643 (September 2–3, 1953), p. 7. Laniel's allusion to Chinese interest in negotiations in his speech of October 27, 1953 seems to have been somewhat premature. The French Premier based his belief on a statement of August 24 by Chou En-lai, who urged the convening of a political conference to arrange a final Korean settlement. See NCNA, August 24, 1953, in *SCMP*, No. 638 (August 25, 1953), p. 1.

5. THE ROAD TO DIENBIENPHU: DIPLOMACY AND STRATEGY, FEBRUARY–MARCH 1954

1. Robert Guillain, "Les Erreurs et les malheurs de Dien-Bien-Phu," *Le Monde*, May 4, 1954, p. 1.

2. Vietnam Home Service (Saigon) broadcast, January 30, 1954.

3. Roy, pp. 103–4.

4. Guillain, "Les Erreurs et les malheurs de Dien-Bien-Phu," p. 1.

5. *New York Times*, February 7, 1954, p. 14. The technicians joined 125 others already in Vietnam under MAAG. The technicians were also necessary because French pilots were not familiar with the planes. Although Americans were engaged in flying supply sorties to French outposts, the crews were civilian, attached to Civil Air Transport of Taiwan. *Ibid.*, May 11, 1953, p. 4; *ibid.*, February 3, 1954, p. 5.

6. Senator Leverett Saltonstall of Massachusetts received such assurances from the Secretary of Defense. *Cong. Rec.*, C, Pt. 2, 1506. The French had requested 400 men.

7. Dwight D. Eisenhower, *Public Papers of the Presidents of the United States: 1954* (Washington, D.C., 1960), p. 250. Hereafter cited as *Public Papers 1954*.

8. *New York Times*, February 14, 1954, p. 1; *The Times* (London), February 13, 1954, p. 6.

9. The French opposed the use of Rhee's troops for fear of triggering a massive Chinese intervention. See *Manchester Guardian Weekly*, February 18, 1954, p. 3.

10. *New York Times*, January 31, 1954, p. 17.

11. *Ibid.*, February 15, 1954, p. 2.

12. *Ibid.*, February 16, 1954, p. 19.

13. *Ibid.*, January 18, 1954, p. 4.

14. For details, *ibid.*, February 10, p. 2; February 16, p. 3; February 22, p. 1; February 28, p. 4.

15. Regional Service (Dalat) broadcast, February 14, 1954.

16. Great Britain, Foreign Office, *Papers Relating to Foreign Affairs Laid before Parliament* (hereafter cited as GB, *Papers*), "Further Correspondence . . . regarding the International Situation," Misc. No. 22, Cmd. 9022, No. 1 (November 26, 1953).

17. *Ibid.*, "Documents relating to the Meeting of Foreign Ministers . . . ," Misc. No. 5, Cmd. 9080, No. 3, pp. 7–14.

18. *Ibid.*, Nos. 1, 4, pp. 17, 22.

19. *Ibid.*, No. 2 (January 27), p. 23 (Eden); No. 5 (January 28), p. 30 (Bidault).

20. These preconditions were mentioned first by Dulles in a press conference; see *New York Times*, May 23, 1953, p. 1. They came forward again at the December Bermuda Conference; *ibid.*, December 9, 1953, p. 4.

21. The Laniel cabinet's margin reduced to 319–249 following his January 8 speech. Ambassade de France, Doc. No. 18, p. 3.

22. This threat was expressed in his famous speech of December 14, 1953. By a "reappraisal" Dulles had in mind a reconsideration of the disposition of United States forces in NATO and a cutback on defense aid. See *New York Times*, December 15, 1953, p. 14, for the text and Harold Callender, "France Is Divided on Coming Parley," *New York Times*, February 20, 1954, p. 3, for insights into the relationship of EDC to France's position at Berlin.

23. Raymond Aron, "Historical Sketch of the Great Debate," in Daniel Lerner and Raymond Aron, eds., *France Defeats EDC* (New York, 1957), p. 16.

24. Interview with Hanson W. Baldwin.

25. *New York Times*, February 10, 1954, p. 1.

26. *Ibid.*, February 22, 1954, p. 2.

27. See Jacques Vernant, "Avant la Négociation internationale sur l'Asie," *Revue de Défense Nationale*, XVIII (April, 1954),

477. The Assembly backed the Berlin decision by increasing the government's pre-Berlin (January 8) margin, 349–263. Ambassade de France, Doc. No. 19, p. 4.

28. The quadripartite communiqué from the conference is in *AFP*, II, 2372–73.

29. *Izvestia*, February 28, 1954, in *CDSP*, VI, No. 9 (April 14, 1954), 25.

30. See *People's Daily*, February 22, 1954, p. 1; also, a speech by Ch'en Yun, member of the CCP Central Committee Secretariat, NCNA, March 5, 1954, in *SCMP*, No. 761 (March 6–8, 1954), pp. 6–7.

31. *New York Times*, February 10, 1954, p. 1.

32. Testimony of May 17, 1954 before U.S. Congress, Senate, Subcommittee of the Committee on Appropriations, *Hearings on H.R. 8067 Making Appropriations for the Departments of State, Justice, and Commerce and the United States Information Agency*, Pt. 2, Vol. 91, 83d Cong., 2d Sess., 1954, p. 2131; U.S. Congress, Senate, Committee on Foreign Relations, *Hearings on the Mutual Security Program for Fiscal Year 1955*, Vol. 11, 83d Cong., 2d Sess., June 4, 1954, p. 32. (Hereafter cited as *Senate MSP Hearings 1954.*) The *Christian Science Monitor* (February 18, 1954, p. 1) attributed to the "highest American sources" the belief that the war would intensify as a result of the Berlin decision, with the Communists, as in Korea, making "a last-minute bid for territorial and military advantages to strengthen [their] hand at the conference table."

33. Paul Ély, *Mémoires* (Paris, 1964), chapter 2.

34. Interview between Jules Roy and Navarre, in Jules Roy, *La Bataille de Dien Bien Phu* (Paris, 1963), p. 610.

35. Quoted in Guillain, "Les Erreurs et les malheurs de Dien-Bien-Phu," p. 1. It was also reported that Navarre "was convinced that they [the French forces] would be able to seize all the vital areas upon which he [the enemy] depended to maintain his front line troops." *The Times* (London), February 20, 1954, p. 6.

36. Eisenhower, *Mandate for Change*, p. 344. The cable was sent February 10.

37. *New York Herald Tribune*, February 19, 1954, p. 3.

38. *The Times* (London), March 10, 1954, p. 8.

39. *New York Times*, March 6, 1954, p. 3.

40. Department of State Press Release No. 3, March 23, 1954, p. 6, in Dulles Papers [File I.B.1].

41. Bernard B. Fall, "Indochina: The Last Year of the War—

The Navarre Plan," *Military Review,* XXXVI, No. 9 (December, 1956), 55–56.

42. *New York Times,* February 18, 1954, p. 22.

43. *Ibid.,* April 3, 1954, p. 5.

44. *Ibid.,* February 18, 1954, p. 10.

45. *Ibid.,* February 20, 1954, p. 2; *The Times* (London), February 20, 1954, p. 6.

46. Eisenhower, *Public Papers 1954,* p. 306.

47. Ély, p. 59.

48. *Ibid.,* p. 60.

49. *Ibid.,* pp. 60–61.

50. *Ibid.,* p. 64.

51. *Ibid.,* p. 77.

52. According to Laniel, VULTURE was the product of joint planning in Saigon and Hanoi. But the original plan called for 300 fighter-bombers, not 150, and for raids on a wider scope than Dienbienphu alone. Laniel, p. 88. Despite the accounts of Ély, Laniel, and other Frenchmen, Admiral Radford has stated in an interview that no Operation VULTURE existed, since the plan to save Dienbienphu by an air strike never reached the operational stage. In light of subsequent events, his contention is technically correct; the use of "VULTURE" hereafter is therefore only for the sake of brevity.

53. Ély, pp. 76–77, 82–83; Jean Lacouture and Philippe Devillers, *La Fin d'une guerre* (Paris, 1960), p. 73.

54. Interview with Admiral Radford. According to Ély, Radford indicated he would push for favorable American action and believed he had Presidential backing. Ély, pp. 83–84.

55. Lacouture and Devillers, p. 73.

56. Ély, pp. 75–76.

57. *Public Papers 1954,* p. 341.

58. Draft of Dulles' Overseas Press Club speech, dated March 24, 1954, p. 5, in Dulles Papers [File I.B.]. According to Tanham, the pre-Dienbienphu level was 1500 tons monthly, with 4000 tons in June. Tanham, p. 69.

As a comparison, it might be noted that at the time one American Army division used daily between 600 and 700 tons when in combat. See Robert Murphy, Deputy Under Secretary of State, to Dulles, March 26, 1954, p. 1, in Dulles Papers [File I.B.].

59. U.S. Congress, Senate, Subcommittee of the Committee on Appropriations, *Hearings on H.R. 8067,* pp. 2131–32.

60. Ély, p. 66. Dulles further indicated that any Indochina solution would only be possible upon removal of the colonialism issue. Ély replied that France had already proven its determination to give the Associated States real independence. *Ibid.,* p. 67.

61. *New York Times,* March 30, 1954, p. 4. Emphasis supplied in all cases.

62. Eisenhower, *Public Papers 1954,* p. 366. Eisenhower said: "Well, I have said time and again that I can conceive of no greater disadvantage to America than to be employing its own ground forces, and any other kind of forces, in great numbers around the world, meeting each little situation as it arises. What we are trying to do is to make our friends strong enough to take care of local situations by themselves. . . ."

63. For an informed French opinion on the substance of the united action strategy, see Jacques Vernant, "Paris, Washington et Londres devant le drame indochinois," *Revue de Défense Nationale,* XVIII (June, 1954), 738.

64. Eden, p. 103.

65. Lacouture and Devillers, p. 74 and p. 74, n. 1.

66. Ély, p. 72.

67. Interview with Admiral Radford.

68. NCNA, February 8, 1954, in *SCMP,* No. 744 (February 10, 1954), pp. 3–4.

69. NCNA broadcasts, February 15 and 21, 1954.

70. See, for instance, *SCMP,* No. 750 (February 18, 1954), p. 2; No. 746 (February 12, 1954), p. 3; and No. 745 (February 11, 1954), p. 4.

71. The Chinese even speculated that General James A. Van Fleet, an old nemesis from Korean War days, would eventually be named supreme United States commander in Indochina. NCNA, March 21, 1954, in *SCMP,* No. 771 (March 20–22, 1954), p. 20.

72. See, for instance, NCNA broadcast, February 25, 1954.

73. NCNA (Canton), March 13, 1954, in *SCMP,* No. 766 (March 13–15, 1954), p. 26.

74. NCNA, April 1, 1954, in *SCMP,* No. 780 (April 2, 1954), pp. 1–2.

75. NCNA, March 21, 1954, in *SCMP,* No. 771 (March 20–22, 1954), p. 3.

76. *People's Daily* editorial, April 3, 1954, p. 1.

77. *People's Daily* editorial broadcast by NCNA, February 22, 1954.

78. NCNA, March 21, 1954, in *SCMP*, No. 771 (March 20–22, 1954), p. 4.

79. NCNA, March 25, 1954, in *SCMP*, No. 775 (March 26, 1954), pp. 1–2.

80. *People's Daily*, March 30, 1954, p. 4. The article was accompanied by a map which indicated forty-four American bases in the Far East.

81. See, for example, Bulganin's speech of March 10. *Pravda* and *Izvestia*, March 11, 1954, in *CDSP*, VI, No. 10 (April 21, 1954), 11–12.

82. *Pravda* and *Izvestia*, March 13, 1954, in *CDSP*, VI, No. 11 (April 28, 1954), 7–8; Dinerstein, p. 71.

83. *Kommunist* (Erevan, Armenia), March 12, 1954. This organ, cited by Dinerstein, was the only one to print the full text of Mikoyan's remarks. See Dinerstein, pp. 71–72.

84. Issue of March 17, 1954, in Dinerstein, p. 107.

85. *Ibid.*, p. 109.

86. *People's Daily*, March 8, 1954, p. 1, paraphrasing an editorial in the North Korean paper, *Minju Choson* [Democratic Korea].

87. NCNA, March 13, 1954, in *SCMP*, No. 766 (March 13–15, 1954), p. 13; also NCNA, March 3, 1954, in *SCMP*, No. 760 (March 5, 1954), pp. 4–5.

88. NCNA, February 28, 1954, in *SCMP*, No. 756 (February 27–March 1, 1954), p. 9.

6. THE PROBLEM OF INTERVENTION: APRIL 1954

1. Ély, pp. 85–86.

2. Navarre, p. 210.

3. *Ibid.*, p. 219.

4. Laniel, p. 45.

5. See, for instance, *Cong. Rec.*, C, Pt. 3, 4207–8.

6. *Ibid.*, p. 4210.

7. Reston, "Art of Sudden Diplomacy," *New York Times Magazine*, April 11, 1954, p. 10.

8. Donald Lancaster, *The Emancipation of French Indochina* (London, 1961), pp. 296–97.

9. Chalmers M. Roberts, "The Day We Didn't Go to War," *The Reporter*, XI (September 14, 1954), 31; Chalmers M. Roberts, "United States Twice Proposed Indochina Air Strike—Blocked

by British 'No,'" *Washington Post and Times Herald,* June 7, 1954, pp. 1, 4. Another, though much less detailed, account is given in John Robinson Beal, *John Foster Dulles* (New York, 1957), p. 207; the ships involved are said to have been the *Boxer* and the *Philippine Sea,* however.

According to Roberts' accounts, those present at the meeting were Secretary Dulles; Admiral Radford; Under Secretary of Defense Roger Keyes; Navy Secretary Robert B. Anderson; Senators William F. Knowland, Eugene D. Millikin, Lyndon B. Johnson, Richard B. Russell, and Earle C. Clements; and Representatives Joseph P. Martin, John McCormack, and J. Percy Priest.

10. Beal has written (Beal, p. 207): "Targets had been selected; the aircraft carriers . . . were in the area with their tactical air groups and atomic weapons aboard. . . . The airplanes would strike at staging areas where the Chinese Communists grouped the forces they were pouring behind the Vietminh, but would not attempt to carry warfare to the big Chinese population centers. The plan was to hit where it would be militarily vital." Despite Beal's statement, it is doubtful that atomic warheads would have been utilized in the absence of a direct armed attack by Chinese Communist troops (see below). As Representative McCormack subsequently confirmed, the discussion on April 3 centered about "a mass air attack upon the Communists who were besieging Dienbienphu." *New York Times,* January 23, 1956, p. 3.

11. Admiral Radford has stated in an interview with the author that some carriers were equipped with atomic weapons; if the *Essex* and *Boxer* had them, they were not allotted for use in any particular situation.

12. Roberts, "The Day We Didn't Go to War," pp. 31–32; Beal, p. 208.

13. Roberts, "The Day We Didn't Go to War," p. 32.

14. *Ibid.*

15. *Ibid.,* p. 31; McCormack statement in *New York Times,* January 23, 1956, p. 3.

16. McCormack statement in *New York Times,* January 23, 1956, p. 3; Beal, p. 207; Roberts, "The Day We Didn't Go to War," p. 31.

17. Eisenhower, *Mandate for Change,* p. 347.

18. Beal, p. 207; Adams, p. 122. As will be elaborated upon subsequently, the President was far more conscious of, and influenced by, allied and Congressional attitudes than was Dulles.

Sherman Adams, the Special Presidential Assistant and therefore a close associate of Eisenhower, has observed: "Having avoided one total war with Red China the year before in Korea when he had United Nations support, he [Eisenhower] was in no mood to provoke another one in Indo-China by going it alone in a military action without the British and other Western Allies. He was also determined not to become involved militarily in any foreign conflict without the approval of Congress. He had had trouble enough convincing some Senators that it was even necessary to send small groups of noncombatant Air Force technicians to Indo-China." Adams, p. 121.

19. Eisenhower, *Mandate for Change*, pp. 346–47. The published version deletes probable reference to a joint warning of potential action against the CPR. The State Department was, in fact, reported to be working on such a warning in early April. *New York Times*, April 7, 1954, p. 1.

20. Lacouture and Devillers, p. 75.

21. *Ibid.*, p. 80; *Le Monde*, April 7, 1954, p. 2.

22. Lacouture and Devillers, p. 75.

23. Ély, pp. 87–88.

24. Navarre, p. 243 and p. 243, n. 1. The draft of the speech, dated 4/5/54 and labeled "top secret," in Dulles Papers [File I.B.1]; official text is in *DSB*, XXX, No. 773 (April 19, 1954), 579–83.

25. Eisenhower, *Public Papers 1954*, pp. 72–73.

26. Lacouture and Devillers, p. 81.

27. Eisenhower, *Mandate for Change*, p. 347.

28. Eden, p. 104.

29. *Ibid.*, p. 105.

30. *New York Times*, April 9, 1954, p. 8.

31. See his remarks before the Republican Women's Centennial Conference, April 7, 1954, Department of State Press Release No. 182, p. 7, in Dulles Papers [File I.B.1]. Under Secretary Smith confirmed the policy switch. In a statement issued to the press April 10 prior to a televised interview the next day, Smith said in reference to the April 7 comments by Dulles: "The position of the United States is that, if there is a united will among the free nations East and West, a will that is made clear to the Communists so there can be no misunderstanding on their part, that this of itself would give pause for further adventures and aggression." *DSB*, XXX, No. 773 (April 19, 1954), 590.

32. Statement of April 10, 1954, pp. 1–2, in Dulles Papers [File IX].

33. Eden, p. 107.

34. *Ibid.*, pp. 107–9. Eden was also informed about, and must certainly have been influenced by, the armaments aboard the carriers (*ibid.*, p. 55). According to James Shepley, chief of the Time-Life Washington Bureau in 1956, the carriers *Boxer* and *Philippine Sea* (the same ones cited by Beal) were en route to the South China Sea on April 10. "On board were their tactical air groups armed with atomic weapons. It was a modern version of the classic show of force, designed both to deter any Red Chinese attack on Vietnam and to provide weapons for instant retaliation if it should prove necessary." James Shepley, "How Dulles Averted War," *Life*, January 16, 1956, p. 72.

35. *DAFR 1954*, p. 257; *New York Times*, April 14, 1954, p. 3.

36. Ély, p. 88.

37. *Le Monde*, April 10, 1954, p. 2.

38. Jacques Chastenet, "Comment conclure la guerre d'Indochine?" *Hommes et Mondes*, No. 93 (April, 1954), p. 5.

39. *Le Monde*, April 11–12, 1954, p. 3.

40. This interpretation is given by Vernant, "Paris, Washington et Londres devant le drame indochinois," p. 739. Cf. also Ély, p. 89.

41. *New York Times*, April 15, 1954, p. 2 (English version); *Le Monde*, April 16, 1954, p. 4 (French version).

42. Statement of April 10, 1954, p. 2, in Dulles Papers [File IX].

43. Quoted in Eisenhower, *Mandate for Change*, p. 350. The Administration's ranks were not lacking contributors to publicizing the value of the fortress, however. Under Secretary of State Smith declared, in answer to questions prepared for a television broadcast: "I would like to emphasize that . . . insofar as the free world is concerned, the French Union forces at Dien Bien Phu are fighting a modern Thermopylae." *DSB*, XXX, No. 773 (April 19, 1954), 3.

44. *New York Times*, April 18, 1954, p. 3.

45. *Ibid.*

46. "Mr. Dulles Answers Some Questions," *US News & World Report*, April 30, 1954, p. 63.

47. Nixon himself later backtracked on his statement when he said that the aim of the United States was to avoid involvement if at all possible and seek an "honorable and peaceful settlement" of the crisis at Geneva. *New York Times*, April 21, 1954, p. 4.

48. Roberts, "The Day We Didn't Go to War," p. 34.

49. Eden later told the Commons that the meeting "seemed to me . . . must inevitably prejudge the question of membership at the outset, and I thought it important not to do this." Speech of June 23, 1954, in *New York Times*, June 24, 1954, p. 4.

50. Earlier on the twentieth, Dulles reportedly conferred with a group of Democratic and Republican Congressmen for a second time. He was said to have informed them that "American intervention in Indochina was not imminent or under active consideration at present." Roberts, "United States Twice Proposed Indochina Air Strike," p. 4.

51. Eisenhower, *Mandate for Change*, p. 350. Navarre wanted United States planes to take out the Vietminh supply base of Tuan Giao with a sustained 48-hour assault. Tuan Giao, northeast of Dienbienphu, was an important feeding point along the Dienbienphu-Lai Chau-Son La triangle. The general believed the elimination of Tuan Giao would give him the three weeks which he needed to save his garrison. See the Roy-Navarre interview in Roy, *La Bataille de Dien Bien Phu*, p. 611.

52. Quoted in Beal, p. 211.

53. Eisenhower, *Mandate for Change*, p. 350.

54. *Ibid.*, p. 351.

55. Eden, pp. 112–13.

56. *Ibid.*, p. 114.

57. Laniel, p. 87.

58. Eden, pp. 114–15.

59. Roberts, "The Day We Didn't Go to War," p. 35; Tournoux, p. 55.

60. Eden, p. 115.

61. Roberts, "The Day We Didn't Go to War," p. 35.

62. Tournoux, pp. 462–63; cf. Roberts, "The Day We Didn't Go to War," p. 35, which substantiates the existence of the Dulles letter and its contents as given by Tournoux.

Dulles' final position on the feasibility of an air strike was probably the result of a Joint Chiefs of Staff report to the President, which cited the danger of annihilating both defenders and attackers. *New York Times*, April 26, 1954, p. 4.

63. Tournoux, p. 463.

64. *The Times* (London), April 26, 1954, p. 6.

65. *Ibid.* See also Eden, p. 104.

66. *Ibid.,* p. 117; also, Eden's speech of June 23, in *New York Times,* June 24, 1954, p. 4.

67. The phrase is from the final Colombo Conference communiqué of May 2. *Ibid.,* May 2, 1954, p. 2.

68. See Eden's speech of June 23. *Ibid.,* June 24, 1954, p. 4.

69. *The Times* (London), April 19, 1954, p. 6.

70. *Ibid.,* April 24, 1954, p. 6.

71. This report was attributed "to the best informed diplomatic [sources] in London." *Le Monde,* April 24, 1954, p. 2.

72. Eisenhower, *Public Papers 1954,* pp. 421–22.

73. Adams, p. 123.

74. Churchill's remarks effectively summarized British thinking. He said: "No decisions were taken in advance of the conference at Geneva. . . . The episode of the siege of the French fortress of Dien Bien Phu . . . creates a violent tension in many minds at a time when calm judgment is most needed. The timing of the climax of this assault with the opening of the Geneva conference is not without significance; but it must not be allowed to prejudice the sense of world proportion which should inspire the conference and be a guide to those who are watching its progress. . . . The Government are not prepared to give any undertakings about United Kingdom military action in Indo-China in advance of the results of Geneva. (Cheers.) We have not entered into any new political or military commitments. . . ." *The Times* (London), April 28, 1954, p. 4.

75. Eisenhower, *Public Papers 1954,* p. 428.

76. *New York Times,* May 1, 1954, pp. 1, 3.

77. Eden, p. 126.

78. James Reston, "Dulles Returning to Face Criticism on Asiatic Policy," *New York Times,* May 4, 1954, p. 1.

7. TOWARD A SETTLEMENT

1. The capitulation was not complete in that Malenkov spoke of capitalism's "collapse" in lieu of its "destruction." Dinerstein, p. 74.

2. *Ibid.,* p. 112.

3. Alice Langley Hsieh, *Communist China's Strategy in the Nuclear Era* (Englewood Cliffs, N.J., 1962), p. 25.

4. See *DAFR 1954,* pp. 327–28.

5. Text of this agreement is in NCNA, April 29, 1954, in *SCMP*, No. 798 (April 30, 1954), pp. 3–5.

6. NCNA, April 11, 1954, in *SCMP*, No. 786 (April 10–12, 1954), p. 1.

7. *People's Daily*, April 21, 1954, p. 1. The editorial also pointed out that Radford "has proposed sending aircraft carriers and planes to participate directly in the Indochina war," while Nixon "has actually shouted about dispatching American [ground] forces to Indochina."

8. "America's Destructive Actions on the Eve of the Geneva Conference," *Shih-chieh chih-shih* [World Culture], No. 8 (April 20, 1954), p. 12.

9. NCNA, May 9, 1954, in *SCMP*, No. 804 (May 8–10, 1954), p. 38.

10. *Jih-nei-wa hui-i wen-chien hui-pien* [Collection of Documents of the Geneva Conference] (Peking, 1954), p. 163.

11. James Reston, "Dulles Returning to Face Criticism on Asiatic Policy," p. 4.

12. *AFP*, II, 2383.

13. *New York Times*, May 8, 1954, p. 4. This was not the first time an Administration official had mentioned the conditions for a settlement. Addressing the American Academy of Political and Social Science in Philadelphia on April 2, the State Department's Officer in Charge for Chinese Political Affairs, Alfred le Sesne Jenkins, said: ". . . we are keenly sensible to the Communist habit of waging war by cease-fire and do not discount the possibility that they might use a cessation of hostilities merely as an opportunity to build up for renewed attacks. In our view, any settlement in Korea or Indochina would have to provide effective guarantees against such a possibility." *DSB*, XXX, No. 774 (April 26, 1954), 627.

14. Press and radio news conference, May 11, 1954, Department of State Press Release No. 4, same date, p. 6 in Dulles Papers [File I.B.1].

15. *Ibid.*, p. 4.

16. *DSB*, XXX, No. 778 (May 24, 1954), 782.

17. *New York Times*, May 12, 1954, p. 6.

18. *Ibid.*, May 13, 1954, p. 14.

19. Hanson W. Baldwin, "Indochina Peril Grows," *New York Times*, June 7, 1954, p. 5.

20. *New York Times,* May 16, 1954, p. 3. Dulles elaborated on these conditions at a news conference May 25. He said: "We are not prepared to go in for a defense of colonialism. We are only going in for defense of liberty and independence and freedom. . . . We don't go in alone, we go in where the other nations which have an important stake in the area recognize the peril as we do. . . . We go in where the United Nations gives moral sanction to our action." *AFP,* II, 2392.

21. See testimony by Dulles in U.S. Congress, Senate, Subcommittee of the Committee on Appropriations, *Hearings on H.R. 8067,* p. 2131.

22. *New York Times,* June 3, 1954, p. 1.

23. *Washington Post and Times Herald,* June 8, 1954, p. 2.

24. The five-power military discussions lasted from June 3 to June 11. The final communiqué made no mention of the subjects discussed or the decisions taken. See *New York Times,* June 12, 1954, p. 2.

25. *Ibid.,* June 9, 1954, p. 1.

26. Speech before a convention of the Rotary International in Seattle. *Ibid.,* June 11, 1954, p. 2.

27. U.S. Congress, Senate, Subcommittee of the Committee on Appropriations, *Hearings on H.R. 8067,* pp. 2130–31.

28. *Senate MSP Hearings 1954,* p. 21. Radford held similar convictions. Democratic members of the Senate Foreign Relations Committee confided that the Chief of Staff had testified in March 1954 that it would be ten years before the Indochinese states would be ready for independence. *New York Times,* May 13, 1954, p. 3.

29. Matthew B. Ridgway, *Soldier* (New York, 1956), p. 276.

30. Interview with Hanson W. Baldwin. Cf. also Hanson W. Baldwin, " 'New Look' Re-Examined in Light of Indo-China," *New York Times,* IV, May 2, 1954, p. 5.

31. Ridgway, *Soldier,* pp. 276–77.

32. "What Ridgway Told Ike—War in Indo-China would be Tougher than Korea," *US News & World Report,* June 25, 1954, pp. 30–33.

33. *Cong. Rec.,* C, Pt. 7, 8905.

34. "What Ridgway Told Ike," pp. 30–33.

35. Ridgway, *Soldier,* p. 277.

36. Radford was unimpressed by the Ridgway Report. He ques-

tioned whether the raising of sufficient manpower would be as difficult as the report stated. Interview with Admiral Radford.

37. McClintock to Dulles, "confidential" action copy telegram, May 4, 1954, in Dulles Papers [File I.B.].

38. The view that partition was the best possible solution under the prevailing military circumstances was held, for instance, by Ambassador Heath (interview).

39. *New York Times,* June 29, 1954, p. 2.

40. A communiqué issued at the conclusion of these talks stated simply that Chou and Ho had "fully exchanged opinions" on the war "and other related questions. . . ." Hoang Van Hoan and an advisor to the CPR delegation to Geneva, Ch'iao Kuan-hua, were in attendance. *Jen-min shou-ts'e 1955,* p. 340.

41. Eden, pp. 133–34, 143–45.

42. London proposed an exchange of ambassadors June 17, 1950; Peking replied June 17, 1954 with an agreement to exchange chargés d'affaires. *New York Times,* June 4, 1954, p. 5 and June 18, 1954, p. 1. It is noteworthy that Eden, addressing the Commons June 23, said at one point: "There is no doubt that one result of the conference has been an improvement in Anglo-Chinese relations." *Ibid.,* June 24, 1954, p. 4.

43. NCNA (New Delhi), June 28, 1954, in *SCMP,* No. 838 (June 29, 1954), pp. 5–6.

44. NCNA (Rangoon), June 30, 1954, in *SCMP,* No. 839 (June 30, 1954), pp. 2–3.

45. NCNA, July 2, 1954, in *SCMP,* No. 841 (July 3–4, 1954), p. 3.

46. Ambassade de France, Doc. No. 25, pp. 2, 4.

47. NCNA, July 13, 1954, in *SCMP,* No. 848 (July 15, 1954), p. 3.

48. Full documentation may be found in GB, *Papers,* "Further documents relating to the discussion of Indo-China at the Geneva Conference," Misc. No. 20, Cmd. 9239.

49. From Ho's nation-wide appeal of July 22, 1954, in *Statements by President Ho Chi-Minh After the Geneva Conference* (Hanoi, 1955), p. 5.

50. Tillman Durdin, "Some in Vietminh, Angered, Say Red Allies Forced Pact," *New York Times,* July 25, 1954, p. 1.

51. Emmet John Hughes, *The Ordeal of Power* (New York, 1964), p. 182. The remark was made by Dulles to Hughes.

8. THE CRISIS IN VIETNAM

1. "Lessons of Dienbienphu: Too Little and Too Late," *New York Times,* IV, May 16, 1954, p. 5.
2. Interview with Ambassador Heath.
3. Interview with Hanson W. Baldwin.
4. *Ibid.*
5. Interview with Ambassador Heath.
6. Interview with Hanson W. Baldwin.
7. Statement of June 4, 1954 by Secretary Dulles, in *Senate MSP Hearings 1954,* p. 33.
8. Interview with Admiral Radford.
9. Robert Guillain wrote from the front that massive air bombardment and tactical air support could neither markedly alter the military situation on the ground nor relieve French troops. The trench system and underground strongholds, he reported, protected the guerrillas and at the same time prevented rapidly moving planes from being effective. Robert Guillain, "Sauver l'Armée française," *Le Monde,* April 29, 1954, pp. 1–2.
10. Eisenhower-Cronkite interview.
11. The only sizable Asian armies were the South Korean (about 600,000 men) and Nationalist Chinese (about 500,000) forces. For security and political reasons, neither the United States nor France wanted to use them or bring their governments within the proposed SEATO pact.
12. Comment by Senator Mansfield during testimony by Secretary Dulles, in *Senate Foreign Policy Hearing 1954,* p. 41.
13. Admiral Radford claimed, in a speech during December 1953, that "atomic weapons have virtually achieved conventional status within our Armed Forces. Each military Service is capable of putting this weapon into military use." *DAFR 1953,* p. 65. Eisenhower had also spoken of conventional atomic weapons in his "Atoms for Peace" address. *Ibid.,* p. 46. But General Ridgway thereafter replied that, in fact, new weapons were "extremely limited" in number with the exception of air-deliverable atomic weapons. Ridgway, "My Battles in War and Peace," *The Saturday Evening Post,* January 21, 1956, p. 48.
14. Interview with Hanson W. Baldwin.

15. As will be argued below, the signal achievement of the Administration lay in *not* having intervened. Ridgway, it should be noted, strongly disapproved of intervening even though the United States could have fought and won; the costs were simply too great. Ridgway, *Soldier*, p. 277. Ridgway wrote to the author: "I did not then believe that intervention with U.S. ground troops would have provided an effective solution, and I have never since changed that opinion." Letter from General Ridgway, Pittsburgh, Pennsylvania, June 16, 1964.

16. The phrase is from Ridgway, *Soldier*, p. 278.

17. Eisenhower, *Mandate for Change*, p. 340.

18. The probable impact of independence upon the French military and civilian sectors in Vietnam is discussed in Devillers, in Holland, ed., pp. 205–7, 260. The French might have drawn a lesson from the Cambodian experience, where the extension of total independence by February 1954 redounded to France's credit. See U.S. Congress, Senate, Committee on Foreign Relations, *Viet Nam, Cambodia, and Laos: Report by Senator Mike Mansfield*, 84th Cong., 1st Sess., October 6, 1955, p. 16.

19. The texts are in *New York Times*, May 13, 1954, p. 6.

20. See Eisenhower's letter to General Alfred Gruenther (NATO Supreme Commander) in Eisenhower, *Mandate for Change*, p. 364.

21. Ély, p. 74.

22. Eisenhower, *Mandate for Change*, p. 373.

23. *Cong. Rec.*, C, Pt. 4, 5116.

24. Hughes, p. 297.

25. Eisenhower, *Mandate for Change*, p. 341.

26. "On 'the Tragedy of Timidity,'" *New York Times*, IV, May 23, 1954, p. 10.

27. In his May 7, 1954 address, for example, Dulles observed that the Chinese "have, however, stopped short of open intervention. In this respect, they may have been deterred by the warnings which the United States has given that such intervention would lead to grave consequences which might not be confined to Indochina." Address by Dulles, May 7, 1954, in Dulles Papers [File I.B.].

28. The comment was made in response to the above-quoted statement on deterrence of the Chinese. See the copy of the May 7 address marked for Livingston J. Merchant (Assistant Secretary for European Affairs), "Draft—5/6/54," p. 21, *ibid.* Eden made essentially the same comment in 1952. See Eden, p. 92.

29. Feng-hwa Mah, "The First Five-Year Plan and its International Aspects," in C. F. Remer, ed., *Three Essays on the International Economics of Communist China* (Ann Arbor, 1959), pp. 41, 44.

30. "Questions of Tactics in the Present Anti-Japanese United Front" (March 1940), in Mao, *Selected Works*, III, 199. Cf. also Truong Chinh, *Primer for Revolt*, p. 56, for this same tactic.

31. Beal, p. 212.

32. Eden, pp. 131–32.

33. Isaac Deutscher, "How the Russians Bet a Little in Asia to Win a Lot in Europe," *The Reporter*, II, No. 5 (September 23, 1954), 19–20; David J. Dallin, *Soviet Foreign Policy After Stalin* (Philadelphia, 1961), pp. 153–54; Aron, "Indo-China: A Way Out of the Wood," p. 10. The possibility that, by secret agreement, working to defeat EDC became France's quid pro quo for Moscow's support of lenient terms should not be overlooked.

34. These agreements included Soviet withdrawal from the Port Arthur naval base by May 31, 1955; Soviet removal from co-sponsorship of several joint companies, and surrender of full control to the CPR in furtherance of the Five Year Plan; exchange of scientific and technical information; and construction of two rail lines. *DAFR 1954*, pp. 328–32. The Soviets also gave a long-term credit.

35. I am indebted for this point to O. Edmund Clubb.

36. It will be recalled that the ICP of 1930 embraced all Indochina, that a National United Front existed even when the ICP was officially dissolved, and that the Vietminh supervised and inspired the Pathet Lao and Khmer resistance forces. In addition, a Vietminh agent had been the guiding light behind an abortive Southeast Asia League formed at Bangkok in September 1947 to include Thailand and Burma as well as the Indochinese states. Richard Butwell, "Communist Liaison in Southeast Asia," *United Asia*, VI, No. 3 (June, 1954), 150. The unification of Vietnam under Vietminh auspices may therefore have been considered by Peking as a threat to China's unquestioned paramountcy in Southeast Asia.

37. The suggestion of such a deal has been made by Nguyen Ngoc Bich, "Vietnam—An Independent Viewpoint," in P. J. Honey, ed., *North Vietnam Today* (New York, 1962), p. 129.

38. See Hsieh, chapter 2.

9. EPILOGUE: THE INDOCHINA LEGACY

1. The military lessons of the war are recounted in Prosser, p. 30, and in Fall, "Indochina: The Last Year of the War—Communist Organization and Tactics," *Military Review*, XXXVI, No. 7 (October, 1956), 11.

2. Ridgway, "My Battles in War and Peace," p. 48.

3. A. Doak Barnett, *Communist China and Asia* (New York, 1960), p. 101.

BIBLIOGRAPHY

Chinese names are alphabetized by the first element. Vietnamese names are alphabetized by the first element when there are only two parts to the name, by the last element when there are three.

MEMOIRS, COLLECTED WRITINGS, AND PAPERS

Ch'ang-cheng [Truong Chinh]. *Lün Yüeh-nan pa-yüeh ke-ming* [On Vietnam's August Revolution]. Hong Kong: Li-ming ch'u-pan she, 1948.

Chi, Hoang Van. *From Colonialism to Communism: A Case History of North Vietnam.* Introduction by P. J. Honey. New York: Praeger, 1964.

Dulles, John Foster. Papers. Princeton University Library, Princeton, New Jersey.

Eden, Anthony. *Full Circle: The Memoirs of Anthony Eden.* Boston: Houghton Mifflin, 1960.

Eisenhower, Dwight D. *The White House Years; Mandate for Change: 1953–1956.* Garden City, N.Y.: Doubleday & Co., 1963.

Ély, Paul. *Mémoires: L'Indochine dans la tourmente.* Paris: Plon, 1964.

Giap, Vo Nguyen. *Dien Bien Phu.* Hanoi: Éditions en Langues Étrangères, 1959.

Ho Chi Minh. *Selected Works.* 3 vols. Hanoi: Foreign Languages Publishing House, 1961. All references are to Vol. III.

Laniel, Joseph. *Le Drame indochinois: De Dien-Bien-Phu au pari de Genève.* Paris: Plon, 1957.

Mao Tse-tung. *On Guerrilla Warfare.* Translated by Brig. Gen. Samuel B. Griffith, USMC. New York: Praeger, 1961.

—— *Selected Works.* 5 vols. New York: International Publishers, 1956.

Navarre, Henri. *Agonie de l'Indochine (1953–1954).* Paris: Plon, 1956.

Ridgway, Matthew B. *Soldier: The Memoirs of Matthew B. Ridgway.* As told to Harold H. Martin. New York: Harper and Bros., 1956.

Truong Chinh. *Primer for Revolt: The Communist Takeover in Viet-Nam.* A facsimile edition of *The August Revolution* and *The Resistance Will Win.* Introduction and notes by Bernard B. Fall. New York: Praeger, 1963.

UNITED STATES GOVERNMENT PUBLICATIONS

Bureau of Intelligence and Research. *Chinese Communist World Outlook; A Handbook of Chinese Communist Statements: the Public Record of a Militant Ideology.* Washington, D.C.: Department of State Publication 7379, 1962.

Eisenhower, Dwight D. *Public Papers of the Presidents of the United States: 1953; 1954.* Washington, D.C.: U.S. Government Printing Office, 1960.

U.S. *Congressional Record.* Vols. XCIX, C.

U.S. Department of State. *The Department of State Bulletin.* Vols. XXII, XXVI, XXX (1950, 1952, 1954).

—— *Foreign Ministers Meeting: Berlin Discussions, January 25– February 18, 1954.* Washington, D.C.: Department of State Publication 5399, 1954.

—— *Foreign Relations of the United States; Diplomatic Papers: The Conference of Berlin (The Potsdam Conference) 1945.* 2 vols. Washington, D.C.: Government Printing Office, 1960.

—— *Foreign Relations of the United States; Diplomatic Papers: The Conferences at Malta and Yalta 1945.* Washington, D.C.: Government Printing Office, 1955.

—— *Indochina: The War in Viet-Nam, Cambodia, and Laos.* (pamphlet) Washington, D.C.: Department of State Publication 5092, Far Eastern Series 58, 1953.

U.S. House of Representatives, Committee on Foreign Affairs. *Hearings on H.R. 5710 to Amend Further the Mutual Security Act of 1951, as Amended, and for Other Purposes.* Vol. 9, 83d Cong., 1st Sess., March 11–June 6, 1953.

—— *Report of the Special Study Mission to Pakistan, India, Thailand, and Indochina, Pursuant to H. Res. 113, a Resolution Authorizing the Committee on Foreign Affairs to Conduct*

Thorough Studies and Investigations of All Matters within The Jurisdiction of Such Committee. House Report No. 412. 83d Cong., 1st Sess., May 6, 1953.

—— *Report on H.R. 5710 a Bill to Amend Further the Mutual Security Act of 1951, as Amended, and for Other Purposes.* House Report No. 569. 83d Cong., 1st Sess., June 16, 1953.

—— *Special Study Mission to Southeast Asia and the Pacific: Report by Hon. Walter H. Judd, Minnesota, Chairman; Hon. Marguerite Stitt Church, Illinois; Hon. E. Ross Adair, Indiana; Hon. Clement J. Zablocki, Wisconsin.* 83d Cong., 2d Sess., January 29, 1954.

U.S. House of Representatives, Subcommittee on Department of the Army Appropriations of the Committee on Appropriations. *Hearing.* Vol. 254. 83d Cong., 2d Sess., February 8–March 29, 1954.

U.S. Senate, Committee on Foreign Relations. *Hearing on Foreign Policy and its Relation to Military Programs.* Vol. 11. 83d Cong., 2d Sess., March 19 and April 14, 1954.

—— *Hearing on the Mutual Defense Assistance Control Act of 1951.* Vol. 11. 83d Cong., 2d Sess., April 9, 1954.

—— *Hearing on the Mutual Security Program for Fiscal Year 1955.* Vol. 11. 83d Cong., 2d Sess., June 4–22, 1954.

—— *Indochina: Report of Senator Mike Mansfield on a Study Mission to the Associated States of Indochina—Vietnam, Cambodia, Laos.* 83d Cong., 1st Sess., October 27, 1953.

—— *Report on Indochina: Report of Senator Mike Mansfield on a Study Mission to Vietnam, Cambodia, Laos.* 83d Cong., 2d Sess., October 15, 1954.

—— *Viet Nam, Cambodia, and Laos: Report by Senator Mike Mansfield.* 84th Cong., 1st Sess., October 6, 1955.

U.S. Senate, Subcommittee of the Committee on Appropriations. *Hearings on H.R. 5969 Making Appropriations for the National Security Council, the National Security Resources Board, and for Military Functions Administered by the National Military Establishment for the Fiscal Year Ending June 30, 1954, and for Other Purposes.* Part 1. Vol. 84. 83d Cong., 1st Sess., May 19–June 18, 1953.

—— *Hearings on H.R. 8067 Making Appropriations for the Departments of State, Justice, and Commerce and the United States Information Agency for the Fiscal Year Ending June 30, 1955.* Part 2. Vol. 91. 83d Cong., 2d Sess., 1954.

―――― *Hearings on H.R. 8873 Making Appropriations for the Department of Defense and Related Independent Agencies for the Fiscal Year Ending June 30, 1955, and for Other Purposes.* Vol. 89. 83d Cong., 2d Sess., March 15–26, 1954.

U.S. Senate, Subcommittee on the Far East of the Committee on Foreign Relations. *The Far East and South Asia: Report of Senator H. Alexander Smith, Chairman on a Study Mission to the Far East.* 83d Cong., 2d Sess., January 25, 1954.

DOCUMENTS AND RELATED MATERIALS

Accords Franco-Viêtnamiens du 8 Mars 1949: Conventions d'Application. N.p.:n.d.

Ambassade de France, Service de Press et d'Information. Speeches and Press Conferences (New York). 1952–1954.

American Consulate General, Hong Kong. *Current Background.* 1950, 1953–1954.

―――― *Survey of China Mainland Press.* 1953–1954.

China and the Asian-African Conference (Documents). Peking: Foreign Languages Press, 1955.

Curl, Peter V., ed. *Documents on American Foreign Relations 1953; 1954.* New York: Harper and Bros., for the Council on Foreign Relations, 1954, 1955.

The Current Digest of the Soviet Press. Vols. V–VI, 1953–1954.

Great Britain, Foreign Office. *Papers Relating to Foreign Affairs Laid before Parliament.* London: Her Majesty's Stationery Office, 1953–1954.

Jen-min shou-ts'e 1952; 1955 [People's Handbook 1952; 1955]. Tientsin: *Ta-kung-pao,* 1952, 1955.

Jih-nei-wa hui-i wen-chien hui-pien [Collection of Documents of the Geneva Conference]. Peking: Shih-chieh chih-shih she, 1954.

New China News Agency. Weekly Bulletin. 1949–1950.

Shih-chieh chih-shih shou-ts'e 1954 nien [Handbook of World Knowledge, 1954]. Peking: Shih-chieh chih-shih ch'u-pan she, 1954.

U.S. Department of State. *American Foreign Policy 1950–1955: Basic Documents.* 2 vols. Washington, D.C.: Department of State Publication 6446, 1957.

NEWSPAPERS

Christian Science Monitor. 1954.
Jen-min jih-pao [*People's Daily*, Peking]. 1953–1954.
Le Monde (Paris). 1954.
Manchester Guardian Weekly. 1954.
New York Herald Tribune. 1952, 1954.
New York Times. 1950–1954, 1956.
The Times (London). 1954.
Washington Post and Times Herald. 1954.

BOOKS AND OTHER PUBLISHED WORKS

IN ENGLISH AND FRENCH

Acheson, Dean. *A Democrat Looks at His Party.* New York: Harper and Bros., 1955.
Adams, Sherman. *Firsthand Report: The Story of the Eisenhower Administration.* New York: Harper and Bros., 1961.
Barnett, A. Doak. *Communist China and Asia: Challenge to American Policy.* New York: Random House, 1960.
———, ed. *Communist Strategies in Asia: A Comparative Analysis of Governments and Parties.* New York: Praeger, 1963.
Beal, John Robinson. *John Foster Dulles: A Biography.* New York: Harper and Bros., 1957.
Bell, Coral. *Survey of International Affairs 1954.* Edited by F. C. Benham. London: Oxford University Press, 1957.
Beloff, Max. *Soviet Policy in the Far East 1944–1951.* London: Oxford University Press, 1953.
Buttinger, Joseph. *The Smaller Dragon: A Political History of Vietnam.* New York: Praeger, 1958.
Childs, Marquis. *The Ragged Edge: The Diary of a Crisis.* Garden City, N.Y.: Doubleday & Co., 1955.
Cole, Allan B., ed. *Conflict in Indo-China and International Repercussions: A Documentary History, 1945–1955.* Ithaca: Cornell University Press, 1956.
Communist China 1949–1959. 2 vols. Kowloon (Hong Kong): Union Research Service, 1961.
Dai, Shen-Yu. *Peking, Moscow, and the Communist Parties of*

Colonial Asia. Cambridge, Mass.: Center for International Studies, Massachusetts Institute of Technology, 1954.

Dallin, David J. *Soviet Foreign Policy After Stalin.* Philadelphia: J. P. Lippincott Co., 1961.

Dan, Dr. Phan Quang. *The War in Indochina: A Comparative Study of the Vietminh and the French Union Forces.* N.p.: March 18, 1954.

Danh, Tran-Ngoc. *Two Years' Achievement of the Viet-Nam Nationalist Government.* N.p.: Vietnam Information Service, September 1947.

Daniels, Robert V., ed. *A Documentary History of Communism.* 2 vols. New York: Vintage Books, 1962.

Dinerstein, Herbert S. *War and the Soviet Union: Nuclear Weapons and the Revolution in Soviet Military and Political Thinking.* Rev. ed. New York: Praeger, 1962.

Donovan, Robert J. *Eisenhower: The Inside Story.* New York: Harper and Bros., 1956.

Drummond, Roscoe and Caston Coblentz. *Duel at the Brink: John Foster Dulles' Command of American Power.* Garden City, N.Y.: Doubleday & Co., 1960.

Dulles, John Foster. *War or Peace.* New York: Macmillan, 1950.

Dutt, Vidya Prakash and Singh, Vishal. *Indian Policy and Attitudes Towards Indo-China and S.E.A.T.O.* Paper submitted to the Twelfth Conference of the Institute of Pacific Relations, Kyoto, Japan, September–October 1954, by the Indian Council of World Affairs. New York: Institute of Pacific Relations, 1954.

Facts and Dates on the Problem of the Reunification of Viet-Nam. Hanoi: Foreign Languages Publishing House, 1956.

Fall, Bernard B. *Street without Joy: Insurgency in Indochina, 1946–1963.* 3d ed., rev. Harrisburg, Pa.: The Stackpole Co., 1963.

——— *The Two Viet-Nams: A Political and Military Analysis.* New York: Praeger, 1963.

Finletter, Thomas K. *Power and Policy: U.S. Foreign Policy and Military Power in the Hydrogen Age.* New York: Harcourt, Brace & Co., 1954.

Giap, Vo Nguyen. *One Year of Revolutionary Achievement: Report to the Viet Nam People at Hanoi.* Bangkok: *Vietnam News,* 1946.

——— *People's War People's Army: The Viet Cong Insurrection Manual for Underdeveloped Countries.* Foreword by Roger Hilsman; profile of Giap by Bernard B. Fall. New York: Praeger, 1962.

Greene, Lt. Col. T. N., ed. *The Guerrilla—and How to Fight Him.* New York: Praeger, 1962.

Guillain, Robert. *La Fin des illusions: notes d'Indochine (février-juillet 1954).* Paris: Centre d'Études de Politique Étrangère, 1954.

Hammer, Ellen J. *The Struggle for Indochina.* Stanford: Stanford University Press, 1954.

Hinton, Harold C. *China's Relations with Burma and Vietnam: A Brief Survey.* New York: International Secretariat of the Institute of Pacific Relations, 1958.

Holland, William L., ed. *Asian Nationalism and the West: A Symposium Based on Documents and Reports of the Eleventh Conference Institute of Pacific Relations.* New York: Macmillan, 1953.

Honey, P. J., ed. *North Vietnam Today: Profile of a Communist Satellite.* New York: Praeger, 1962.

Hsieh, Alice Langley. *Communist China's Strategy in the Nuclear Era.* Englewood Cliffs, N.J.: Prentice-Hall, 1962.

Hughes, Emmet John. *The Ordeal of Power: A Political Memoir of the Eisenhower Years.* New York: Dell Publishing Co., 1964.

Isoart, Paul. *Le Phénomène national viêtnamien: de l'indépendance unitaire à l'indépendance fractionnée.* Paris: Librairie Générale de Droit et de Jurisprudence, 1961.

Kissinger, Henry A. *Nuclear Weapons and Foreign Policy.* Garden City, N.Y.: Doubleday & Co., 1957.

Lacouture, Jean and Philippe Devillers. *La Fin d'une guerre: Indochine 1954.* Paris: Éditions du Seuil, 1960.

Lancaster, Donald. *The Emancipation of French Indochina.* London: Oxford University Press, under the auspices of the Royal Institute of International Affairs, 1961.

Lerner, Daniel and Raymond Aron, eds. *France Defeats EDC.* New York: Praeger, 1957.

Lieu, Tran Huy. *Les Soviets du Nghe-Tinh de 1930–1931 au Viet-Nam.* Hanoi: Éditions en Langues Étrangères, 1960.

Millis, Walter. *Arms and Men: A Study of American Military History.* New York: New American Library, 1956.

Morgenthau, Hans. *Politics Among Nations: The Struggle for Power and Peace.* 2d ed., rev. New York: Knopf, 1955.

Mus, Paul. *Le Destin de l'Union Française: de l'Indochine à l'Afrique.* Paris: Éditions du Seuil, 1954.

*On the Reestablishment of Normal Relations between the North-
ern and Southern Zones of Vietnam.* Hanoi: Foreign Languages
Publishing House, 1955.

Osgood, Robert Endicott. *Limited War: The Challenge to American Strategy.* Chicago: University of Chicago Press, 1957.

Panikkar, K. M. *In Two Chinas.* London: George Allen & Unwin,
Ltd., 1955.

Pentony, DeVere E., ed. *China, the Emerging Red Giant:
Communist Foreign Policies.* San Francisco: Chandler Publishing Co., 1962.

Pye, Lucian W. *Guerrilla Communism in Malaya: Its Social and
Political Meaning.* Princeton: Princeton University Press, 1956.

Rees, David. *Korea: The Limited War.* London: Macmillan, 1964.

Remer, C. F., ed. *Three Essays on the International Economics of
Communist China.* Ann Arbor: University of Michigan Press,
1959.

Renald, Jean. *L'Enfer de Dien Bien Phu.* Paris: Flammarion, 1955.

Rigg, Lt. Col. Robert B. *Red China's Fighting Hordes.* Harrisburg,
Pa.: Military Service Publishing Co., 1951.

Roy, Jules. *La Bataille de Dien Bien Phu.* Paris: René Julliard,
1963.

—— *The Battle of Dienbienphu.* Translated from the French by
Robert Baldick. Introduction by Neil Sheehan. New York:
Harper & Row, 1965.

Salmon, Malcolm. *Focus on Indo-China.* Hanoi: Foreign Languages Publishing House, 1961.

Schilling, Warner R., Paul Y. Hammond, and Glenn H. Snyder.
Strategy, Politics, and Defense Budgets. New York: Columbia
University Press, 1962.

Starobin, Joseph. *Eyewitness in Indo-China.* New York: Cameron
& Kahn, 1954.

*Statements by President Ho Chi-minh After the Geneva Con-
ference.* Hanoi: Foreign Languages Publishing House, 1955.

Steinberg, David J., et al. *Cambodia: Its People, Its Society, Its
Culture.* New Haven: Human Relations Area Files Press, 1957.

Strausz-Hupé, Robert, et al. *Protracted Conflict.* New York: Harper and Bros., 1959.

Tanham, George K. *Communist Revolutionary Warfare: The
Vietminh in Indochina.* New York: Praeger, 1961.

Taylor, Maxwell D. *The Uncertain Trumpet.* New York: Harper
and Bros., 1959.

Thanh, Nguyen Duy. "My Four Years with the Viet Minh." Bombay: Democratic Research Service, n.d.

Thompson, Virginia and Richard Adloff. *The Left Wing in Southeast Asia*. New York: William Sloane Associates, under the auspices of the Institute of Pacific Relations of the International Secretariat, 1950.

Tournoux, J.-R. *Secrets d'État: Dien Bien Phu, les Paras, l'Algérie, l'Affaire Ben Bella, Suez, la Cagoule, le 13 Mai, De Gaulle au Pouvoir*. Paris: Plon, 1960.

Trager, Frank N., ed. *Marxism in Southeast Asia: A Study of Four Countries*. Stanford: Stanford University Press, 1959.

Vizetelly, Henry E., ed. *The New International Yearbook: A Compendium of the World's Progress for the Year 1952; 1953; 1954*. New York: Funk & Wagnalls, 1953–1955.

Warner, Denis. *The Last Confucian*. New York: Macmillan, 1963.

Whiting, Allen S. *China Crosses the Yalu: the Decision to Enter the Korean War*. New York: Macmillian, 1960.

IN CHINESE

Ch'en I-ling. *Yüeh-nan hsien-shih* [The Present Situation in Vietnam]. Taipei: Chung-hua wen-hua ch'u-pan shih-yeh wei-yuan-hui, 1957.

Figuères, Leo, et al. *Yüeh-nan ti chieh-fang yün-tung ho ti-kuo chu-i ti ch'in-lüeh* [Vietnam's Liberation Movement and Imperialism's Aggression]. Translated from the French by Sung Kuei-huang. Shanghai and Peking: Wen-kuang shu-she, 1951.

Hsiao Yang. *Chieh-fang chung ti Yüeh-nan* [Vietnam in Liberation]. Shanghai: Chun-lien ch'u-pan she, 1951.

Liang-t'ien. *Yüeh-nan Lao-chua ho Chien-pu-chai ti min-tsu chieh-fang yün-tung* [The National Liberation Movement in Vietnam, Laos, and Cambodia]. Peking: Chung-wai ch'u-pan she, 1951.

Lü Ku. *Yüeh-nan jen-min fan-ti tou-cheng shih* [History of the Vietnamese People's Anti-Imperialist Struggle]. Shanghai: Tung-fang shu-she, 1951.

Mai Lang. *Chan-tou chung ti hsin Yüeh-nan* [New Vietnam in Struggle]. Hong Kong: New Vietnam Press, 1948.

Su Tzu-pien. *Chin-jih Yüeh-nan* [Vietnam Today]. Hong Kong: Freedom Press, 1952.

Wu Chih-ying, ed. *Hu Chih-ming ch'uan* [Biography of Ho Chi Minh]. Shanghai: Pacific Press, 1951.

PERIODICAL AND NEWSPAPER ARTICLES

Adloff, Richard, and Virginia Thompson. "Cambodia Moves Toward Independence," *Far Eastern Survey*, XXII, No. 9 (August, 1953), 105–11.

—— "Laos: Background of Invasion," *Far Eastern Survey*, XXII, No. 6 (May, 1953), 62–66.

"America's Destructive Actions on the Eve of the Geneva Conference," *Shih-chieh chih-shih* [World Culture], No. 8 (April 20, 1954).

"L'Amérique et l'Indochine du débarquement japonais de 1940 à Dien Bien Phu," *Chronique de Politique Étrangère*, VII, Nos. 4–5 (July–September, 1954), 485–505.

Aron, Raymond. "Indo-China: A Way Out of the Wood," *Réalités*, No. 40 (March, 1954), pp. 8–12.

Baldwin, Hanson W. "Air Power Controversy–III," *New York Times*, June 11, 1953, p. 22.

—— "The Bomb and the Battle," *New York Times*, April 1, 1954, p. 21.

—— "Defense Picture Drawn in Debate on the Budget," *New York Times*, IV, June 14, 1953, p. 12.

—— "Indochina Peril Grows," *New York Times*, June 7, 1954, p. 5.

—— "Lessons of Dienbienphu: Too Little and Too Late," *New York Times*, IV, May 16, 1954, p. 5.

—— " 'New Look' Re-Examined in Light of Indo-China," *New York Times*, IV, May 2, 1954, p. 5.

—— "The New Reserve Plan–II," *New York Times*, June 26, 1954, p. 6.

—— "Pentagon's 'New Look' Much Like the Old One," *New York Times Magazine*, November 1, 1953, p. 10.

—— "Warning on Indo-China," *New York Times*, September 10, 1953, p. 2.

Butwell, Richard. "Communist Liaison in Southeast Asia," *United Asia*, VI, No. 3 (June, 1954), 146–51.

Buu Loc. "Aspects of the Vietnamese Problem," *Pacific Affairs*, XXV, No. 3 (September, 1952), 235–47.

Callender, Harold. "France is Divided on Coming Parley," *New York Times*, February 20, 1954, p. 3.

—— "Indo-China Showdown Clarifies Paris Policy," *New York Times*, IV, November 1, 1953, p. 4.

Chang T'o-jo. "New China's Peaceful Foreign Policy," *Shih-chieh chih-shih* [World Culture], No. 39 (October 4, 1952), pp. 5–6.

Chastenet, Jacques. "Comment conclure la guerre d'Indochine?" *Hommes et Mondes*, No. 93 (April, 1954), pp. 1–13.

Cheng Wan. "On America's So-Called 'New Look' Foreign Policy," *Shih-chieh chih-shih* [World Culture], No. 4 (February 20, 1954), pp. 6–8.

"China Hails the Truce," *People's China*, No. 16 (August 16, 1953), p. 3.

Dai, Shen-Yu. "Peking and Indochina's Destiny," *The Western Political Quarterly*, VII, No. 3 (September, 1954), 346–68.

"Defense and Strategy: New Accents in Military Thinking and Spending," *Fortune*, XLVIII (December, 1953), 77–84.

Dejean, Maurice. "The Meaning of Dien Bien Phu," *United States Naval Institute Proceedings*, LXXX, No. 7 (July, 1954), 717–25.

Deutscher, Isaac. "How the Russians Bet a Little in Asia to Win a Lot in Europe," *The Reporter*, II, No. 5 (September 23, 1954), 19–22.

Dulles, John Foster. "A Policy of Boldness," *Life*, May 19, 1952, pp. 146–60.

—— "Policy for Security and Peace," *Foreign Affairs*, XXXII, No. 3 (April, 1954), 353–64.

Dunn, William B. "How West Could Win Vietnam's Support," *Foreign Policy Bulletin*, XXXIII, No. 17 (May 15, 1954), 1–2.

Durdin, Tillman. "Some in Vietminh, Angered, Say Red Allies Forced Pact," *New York Times*, July 25, 1954, pp. 1, 3.

Ennis, Thomas E. "The French Empire I: In Asia," *Current History*, XXVIII, No. 165 (May, 1955), 282–87.

—— "Indo-China at the Crossroads," *Current History*, XXV, No. 147 (November, 1953), 301–5.

Fall, Bernard B. "The Cease-Fire in Indochina—An Appraisal," *Far Eastern Survey*, XXIII, No. 9 (September, 1954), 135–39.

—— "Indochina: The Last Year of the War—Communist Organization and Tactics," *Military Review*, XXXVI, No. 7 (October, 1956), 3–11.

—— "Indochina: The Last Year of the War—The Navarre Plan," *Military Review*, XXXVI, No. 9 (December, 1956), 48–56.

—— "La Politique américaine au Viet-Nam," *Chronique de Politique Étrangère*, XX, No. 3 (July, 1955), 299–322.

214 BIBLIOGRAPHY

—— "Red China's Aims in South Asia," *Current History*, XLIII, No. 253 (September, 1962), 136–81.

Favrel, Charles. "Pratiquement privée du secours aérien, la défense de Dien-Bien-Phu se resserre sur quelques kilomètres carrés," *Le Monde*, April 22, 1954, pp. 1, 3.

Fitzgerald, C. P. "East Asia After Bandung," *Far Eastern Survey*, XXIV No. 8 (August, 1955), 113–19.

"For Collective Peace in Asia," *People's China*, No. 20 (October 16, 1954), pp. 32–35.

"La Guerre d'Indochine," *Sondages*, No. 3 (1953), pp. 3–6.

Guillain, Robert. "Dien-Bien-Phu: Qui? Pourquoi? Comment?" *Le Monde*, May 2–3, 1954, pp. 1–2.

—— "Les Erreurs et les malheurs de Dien-Bien-Phu," *Le Monde*, May 4, 1954, pp. 1–2.

—— "Sauver l'Armée française," *Le Monde*, April 29, 1954, pp. 1–2.

Halpern, A. M. "The Foreign Policy Uses of the Chinese Revolutionary Model," *The China Quarterly*, No. 7 (July–September, 1961), pp. 1–16.

Hinton, Harold C. "Communist China's Military Posture," *Current History*, XLII, No. 253 (September, 1962), 149–55.

Hunter, William H. "The War in Vietnam, Luce Version," *The New Republic*, March 23, 1963, pp. 15–17.

"Intervention in Indo-China: Radford Knows What He Wants, But Will His Policy Work?" *The New Republic*, June 14, 1954, pp. 3–7.

"Interview with General Nathan F. Twining," *US News & World Report*, December 25, 1953, pp. 40–45.

"Interview with Admiral Arthur W. Radford: Strong U.S. Defense for 'Long Pull,'" *US News & World Report*, March 5, 1954, pp. 48–55.

Jacquet-Francillon, Jacques. "The Borders of China: Mao's Bold Challenge to Khrushchev," *The New Republic*, April 20, 1963, pp. 18–22.

Johnson, Dr. Hewlett. "China Works for Peace," *People's China*, No. 19 (October 1, 1954), 42–45.

Katzenbach, Edward L. Jr. "Indo-China: A Military-Political Appreciation," *World Politics*, IV, No. 2 (January, 1952), 186–218.

Kissinger, Henry A. "Military Policy and Defense of the 'Grey Areas,'" *Foreign Affairs*, XXXIII, No. 3 (April, 1955), 416–28.

Kuo Mo-jo. "The Korean Armistice and World Peace," *People's China*, No. 16 (August 16, 1953), pp. 4–6.

Lindley, Ernest K. "Dulles Struggles Ahead," *Newsweek*, May 17, 1954, p. 37.

Lippmann, Walter. "First a United American Front," *Washington Post and Times Herald*, June 10, 1954, p. 15.

Liu Ning-i. "On the Eve of the Peace Conference of the Asian and Pacific Regions," *People's China*, No. 19 (September 1, 1952), p. 7.

Martin, Robert P. "Uncensored Story of Indo-China," *US News & World Report*, June 25, 1954, p. 36.

McCormick, Anne O'Hare. "The President's 'New Policy' of Long-Term Defense," *New York Times*, May 2, 1953, p. 14.

Morley, Lorna. "Menaced Laos," *Editorial Research Reports*, II, No. 12 (September 23, 1959), 717–34.

"Mr. Dulles Answers Some Questions," *US News & World Report*, April 30, 1954, p. 63.

"Must We Fight in Indo-china?" *The New Republic*, May 3, 1954, pp. 7–8.

Nguyen Thai. "The Two Vietnams and China," *The Harvard Review*, II, No. 1 (Fall-Winter, 1963), 26–32.

Nitze, Paul H. "Atoms, Strategy and Policy," *Foreign Affairs*, XXXIV, No. 2 (January, 1956), 187–98.

Pouillon, Jean. "Illusions avant Genève," *Temps Modernes*, No. 101 (April, 1954), pp. 1903–14.

Prosser, Major Lamar McFadden. "The Bloody Lessons of Indochina," *The Army Combat Forces Journal*, V, No. 11 (June, 1955), 23–30.

Reston, James. "The 'Agonizing Reappraisal' Has Already Begun," *New York Times*, IV, May 2, 1954, p. 8.

—— "Art of Sudden Diplomacy," *New York Times Magazine*, April 11, 1954, p. 10.

—— "Candor or Confusion?" *New York Times*, October 7, 1953, p. 7.

—— "Dulles Returning to Face Criticism on Asiatic Policy," *New York Times*, May 4, 1954, p. 1.

—— "Dulles Talks Reflect Basic Policy on Asia," *New York Times*, March 30, 1954, p. 1.

—— "Dulles to Assure Congress Critics on Asia Strategy," *New York Times*, February 22, 1954, pp. 1, 3.

—— "Errors on Indo-China," *New York Times,* February 12, 1954, p. 2.

—— "On 'the Tragedy of Timidity,' " *New York Times,* IV, May 23, 1954, p. 10.

—— "Uninspiring Bao Dai Regime Held Weak for War on Reds," *New York Times,* July 17, 1953, p. 3.

—— "U.S. Plan to Reduce NATO Force Denied," *New York Times,* October 21, 1953, pp. 1, 22.

Ridgway, General Matthew B. "My Battles in War and Peace," as told to Harold H. Martin, *The Saturday Evening Post,* January 21, 1956, pp. 17–19, 46–48.

Roberts, Chalmers H. "The Day We Didn't Go to War," *The Reporter,* XI (September 14, 1954), 31–35.

—— "United States Twice Proposed Indochina Air Strike— Blocked by British 'No,' " *Washington Post and Times Herald,* June 7, 1954, pp. 1, 4.

Shepley, James. "How Dulles Averted War," *Life,* January 16, 1956, pp. 70–80.

Sulzberger, C. L. "Eisenhower Wins on Defense Plank," *New York Times,* July 11, 1952, p. 9.

—— "Europe is Reappraising Both U.S. and Russia," *New York Times Magazine,* April 11, 1954, p. 3.

Szu, Li. "Restore Peace in Indo-China," *People's China,* No. 7 (April 1, 1954), pp. 7–9.

"U.S. to Fight More 'Little Wars'?" *US News & World Report,* April 30, 1954, pp. 21-23.

Vernant, Jacques. "Avant la Négociation internationale sur l'Asie," *Revue de Défense Nationale,* XVIII (April, 1954), 473–78.

—— "Paris, Washington et Londres devant le drame indochinois," *Revue de Défense Nationale,* XVIII (June, 1954), 735–42.

"What Comes After Dienbienphu," *US News & World Report,* May 7, 1954, pp. 21–23.

"What Ridgway Told Ike—War in Indo-China Would be Tougher Than Korea," *US News & World Report,* June 25, 1954, pp. 30–33.

"Why U.S. Steers Clear of a Fight in Asia," *US News & World Report,* December 10, 1954, pp. 62–64.

"Why War Talk is Fading," *US News & World Report,* May 7, 1954, pp. 25–26.

Zhukov, Ye. "China's Revolutionary Victory and Its Influence on the Liberation Movements of the Various Asian Peoples," *Shih-*

chieh chih-shih [World Culture], No. 38 (September 27, 1952), pp. 7–9.

INTERVIEWS AND CORRESPONDENCE

Columbia Broadcasting System (Television). Interview between Dwight D. Eisenhower and Walter Cronkite. New York, New York, November 23, 1961.

Interview with Hanson W. Baldwin. New York, New York, July 14, 1965.

Interview with Donald R. Heath. New York, New York, June 28, 1965.

Interview with Admiral Arthur W. Radford. Washington, D.C., July 13, 1965.

Letter from Everett F. Drumright. Poway, California, July 15, 1965.

Letter from General Matthew B. Ridgway. Pittsburgh, Pennsylvania, June 16, 1964.

Statement by Donald R. Heath. New York, New York, July 5. 1965.

MISCELLANEOUS

MacAlister, Robert J. "The Great Gamble: United States Policy Toward South Vietnam from July, 1954 to July, 1956." Unpublished Master's essay, Department of Political Science, University of Chicago, 1958.

INDEX

Dai, Shen-yu, 169
Dan, Phan Quang, 49
Dang Lao Dong (Vietnam Labor
Party), 13–14
Declaration of July 3, 43, 49, 124
Defense program, U.S.: Eisenhower Administration policies,
53–56; weaknesses in, 158–60
Dejean, Maurice, 69, 92
Democratic Republic of Vietnam
(DRV): formation, 3; motivations for war, 5–6; Chinese Communist commitment in, 6–19,
167–68; peace feelers, 18–19,
46–48, 180; popular opinion
control campaign, 43–44, 179;
British proposal for, 111–12; partition, 126–27, 129–30; unified, as
threat to CPR, 154, 121; see also
Associated States of French Union; Indochina; and under specific topic or nation involved in
Dienbienphu, 18; attitudes on holding, 50–51, 75, 110, 180–81, 194;
heavy fighting, 68–69; encirclement, 71; siege, 78; U.S. aid for
defense of, 79–80, 188; March 13
attack, 81; military tactics at, 93;
Chinese at, 93, 98–99, 155; plans
for saving, 94–95, 135–36, 190–91;
symbolic value of, 105–6, 193;
requests for U.S. aid at, 108–10,
113, 194; fall of, 115, 118, 150,
151–52; CPR on, 118, 150, 151–52
Dillon, Douglas, 97
Dinerstein, Herbert, 89, 183
Dirksen, Everett M., 37
"Domino reaction," 26, 121, 143,
147, 160
Dong, Pham Van, 2
Drumright, Everett F., 148, 176
DRV, see Democratic Republic of
Vietnam
Dulles, Allen, 182
Dulles, John Foster, 75, 104, 139,
147, 170, 191; on Indochina pol-
icy, 25–26, 27–28, 30, 80–82, 99,
101–2, 115, 120, 121, 122–24, 126,
189, 197; on Chinese Communists,

29, 31–32, 71–72, 80–82, 98–99, 138,
148, 151, 161, 186, 189, 200; on
Thailand and Laos, 30; on Southeast Asia security, 30, 107–8,
121, 122; on Navarre Plan, 50,
75, 77, 98–99; foreign policy influence and importance, 53, 131;
on use of native forces, 54;
January 12, 1954 speech, effects
on West, 57–60, 182; on France
in EDC, 72–73, 186; acceptance
of CPR in international conference, 73, 74; on unilateral vs.
united action, 97, 100, 106, 108,
122–24, 126, 192, 194, 197; on importance of Dienbienphu, 106;
on military aid for Dienbienphu,
108, 109–10, 115, 136, 194; attitudes on British at Geneva, 114;
domestic criticism of Asian
policy, 119–20; on Vietnam
partition, 130; on air power in
Vietnam, 135; on political concession to Associated States, 142;
agreement with Korea, 174
Dunn, William B., 178

EDC, see European Defense Community
Eden, Anthony, 114, 136, 139, 147,
155; on Indochina settlement, 47,
153; on united action, 100, 102,
108–9, 110–11, 193; on Communist activity, 105, 200; on American military aid for Dienbienphu, 108–9; on Southeast Asia
defense body, 194; on Anglo-
Chinese relations, 198
Eisenhower, Dwight David, 27, 48,
127; on Truman's Indochina
policy, 24–25; on Korean conflict, 29; on Asia and U.S. security, 31, 80, 99, 112–13, 121–22;
on French Indochina policy, 39,
41, 42; on involvement in Indochina, 69, 78, 83, 87, 151, 189,
191–92; on united action in Vietnam, 96–97, 119–20, 145, 146–47,
192; on Chinese Communists,

"Anything helps. The more wild fruit you girls find, the more of our apples we can dry for winter. Then, in the morning, you can be out in the corn early and work till it starts getting really hot."

"I'll finish plowing this week." Jonathan grinned. "Then, my girl, I'll get a corn knife and race you!"

Christy laughed. "I don't care if you win." She already felt better at the prospect of spending the sweltering afternoon wandering after fruit, instead of bending to hack away with the vicious blade. John Brown and his sons had killed those men at Osawatomie with short swords that must not have looked much different.

"Leave some for the birds and wild creatures!" Ellen called as the girls departed with oak split baskets and a jubilant Robbie. If anything made him prouder than protecting Beth, it was guarding two of his humans. For a dog, he was approaching old age. Christy didn't want to think of the time when he wouldn't dash along ahead, behind, and on all sides of them.

Beth giggled and caught Christy's hand, swinging it so joyfully that Christy realized with a stab of compunction that she hadn't paid much attention lately to her little sister. Giving Beth's hand an answering squeeze, Christy laughed down at her. "You must already know where the best trees and bushes are."

Beth's sunbonnet bobbed denial. "I don't go 'way far away. I'm scared of bears and panthers and water moccasins and copperheads." She shivered. "I saw a wolf watching me yesterday. He was on a bluff across the creek. Could he eat me, Christy?"

"Maybe he could, but I don't think he would," Christy teased. "You're much too tough and skinny to interest any self-respecting wolf."

31

When Beth didn't laugh, Christy knelt and looked into solemn eyes that were more green now than brown or gold. "Honey, Father says he's never heard of wolves killing a person in this country. They may have a long time ago in France, during a famine, and perhaps in Russia when they're starving, but. . . ."

"S'pose they get to starving here?" Beth shuddered.

"Then we won't go out in the woods. But they're not starved, Bethie, or they wouldn't let Robbie run them off from the sheep."

"I don't want them to eat Nosey or Cleo or Mildred or any of their lambs." Beth sniffled and rubbed her face on Christy's shoulder.

"Gracious, it's way past time we had a talk, sweetheart. Here I thought you were having a grand time in the timber!"

Beth cast her a searching look. "I . . . I took Lambie. Do you think I'm a scaredy-cat?"

"I think you're brave as a lion." Christy held the thin child tightly and tucked some dark curls under the shabby sunbonnet. "To hunt berries when you're scared is heaps braver than if you were never afraid to start with. What other peculiar notions have you got in that funny little head of yours?"

"Oh, I make believe Charlie and Thos are back!"

"They're growing up, Bethie."

"I wish they weren't!"

"So do I, but we can't change it."

Beth grabbed Christy around the waist. "You're almost grown-up, too, Christy! You . . . you won't go away, will you?"

"Not for a long time." Christy thought of Dan with a wrench of longing, but she couldn't imagine leaving home even to be with him. Not yet. Maybe she wasn't as grown-up as she thought she was. "Anyway, honey, I hope to always live where I can see you and our folks real often. So you just be sure you don't move to California or Oregon!"

Beth chortled at that and they were soon picking purple gooseberries from a big bush that concealed an old nest, possibly a cardinal's. Those scarlet birds favored the dense bushes for nesting.

"When Danny comes, it's almost as good as having Thos or Charlie . . . and some ways it's better 'cause he plays the fiddle and sings so pretty." Beth slanted a hopeful glance at Christy. "When you're grown-up, why don't you marry him? Then we'd have you both!"

"Don't you say anything like that to him!" Christy warned, but it was good to have someone to confide in, even a small sister. "I don't mind his broken nose. It shows he's been through a lot. Do you know, Bethie, the first time he ever spoke to me was to bawl me out because I hadn't jumped up fast enough to change your diaper?"

"Christy!" shrieked Beth. Curiosity triumphed over chagrin. "Did Danny have a sister over the sea?"

"He did." Christy told what she knew of Dan's childhood as they moved on to a beautiful black cherry tree on the creekbank. A squirrel finished gnawing open a cherry stone to get to the kernel and feasting blue jays scolded as the girls began to pick.

"Don't fret," Beth promised the birds. "We'll leave you all the cherries we can't reach." She looked gravely at Christy. "If you marry Danny, I'll try to be like his sister and make up a little for Bridget."

They talked as they roamed, shunning the raccoon grapes that even the animals wouldn't eat, squealing at the discovery of elderberries, a black haw tree — although it had precious little fruit — and wild plum thickets. Well before sunset, their baskets were filled.

"Let's take some spicebush home for tea," Christy suggested as she brushed against the dark green leaves. Fragrance filled the air as they broke off a handful of twigs.

They went home well content in a closeness they had lost as Beth grew out of babyhood. Brave, funny little Beth, hiding all those fears as she tried to help feed the family! Christy resolved to be a better sister, especially since it was clear that Beth didn't tell her parents her deepest worries.

Beth joined her in the cornfield next morning, planting her foot on the stalks beneath the ears and twisting them off. Although Christy tried to send her to the house after a few hours, Beth persisted till their mother called them in to help pit the fruits that were large enough for drying, cut them in half, and spread them to dry on a clean sheet in the loft. The plums went into a big crock filled with water. Scum would form after a while and the fruit would keep for months.

Now that the corn was too hard for roasting ears, Christy helped her mother make sweet cornmeal by rubbing the ears over a piece of tin pierced with nail holes. This grating, or "gritting" as Hester called it, made delicious bread and tasty grits and some was dried for later use.

After Jonathan finished plowing, it only took a few days to finish cutting the stalks, haul them to the barn, and crib the ears. At night, the family gathered around a tub and shelled corn by rubbing ears against each other or scraping them against the rim of the tub. Beth put four or five ears in a sack and tromped up and down on them till most of the kernels came loose and she could easily rub off the remainder.

"Wouldn't it be grand if the mill could take out the hulls?" Christy asked. The unbolted meal had to be sifted to get rid of the tough bits.

"Goodness, dear," twinkled her mother, "I'm grateful not to have to grind the corn in a hand mill! And we're mightily